EMISSARY

EMISSARY

THOMAS
LOCKE

Revell

a division of Baker Publishing Group
Grand Rapids, Michigan

© 2015 by T. Davis Bunn

Published by Revell
a division of Baker Publishing Group
P.O. Box 6287, Grand Rapids, MI 49516-6287
www.revellbooks.com

Printed in the United States of America

All rights reserved. No part of this publication may be reproduced, stored in a retrieval system, or transmitted in any form or by any means—for example, electronic, photocopy, recording—without the prior written permission of the publisher. The only exception is brief quotations in printed reviews.

Library of Congress Cataloging-in-Publication Data
Locke, Thomas, 1952–
    Emissary / Thomas Locke.
        pages cm. — (Legends of the realm ; #1)
    Includes bibliographical references.
    ISBN 978-0-8007-2447-4 (cloth)
    ISBN 978-0-8007-2385-9 (pbk.)
    I. Title.
  PS3552.U4718E46 2015
  813'.54—dc23   2014029802

This book is a work of fiction. Names, characters, places, and incidents are the products of the author's imagination or are used fictitiously. Any resemblance to actual events, locales, or persons, living or dead, is coincidental.

15 16 17 18 19 20 21   7 6 5 4 3 2 1

This Book Is Dedicated To

Nicholas Burgess-Jones

Who shares in the vision

And the quest

1

Most people were given a new world for their twenty-first birthday. Coming of age meant celebration and beginnings and vast horizons. Any man or woman could join with the partner of their choosing, claim a profession, leave their apprenticeship, or even take a different name. Hyam was given one choice, which of course was no choice at all. He was invited to walk away from everything he had ever known.

His mother had been ill for almost a year, and the village healer could do little save bar pain's specter from her chamber. Which was an immense boon, Hyam knew, because the agony his mother did not feel was etched deep into her features. The hurt might be banished, but the wasting still ate at her.

Two nights before her son's adulthood began, the lady breathed her last. There was a palpable sense of relief in the village, for his mother had been much loved and the ending had been too long in coming. Hyam's first act as an adult was to help lower his mother into the ground. He said the proper words, he allowed the village women to embrace him and weep, and he heard anew his mother's final request. Her softly whispered entreaty had carried such a sense of repulsion he almost refused. But in the end Hyam packed the six meals he would require for the journey, as he was not allowed to hunt upon this trail, and took the lonely route east, rimming the forest, over the knob, along the forbidden ridgeline, and into the wizard's vale.

The journey proved an immense gift, for Hyam had always been private with his thoughts and his emotions. He wept over his loss. He stamped and fought the trail, and bemoaned his lonely fate, and worried over what would become of him. He was free to shout his rage. None heard him. The trail only led to one place and was busy just during the festival seasons. Hyam was safe, he was isolated, and by the time he reached his destination, he was almost comfortable with the burden of grief.

The region's Long Hall was larger than his village. All such places bore the same name, right the world around. For centuries all magic save the healing arts had been banned from the realm. Only within communities known as Long Halls was magery still taught and practiced.

From a safe distance, the hamlet was beautiful but austere. The stone dwellings were precisely laid out, the surrounding walls rising and falling with the hills. The community overlooked the same stonewashed river as his village. As far as Hyam was concerned, that was the only thing they shared.

He pulled the leather cord, and the bell by the community's only portal rang a lonely note. He shivered against the onslaught of memories. When the small barred gate opened, he said to the old man, "I am here to see a wizard of the Long Hall."

"How is this one known?"

"Shard."

"There is none here by that name."

"I don't understand. Shard is my father. I was here as an acolyte myself for five years."

"How are you called?"

"Hyam."

The portal clicked shut. Hyam did not ever recall having seen that face before. But most of the community was barred from the acolytes. He turned his back to the door and resisted the urge to simply walk away. Perhaps the elders received a second name at some point. His father had been renamed when he became a mage, signifying one who was only complete as part of a greater whole. Such naming was part of the Long Hall tradition, all of which Hyam roundly despised.

The portal's lock rattled, and the door creaked open. A white-haired woman stood before him. "One who is expelled from these walls may not enter again."

Hyam did not need to see the blue band rimming the woman's cowl and sleeves to know he stood once more before the Mistress. He might despise the place and the secrets they jealously guarded, but there was no future in riling one so powerful.

He bowed low. "I came at my mother's request. She wished for me to tell her husband—"

"There are no husbands here. Nor wives. Nor children. Nor vows recognized by the outer world. We are our own realm."

Hyam recognized the words as part of the lessons he had been forced to endure. The memories returned with a rush of old regret. "I should not have come."

The woman caught his bitterness. "You hated it here so much?"

Hyam saw no need to respond.

She seemed to find the answer she sought in his silence, for she stepped through the portal and led him to a stone bench overlooking the river. "Sit with me."

Hyam hesitated, wanting only to be away. But there was nothing to be gained from rudeness. He sat.

"I remember you. Your task was languages, was it not?"

Acolytes were only permitted to study tiny hints of the arcane arts. Their time not spent performing chores was given over to lessons in one specific area, which the senior mages saw as the avenue they might follow the rest of their lives.

"For my first year, I watered the fields and fed the animals and carried stones from the quarry. Languages came after."

"What did you study?"

"Ashanta. Milantian." He found it hard to utter the third name. "Elven."

"A worthy task."

He turned and inspected the seamed face. Acolytes were not permitted to look directly at any elder save their teachers. "To force a child to learn a language dead for over a thousand years and beat him until he bled when he erred—I would not call this worthy."

She might have shrugged. "You were also a hunter."

"Arrow and knife." His one outlet, his one chance to escape. For brief periods.

"You learned the forest ways."

"Some of them." From a taciturn man who smelled like a goat and spoke less than his father.

"And then you were passed over."

He smiled at the recollection. "My finest hour."

She was untouched by his satisfaction. "Did you ever wonder why you were not invited to join with us?"

"No, Mistress. I was too glad to leave you behind."

"And yet it is strange, is it not? You were an excellent pupil. You were adept at all your lessons. Your ability with the languages was astonishing."

"I do not recall my teachers ever using that word to describe me."

"Astonishing," she repeated. "Even with Milantian, which some claim can only be truly used by one of that race."

"I have returned because it was my mother's last request. Please tell the one called Shard that his former wife is no more. I thank you for seeing me and bid you—"

"Shard passed away four years ago."

Hyam settled back onto the bench and absorbed the news. And felt nothing. "So I am an orphan."

She looked at him then, with eyes of smoky brilliance. "You have been that for far longer than these few days."

"I don't understand."

"Shard did not sire you, the woman who raised you did

not birth you." The leader of Long Hall spoke with a calm firmness. "You know who we are. You know I do not lie."

He met her gaze and recalled more of the reasons he loathed this place. "You and your kind already stole five years of my life. You will not take my birthright as well."

She watched him rise and asked, "Your mother's dying bequest means so little?"

"You just said she was not that."

"I said she did not birth you. The love she gave, the home, the nurturing, what does that make her if not your true parent?" She patted the stone bench. "Sit. Please."

When he remained standing, she said, "You were brought to your parents by a Traveler."

Hyam laughed out loud. "Why not a wolf? Carried in his great fangs and deposited—"

"A Traveler," she repeated.

"That is a legend more dead than the Elves."

"They live, they are, and this happened."

"A wandering wizard dropped a baby boy on my parents' doorstep." Despite himself, he was drawn back down to the bench. "And what, they just happened to think it would be a nice idea to raise me?"

"Your father was against it. Your mother insisted. The argument lasted for the first six months of your life. Then the mages' ability woke within him and he came here." She showed him a vague smile. "Many who join us bring such tales of loss and woe."

"She never told me why he left."

"Why should she?"

"I drove my father away."

"You served him well, as he would have told you, were he still with us." She hesitated, then added, "There is something you should know. Perhaps it is the real reason you were drawn here this day. So that I might inform you that you are not human."

The wind sighed through the trees on the narrow valley's other side. An emerald slope descended to the sparkling river below. Wildflowers shivered and danced in the cool breeze. Overhead ships of froth and mist drifted in a blue realm.

"What are you saying?"

"We think Milantian. But we cannot be certain. There is a powerful veil cast over your heritage. To have your blood tested would have meant alerting officials of the realm. And you know what they do to Milantians."

The world and the day no longer seemed capable of holding him. Beyond the forest, his village was busy with the spring planting. New homes were being raised to hold the families that would soon grow and claim their place among their clan. There would be the season's first feast. There would be music and laughter and a sense of belonging. Maidens would weave flowers into their hair and laugh over which man might claim the dance, the kiss, the night. And here he sat. Learning that there was indeed a reason for why he had never belonged.

"Milantians are killed on sight."

"Throughout the realm," she agreed. "They are safe from no one. They are the scattered people. Only a few remnants survive of the mighty warrior clan who once brought havoc and woe to our land."

"But you don't know for certain I'm—" He arched back so far he would have toppled to the earth save for his frantic grip on the stone. "The language."

"No one save a Milantian can learn their tongue."

"That is only a saying."

"None of our scholars can speak more than a few words, even after studying it for years. And yet you gobbled it up. You learned all the elders had to teach in weeks, and you raced through all our books and scrolls in a single winter."

"Then you took that from me as well."

"We could not risk word slipping out that we harbored an adept. Because that is what you most certainly were. A child gifted in the forbidden tongue. None could ever recall such a feat. So we hid you the only way possible. We forbade you to ever speak it again."

Old anger formed a cold fist in his gut. "And forced me to learn Elven."

"We did. Yes."

"The Milantians destroyed the Elves."

"So our history says."

"I don't understand. What's more, I don't want to understand."

Once again she showed him a gaze of crystal smoke. Her eyes held no guile and less remorse. It was the gaze of a woman who could consign a child to the misery of useless lessons and beat him until he succeeded, without a moment's hesitation or regret. "Some say Milantian is not so much a language as a means of drawing power from beyond. Which is precisely how the ancient texts describe Elven. Our elders hoped one tongue might eventually balance out the other in you. Or grant you the wise usage of both."

The logic assailed him, as did the wizard's utter absence of concern over the distress Hyam had known. "No one ever told me any of this."

"You were a child. You did as you were ordered. It is a child's place to obey without question."

"What happens now?"

"Milantians are said to come into their powers in their twenty-first year. If this is indeed your blood, you will know soon enough. If you need to know more, there is a scholar at our community in Havering. A historian named Trace. Tell him I sent you." She rose and gathered her hands within the folds of her grey robe. "If your horizons are to grow beyond the safety of this valley, you should know that war is coming. Your new powers will challenge you in ways you cannot fathom and most certainly will not find either comfortable or pleasant. Nonetheless, it is time for all who cherish peace or truth to prepare."

She left him without either farewell or backward glance. The door clicked shut, sealing him out. He remained where he was, trying to rejoin with the wind and the sunlight and the world beyond the forbidden portal. Only when he hefted his pack and started back down the trail did he realize that he had neglected to ask her name so he could tell this Trace who had sent him. Then Hyam decided that it did not matter. He had no intention of speaking with another member of any Long Hall. For as long as he lived.

2

Hyam's cottage was called Far Field and had been in his mother's family for centuries. The village of Honor stood in a broad region of river-bottom land, the earth rich and fecund and well-watered. Honor was prosperous and complacent and set in its ways. The village fields were bounded by a forest that few locals ever entered. Boars and wildcats were far from the worst woodland dwellers. Some claimed the other beasts were mere legends. Hyam knew better. He had seen the prints, read the signs, and twice smelled the acrid stench of passing creatures he dared not name. But he entered the forest because his family's survival demanded it.

He had never known fear within its shadows. The rustling passage of animals that lusted after fresh blood did not paralyze him with terror. He burrowed into piles of dried foliage and waited for the danger to pass. Once he had found himself sharing his burrow with an injured baby deer. He had stroked the animal until the threat departed, then rejoined the trail and discovered one haunch of what had most likely been the fawn's mother. The deer's hind leg had been severed in one bite, which meant the mouth had been six hand-widths across. Hyam had carried the fawn home and hand-fed it and slept in the corral with it. Then one night he had woken to discover a full-grown stag standing over him, with antlers so broad they etched two dozen streaks among the stars. The stag had inspected him a long moment, then bent down and licked his ear. The next morning the fawn had been gone. Since returning from the Long Hall, Hyam thought of the animal every time he traversed the forest trail.

Two hours' hard trek beyond the forest border, the trail opened into an oval field. The size was as mysterious as how neither the forest nor its occupants ever encroached. The earth was immensely fertile. The surrounding woodland shielded the winds and trapped much of the heat. Hyam and his mother and his uncle could plant a month earlier than all the other village fields, and if the snows held off, they could often bring in two crops. His uncle's two sons had hated the forest and married into families with good land closer to home. Hyam had lost his uncle the year before his mother took ill, and now he walked the trail alone.

It was not just the memory of the stag that clouded his mind this morning. For the two weeks since his trek to Long Hall, Hyam's dreams had been awful. Great swirling mists filled his nights, streaked by lightning and powers beyond his ken. Images shouted to him in half-remembered tongues, luring him down false trails. Sirens with weaving heads of snakes offered smoking elixirs intended to unlock the beast within. Vixens with pearl-white bodies sought to consume him in lustful wrath. Warriors with blades of fire and eyes like devouring coals laughed at his defenseless state and swooped down atop vultures the size of houses. He woke most dawns streaked in sweat and panting from battles he seldom won.

This morning proved the worst of all. Hyam had a dream so real he thought he had somehow woken and been transported to the border of his oval field. In the dream, he held his shovel in his hand, but not in order to till the earth. Instead, he extended it out like a wand and shouted words the Long Hall wizards had forbidden him to ever utter again. Paths of fire had leapt out from his feet and formed shimmering patterns that covered the field and extended on through the forest to the realms beyond. Wherever the triangular designs went, there too went his vision, until it seemed that Hyam could peer to the empire's farthest reaches.

Then the flaming paths had risen up like snakes, writhing around him, binding and blistering with savage glee.

The moon cast a silver wreath over the cottage and garden and barn, just as it had in his dream. Hyam pulled bucket after glistening bucket from the well and poured them over his head, doing what he could to wash the images away. The cows had grown used to his early arrival and shouldered in beside him to drink from the trough. He milked them and the goats, filled the byre with fresh fodder, and ate a meal of flatbread and fresh cheese and plums. By daybreak he was ready to set off for the fields, when he heard a distant voice call his name.

Norvin was a broad-shouldered man with a ready grin. The mayor ruled through good humor and strength of will. Hyam's mother had considered him a dear friend.

Norvin swallowed Hyam's hand in his own and demanded, "How are you keeping, boy?"

"Working hard." He hesitated, then added, "Nights are a trial."

"Loss will do that to you. Stand fast. It will pass."

"I hope you're right."

"And I'll wager you've forgotten what happens in four days' time."

Hyam had to search hard. "The planting festival."

"We brought down a boar two days back. He should be good and hung by then. We'll bury him in coals and roast him all day. Good wine, pretty lasses, two fiddlers who've put down roots for the season." He clapped Hyam hard enough to almost buckle his knees. "You'll be right as sunrise. Or too hungover to care."

"I'll be there," Hyam promised. "Is that why you came?"

"Eh, yes, well, no." Norvin cast a wary gaze over the empty pastures. "The women elders are setting their eye on you, lad. They say your mother didn't want to marry you off, but she's gone, and it's time."

"It's none of their business."

"They tend to decide for themselves what is theirs to worry over. Mark my words, lad. You're a catch, and they aim to land you. I wouldn't want any man to go into such a battle blind."

Hyam caught the furtive looks and said, "You might as well give me the other half."

Norvin sighed. "You remember my niece Irvette."

"We grew up playing together." Hyam recalled a girl with a smile too broad for her face and copper pigtails that always seemed to dance with unbridled joy. "She married downriver."

"She lost her man to the midwinter fevers. And her own parents two years back. There's been some trouble with her man's family she won't discuss. Now she's back home, arguing with my wife over who has dibs on our loom and raising her little one in our little shed out back."

Hyam searched his heart, which was what the mayor's unspoken invitation deserved. All he felt was emptiness. "Come with me."

He led Norvin into the cottage and over to the alcove by the two windows. He opened the shutters, revealing his mother's loom and spinning machine and the half-finished tapestry. "Irvette can have it if she wants."

"Son, this is too much. Your mother—"

"Is gone. Irvette had a good hand with the weaving." The unfinished tapestry showed a mystery Hyam had pondered for over a year. A young man who looked remarkably like Hyam sat upon a massive warhorse. He was dressed in finery the color of royal purple. In his right hand was a staff, and atop the staff was a purple orb that shot brilliant light over the landscape. Hyam had twice asked his ailing mother about it, but the question had only caused her to weep.

He shuddered anew from the burden of lost hopes and said, "Irvette should complete what my mother couldn't. I will count that as payment enough."

The mayor of Honor village inspected him. "You know

what the elder ladies will say. That's the sort of gift a man uses to lay claim."

Hyam nodded and wished he could care one way or the other. Still . . . "We were friends. She's in mourning. As am I. We'll speak of our futures when the time is right."

Norvin puffed out his cheeks. "I could bring my wagon up tomorrow, if you're certain."

"It's the right thing. Take it."

They walked back outside. But Norvin made no move to rejoin the road. "There's something else. We've heard rumors, carried by tinkers I trust and a caravan making their way west."

The man's somber tone said it all. Hyam spoke the word, "War."

"How did you know?"

"My mother's dying wish was that I go tell my father of her passage. After the funeral I went back to Long Hall. My father was gone. But the Mistress of Long Hall saw me." He shuddered anew at the impact of her words. "She said war was coming."

Norvin took a moment digesting the news. Hyam did not rush him. The mayor finally asked, "You speak Ashanta?"

"I learned the tongue at Long Hall."

"Your mother had contacts with the Ashanta, as I recall."

"She claimed they were my father's connections, from his merchant days. She traded village weavings for their soaps and oils." He smiled at the memory. "I had a friend, Bryna. I haven't seen her in almost two years, not since Mother took ill."

"Rumors point to battles being fought throughout the bad-lands far to the east. Some say the troubles won't touch us, but too often trouble has a habit of spreading where it's not welcome. Will you go and ask if they have news?"

It was a sensible request. The Ashanta were telepaths, and legends claimed they could communicate with others of their race throughout the realm. Little was known about them for certain. The Ashanta themselves said nothing at all. They did not forbid contact. They did not dislike others. They simply lived apart. In every sense of the word.

Hyam replied, "I'll leave tomorrow at first light."

The hand on his shoulder was gentle this time. "You are a friend to our village. And to my clan." The mayor of Honor started off, then turned back to ask, "How long has it been since you've seen Irvette?"

"The summer we both turned ten," Hyam recalled. "She was betrothed the year I returned from Long Hall. We might have spoken before she left Honor. I don't remember much of that time, except how happy I was to be rid of the mages."

"The lass has changed. Even carrying her sorrow she's a lovely woman." Norvin inspected him anew. "You were apprenticed to the wizards for five years?"

"An eternity, more like."

"Did any of it catch?"

"Very little magic, if that's what you mean. The elders of Long Hall share few secrets with acolytes."

"Pity, that. If we're to raise a militia, having a bit of wizardry on hand could make all the difference."

"Magic is outlawed," Hyam pointed out.

"So is war, lad." The mayor of Honor kicked at a stone. "So is the killing of one's own."

3

Hyam's two horses and the oxen would pull his wagon along the forest trail, but they did so reluctantly. Hyam found it hard to pay attention to genuine threats, with them jerking and pulling and veering. Horses and oxen alike loathed the forest and moaned at each scrape of branch upon branch. Leading a team on his own was nigh on impossible. The previous harvest season, Hyam had almost been trampled when some beast had howled in the distance and the team bolted. So far this spring he made do with a handcart. He had erected a lean-to where the trail entered the clearing and left his tools there. Most farmers dared not leave valuable implements laying about. But in all his life he had only met a handful of others upon the trail, and none since his uncle had passed away.

Today he carried just his bow. A quiver hung from his back, and a knife long as his forearm was strapped to his waist. It was more a sword than a knife, but peasants were forbidden to own weapons of war. Hyam had learned to wield it from the Long Hall forester, a silent mage whose few words would still the most feral of beasts.

Hyam's bow was as tall as he, and only three people he knew could string it, much less bring it to full draw. He had made the bow himself, fashioned on the instructions of his uncle, the most patient man Hyam had ever known. His mother's brother had once served as archer to the king. The year Hyam had returned from his banishment to the Long Hall, while the nightmares plagued him and he feared he would never be free from his stone prison, his uncle had taken him deep into the forest. There a lightning bolt had split a yew so vast ten men could not have joined hands around its girth. Together they had fashioned three bows, one for his uncle and two for Hyam. Each had been formed from the point where the supple exterior wood joined the stronger heartwood. Hyam's first bow had been a third smaller and so slender he feared his uncle was mocking him. But his uncle had explained that Hyam was coming to archery late in life and needed a youth's implement to develop the skill. Two years he had drawn and shot, drawn and shot. In the process he had developed shoulders broad as his larger ox and a chest to match. Then his uncle had declared him an archer and shifted him to the second bow. Somewhere along the way, the nightmares had stopped. They'd never returned. Until now.

He stepped into the oval farmland in the heat of mid-morning. He set his bow and quiver by the lean-to and reached for his tools. But when his hand settled upon the spade, Hyam faltered. He told himself it was only a dream, that no night

26

specter was waiting to shout in the forbidden tongue and pounce. He forced himself to grip the implement.

Farming was all about meeting the most urgent need. Chores were never done. Accepting this was part of sleeping at night. Since his uncle had passed away and his mother took ill that final time, Hyam had limited his crops to less than half the field. He planted a border of fruit trees around the tiny spring that bubbled up near his shed. He raised some wheat but gave most of his time to vegetables. Every season he debated whether he should put the pastures surrounding his cottage to the plow and forget the oval field entirely. But he knew it was idle chatter. There was no other farm that came close to his yield or quality.

He had been debating whether to add a few rows of corn. It meant reclaiming some of the fallow earth, which had not been touched in more than two years. Not to mention forcing a terrified ox to walk the forest trail so the beast could drag the plow. And he was going to put in some blackberry vines that he had clipped from wild bushes growing along the forest perimeter. They had rested in a shallow watering trough for three days, and all had sprouted roots.

Hyam walked to the point where his farthest row of carrots met the knee-high weeds. This field contained mystery upon mystery—how the wild growth never rose higher, how brambles never took hold, how neither ravens nor wild mice attacked his ripening crops. He often wondered about such things as he worked. Imaginings about some long-forgotten heritage and a possible tie to his mother's forebears did much to shove his loneliness aside.

He settled into the simple, satisfying routine of hard work and sweat. The heat grew with the sun's approach to zenith. He stripped off his shirt, drank deep, and started on another row. When it happened.

The shovel in his hand vibrated like a water-seeker's implement. Hyam dropped it and jumped back. The spade lay at his feet, mocking his jolt of genuine terror. He hesitated a long moment, then picked it up once more. The sense of power returned, but muted.

He stood there in the baking heat, wondering. Either he confronted this or he packed up and left for the day. And then . . . what? Return the next day and let his fears dominate again?

Angrily he stabbed the shovel into the earth. And leapt back a second time, shouting as he did. Because the earth came alive before him.

The furrow opened with a rustling sound, like a river of dry earth, which in a way was precisely what he saw.

Two years of weeds and wildflowers disappeared as the earth turned upon itself. The furrow opened at the pace that Hyam could run, quiet and easy and smooth. It reached the field's far end and stopped. The forest beyond remained silent. The furrow lay straight as a sword. Open. Waiting.

Hyam reached down and hefted the spade. The same thrilling energy vibrated through his hand, up his arm, through his entire body. He sensed it more clearly now. The force seemed to be coursing in both directions, from the spade to him, and back down again.

Hyam took two steps to his left and gingerly planted the

28

blade into the earth. Another furrow opened up before him. Running with impossible precision across the expanse. The oval field was at its longest here, almost a mile in diameter. No trained team could plow such a line. It did not waver nor vary an inch. He stepped over and started another, not even waiting this time. Again and again, until he had a dozen furrows all opening before him simultaneously. The air was filled with the sound of softly ripping roots, of earth tumbling and opening and turning.

He reached the field's far side and halted. Now that he was done, he could not believe his own audacity. The shovel continued to vibrate softly. The coursing energy was no longer content to flow from his body to the dirty handle and back. Hyam felt it rise up from the earth now, filling him with an immense awareness of his connection to this place. A bonding that ignored time or logical limits.

Hyam jerked again as the dream flashed behind his eyes. He recalled how it had ended, the lines of power rising from the earth and lashing him with cords of flame and vengeance.

At that very moment, a voice cried merrily, "Do my eyes deceive me? Have we found ourselves a farmer practicing the forbidden arts?"

4

The first man who emerged from the woods was a knight of the realm. Even from this distance, Hyam could see the gold chain of office that looped around his neck and under his sword arm. The chain was linked to a mail coat that sparkled like polished silver. He kneed his horse forward. The sunlight caught the gemstones on his sword's hilt and flickered off the rings upon his gloved hands. He wore no helmet but rather a fanciful cap of black leather. A black feather sprouted from the cap and waved jauntily as his steed trod upon the perfect furrows.

"Stand still, you," he called. "It's far too hot to give chase."

Hyam measured the distance to the bow leaning against the shed, then gave up the thought when eight men-at-arms emerged between him and his weapon. The knight must have seen him tense for the race, for he grinned and shouted to his fellows, "I say, we have come upon a fighter as well as a farmer."

All nine warriors rode destriers. Hyam had never seen one before, but he had heard tales. The beasts were massive, fully twice the size of his own workhorses, heavier even than his largest ox. Destriers were trained to obey their riders' commands even in the heat of battle. They were bred for ferocity and fury and fought with teeth as well as hooves. Such horses would not be spooked by forest scents or sounds.

One of the men-at-arms held back and called, "Perhaps he is a mage, sire."

"Don't be foolish. Look at the man. He is a peasant with a forbidden gift." The knight ambled across the field. "Which explains his tilling this forest pasture. Doesn't want anyone else to know his dirty little secret."

The first warrior did not share his mate's qualms. The blade snickered as he drew his sword from its scabbard. The warhorse snorted in anticipation and stepped forward. The other knights made a line behind him, tracking around the forest perimeter.

"Hold there a moment." The knight's smile was a carelessly tossed lie. "We are tasked with ferreting out the Ashanta village. Point us in the right direction, that's a good lad."

Hyam remained silent.

"Come, come, peasant. We know one exists around here. Don't deny it. Give us directions and we'll make your end swifter than you deserve."

Hyam still did not speak.

"Well, never mind. We'll find them soon enough. Who has the rope?"

"I do, sire," the second soldier called.

"Well then, stop your shilly-shallying and string the fellow up." He gave Hyam a cheery wave. "We'll burn your village while we wait for my brother the prince to arrive with our full force. Of course, we could aim straight for the Ashanta, if you'd do us the kindness. Still refuse to speak? Well, never mind. A village roasting is as good a way as any to idle away the hours."

Hyam's racing heart only heightened the sense of connectedness to the power. It coursed through his shabby boots, up his legs, filling his body, pouring into his arms and the fists clenching the shovel's handle. He did not think on what to do. He simply gave motion to the power.

He stabbed the earth with the spade. As he did so, he spoke the first word of Milantian he had uttered in nine long years. The word came as naturally as the power that now rushed from his hands, down the handle, through the blade, into the earth. *"Open!"*

Another furrow rippled forward. Only this one was neither straight nor shallow. It coursed forward, reached the tree line, and turned sharp left. Taking aim at the warriors.

The first horse snorted and jerked back. The soldier sawed at the reins, but it did no good. Nothing did. The furrow opened like the maw of a great beast formed from earth and stone. The trees bowed back, their roots exposed like gnarled fangs. The earth was riven by a trough fifteen paces wide and twice as deep. The soldier gave a single hoarse scream, echoed by his steed. Then he tumbled into the depths.

The other warriors were caught in a panic-stricken jumble. They yelled and sought to flee in every direction save toward the opening earth. But to no avail. The furrow swept up and opened farther and swallowed them all.

Hyam lifted his spade. Instantly the cavern closed, smooth as flowing water. The sounds of screaming men and horses were chopped off. The roots returned to their place, anchoring the terrain. Of the men there was no sign.

From behind him, Hyam heard the sound of pounding hooves. He turned in time to see the knight disappear into the woods at the field's far end.

There was no time for worry nor logic. He knew with gut-wrenching certainty what he had to do. Hyam raced to the shed, over earth that now compressed eight warriors and their steeds. He hefted his bow and strung it in one fluid motion. He plucked an arrow from his quiver, lifted the bow, and drew it to his chin, aiming it at the point where the knight had vanished among the trees. He released the arrow and yelled the three Milantian words, *"Fly! Find! Kill!"*

The arrow flew over the silent field and disappeared into the forest. A moment later, Hyam heard a shout followed by a crash.

He raced across the field and into the forest. The branches seemed to lean away from him, as though granting him a momentary free passage. Which of course was impossible. But Hyam was too intent upon his fallen prey to give notice. He had always moved easily through the thickest undergrowth.

He spotted the horse first, standing in trembling fear above its fallen rider. Hyam lashed the horse to a nearby sapling, then examined the knight.

The arrow had taken him straight through the center of

his chest. Blood dappled the indolent mouth as the knight reached up, his eyes and hand pleading since his voice failed him.

Hyam demanded, "Where is your force?"

The knight pointed to his left. Hyam searched for some unseen trail, then realized the man was aiming at his horse.

"How large is your army? When will they arrive?" Hyam asked.

The man continued to point at his steed, his gaze imploring.

Then Hyam noticed the chest. A large lockbox banded in iron was lashed tightly to the saddle. Hyam realized, "You want to pay me for a healing."

The man's gaze grew more frantic still.

"I am no healer." Hyam leaned over the dying man. Words sprang to his mind, a quotation that had once flamed within his young heart. They came from the first Elven scroll he had ever studied. Now the words came to him unbidden. Hyam spoke in a tongue he knew the knight did not understand. "I am vengeance. I am the protector of my people. I am wrath unleashed."

The light in the man's eyes faded, then vanished altogether. Hyam stood there a moment, then turned and walked to the horse, which whickered softly at his approach. Hyam allowed him to smell his hand and wondered if death carried a scent to such animals, for the horse shied away. Hyam spoke softly and remained there, waiting until the horse allowed him to stroke his nose. He took his time, scratching the spot behind each ear, then trailing his hand down along the horse's flank. He then moved to the saddle and unlashed the chest. It tumbled heavily to the ground.

Hyam walked back over and searched the corpse for a key, which he found dangling from the gold chain of station. He slipped it over the inert arm, walked back, and unlocked the chest. And groaned at the sight.

The chest held a fortune in booty. Each item cried in silent woe. Some of the rings still held fingers.

Hyam returned and stripped the man of all his finery, the jeweled rings and the bracelets and the heavy coin purse and another chain hidden beneath the leather vest and the sword and the mail. The hat with its bloodstained feather he left on the ground. He lashed the chest back to the saddle and hung the mail and sword from the pommel. He led the horse back toward the field, then returned to stand over the body.

He had no idea whether the force would work here. Or whether the spade was required. But there was only one way to find out.

Hyam drew his knife and hesitated a long moment. Then he sensed a power emanating from his oval field, coursing through the earth beneath his feet. Ready. Hyam stabbed the ground and spoke the word again. "*Open.*"

The earth ripped and groaned and gave a mighty yawn. The body tumbled in among the roots and shadows.

Hyam withdrew the knife.

The earth closed.

5

Joelle unsheathed her knives and unrolled her stolen scroll. The last two documents she had slipped from the wizard's library had proven useless, for they were written in some archaic script she did not understand. This scroll, however, was about something called "cold fire." She drew in the mage-force, spoke the words, laced her blades with the power, and began her nightly routine. Stabbing the shadows of her windowless room, sweeping down upon foes that were asleep in other areas of the Long Hall. Readying herself for the chance that she vowed would come soon. To fight. To flee. Or die. She no longer cared much either way.

The memories were hot tonight, as brilliantly clear as the magical force her blades weaved in the still air. Normally she did not indulge in either recollection or regret, for both cost her too much resolve. But tonight marked the beginning of her fourth year, the last she would spend here. She was almost ready. Even if she wasn't, she was going. And tonight the memories of her arrival swept her away.

The only part of her former life that the wizards had let her keep was her name. They had even argued over that, but in the end the quarrel had faded into sullen resentfulness. Joelle had still been weak from the ailment that had almost killed her, such that acolytes had carried her on the same stretcher her mother's kin had used to bring her from their homeland. Nine days they had traveled to arrive at this Long Hall, and not once had they spoken to her or even looked her way.

As it was, many of the wizards she met in those early fever-stricken days did not want to take her in. Those who opposed her staying in the Long Hall did not actually come out and say what they thought, which was she would be better off dead and all the problems she represented buried with her. Joelle had silently agreed with them, for she had loathed the stone community at first sight. She had just turned fifteen, and she was to be their prisoner for life.

Her one true friend among the mages was named Trace, and he was the Master who ruled over all the wizards and their community, which was named after the largest structure, a Long Hall.

"None of this is as it should be," he told her six weeks after her arrival, when she was finally strong enough to rise from her bed and walk unaided. "But here at least you are safe. The mages and acolytes are forbidden from bothering you in any way."

Trace pointed across the stone plaza to the oddest element of the entire Long Hall, the door. There was only one way in or out. Even the fields lay within the high stone wall, even the quarry.

"Beyond that portal lies only death," Trace said.

Joelle liked him and she liked his heart, for Trace was not just kindly but a wizard of passion and feeling. So she told him the truth. "You should have left me in the forest to die."

His hand dropped. "That was forbidden to us also."

"But why?"

They were seated by the central fountain. The water sparkled and played a merry tune, mocking her.

Trace asked, "How much did your parents tell you?"

"That their marriage was forbidden, but they were in love and my mother was pregnant with me, so they fled into the forest." She clenched her fists along with her jaw. She had promised herself that she would not shed a single tear in this place. Not ever.

"And then they died."

"Of the fever," Joelle confirmed.

"And you were alone."

"For almost a year."

"Until you caught the same fever. What happened then?"

Faint images came and went behind her eyes, disjointed glimpses of a different world and a hidden folk who sang their speech and melded with the trees and the sunlight. She recalled a journey beyond time and place, one that ended by her being left in a meadow before a city of white stone. Joelle knew he was not mocking her, but still she could not speak of what she was not entirely certain she had seen at all. She simply replied, "I'm not sure. I was very sick."

"Somehow you were brought to your mother's people. And they brought you to us."

"Why did you take me?" When he hesitated, Joelle pressed, "Why do you *keep* me?"

"Our treaty with your people goes back a thousand years." Trace spoke slowly, carefully weighing each word. "Almost as long as the edict that forbade your parents' union. To put it bluntly, we owe them. Your mother's people ordered us to take you in and keep you here all your life. We had no choice but to agree."

She liked how he spoke to her, without guile or any desire to hide even the most painful truths. "Why did my mother's people heal me? Why not just let me die?"

Trace spun a finger, swirling magical force into a ribbon of light that rose to join with the sunlight. "To that, I have no answer. They like to think of themselves as compassionate, I suppose."

Joelle watched the rainbow ribbon and remembered her mother making the same design, a game to delight a child. She fought for control once more, then replied, "I can think of many ways to describe what they've done to me. Compassionate is not one of them."

Trace stilled his hands, the magic faded, and he said, "Your mother's people are known to hold certain abilities."

Instantly she understood this was why the Master of the Havering Long Hall was speaking to her. It was not to reassure or to comfort but to *know*.

Trace went on, "They can see beyond the reach of physical eyes. Can you do that, Joelle?"

She hesitated, then decided she would give him the truth. "Ever since I was a child."

He nodded, as though he approved of her response. But she was certain Trace found her answer most troubling.

"Can you sense anything particular about this place?"

She had perceived it when she first arrived. "A chamber lined in spells. And full of power."

"To approach that place is forbidden upon pain of death." When she did not respond, he continued, "You must be aware that some mages want to cast you out. They do not think you belong any more than you do. These wizards look for a reason to expel you from here. Your mother's people have vowed to kill you, should you ever emerge."

Master Trace gave her a long moment to ponder this, then went on, "Our own acolytes are not told of the hidden chamber or what it holds until they have taken their final vows. If you seek to pierce the forces shielding that room, most likely the protective spells will destroy you. You will not enter, this I can promise you. The spells are as sensitive as they are strong. If you try and survive, you will be sent away. If you leave the Long Hall, you will die."

"That holds a certain appeal."

"You will die," he repeated. "Your mother's people made this very clear."

"And if I stay, what then?"

The Master of Havering Long Hall sighed softly, as though the most difficult part of his day was now behind him. "We train our acolytes in the hidden arts. I will try to have you included among them."

"Try? You are the Master."

"My opponents in this matter are very strong. But I give you my word, I will try."

In the end, though, Trace's best efforts were not enough. The mages who sought her eviction used her heritage as a reason to keep her from studying with the other acolytes. Even so, Trace remained true to his word and secretly taught her all he could. Joelle suspected that all along the Master assumed she would one day use the spells to break out of the Long Hall and then protect herself from her mother's kin. But by the time she grew certain of this, Joelle had learned to hide certain mysteries from everyone, even her one true friend.

Joelle completed her exercises, stowed away her knives and the stolen scroll, and prepared for bed. Her last thought was the same as every night, that this would be her last month of imprisonment. When she awoke, she was thrilled to discover that this was to be one of her special, secret dawns.

Joelle never knew which mornings would liberate her, or even how they happened. But she reveled in her brief spans of liberty, even when she was not in truth free at all. For on many such occasions, she did not *go*. Rather, she was *taken*.

Such journeys always came at the same moment, at night's end, as she gradually transitioned to wakefulness. There was a breath like most breaths, and then she escaped. Free from her body, from her cell, from this place.

There was a tiny crack in the Long Hall's outer barrier, so small that ants could not pass single file, and yet large enough for her to squeeze through. Once beyond the wall, she was both free and not free. Free, because she could sometimes move as she wished, enter the forest, and dwell there until her body demanded she return and rise and begin another dull day. Not free, because she was often taken where she did not want to go.

This morning's travel was not under her control.

Joelle had been brought to this yellow city a number of times. But she still could not say how she came, or why. Only that an enemy lived here. Such journeys carried a weight, a burden, that filled her soul with foreboding. When they were over, and she was back in her windowless stone cell inside the Long Hall, she wondered if it meant that she was to die in that city. Which filled her with a painful hope, since it meant she would succeed in breaking out and being free for a time, and surviving until she arrived there.

So she came, but never of her own accord, and always to the same place. From her perch, the yellow city rose on the opposite side of a broad valley. Ridges rose and fell to the end of the world. The desert was all-consuming. Not even time held much sway here. The years this city had endured were beyond count.

Only this day she was not alone.

A full army was gathered along her ledge, the men of a type she had never seen before. They were bearded and wild, carrying massive swords and double-bladed axes and spears, and riding horses as fierce as the men. The horsemen were flanked by foot soldiers, and all of them glared across the valley at the city. Their gazes were intense and flinty, the same fury burning on every face. Joelle was very glad indeed she could not be seen.

It seemed to her that she viewed a different season than the one in which her body dwelled. This had happened a few times before, and on each occasion Joelle had the distinct impression there was a lesson here, or a warning, such as now. The warriors were dressed in furs, with leggings and boots and gloves beneath their mail. Breath steamed silver-white from beast and man alike. Back in the realm where she slept, it was late spring. Joelle had no idea why this was happening, only that she must observe.

Across the distance, the city gates opened. This was another remarkable component of her journeys, how she could see even remote objects with crystal clarity. She stood on a rock behind the army and watched as a frivolous, chattering mob of knights emerged from the city gates. At their center walked two indolent men with gold chains of royal office looped around their shoulders. One wore a crown, the other a dandy's cap of black leather with a tall black feather. Both wore jeweled rings over gloves and were clutched at by chattering women. The men accepted the other knights' cloying attention as their due. The group laughed and caroused and ignored the army on the opposite ridgeline.

Servants scurried through the gates and set down tables and chairs and two high-backed thrones for their leaders, then lay out silver platters of fruit and poured golden goblets full of wine. A minstrel began playing a lute as a battalion of foot soldiers tromped out and formed up alongside the knights.

The warrior closest to Joelle's perch unsheathed his great sword and shouted words she could not understand. It seemed to her that the very earth trembled as the other warriors took up the roar.

But the knights seated on the valley's other side remained untouched by the ferocity.

The warrior pointed his sword, yelled something more, and all the warriors set off down the ridge into the valley.

At that moment, another figure emerged from the city gates. Though Joelle had never seen him before, still she knew him. The crimson mage carried a scent so fierce she could smell it without her body, a vile stench of all the towns he had burned, all the lives destroyed. The wizard carried a staff, upon which glowed an orb as red as his robes. He turned to the approaching horde and gestured with his free hand. He spoke words that seared Joelle where she stood. As he uttered his spell, what appeared to be metal insects emerged from his shadowed hood and swarmed about him.

The minstrel stopped playing then, and most of the knights could no longer pretend to be enjoying themselves. Only the indolent pair at their center remained at ease.

A putrid mist began spewing from the orb, forming tendrils that slithered down the slope, growing snakelike arms as it raced toward the warriors. The mist was the color of watery blood. It clung to the rocks and the scrub, rising no more than a few inches from the earth.

The warriors saw it and faltered, but before their leader could sound a retreat, the mist was upon them.

As soon as the mist touched their feet, the warriors and

their steeds were bound in place. They and their mounts screamed and struggled, but to no avail.

The mist crept up each of the warriors, blanketing them in the vile shade, until only their heads were free. Then the remaining mist melted into the valley floor.

To the faltering sound of the lute, the indolent knight lifted one hand. Reluctantly the foot soldiers started forward, marching down the ridge, entering the valley. Down to where the army was trapped like screaming pillars.

Joelle could not depart. She knew this from experience. When she was taken somewhere, she remained until she was hauled back. But she could at least turn her face away. There was nothing, however, that she could do about the screams and sounds of chopping meat and metal striking metal. She had no ears, nor hands to cover them.

Only when the valley went silent did she turn back. And even then she did not want to, but her attention was pulled around with the same force that had drawn her here. To her astonishment, the valley floor was covered with nothing save a dark grey ash. Of the warriors and horses, the only sign they had ever existed was the line of blood-spattered foot soldiers who tromped up the opposite ridge and passed through the city gates.

Joelle watched as the two knights rose, drained their goblets, and sauntered back into the city. The day's entertainment was over. A silent clutch of knights and women and servants hastily followed.

The only one who remained was the crimson mage, who lifted his staff and waited as the ash swirled and blew away, though there was no wind to carry it. The mist rose from the earth and swept back up the ridge and was swallowed by the orb. Still the wizard stood there, staring out over the empty valley.

Though the cowl held such shadows that the wizard's face remained well hidden, still Joelle knew he was looking straight at her. He lifted the staff, but at that moment she was drawn away, back, back, over forests and fields, through the crack in the wall, into her cell . . .

Joelle bolted upright. Her chest heaved with such force, each breath carried a tight moan. She never felt the fear until her return.

She forced herself to rise from the bed, the images and the sounds seared upon her brain. As she dressed and walked down the stone corridor to begin her day's work, she wondered if it was all intended as a warning. Leave the Long Hall and face the red wizard. But even this was no longer enough to stop her.

Joelle was leaving. And soon.

6

By the time Hyam traversed the forest trail and arrived home, he found himself defeated by the truth. No amount of mental argument could rid him of the burden he carried. He had killed soldiers of the realm. And a knight. With magic.

The knight's casual brutality rang in his mind. To remain in his home risked destruction of Hyam's entire village. He could not take that chance. He dismounted in the cottage forecourt both heartsore and exhausted, knowing he would be wearier still before the night was done.

Hyam watered and fed the horse, then entered the cottage and stuffed a satchel with clothes, his razor, a few keepsakes from his mother, and an extra pair of boots. To this he added his five sacks of arrows. He then heated water and bathed and dressed carefully. His mother had always insisted upon wearing her finest to visit the Ashanta village. Hyam's festival clothes bore the fragrance of the herbs in which his mother had packed them. He gave the cottage a long look, and his gaze rested upon the tapestry. In the moonlight his mother's final artwork seemed alive, the orb's violet globe shimmering across the stone floor and touching him where he stood. He recalled the way his mother had sung as she worked the loom, a wordless melody from a distant time. The memories added a piercing poignancy to the act of locking his front door.

He rode with his bow packed in a leather slipcover and fitted into a saddle loop probably intended to hold a lance. The satchel and extra arrows and the knight's gear were all lashed behind the chest. Hyam had spent his winters sanding down the ash boughs and hardening the tips in the coals and sharpening the iron bolts he bought from passing tinkers. The feathers came from his own flock of geese that wintered elsewhere but returned each spring and bred their babies in malodorous nests that lined his pond's far side. It did not seem to matter that each summer Hyam trapped a score and more of the geese for his oven. They came without fail, and each autumn he walked the frigid mud and harvested a fine crop of long wing feathers. Some arrow makers claimed feathers drawn from the same wing made for a truer aim, but Hyam discounted that, just as he did the need to sing war tunes while sharpening the heads. He wet his feathers and flattened them beneath a stone for ten days before gluing them into place. He had won enough competitions to be confident of their accuracy.

The sunset was dimming as he pulled up in front of Norvin's home. The mayor's house was larger than most and rimmed by a waist-high wall. The family had raised massive wolfhounds for generations beyond count. Their watchdog barked once, a sound deep as a bear's growl, then whined as Hyam reached over the gate and allowed the beast to sniff his hand. He had always wanted a wolfhound of his own but never managed the price. A trained wolfhound cost as much as a cottage.

"Hyam?" To his surprise, it was not the mayor who approached but his niece. Irvette rounded the corner of the hard-packed yard, an infant in her arms. "What brings you here?"

"I must have a word with your uncle."

"He and Auntie are with the elders." Instead of the girl child he recalled, a beautiful woman stood before him, her features stained from recent loss. "They should be back any minute. I'm making supper. Have you eaten?"

"Not since daybreak."

"Come in and keep me company." She opened the gate, then inspected the heavily laden horse. "What are you carrying?"

"Gifts. I'm sorry for your loss, Irvette."

"And I am grateful for your kind offer. But I can't accept."

His mind was overfull from an impossible day, which excused the fact that he needed a moment to realize she meant his mother's loom. "I ask for nothing in return, Irvette."

"Hyam, you are a fine catch and will make some woman very happy. But it will not be me." Her grey eyes were bronzed by the dusk. "I am in love with a village lad. Neither of us expected this. But it has happened. He is waiting for the mourning to end before asking my uncle for my hand. I am betrothed in all but name."

He followed her into the house. "Do I know him?"

"Probably. So I will not say his name. My uncle should be first to hear. He is a youngest son, which means he has no prospect for land or home." Her smile was guileless, and even with the burden of recent sorrow she carried a maiden's joy. "It's good my uncle is a man of means."

He watched her fill an earthen bowl with stew. "I'm very happy for you both."

"Thank you, Hyam." She set the bowl in front of him, then added a chunk of bread before asking, "Where are you going this time of night?"

"I'm leaving on an errand. Or quest. I'm not sure which." He spoke between bites. "There is no telling when I will return. And whether I'll be permitted to stay in the village if I do."

She settled onto the bench beside him. "What have you done, Hyam?"

"As you say, it's best your uncle hear first."

"The horse you've left out front. It's a warrior's steed, isn't it."

"Yes, and that's all I'll say." He pointed to the pot and the ladle. "May I have more?"

She served him a second bowl and sliced more bread and then seated herself and fed the infant. Midway through his second helping, the mayor of Honor pushed open the door. "Whose beast of war is that out front? Hyam?"

"We need to talk."

The mayor's wife mirrored his girth and utterly lacked Norvin's good humor. She was both rotund and big-boned and greeted the world with the sharp edge of her tongue.

Norvin seemed to enjoy having his mate cut and parry with his foes. This allowed the mayor to show one and all a ruddy good cheer. Hyam doubted that Irvette found it easy dwelling in that woman's garden shed.

Norvin's expression grew as severe as his wife's while Hyam told of killing the knight and his retinue. Hyam did not tell them everything. He wanted to, but each time he strayed from the barest of facts, his throat clenched tight.

Even so, the mayor's wife discerned the truth. "Nine warriors taken down by one bow."

"Hyam is the village's finest archer," Norvin said doubtfully.

"A forest hunter. A farmer. Killing nine armed soldiers. Do you even hear yourself?"

"Hyam claims to have learned little magic at the Long Hall."

"What wizard tells a mere mortal the truth?"

"I have never met one to ask."

She snorted. "You defend him because he killed men he *claims* were going to harm us. But in truth his actions might spell our doom."

Even Irvette was troubled by the exchange and cradled the infant more closely as she observed from the fireplace. Hyam found confirmation of his own decision there in their fearful expressions. He rose from the table and said, "There's more."

He went back outside and retrieved the chest. He opened it on the table and showed them the bloodstained booty. "I have taken a purse full of coins for myself. The rest I give to the village."

"What am I to do with this?" Norvin demanded.

"Protect our hamlet and the valley. Hold this against an uncertain future."

Norvin looked at his wife, who snapped, "We certainly can't keep it here."

Norvin pointed out, "There's a fortune in that chest."

"Aye, more than enough to see the village burned about our ears."

Hyam decided there was nothing to be gained by pointing out the knight had already vowed to do just that. "I could leave it with the Ashanta on deposit."

Norvin brightened immensely. The Ashanta served as bankers to all the outlying regions. They took their cut and made the money available anywhere in the realm. Norvin glanced at his wife, who struggled to find something to criticize but finally shrugged her acquiescence.

"There's not much need in asking the Ashanta to confirm what we already know," Norvin pointed out.

"The knight said they were tasked with destroying the Ashanta settlement," Hyam replied. "I must warn them."

"Will you return?"

"I don't know. Should I?" When the mayor did not respond, he added, "Will you permit it?"

"No," his wife groused. "Harboring a mage is punishable by the razing of the entire village."

"But if the army comes through, he could mean our deliverance," Norvin replied.

"Or our destruction," she countered. "A thousand times no."

"Your wife is correct." Hyam rose slowly, wearied by far

more than the longest day of his entire life. "Thank you for the meal."

Norvin followed him outside. "Give her time. She'll come around. You are not just welcome, but needed."

"What she says is right. It may be too great a risk." He turned and called back through the open doorway. "Irvette, forgive me, but I must speak. Join us, please." When she and Norvin's wife both stepped forward, Hyam went on, "Norvin, your niece is in love with a village boy. She has waited to say something out of honor to your house. But there isn't time. I want Irvette to have my cottage."

The three were once again reduced to astonished silence.

"And the flocks," Hyam went on. "And the pastures. But not the field in the forest. That you must not enter."

"It's too much," Irvette murmured.

"It would give my heart rest to know my home remains a haven for love and new beginnings."

"And if you return?"

He studied the three fine faces, saw the strength and the goodness and the roots sunk deep in the village earth. And knew with visceral certainty that he was closing a chapter of his life. "Let your uncle be witness that I hold no debt over you. I will accept what you wish to give me. If I return."

"When you return," Irvette replied softly, ignoring the swift glance her aunt cast. "When."

It was a hopeful note upon which to take his leave, even if he did not believe it himself. "Be well, Irvette. Stay safe. Be happy. Fill my mother's house with laughter and love and many children."

More than firelight added a flush to her cheeks. "A sweet boy has grown into a man of honor. Be well, Hyam. And remember where your home is."

Hyam walked down the front path. By the gate he offered the mayor his hand in farewell.

"One moment," Norvin said. He turned and walked around his house.

Which meant Hyam was left alone with the mayor's wife. As he lashed the chest back into place, she hissed, "You are a mage. A forbidden one. My husband in his fear of war fails to see the threat directly in front of his face."

"I mean you and yours no harm," Hyam replied.

"Then depart at once." She wheeled about. "And never return."

Norvin appeared soon after, and something in the man's expression said that the mayor had heard every word. In fact, it could well have been that he had intended his wife to speak what he could not utter. For he refused to meet Hyam's gaze as he said, "I've seen you admire my hounds. Take this one. She's the finest of my brood."

The young wolfhound was silver with a white streak running from between her golden eyes to the tip of her tail. She stood almost as tall as Hyam's waist. "She's magnificent."

"Aye, the white streak is said to be the mark of high intelligence. She'd be destined for the king's stables if I took her to market." He snapped his fingers and pointed at the ground by Hyam's feet. The animal loped forward. "I call her Dog, like all my pups. She'll mind you well enough. When you're ready, give her a name that suits you both. Short and sharp works best." He offered Hyam a strip of jerky. "Feed her a bit, let her have a good sniff."

Hyam did as instructed. As he stroked the thick pelt, he saw she stood on paws the size of dinner plates. "She's not yet fully grown?"

"Comes with the pale strip down the back, or so I'm told. Means she's more wolf than dog, with a bit of snow-warg thrown in for good measure."

He fed her the rest of the jerky, then pointed to the ground where she stood. "Stay, girl." Even seated, the dog was taller than the house's surrounding wall. "She's a beauty, Norvin. Thank you."

Norvin hesitated, then swept up the younger man in an embrace as fierce as it was brief. Then he turned and walked away.

Hyam watched the mayor shut the portal without a backward glance. Then he climbed back into the saddle and looked down to where the wolfhound watched him with unblinking golden patience. "Let's go, girl. The road awaits."

The journey to the Ashanta village should have taken two full days. Hyam had no idea how he remained awake through that long night. But he did. What was more, he made good time. The night was utterly still, the sky lit by a moon one sliver off full. Where the valley narrowed, the hills rose to either side like humpbacked beasts. The trail tracked along the river's edge, two ghostly ribbons that cut through the dale.

His thoughts made for foul company. The final words

hissed by the mayor's wife scalded away any regret he might have had over giving up the only home he had ever known. The certainty that he had done the right thing, however, could not chase off the question that had plagued him since returning from the Long Hall. Hyam's lack of knowledge regarding his own heritage was only heightened by his newfound magical prowess. The night echoed with words spoken by a Mistress who lived without deceit. Only the Milantians were said to be adept at their own tongue.

A thousand years of peace had turned the warrior race into legends meant to scare children. But Hyam had studied the remaining scrolls because he had been forced to. Milantians looked like their human kin. But their powers were immense, their destruction still evident beyond the eastern badlands. Or so Hyam had read. He had never been farther from his home than the Ashanta village up ahead. The fact that he was setting off on a journey that might last his lifetime, without either destination or a clear idea of his own past, left his chest aching.

Three hours into the journey he stopped to water the horse and search the surrounds for movement. His body was one huge bruise. Lifting himself back into the saddle was a massive chore. But as they set off, Hyam heard an owl cry, a sound like a baby's wail. He had occasionally caught glimpses of the birds, grey as frost with wings longer than his own arm span. The destrier merely snorted and his unnamed dog kept padding along. He had yet to hear the dog make a sound. The owl's mate cried from the valley's other side. That was how they hunted, spooking small animals with hunting calls from a multitude of directions. The owls kept up their noisy banter until dawn, tracking Hyam down the valley. When the birds finally went silent, Hyam had the sunrise to keep him from drifting off.

The region through which he passed, where he had dwelled all his life, was known as Three Valleys. A trio of broad streams coursed along the narrow vales, joining together ten miles below the Long Hall. Seventeen villages in all found shelter and relative prosperity within the bottom land. They were shielded from the world by forest and ridgeline. Goings-on within the realm beyond the hills was little more than fodder for idle talk. Most of the villagers liked it that way and hoped that all perilous events would long be over before the first tidings even arrived.

The name itself was misleading, as there were not three interconnected vales but four. The Ashanta name for the region was Eagle's Claw, after the fourth talon, short and razor sharp, that jutted from the back of the bird's foot. The Ashanta dwelled in a tight niche of flatland, encircled by forests and steep-sided cliffs. Beyond the ridgeline rose the Galwyn Range, arid and treacherous, home to mountain lions and beasts that had seldom been seen, much less named. The Ashanta were a race apart. They did not show hostility to visitors, they simply did not invite. They never traveled. In all Hyam's life, he had never met an Ashanta outside their village. For some inhabitants of Three Valleys, this silent isolation bred suspicion and hostility. If the Ashanta cared one way or the other what people thought of them, Hyam had not heard.

The sun was almost overhead and baking hot when Hyam reached the Ashanta boundary stones. The pyramids were a uniform white, though there was no such rock or quarry anywhere in the valleys. These chest-high pyramids were planted every three paces, stretching out in steadfast rhythm all the way to the distant cliffs and forests. Each face was carved with the Ashanta symbol for treaty. Their land possessed no fences. And yet their animals did not wander or roam. Ahead and to his left, a flock of sheep bleated softly. Farther up the valley to nowhere milled a large herd of cows. Between them were the crisscrossed patterns of springtime planting. Neither group of animals made any move toward the fresh new growth or approached the boundary stones.

The trail Hyam followed had grown increasingly rugged since the last village. At the stones, the road simply ended. Hyam did as his mother had always done upon arriving at their land. He stopped and waited. There was no need to call, for there was no one to hear. But he had the distinct impression that they knew and that they appreciated the gesture.

Forest and cliffs formed a ragged frame around the valley. Farther in the distance rose the inhospitable peaks, tight patches of snow along the highest reaches, but otherwise the faces were yellow as old teeth. A thin trickle of melt fell from the valley's far end, the waterfall mostly mist by the time it fed the stream that ran to Hyam's right. In another month's time the waterfall would vanish, but the streams remained all summer long, fed by a series of underground springs that flowed from cavern mouths.

Two such rivulets formed natural boundaries for the village that came into view as he passed the first headland. The village between the streams was fashioned from the same white stone as the boundary markers and sparkled fresh and silent in the sunlight. As he had hoped, a figure was seated on the offering stone. The flat white stone, broad as the floor of his cottage's main room, rose at the point where the two streams met. Tiny footbridges, scarcely as wide as a wagon, traversed the streams, almost fairylike in their miniature perfection.

Hyam traversed the bridge and halted before the stone. He did not raise a hand or speak a greeting, for he knew it would not be returned. The Ashanta had no word for hello or farewell.

His mother had often brought the village weavings and her own tapestries here, setting them upon the stone, waiting for a gift of oils and cloves and healing herbs. There was no negotiation with the Ashanta. Hyam had known the woman who sat waiting since childhood. Her name was Bryna, and she had been his favorite playmate. But she was a child no longer.

Bryna's merry laughter had been replaced by the unmoving calm that dominated the Ashanta world. Her eyes had taken on the violet cast of adulthood, a color so dark and rich it could be mistaken for black. There was no white to her eyes any longer. Just the rich, deep, unreadable violet. Hyam knew from the Long Hall's scrolls that this was the sign of Joining.

He could not stifle the groan as he eased from the saddle. Walking to the stone meant easing any number of cramps. He seated himself in gradual stages. "You've joined, then."

"Since last winter." Even Bryna's voice had changed. Gone was any vestige of humor, any emotion save the unreachable calm. "How are you, Hyam?"

"Sore."

"You rode all night?"

"I did. And this after the longest day of my life."

She sat in unmoving calm as he related what he had learned. She asked no questions. He spoke no secrets. For to divulge the means by which he had killed the enemy would have required him to describe the awakening of powers he did not understand. And one thing he vividly remembered from his early lessons. The Ashanta were sworn blood enemies of the Milantians.

When he was done, she rose and said, "The village calls me."

He gestured to the horse. "I've brought quivers of arrows for your hunters. I made them myself. And a coat of mail and a sword decorated with gemstones."

She hesitated a moment, and he had the distinct impression she was discussing this with an unseen host of others. "What will you have in return?"

"Nothing. It is a gift."

She and the unseen others examined him. "You have always been a friend to our people. You and your parents before you."

"There's something else." He forced himself to his feet and walked with her to the wagon. "The chest is full of war booty. Some of it . . . well . . ."

"We understand."

"I haven't had a chance to clean it."

"We can do this. You wish us to hold it in safety for your clan?"

"The mayor of Honor will come. Or another with authority to speak for the Three Valleys."

"Very well." She pointed to the stone. "We ask that you wait here, in case there is more that is required. Are you hungry?"

"Very." As she accepted an armload of arrows, Hyam asked, "Bryna, is there anything left of who you used to be?"

"It's not like that at all." She took a few steps, then added, "And yet it is."

"I miss my friend," he called after her. He waited and watched, but she gave no sign she had even heard.

7

Hyam unsaddled the horse but decided not to tether it. He doubted even a strange animal would stray far in this land. Soon four silent Ashanta arrived, two carrying steaming bowls. They set the food upon the stone and took away his gifts. They did not speak. He fed the dog from his own spoon, then lay down in the shadow of the offering stone and gave in to exhausted slumber.

It seemed as though the dream began the instant he closed his eyes. Only it was unlike anything Hyam had ever known. His eyes remained shut, and yet he still saw the sky. He watched the clouds for a time, he heard the soft rustle of breeze in the grass, he felt the dog settle beside his left leg. He knew all this, just as he was aware that he slept. And then he felt the call. It was not a command, and yet the invitation was strong as a cord that bound him to the village he had never entered. He was drawn away from his slumbering form.

Hyam drifted up, up, rising from himself, his awareness clear in a very odd manner, for he only saw what he focused upon directly. Everything else was not just murky but unseen. He drifted across the pasture fronting the Ashanta village. He felt led, but not in any direct manner. Rather it seemed to him that he followed a current, strong as a river in the rainy season. He entered the village itself and saw how the lanes connecting the structures were shaped from the same white stone as the houses. As were the two squat towers at the center of the village. They were the oddest watchtowers he had ever seen, scarcely rising above the rooflines, and set to either side of the largest building of all. He came to a halt by the left-hand tower, hovering so close that he could have reached out and touched the sentry's shoulder, if he only had a hand.

The sentry before him was a man, the other tower held a woman. Both stared out to the horizon and beyond. And Hyam understood, for the current carried awareness as well as direction. They did not stand guard with their eyes. They sought the unseen, spanning the forests, hunting the trails, searching for the army that Hyam had said was coming.

And at the same time, both sentries were connected to the clan. This bond of awareness flowed in both directions, Hyam realized. The clan could reach out and see what the sentries saw. And the sentries could follow what was happening within.

It was the simplest deed in the world to turn away from the sentry and follow his awareness. Hyam flowed into the large chamber where some stood and some sat, and from there extended out farther still, following now the stronger current of a thousand listening minds.

He traveled some great distance, and yet it was no journey at all. He arrived at a second chamber, long and narrow and high ceilinged, so huge it could have held his entire village. The vast interior shimmered with an astonishing light. The walls and the distant ceiling were decorated with circular symbols fashioned from gemstones. The giant pinwheels and mandalas sparkled and shimmered as clouds passed across windows tall as forest trees.

In the middle of the chamber was a square podium, rising twice the height of his cottage roof. Upon it stood a collection of perhaps three dozen berobed figures. Chairs and benches lined the walls. Otherwise the stone floor was unadorned. Hyam had no idea where he was, nor did he care. He was joined with an Assembly. Thousands upon thousands of Ashanta filled the chamber. Some in bodily form, most not. There was no sound. But the discussion was fierce, and piercing, and multifaceted, and *fast*.

Suddenly a woman shrieked, "He is *here*!"

"Impossible!"

"And yet it is so. The messenger is *in our Assembly*!"

One berobed figure leaned over the podium's railing and glared down. Instantly Hyam's attention shifted so as to look with a hundred thousand other eyes, over to where his childhood friend quailed beneath the leader's glare. "You brought an infidel?"

"I-I sense nothing," Bryna stammered.

"Not her," the woman snapped, and Hyam knew the old

woman who spoke was the Seer of Bryna's village. She had spent years as a sentry and graduated to the ability of seeing beyond space, beyond time. To the heart of matters. "He entered upon a sentry's bond."

"Is that possible?"

"Before this moment, I would have said absolutely not. But my opinion changes nothing. He is among us."

The leader demanded of Bryna, "What is this messenger's name?"

"Hyam."

The leader lifted his head and called through the hall, "I address the human known as Hyam. Can you hear me? If so, identify yourself and be counted."

Hyam had no idea what to do, or how. Even so, he moved toward the podium. "I am here."

"How are you doing this?"

"I have no idea. One moment I was asleep. The next, I came." Hyam hesitated, then added, "I was warned that I might harbor talent as a wizard."

"Who said this?"

"The Mistress of the Three Valleys Long Hall." Hyam wanted to tell them what he suspected, for he longed to know his own identity. But he was checked in a most certain manner by the sudden and fleeting image of Guardians standing among the others. The Guardians were Ashanta warriors trained in arcane methods of utter destruction. The scrolls that had taught him this tongue had revealed much about the Ashanta's thousand-year quest to destroy every vestige of the Milantian race.

The Assembly's leader studied Hyam for a time, then asked the Seer, "Is he Ashanta?"

"I . . . I cannot see. The matter is hidden from me."

"By this one, the interloper, the invader of our Assembly?"

"No. Of this I am certain." Hyam felt a penetrating awareness pass around and through him. Then the Seer added, "He speaks the truth as he knows it."

"About himself or the invading force?"

"Both."

The leader was clearly in a quandary. He turned to Bryna and demanded, "What do you say of this one?"

"I have known him since childhood. He is as you see. He cares. He gives. He has come to warn us."

"It is true what they say, you are fluent in our tongue?" the leader asked him.

"While I was apprenticed at Long Hall, I learned your speech and writing both."

"Hear this, then. We have lived in peace with humans for nine hundred years and more. We allied ourselves with your race against the Milantians in the Great War. When the battle ended, we were granted these lands by treaty. Our fiefdoms are meant to exist for all time."

Hyam had no idea how to respond, so he remained silent.

"Since the period before the war, we were represented among the humans by an outsider. We called this one our emissary. In the same treaty that grants us these lands, the emperor assigned our emissary the title of Knight of the Realm. The last emissary passed on over a century ago. Since then, we have seen neither need nor benefit in naming another. Until now."

Only at this point did Hyam realize what the leader was offering. "Sire—"

"We have no such titles among our people. There are no royal lines, nor any who stand when others kneel."

"I will address the army on your behalf. But I do not seek any title."

"Nonetheless, if you speak for us, it must be official."

"But . . ."

When Hyam did not continue, the leader commanded, "Speak."

But he could not. The same warning image glared before his awareness. Of the Guardians' automatic response to any Milantian. Death.

"I will do as you ask," Hyam said.

The leader asked the Assembly, "Where is the uniform?"

To his astonishment, it was Bryna who answered, "With us."

"What, at Eagle's Claw?"

"Once a generation it is remade. I watched my mother do this task some three years back. She trained me, as she was trained by her mother."

A ripple of astonishment swept through the chamber. The leader demanded of the Seer, "Is this a sign?"

"I don't . . . I can't . . ." The old woman utterly despised being uncertain about anything. "Perhaps. Yes. Perhaps."

The leader turned back to Hyam. "You will speak for us, now and in the future?"

Though the moment was laced with the darkness of half-truths and unspoken dread, Hyam said, "I will."

"You accept the responsibility that comes with this position?"

"Those known to me now and revealed in the future."

"For as long as your service is required?"

He had read the scroll regarding Ashanta oaths and gave the expected answer. "Whenever you call, I will come. Whatever the task, I will do."

"Even if the duty means your certain death?"

"What is death except another transition?" Hyam recited from memory. "What is life but another chance to serve?"

The leader showed astonishment. "Who taught you these words?"

"The Long Hall contains hundreds of your scrolls. I learned them all." What astonished him was the fact that he remembered. He remembered everything.

This time the old woman's response was ironclad. "This is indeed a sign."

"Very well." The leader stood straighter still and gave a regal gesture to the Guardians by the side wall. "It is time to show the new emissary what we are capable of. What we hoped would never be revealed again."

8

When the army appeared four mornings later, Hyam had mostly recovered from the experience of learning how the Ashanta made war. For two days he had wandered about the fields, his head splitting in pain, trailed by Bryna and the horse and the dog. She had repeatedly told him that it was a necessary act, to show their emissary the truth. And Hyam had reluctantly agreed. Though the truth had almost killed him.

The village fed him bowls of a stew that even a toothless babe could manage. And that was how Hyam felt for those first two days. Witless and without strength. Bryna scarcely left his side. Every few hours she spooned in a foul-smelling elixir that burned going down, but it quelled all nightmares and rebuilt his mental strength. Whenever she returned to the village, he walked in solitary circles with his dog and steed for company. He never set foot beyond the boundary stones.

The Ashanta might have rendered him so weak. But they also shielded him. Of that he was mortally certain.

On the fourth morning Bryna arrived with an ancient woman in tow. The Seer who had announced his arrival in the Assembly walked with one hand on Bryna's arm and the other holding a gold-tipped staff. The pole's tip was branded by the same sign that adorned the boundary stones, the symbol for treaty.

Hyam bowed respectfully. When the dog nudged his leg, he pushed the beast away. "I am honored by your presence, Mistress."

She swatted the air, uninterested in his deference. "You have joined with us a second time?"

"No, Mistress."

"He drinks the healing potion," Bryna pointed out. "It stills all gift of vision."

"I know that, girl. I taught you the healing arts, remember? But this one had defied our understanding of bodiless transport." She had a slight milky cast to her violet eyes, and Hyam wondered if she was blind. Then he decided that the loss of physical sight meant less than nothing to her.

"You will tell us if it happens again?" the Seer demanded.

"Yes, Mistress."

"We cannot have an interloper secretly entering our Assembly."

"I understand."

"Being named emissary makes no difference. If you come, you must announce your presence."

"I will do as you say."

She nodded. "You comprehend why we insisted upon your experiencing our response to attack?"

He tasted several responses, but a slight shake of Bryna's head kept him silent.

"It is the test every emissary must endure. So that they speak with true authority." She pointed to the forest beyond the farthest boundary stones. "The army comes. They will be here by midday. There is a mystery that travels with them. A dark force, one that has denied our sentries the ability to detect their approach. A hunter alerted us. If you can, try to discern how they mask themselves."

"I will do as you say."

"If you see anything that speaks of magery, or if you sense an unearthly charge . . ." She waved her hand again. "But you are untrained. Warn this army that they enter our lands at their peril. Return safely. It is enough."

As she turned away, Hyam said, "Mistress, if they refuse my entreaty, if they should attack . . ."

She replied over her shoulder, "Rest assured, Emissary. You will be protected. You have my word as Seer."

"What if . . ."

She continued to walk away. "Ask your question."

"What if this power you fear shields them from your weapon?"

She turned back so as to face him fully. The milky violet eyes carried a charge that peeled away the flesh and seared his bones. "I fear nothing, do you hear me? Nothing! What we revealed to you is not our only weapon. The others have not been used since the dark ages. It would be a terrible day when this power is revealed. An era of annihilation would result. But know this. The Ashanta will not be overcome."

Hyam spent the remainder of the morning watching the army assemble. He had never seen so many people at one time, not even at the harvest festival, when all seventeen villages of the Three Valleys joined together. That was a merry time, the villages competing over which could provide the finest entertainment and food. Because the farthest villagers traveled all day to arrive, the event was in truth a feast that lasted three days.

The army's encampment held a mockery of the valley's complacent good cheer. Colorful flags fluttered atop tall staffs. Hundreds of tents with peaked crowns flapped in the rising wind. Hyam detested the clatter of metal and the shouts of men and the cry of horses and other animals. He despised their careless manner and the way they ignored the boundary stones. Their camp began at the forest edge and extended like a disease into the green pastures. Men-at-arms walked toward the Ashanta flocks and cut down the sheep and cows where they stood. Their brassy laughter carried across the meadows. Hyam ate another meal of stew, fed the dog, then curried and saddled his horse. He missed the silence of the past days, the rustling grass, the low of contented animals, the peace.

When Bryna returned, she was accompanied by two others. Hyam thought he recognized one as the sentry whose attention he had tracked into the Assembly. But the pair simply set down their bundles on the offering stone and stood waiting.

Bryna stood between them, her arms empty, and said, "The time has come for the emissary to speak for us."

The gesture carried a certain formality, and Hyam sensed that her clan was joined with her. "I am ready."

She untied the two bundles. One contained clothes, the other a sword. "We ask that you don the uniform of our representative."

Hyam found himself reluctant to even touch such finery. Pressed by Bryna's gaze, he hefted a quilted leather shirt and instantly his nostrils were filled with the fragrances of childhood. Though the clothes had been aired and tailored to fit him, they still bore the scent of the herbs in which they had been packed. Clove and eucalyptus and rosemary, those his mother had cherished. The leather was supple as cotton and light as air. Its color was the same as the Ashanta eyes, a dark violet, rich and neutral at the same time. The sides were split so as to permit him to mount and ride easily. On the chest was stamped the treaty symbol.

His trousers were a canvas dyed the same shade as his shirt, with leather strips running down both legs. His boots and belt and scabbard were all the same color. The boots were deerskin and so soft they could be rolled up and tucked away like socks. They fit perfectly.

When he was dressed, Bryna motioned to the other pack. "Arm yourself."

The sword itself was unlike anything he had ever known, a pale white blade longer than his arm, slightly curved, the edge holding sharp and true along both lengths, and so light he scarcely felt it, even when holding it straight out.

"Milantian steel," Bryna said.

In his readings he had come across mention of this strange metal, the color of milk and ever sharp. The blade made a musical ring as he slipped it back into the scabbard. The melody of death.

Bryna handed him a triangular flag. The patch of stitched silk showed a rampant beast standing on its hind legs, baring fangs and long claws, breathing flames. "You carry the king's royal standard of peace." She handed him a pair of scrolls. "These are copies of the royal charter, one for the leader of this invading force, the other for you to keep. This decree was set in place by the first Oberon king. It grants our appointed emissary the right to ride beneath the royal banner and claim a place in the king's hall."

He lashed the flag to one end of his bow, then slipped the other end into the pocket behind his right stirrup. The flag flapped crisply in the wind. As Hyam swung into the saddle, he was caught by the similarity to his mother's final tapestry. Only the orb was missing. He wondered at the possible meaning and decided such ruminations would have to wait.

Hyam did not speak. The Ashanta had no interest in empty words. He understood that better than ever before. Hyam pulled the bridle and swung the horse around and kneed it to a trot. The dog loped along to his left. Ahead of him was the army, and beyond that a destiny he could neither fathom nor claim.

9

On an impulse Hyam turned his steed and rode out beyond the boundary stones. His route would be doubled in length, but that did not matter. He wanted to establish a perimeter for his message, for his warning, and for the possible battle to come. He would do all he could to remove this stain from the Ashanta land.

Before it was too late.

Hyam circled around the boundaries, wading carefully through both streams. When he was a hundred paces from the enemy's camp, he halted. And waited.

A shout rose from the camp up ahead. There were several hundred tents of all sizes and shapes, but when the man emerged from the largest and brightest, Hyam knew he faced their leader. The knight confirmed this by calling and then standing with his hands upon his hips as soldiers and stewards raced to do his bidding. A convoy of a dozen horses was formed up, while the man himself was girded in armor that sparkled in the sunlight. A steward cupped his hands, and the man used the servant as a stepladder, climbing atop the largest steed of all. Together the dozen men rode out to meet him.

Beside him, the wolfhound growled.

Hyam glanced down. It was the first sound he had ever heard the animal make. Her lips were drawn back, revealing fangs as long as his little finger. "Go back!"

The hound cast her yellow eyes at him. Uncertain.

Hyam pointed behind them. "Go there! Now!"

Reluctantly the animal loped back, then turned and waited. "Sit! Don't move!"

The lead knight kept to just inside the boundary stones. He halted when the final pyramid stood between him and Hyam. He looked the lone rider up and down. Then he laughed out loud. "What manner of idiot do they send out to meet us?"

The lead knight wore a padded habergeon sewn with metal plates, bright as silver, that fell like a protective robe over the ribs of his mount. On his head he wore an aventail, a hood of mail fashioned from silver links and laced with the intricate design of a gold crown. He pointed a gloved and beringed hand at the flag fluttering from Hyam's bow. "Do you intentionally seek to insult your liege lord?"

"I represent the Ashanta. I carry the banner they gave me."

"Listen to this man's accent, will you." The knight had a close-cropped black beard and eyes that sparked like savage coals. "What are you in real life, a cowherd to this defiled breed?"

"The Ashanta have instructed me to deliver a message."

"Pay attention, cowherd, and receive the only message to be

delivered on this field of battle." He pointed to the triangular flags snapping atop tall lances carried by the next men in line. "Observe my own standard. See the difference? Your ensign represents the Oberons. Their reign is finished. Consigned to history by my father's father. Do you hear what I am saying, cowherd? The Oberons are reduced to ruling over a single fief at the empire's western fringe. They exist at all by the mercy of my brother, Ravi, the newly crowned king."

Hyam's attention was caught by a figure at the far end of the line. He could not even say whether it was a small man or a largish woman. The person wore a crimson cloak whose cowl fell far over the face. The hands were masked by gloves the color of living blood. One hand held reins of red leather, the other held a red staff topped by an orb the size of two fists, perfectly round. It glowed rich and crimson, like a single furious eye. The horse was russet in color and was both hooded and blanketed by more of the fiery fabric. Horse and rider stood so still they might have been a statue. Then the hand holding the staff moved slightly in his direction, and Hyam sensed an unwanted presence glide over him, probing gently, taking his measure. Abruptly the crimson rider turned the horse and headed back to camp.

Hyam raised his voice and called, "Here is the Ashanta's message. Remove your camp beyond the boundary. And you will be spared."

The crimson rider slowed, then turned back. Observing him again from beneath the masking hood.

"Your manner of dress is like the drawings from my history books. I detested history." The prince kneed his horse closer to Hyam. He sniffed delicately. "What is that I smell, herbs? Oils? Are you arthritic, cowherd?" He flicked his fingers. "Go back to the forbidden ones. Deliver my terms. They have until dawn to leave their village. They may take nothing. They must follow the east route. They may not stop until they pass the realm's frontiers. Their kind are no longer welcome here. They have no place. Not now, not ever again. They are banished. Upon pain of death."

Hyam pitched his voice so the crimson rider could hear. "Heed my words. The Ashanta were granted this land by royal charter—"

"The treaty holds no force! The lineage who signed it has been banished!"

"—for coming to the aid of humans in their hour of direst need."

"Legends," the prince spat. "Tales not worthy of children."

"Our records claim we humans vanquished the Milantian hordes. But this history is false. The human armies were almost overwhelmed, and the Ashanta rescued—"

"Lies!"

"They rescued us. Why? Because the Milantians intended to enslave us. The Ashanta had witnessed what the Milantians had done to the Elves when this race proved unwilling or unable to accept slavery. The Ashanta knew we would prove more malleable. And the Ashanta despise the binding of any sentient being."

"You dare utter such heresies in my presence?" The prince drew his sword. "I will split you and your stinking shirt, cowherd."

The knight holding his banner protested, "Sire, we speak beneath the standard of peace."

"This one deserves no peace! He is worse than the Ashanta. He is a turncoat, a cowherd to the banished few." The prince reared back, intending to plunge his sword straight through Hyam's breast.

Hyam gripped his own sword and unsheathed it in one fluid motion. It was the instinctive response of a hunter to the sudden assault. But what happened next astonished Hyam as much as the others. His sword flashed in a swift parry, but instead of merely checking the prince's blade, it sliced through like cutting cloth. The dismembered blade clattered upon the boundary pyramid and fell to the ground.

The prince gaped at the empty pommel in his grip. "What magery is this?"

"That is not magic, sire." The knight to his left was a greybeard with a battle scar that sliced across his cheek and brow. "Their representative carries a blade of Milantian steel," he breathed.

"Another myth," the prince spat. He thrust the empty pommel at Hyam, his entire arm trembling. "This one is a mage!"

"It is no myth, sire. I have myself touched such a blade. Once."

The prince glanced back, uncertain now.

The knight went on, "Sire, the entire camp is observing you. I implore you to respect the banner of peace."

Hyam held to his overloud voice. "I beseech you to heed my words! The Ashanta defeated the Milantians with powers beyond your ability to understand. If you do not retreat beyond the boundary stones, every one of you will perish!"

The prince leaned across the pyramid and snarled, "I will see you flayed and quartered before this day is over."

Hyam knew a crushing sense of defeat but forced himself to finish the message. "You have one hour."

"Silence, you filth! I command this field!" Spittle flew with his enraged words. "We attack!"

"Sire," the knight protested. "You promised them until—"

"The offer is retracted!" He spurred his horse about, still gripping the empty pommel in one hand. "We attack now, do you hear me? This very instant! Sound the battle horns. We go to war! And a thousand gold florins to the warrior who brings me the cowherd in chains!"

The battle lines formed with remarkable swiftness, galvanized by the prince's ire. He stomped and shouted before the ranks, spurring his men to ever greater speed. Trumpets sounded and officers barked. Then there was a final burst of noise, trumpets and officers together, and the assembled ranks went silent. In the abrupt stillness, Hyam realized his dog was growling, probably had been for some time. He glanced back and saw the animal was still planted on her haunches, right where Hyam had directed her to sit. He whistled softly and said, "Come, girl."

The dog padded over, still growling, a soft rumbling deep in her chest. Hyam reached down and ruffled the pelt between her ears. "We are going to name you soon. Would you like that?"

But the dog did not pay him any attention. Instead, she remained focused on something beyond the encampment.

"What is it, girl?" He straightened in his saddle just in time to observe the crimson rider break from the camp. The hooded stranger did not move toward the battle line. Instead, the rider sped to the forest boundary.

Where the pasture ended, the rider wheeled about and faced Hyam. The cowl still held the shadows like a fist, but even so Hyam again sensed the unwanted touch. The crimson glove raised the staff in Hyam's direction, and the strengthening wind carried a moaning whisper of words he could not make out. It seemed to Hyam as though an unseen cloak was abruptly stripped from his shoulders. Then a giant's fist clenched his lungs, and the breath left his body in a quick huff.

The dog roared then, more a wolf's howl than a bark, loud enough to silence the prince in the middle of his harangue. The knight glared furiously in Hyam's direction, pointed with a new sword, and said something that was rewarded with a hungry cheer. A trio of riders broke free and started toward him.

Hyam was still trying to find his breath as he pulled the reins about. "Time to ride," he managed.

Then it happened.

The Ashanta assault began in an almost gentle mode. The wind strengthened and seemed to collect footfalls from just beyond the range of human hearing. The brassy trumpets of the prince's army were echoed by a plaintive note that rose and fell and rose again. Hyam turned in time to see his three assailants slow and gaze about them, hunting for those who hunted them.

The Ashanta army arrived then, carried upon the wind. The sky grew yellow and shrouded. The wind called a different note, a moan so vast and horrible it could only mean the arrival of doom.

Hyam tried to tell himself that all was well. That he could turn and watch in the safety promised by the Seer. And yet he was filled with a dread for the fate that awaited the prince and his army. And a genuine terror of being forced to relive how the Ashanta made war. He leaned over the horse's neck and gripped the mane with such fierceness his knuckles were turned bone white. "Ride!"

The destrier bolted, as though the warhorse had spent days waiting for this precise command.

Behind Hyam rose the first shrieks of terror and pain. He clenched his eyes shut, only to have them drawn open by the sudden awareness that he was being chased. Hyam glanced back and saw anew what he had hoped would never be visible again.

The Ashanta army rose like coagulated mist, a dread pestilence that took on the form of spectral warriors. They swept into the line and joined with the warriors into a parody of battle. Every soldier became an enemy. Every sword was aimed at their former mates. Every knight became just another target. Arrows swooped and flames rose and swords fell. Over and over and over. Even when mutilated and dead, the bodies continued their parody of battle.

Even when he shut his eyes again, Hyam still saw it all. For he was among them. Riding away did not remove him from the fray. Nothing would save him. He was doomed.

Then he felt spectral hands reach over his face and claw back his clenched eyelids. And he saw that he did not ride alone.

Ghoulish warriors rode before and behind him. Two more rode the dog. They reached and they clenched and they tore at his clothes and his skin and his bones. Determined to make room in his being for their dark force. Gripping his arms with a fierce passion that defied even the grave, struggling to turn the reins.

Then from behind him there came a light of blinding ferocity. It was violet and it was without color. And a voice cried across the distance. Commanding the forces that it had unleashed. Demanding they relinquish their hold and return to the shrouded earth.

The spectral warriors lashed and groaned and wailed. The knifelike hand that worked inside his skull was the last to relinquish its death grip. One by one the ghouls dropped off his steed and fell smokelike into the earth. Hyam was left blinded by pain and a final wailing note, a promise that the ghouls would return and claim him on another day, when the light of Ashanta was not there to save him. This sinister oath and the pounding of great hooves were the last things he knew before darkness swept over him and carried him away.

10

Joelle swept the flagstone corridor and counted as she moved. The actions were ingrained now, so well known not even a passing mage gave her any notice. There used to be problems with some of the wizards, especially those newly graduated from the ranks of acolytes. The young women saw her as a threat, the young men as an opportunity. They were, after all, inducted into the Long Hall's source of power. They could do anything. Even conquer the silent servant, the imprisoned one. Or so they thought.

She had learned to defend herself, then Trace had noticed and made sure no one ever touched her again. What happened to the ones who ganged up and sought to ensnare her, she had no idea. Trace was a gentle soul by nature. But when angry he could grow in power until his menace filled the halls and made him appear a giant in human skin. And Trace had been very angry indeed. Seven young mages had vanished, and Joelle no longer worried about her safety when passing shadowed alcoves or when working alone. Now her lessons of defense had been turned into strategy for the coming battle.

Soon after the young men vanished, Trace began feeding her scrolls. Not directly, there was too much risk in that. But in their quiet moments by the fountain or seated together in the scullery after the final bell, he would ask what she studied, which of course was forbidden, but he paid such orders no mind. Which was decidedly odd for a Master Mage. Yet Trace remained utterly opposed to her situation and still sought on occasion to have her included among the acolytes. But Joelle now knew that her mother's kind were forbidden from joining the Long Hall mages. And the wizards who wished she had been left to the forest wolves had grown in power, bitter men and women with pinched features and hands that wove gossip and pain far better than any spell. They were led by the Librarian and the Doorkeeper, holders of the two portals she most wanted to open. Trace could neither vanquish their clique nor win them over. But he could and did work around them.

As Joelle worked her way down the hall, she counted off the steps to the most complicated spell she had ever fashioned. She had discovered the scroll stretched out on a library table, where the senior acolytes had been perusing it before their exams. Trace had mentioned this in passing, a casual gesture between friends. How he despaired of teaching this crop of young ones anything at all. How their heads—

"Your heads are empty! Your brains have been wasted away by all the drivel you pour in them when you should have been studying!"

Even before she could make out the words, she knew it was Trace, for the acolytes laughed in response. They loved the old man as fiercely as the Doorkeeper and the Librarian loathed him, perhaps even more. Trace remained Master of the Havering Long Hall because his friends were also his allies, and his allies were the strongest group within the fractious hall. But Trace often confided to her that being Master was like trying to herd goats—simply because they were tethered did not mean the beasts would go where you wanted.

Joelle worked her way closer to the classroom, her gaze focused on the sweeping broom, her heart twisted by angry longing. She heard Trace shout in mock rage, "No, no, no! Dunderheads, the lot of you. Stop kneading the spell like it's bread you're making! *Weave* the power. Let it *flow* from your hands!"

Joelle busied herself outside the doorway, just in case another wizard happened by. She had traveled again at dawn, arriving at a point where the crimson mage rode alone through some great forest. The red-cloaked wizard had sensed her presence and turned. The glinting black insects had risen like a cloud from his hood, hunting, hunting. Instantly Joelle had been drawn away, returning to relative safety within the Long Hall. Even so, the dread remained.

And then there was the other problem. Joelle could not get the spell to work.

It was the first time she had been stymied, and it infuriated her. The scroll outlined a weapons spell, an implement of warcraft. It claimed to transform a blade into lightning, a hammer into a mace that could bludgeon through stone. It was what she had been hunting, the last item she required before escaping. But she could not make it work.

Joelle counted the stages as she swept, reciting them under

her breath, seeking what she had missed. She knew she had done it correctly, but there was something . . .

"No, no, *no!* You are the worst crop of dunderheads it has ever been my misery to instruct. And you, you imbecile, you are the worst dunderhead of them all! Come over here so I can thump that great lump growing between your shoulders."

A voice she recognized retorted, "I am doing what the scroll says to—"

"*Forget* the scroll. Did you not hear a single word I said?"

"I heard *everything* you said, Master. You said—"

"I said that when it comes to warcraft, no scroll is complete."

Joelle froze in mid-sweep.

"One crucial element is always missing. It is intended as a safety mechanism, like the lock that requires a key. And it is intended to instruct. Because an intelligent student, which you most certainly are *not*, would know that in order for the spell to work upon an inanimate object, it requires . . . what? Anyone?"

The insight was so powerful, Joelle actually spoke aloud. "A binding spell."

"Precisely! Who said that? Perhaps I was wrong, and there is at least one student here who is not a complete waste of my time. Come, come. Who spoke?"

Joelle heard footsteps farther down the hall and resumed her sweeping just as a mage rounded the corner. Trace's voice continued to drone on behind her. But the key was now in the lock, and she would soon open the portal.

And go free.

11

Hyam's awareness came and went in fleeting waves. He knew only brief glimpses of a world beyond his eyelids. Each hint was lanced by the agony in his head, so deep it hurt to rise to wakefulness. He departed as swiftly as he arrived.

He had no idea how often he came and then left again, for in those early days he could not think clearly enough to count. All he knew for certain was that he had seen stars and sunlight both. How many days passed, Hyam had no idea. But gradually he lingered for longer periods, and his other senses began to return. He felt his head being lifted, and he swallowed a putrid brew that burned as it went down. He had the impression of figures that drifted about him. He smelled woodsmoke at night and heard soft conversation—a man's voice and occasionally a gentle speech in return. There was something to this second voice that touched his heart, reaching through the herbal fog and sparking a mysterious yearning for what he had never known before.

The next time he woke Hyam felt sunlight upon his face. He recalled a dream of musical chimes, but when he opened his eyes the melody became a metallic clatter. He saw pots and pans and knives strung from a rafter overhead. The world rocked gently, and there was a rhythmic creaking timed to the swaying motion. Hyam lifted his head a fraction and sensed that he was back for good.

"Ah, finally! Beloved, observe, the stranger decides to join us. Is that not wonderful? No, no, lad, don't try to sit up on your own." The rocking ceased, and strong hands helped him rise to a seated position. A bearded face, seamed by years and miles and hardship, smiled with astonishing tenderness. "Welcome back to the land of the living. It is not altogether a delightful place, I admit. But better than the alternative, wouldn't you agree?"

The man was squat and rotund as a barrel with legs. He wore a tinker's garb, simple brown homespun with a broad trader's belt about his middle. He drew a ladle from a water barrel lashed above the wagon's rear wheel and watched approvingly as Hyam drank. "More?"

"Please."

"Elixir of life, this. Nice to see you drinking on your own, isn't it. Oh my, yes. For a time, my dear one and I feared we had lost you to the world of shadows."

Hyam finished off a second ladle, then croaked, "How long have I been out?"

"Oh, I don't have much interest in the counting of days,

young man. The forest keeps a different sort of time. Day follows night, I walk, I enter another hamlet, I sell my wares, I move on. You have been with us for a time, hasn't he, my dear. You have been with us long enough to finish off two jugs of my sweet one's strongest elixir. Four days? Six? Such tallies are beyond me." The tinker pointed into the woodland bordering the trail. "There's a creek up ahead, in case you're ready for a wash."

He'd been down long enough for his limbs to feel watery as he climbed from the wagon. Only when he stood on trembling legs did he realize he was stark naked. He decided it did not matter and gratefully allowed the tinker to slip beneath his arm and support much of his weight as he walked to where the creek formed a waist-deep pool. The twenty paces were enough to leave him panting. He lowered himself into the cool water, groaning from the pleasure.

The tinker brought a jar of soap and some pungent herb that he claimed would aid in the healing. Hyam mixed it with clean sand and spent more than an hour scrubbing his hair and skin. The tinker handed him a straight razor, and Hyam scraped away his beard. Being clean shaven left him feeling immensely better. The tinker made camp in a miniature clearing nearby, one that bore the shadow of a fire pit that had not been used in a long time, certainly not that season. Hyam was hugely glad his mind was returning to a state where he could notice such matters.

The tinker offered him a clean blanket with which Hyam could dry and then cloak himself. As he made his slow way back to the wagon, a shadow flitted in from the forest and bounded through the camp. The wolfhound's appearance filled Hyam with such abrupt joy his eyes filmed over. He fell to his knees and embraced the thick neck with all the strength he could muster.

"The beast leaves you for a hunt, then returns and fits himself to your side." The tinker stirred a metal pot, tasted, and nodded his satisfaction. "Kit yourself out and come grab a plate."

Hyam noticed his Ashanta gear was freshly washed and draped upon the wagon's side. He drew simpler garb from his satchel and dressed, though the effort left him exhausted. When the dog nudged his thigh, he almost toppled over. The tinker waited as he settled on a stump, then offered him a tin plate of stew. The scent left him giddy with hunger. Hyam tasted a wealth of flavors—forest roots and a meat he thought was probably quail.

"This is wonderful."

"Aye, my dear one is a fine hand at woodland feasts." The tinker seated himself on a neighboring log and dug in. Otherwise the clearing was empty. "Do you want to tell me your name, lad?"

"Hyam," he replied. "And I will tell you whatever else you want to know."

"I'm just a simple tinker, lad." He turned so as to inspect the purple clothes hanging from the side of his wagon. But all he said was, "Most things about this world are beyond my ken. More stew?"

"Please." Hyam accepted the plate and said, "I don't know the words to thank you. I doubt they exist."

The tinker ladled himself another helping, settled comfortably, ate a few bites, then said, "There we were, making our way along a trail so empty we could claim it as our own. Heading east from the Three Valleys, we were, wondering if we would meet another soul before we crossed the forest. When the most dreadful noise rose from behind us. Banshee wails, strong enough to wake the dead."

The recollection of what he had experienced left Hyam unable to eat another bite or even hold the plate steady. The dog sensed his distress and fitted her head between Hyam's arm and knee. She huffed softly and licked his face, drawing him back.

If the tinker noticed, he gave no sign. "I did what anyone would do in my place, which was to quake in my boots and push on hard as my nags could manage. When all of a sudden I heard hooves bearing down upon us. Suddenly this great beast of a warhorse appeared, and beside it ran the largest wolfhound I had ever seen or heard of. And there upon the back of that steed was a man. He was completely gone from this earth, and yet he was still alive. I was certain of that by the way he kept hold of the horse's mane. I was so astonished by the sight I froze. Your horse was smarter than me, for it slowed and halted and nudged me with its nose. And then to my astonishment this great wolf stepped forward and did the same. Pressing me to do what I could for the man they clearly loved." The tinker's grin shone in the firelight. "There was little else I could do but obey. My dearest one agreed. Otherwise your two companions might have trampled me to the earth and devoured me on the spot."

Hyam glanced around the thickening gloom. His destrier was cropping grass on the clearing's other side, along with the tinker's two swayback mares. The dog lay beside him, panting softly and staring at the fire. Otherwise there was no life, no sound. Hyam glanced at the tinker and decided he was more than comfortable with a bit of lonely daftness.

The dog lifted her head and searched Hyam's face with eyes that gleamed golden in the firelight. Abruptly Hyam decided it was time for the naming. And he knew what that name must be.

He stroked the fine pelt and said, "Your name is Dama."

The word was Elven and signified a lifelong friend, and far more besides. A dama was bound by blood and bone and life's breath. Where one went, there went the other. The Elven word for trust was drawn from the same root.

The wolfhound woofed her approval and licked his face.

Then Hyam noticed how the tinker was studying him.

A smile flitted across his features, and he asked, "You speak the forest tongue, lad?"

"Aye, I do."

"Well then." The tinker turned and addressed the shadows beyond the clearing. The hair on Hyam's neck rose as he heard the tinker speak in Elven. "You hear that, my dearest one? We have a new friend. One that honors the forest ways. Come, come, my dear. There is no need for shyness. Join us in the joy of new amity."

Hyam wondered momentarily if he had reentered the drugged dream state. And his confusion was certainly excusable. For at the clearing's other side appeared an impossibility.

The woman's skin was the color of minty springtime leaves. Her eyes were slanted above high cheekbones and colored as golden as the dog's. Her body was slender and supple as a young sapling, her hair woven with forest blooms.

"This can't be," Hyam breathed. For according to the Long Hall scrolls and valley lore both, no Elf had walked the earth for over a thousand years.

"Aye, I could not agree more, lad. How could one so beautiful love the likes of me? But she does, and I count myself the luckiest of men. And not just men either! The most fortunate being to ever have walked a forest trail." His boundless joy sent him to his feet, where he extended his arms in grateful welcome. "Meet my Aiyana. My beloved. My Elven delight."

12

The tinker's name was Yagel, and he greeted Hyam each morning with the easy cheer of lifelong friends. They spoke only Elven now, which Hyam disliked but used out of courtesy. The tinker was kind as he corrected Hyam's pronunciation and offered finer points of grammar and speech. For a tinker he was remarkably well versed, even spouting bits of Elven poetry when the mood came upon him. But when Hyam ventured to ask of his background, Yagel laughed off such questions as inconsequential. "My beginnings are so far behind me it would be like describing the flow of a forgotten river. I have trekked these forest trails so long, I know no other life."

The Elf remained shy and silent. Occasionally Hyam heard a soft murmur as she addressed her mate, gentle as a dawn breeze, mellifluous as birdsong. He never made out the words. Aiyana never spoke to him at all. Even meeting his gaze for an instant was a trial. She was most comfortable drifting through the forest to one side of the route or the other. From time to time he felt her gaze touch him. Hyam did his best not to show he noticed. Whenever he forgot himself and glanced her way, Aiyana was already gone.

His strength returned gradually. On the third night after his awakening, he refused the elixir and Yagel did not insist. Three times that night he woke from terrible dreams, fighting ghouls he hoped could not track him on these forest trails. The third time, as he forced himself back down onto the sweat-stained pallet, he noticed Aiyana standing by a nearby tree, watching him with sympathy and sorrow. He drifted away, wondering if Elves slept at all, and if so, did they dream.

Dama adored the green woman. The wolfhound greeted her rare appearances with a glance at Hyam, clearly asking permission to sidle over. Aiyana petted the dog with feather-light strokes. It was the only time she willingly met Hyam's gaze. Once she even smiled, and Hyam carried the memory as he would a treasure.

Twice Hyam tried to describe what had happened—the army and the assault and the Ashanta response. Both times the tinker shook himself like a dog rising from a pool. "I am not fit for such goings-on, lad. I know some tinkers trade in news like I do cutlery and mirrors. I am not one of them."

"There are things I need to relate, and more I need to know," Hyam replied stubbornly.

"I'm sure that's so, lad. But such matters trouble my be-loved. So I have found it best to remain blind to the outside world. Which is a good thing, since my addled head could scarcely make heads or tails of it when I was at my best. Which I most certainly am not now."

"What about the Elves? I'd always heard they are no more."

"My darling Aiyana does not speak of her heritage," he replied firmly. "I am grateful that she remains beside me. My heart is full, my days peaceful, my mind content. She has her secrets, Aiyana does. And I respect that. What she wishes me to know, she will tell me." He could see his response did not satisfy Hyam, so he added, "What you need is one of the educated folk. A person whose head is trained to hold all manner of arcane knowledge."

Hyam felt a different sort of dread. "I was told to visit a Master Trace, head of the Long Hall in Havering."

"There you are, then." The tinker pointed ahead. "Five days farther on, the road forks. The northern trail borders the forest on to Mineral Springs, then Gotha, and finally the provincial capital of Calvert. The southern route passes through Melcombe town, climbs the Galwyn Ridge, and heads straight as an arrow to Havering."

Hyam found it noteworthy how the supposedly simple-minded tinker could know their precise position. "How far from the fork to the city?"

"Three days past Melcombe, four if you take it slow. Which you should. The Galwyn Hills are steep and the terrain harsh, mostly desert ridges, shaped by wind and time. I went there once in earlier days. Dreadful place. But to go round the hills southward is a month's trek. Take the Galwyn Road, but slow, lad, slow." The tinker gave a ponderous nod. "We go north along the forest route. I dislike straying more than a few paces from my Aiyana, and my Elven sprite never leaves her forest. Not for an instant nor a breath."

Each day Hyam took long loops through the forest, walking

farther and faster, pushing hard, strengthening himself. He carried his bow and had his dog for company, and he managed to bag several birds for the stew pot. But mostly he just walked and healed and reveled in the forest peace. He suspected Aiyana was never far off, even when he saddled the destrier and rode farther afield. He welcomed the company, though he suspected her presence was what kept away the larger game.

The forest here was ancient indeed. The trees towered so high that on the stillest mornings their boughs were wrapped in mist, like they had managed to trap the clouds themselves. The undergrowth was springy soft with eons of untouched mulch. The air was sweet and pungent. Several times each day Hyam stood still and silent, breathing in the air, wondering if he might ever feel the power rise from the earth and course through him again. Perhaps it had been somehow tied to his field and his valley. Or perhaps the spectral battle had left his spirit too wounded to ever know such things again. No doubt there would come a time when he would mourn the loss. For the moment, however, he was simply grateful to be alive and walking the verdant woodlands, with the sunlight sparkling through high distant leaves, and with an Elf for an unseen companion.

Four mornings later he left the destrier tied to the rear of the tinker's wagon, though his horse snorted and pawed the trail in wordless entreaty. He carried his bow and a quiver as he set out with Dama. South of the trail, the first jagged edges of the hills encroached into the forest. The ridges rose in forested waves, though the rocky earth seemed capable of giving a mighty shrug and divesting itself of all growth. Dama moved ahead of him, startling two grouse hiding in a thicket, but otherwise finding no scent worth tracking. Hyam found himself too busy bidding the woodlands a silent farewell to shoot the birds. He walked and sought to ingest as much as he could of the stillness and healing green.

At midafternoon when he started back toward the trail, a movement flitted across the ridgeline to his right. He glanced at Dama, who seemed to notice nothing out of the ordinary. But something about the fleeting image had set Hyam's heart to racing. He merged with the shadows and signaled for the dog to join him. Together they stood motionless, Hyam scarcely breathing, the dog panting softly and glancing about, utterly calm. Just as he was about to dismiss the image as a fragment of unwanted memory, he saw it again.

This time Dama saw it as well, and her only response was to glance up at Hyam. Which only added to his astonishment. For there upon the ridgeline walked a stag of monumental proportions. The beast looked straight at him, as though inviting Hyam to join him. Willing him forward.

Hyam stalked slowly, checking each footstep, moving with silent stealth. Dama continued to watch Hyam more than the prey.

The stag did not move. Finally Hyam reached the last stand of trees. When he hesitated, the stag lowered its head and snorted gently. Then Dama nudged his thigh. Pushing him forward. Alone.

This made no sense at all. A stag of this size would have had ample experience fleeing hunters. And Dama was a beast made for bringing down such prey. Hyam knew the stag could smell them both. Yet the animal did not take flight. Instead, it raised its head. And in that moment, Hyam felt a chill course through him.

The same antlers cut the sky as had last scripted against starlight and moon when he had been a child, sleeping with his arms wrapped around the fawn. Standing before him now was the same proud head. The same august bearing.

"Stay, Dama," he murmured, and bent over to deposit his bow and quiver on the earth. The dog panted softly and went prone.

Hyam climbed the final rise and stepped onto the ridge. The stag did not move.

Hyam had no idea what to do. The deer snorted softly. Hyam raised his arms and spoke the words in Elven. "I greet you, noble stag."

The deer snorted again and closed the distance between them. Only then did Hyam realize the stag was lame.

He dropped to his knees. The stag responded by lifting its injured limb. The foreleg had been gashed to the bone, and now it festered. The gash ran from hoof to knee. The flow from the wound was yellow, the stench soft and strong at the same time.

Hyam found it difficult to deliver such news to such a noble beast. "There is nothing I can do."

The deer lowered its head and licked him across his cheek, then on the same ear he had touched before departing with the fawn.

The stag waited, snorting softly, as Hyam rose to his feet and drew his knife. He stroked the beast for a long moment, then wrapped his arms around the stag's neck. "I am sorry. And I thank you."

Hyam sliced the vein where it pulsed in the stag's strong neck. And then held him as the animal bled out.

13

Hyam did not rise until Aiyana crested the ridge. The stag's blood coated his entire front and most of his back, and it had dried and hardened while he had knelt beside the fallen animal. He stood, awkward in his stained clothes and blood-smeared face. Dama walked alongside the Elf, who looked at the stag and then at him. Aiyana's expression carried the same sense of calm tragedy that he felt. She addressed him directly for the very first time. "Come."

He started to ask if they shouldn't dress the deer first, then decided that an invitation spoken by a silent Elf demanded obedience. She led him down the slope and deeper into the forest. He followed her through a thicket that seemed to lean away from them both, then spring back afterward. They passed through a wooded gorge that grew narrower the farther they proceeded. Somewhere far above, a sun shone, but here all was emerald shadows. They reached a point where Hyam could have touched both sides of the gorge at the same time, and Dama was forced to follow a pace behind. Abruptly the walls fell back, revealing a forest pool. A spring bubbled constantly at its center.

Aiyana pointed to the water and said, "Disrobe and wash. I will return."

She stepped through a crevice and disappeared. Hyam found the pool to be one degree off scalding, obviously fed from an underground spring. He scoured himself with sand, washed, and scoured again. As he doused himself a second time, Aiyana appeared carrying a robe the color of forest mist. She set it and a broadcloth down on a rock and turned her back. Waiting.

Hyam dried himself with the cloth, then slipped the robe over his head. The garment was small in the shoulders and short in the sleeves. But it did not matter. Hyam left his bloodied clothes and boots there by the pool and followed her barefoot through the crevice. On the other side, the ridge fell away, revealing more forest. Only there was an unmistakable difference to this woodland. The silence was not as it had been. Everything *listened*. Each blade of grass, every bird, all the trees—they were *aware*.

Aiyana lifted her hands and began to chant. If her speech had sounded musical before, this was wondrous. Hyam was left breathless from the simple spectacle. Her words flowed together into a single long utterance. He thought he could probably have dissected it and drawn out the individual words. And yet he was too immersed in the experience of listening to care. As she stopped speaking, he realized that for the first time since leaving his field, he was joined again with the forest and the earth. By the simple act of *listening*.

Aiyana went silent. In response, the trees directly before her parted. There was no tearing of the earth nor bending of trunks. This was something else entirely. Hyam's vision seemed to stretch, allowing more space between impenetrable trunks. A new lane was revealed, narrow as the gorge, and lined on both sides by trees as old as time. The boughs intertwined overhead, so thick the sun was utterly blocked. Aiyana motioned him forward.

The light was cathedral soft, and the ground underneath was covered by a supple blanket of moss. After a few steps Hyam realized he walked alone. He turned back and saw that Dama sat beside Aiyana, who said, "It is forbidden for me or your friend to enter. Go. We will await your return."

The lane was long, miles perhaps. At its end rose two stone sentinels, set to either side of a towering iron gate. The statues were giant Elves, armed with staves that ended in circular orbs. They stared in stern vigilance in the direction from which Hyam had come. As he approached, he felt as though he passed through a veil of awareness, one that carried a deadly force. It held him for a brief moment, then parted, gentle as an assembly of fairy wings. He passed through the gates and entered the kingdom that was no more.

The city of the Elves was a poem of natural beauty. Several, in fact. Many different lyrical forms joined together like pages of a lovely tome. The Elven kingdom spanned a great valley, covered a forest, surrounded a lake, and rose up the ridges that framed the valley and the woods and the waters. In each area, the Elves took the natural features and converted them into their dwellings. They sculpted woodland havens high in the trees. They made crystal islands in the lake's midst. They carved sculptures of delicate grace from the rock. They lined the shore with sandcastles. And all were bound together by bridges and carvings where form met form in lissome charm.

Hyam was led to the palace at the lake's center. To his awestruck mind, it seemed as though the waters had been crafted into structure, and perhaps they were, but without the chill of ice. The palace was clear and blue like the waters from which it rose. All the surroundings shimmered and glowed, as though the walls and ceilings had managed to catch the sunlight and hold it in safekeeping. For that was one of the most powerful impressions Hyam had as he stepped into the crystal audience hall—that he was safe.

The other impression was that everything here had significance. The meeting was here because there were no shadows, nowhere to hide or be hidden. Through transparent and light-flecked walls, he saw a multitude of Elves gather and watch and listen as the regal figure upon the throne greeted him.

"Welcome to the Hidden World. I am Darwain, ruler of the Elves. Your name?"

"Hyam, sire. Of the Three Valleys."

To Darwain's right was a second throne, this one occupied by a regal lady whose brow held a crystal diadem. Darwain took hold of her hand as he said, "Tell us why you are here."

"The Elf called Aiyana, she brought me to the path. I came."

"No. That is *how* you came to be the first stranger to enter our gates in ten centuries. I wish to know *why*."

Hyam pondered that a long moment. The crowded audience hall and all the Elves who observed waited with him. Finally he said, "The statues that guard your gates. They hold staffs that are topped by stone orbs. I have seen another. Only this one was not stone. It was made from glass or crystal or gemstone."

A ripple passed through the multitude. The Elven king asked, "Its color?"

"Red. The shade of living blood. It glowed like fire." With each word the current of consternation and anxiety grew louder, and Hyam knew he had spoken rightly. "The one who held it was dressed in a crimson robe that kept the rider's face in constant shadow. I know not whether I confronted a man or woman."

"It may have been neither," Darwain replied. "Tell us how you came to witness the orb. Leave out nothing. For all our sakes."

Hyam did as he was commanded. He began with his mother's death and the unwanted revelation from the Mistress of Long Hall. The dreams. The spade. The warriors. The trek to the Ashanta village. He described falling asleep beside the offering stone, the rising up and traveling to the Assembly. He recounted his appointment as emissary. He told of meeting the crone there where the creeks joined and her assurance of safety. He described confronting the king's brother, the crimson rider, the battle, his near defeat, the tinker, the Elf, the stag. There was a great release in telling them everything, even his doubts over his heritage, even his fears that he might be Milantian, one of the race blamed for the Elves' demise. The act of confession left him both weightless and ready for whatever came next.

The ruler and his queen neither spoke nor moved during

the telling. When Hyam went silent, Darwain said to an attendant, "Go to the entryway where Aiyana waits. Inform her that Hyam must remain with us awhile longer. Wish our daughter and the mage every joy. Thank them for bringing us the Ashanta emissary. Tell them they did rightly."

Hyam was uncertain he had heard rightly. "What mage?"

Darwain and his wife showed quiet humor. "You thought we would permit a child of the hidden realm to marry a simple tinker?"

"I don't know what I thought, sire."

"Or that a common tradesman would know the potions to heal your spirit from such an attack?" He shared soft laughter with the woman seated to his right. "Aiyana is not the only one who sacrificed everything for love. Yagel was destined to become Master of the Havering Long Hall. All senior mages are required to spend a year at some craft within the human realm. He chose to travel. He met our daughter, who loved to wander farther than we would have liked from our gates. They fell in love. Yagel asked and received our blessing. In return, he has spent his years binding the forest trails, keeping them safe, and ensuring that the hated ones do not hide among our woodlands."

Hyam cringed at the prospect that he might be one so named. "I have not thanked him for saving my life."

"You survived. You came. You delivered news we have dreaded ever hearing but needed to know. Yagel will call this thanks enough." He motioned to an attendant, who moved to stand beside Hyam. "Now you will rest, and our healers will ensure you are fully restored. We will meet again."

14

"At some point in the distant shadows of time, our sworn enemies found the first orb," the Elven ruler told him. "The first we knew of this was when the Milantians attacked, and we were unable to repulse them. We feared they had created the crystal globes, but we since learned they never held this ability. Perhaps none do. We still don't know where the orbs originated. Perhaps they are natural, grown from the earth itself, fashioned over eons by the tides of energy that they mark. But our most ancient records speak of a fifth race, one that either died away or simply departed long before either Elf or Man or Ashanta came to walk upon this earth. We think they created the orbs and then planted them in order to heighten the flow of power. What we know for certain is this. The earth is rimmed by lines of force."

They were seated in the great audience hall, where long tables of crystal were laid out beneath a moonlit night. The light creasing the walls danced and flowed, mimicking the torches that rimmed both the hall and the lakeshore, where more tables had been raised. The ruler spoke in a voice that was comfortable to Hyam's ear. And yet he was certain even the farthest Elf could hear their ruler clearly.

"I have seen these lines," Hyam said, wondering if he was wrong to interrupt. "In a dream."

A quiet murmur drifted through the chamber. Darwain glanced at his silent queen, then went on, "Where these lines of power come together, the orbs were found. In the years that followed the Milantians' first assault, we learned much about them. They are so light as to be almost weightless. They cannot be duplicated. Nor do they hold a particular *kind* of power. Each globe is a receptacle. The *user* determines how this force is applied. And for those who desire the orbs for the purpose of destruction, they take on the color . . ."

"Red," Hyam supplied. "Like crystal flames."

Hyam had been given a sandstone villa on the lake's broad shore. Healers had come and prescribed baths and unguents and potions. Their ministrations complete, they gave him a mint-green shirt that laced up the front, and trousers and boots cut in the human fashion. All were made from a fabric soft as clouds, yet the boots protected his feet from the sharpest rocks. He had tried to go for a walk, but two dozen paces from his doorway, he had turned back. Nothing had been said, but it was evident that the Elves were distressed by his walking among them. They had survived by being invisible. Clearly his appearance made many fearful of greater changes to come.

"The Ashanta entered the war too late to save most of our

people. Why they waited, we do not know. They have always been a race apart. But we held no enmity, then or now. In the days following the Milantians' defeat, they helped bring our remnants together. They have held the secret of our existence for ten centuries."

The ruler's manner of speech shamed him. For Hyam spoke their tongue as a carpenter might wield a hammer. Darwain gave each utterance a mystical beauty, in keeping with wind and chimes and waterfalls and birdsong. His every word carried the magic of woodlands and nature. That they listened to Hyam without wincing or disgust, he took as a measure of their kind nature.

Darwain continued, "After the Milantian hordes were crushed, their remaining orbs were taken and destroyed. Most of the others we could locate were demolished as well, to keep the Milantian remnants from ever wielding such dread power again. Only a few remain, and those were carefully locked away and guarded. We have no idea how many orbs originally existed. We have four, used to protect our kingdom and keep it hidden. These too were gifts of contrition from the Ashanta. Each of the Long Halls was established to safeguard an orb and study its force. Learning the orb's true functions and potential is the responsibility of each Master or Mistress. Whether the Ashanta hold orbs of their own, we do not know. Unlike humans, their magic does not seem to be either drawn from or magnified by orbs. Which is what saved us."

The meal had been as magnificent as it had been mysterious. Hyam had dined upon dishes concocted from fruit and fish and fowl and root and vine. And yet he could not name anything. Nor could Hyam say how long he had been a guest here. It was clear to him now how Yagel had refused to discuss the counting of hours or days. In the Elves' presence, time's passage was a distant memory.

"There is much more we could tell you," Darwain finished, "but all that must wait until this peril is met and vanquished."

Hyam replied, "First I want to discover what I can about my heritage."

Darwain's displeasure was a fearsome spectacle. "You dare delay our quest for such petty issues as your heritage?"

"It's not petty to me."

"The last time we confronted Milantian mages, they crushed our armies and almost wiped our race off the earth. Your past is of no importance here. None!"

Hyam knew a farmer's stubborn resistance, even when faced with what he knew to be the truth. "I just want—"

"You want, you want. What about any of this is the way we want? Heed my words, young human. You must rise up to the challenge of living *now*. You must ask the questions that deserve answers *now*. You must heed the clarion call of this present crisis and grow into the role you yourself accepted. *Now*."

Hyam disagreed with the king. And utterly disliked Darwain's assumption that he could proclaim edicts over Hyam's life. But he also knew there was nothing to be gained from arguing. "What would you have me do?"

The Elven ruler subsided. "Continue your duties to the Ashanta. Tell them what you have learned. They will be as distressed as we to hear that a dark mage uses an orb to wreak havoc. Seek their wisdom."

"I will do as you say."

"Discover if you can the purpose of this crimson rider. Who among the humans serve him, and why. That too we must determine. When you are ready, report back to us." He passed over a sliver of carved crystal, the length and breadth of Hyam's little finger, hung from a slender chain. "Enter any forest glade alone. Blow on this. A gate will appear. Speak to the one who arrives. He will come to you in my name and with my authority."

Hyam slipped the chain around his neck. He knew his time here was ending and forced himself to ask the dreaded question. "What if I am another Milantian mage?"

"We have discussed this and can only tell you that the answer is sealed away. Why, we do not know, but we suggest you not probe this further. Some great force hides the answer, and we suspect there is a reason as powerful as the shield that hides the truth." When he saw that Hyam disliked the answer, Darwain added, "What if you are the Elves' only hope? Will you squander your life and ours as well on questioning your past? What if these inquiries blind you to the future? Your challenge, human, is to grow beyond whatever yesterday held and accept the challenge of tomorrow!"

The palace rang long after the king's words faded, or perhaps it was just how their force echoed in Hyam's mind. "I will."

"Then we thank you for your presence, and for your bond." The ruler rose to his feet. "Your coming portends a dark time. Allies are vital. We are grateful to count you among the few and the honorable."

15

Joelle required two more weeks to prepare. She needed a calm night for one thing, but spring storms ravaged the land for three long windswept days. She needed to prepare food and steal a map of the region, for she had little idea where she was or where she might find safety. And she needed to practice the pesky spell.

There were moments when she almost gave up. The spell required growing the mage-force and then bundling it up, tighter and tighter. Finally it had to be bound to the weapon. But the energy of wizardry was not meant to be trapped. It was the force of nature, unbounded by any restrictions, surging and rampant and desperate to be free. Which was perhaps why she loved working spells as much as she did, even when they were as frustratingly difficult as this one.

After many arduous nights she managed to bind the power to one knife, though the other remained as unrepentantly dull and metallic as ever. Her one success, however, shone with such brilliance she was almost afraid to handle it. The blade shimmered with a passionate fire, humming with a force she felt through her fingers, begging for her to release it. But she dared not, since the last thing she wanted was to demolish an interior wall and bring all the mages down on her head. So she released the spell, which was as frustrating as it was difficult, given all the work she had put into making it happen. Then she kept at it, night after night, until both blades hummed with the fierce song of her heart, impatient to fly, to wreak havoc, to break free.

Joelle knew the Long Hall had originally required a night watch of three mages, two of whom patrolled the perimeter, with a third stationed in the central bell tower. She also knew the practice had been ended by the Master before Trace. When Trace had tried to reestablish it, he had faced a sullen mutiny.

Perhaps Trace shared such gossip with her simply because she was not a part of his world, though intimately aware of most things. Or if indeed he was preparing her for what he knew must eventually come and, in truth, wanted her to succeed. In any case, she knew that each night, when the bell sounded the midnight hour, the portal was sealed with spells. Then the perimeter defenses were checked once more, and all the mages including the Doorkeeper retired for the night. There was nothing in Joelle's opinion that spoke of the wizards' smug complacency more clearly than how, every night, they treated the Long Hall as a realm apart, safe from every threat.

The watches might be a thing of the past, but the bell continued to sound and the watchtower continued to hold the mage-force intended to repel attackers the wizards thought would never come. That night Joelle took the bell's chime as her cue. She dressed and hefted the pack she had sewn, which contained the stolen food and map, the robe she would use as an outer cloak, and her bedroll. Her knives and the scroll were in a separate bundle that she gripped to her middle. She emerged from her chamber and tried to listen, but her heart beat so loudly she could scarcely hear her own footsteps as she hurried down the empty corridor.

The courtyard was empty of all save moonlight. The ancient stones shone like purest silver, or perhaps it was merely her excitement that made the place beckon so. Joelle did not feel any regret over leaving such a lovely place. She had always considered her prison to be beautiful.

She rested her pack where she had sat next to Trace for their first conversation, and used it to anchor the scroll open. She had read the words so often they felt imprinted on the back of her eyes, but she needed to get this right, and do so the very first time. Joelle had no idea whether the watchtower would sound an alarm when the portal was attacked from within. But she needed to break down the door and escape before the mages were awakened.

She had not slept for the past two nights, and her eyes were grainy and her hands unsteady. She gripped her fists tight against her chest and clenched herself hard as she could, from toes to hairline, every muscle in her body taut and electric. Then she set her two favorite knives on the stone next to the scroll and began weaving the spell.

Joelle had walked the perimeter wall enough to know that

it ran in a virtual circle, with the secret chamber at its center. She had long wondered if the wall traced a boundary, beyond which the mage-force could not be drawn upon. In the lonely hours, especially on dawns that did not offer the momentary freedom of travel, she wondered how she would feel once she left and the magic was no longer there for her to call upon. But such internal dialogue had no place now. The same moon that turned the courtyard silver played over the world that had been denied to her for three long years. Its draw was magnetic and not to be denied.

Joelle had practiced the spell enough for the stages to flow almost smoothly. Now she drew the force from the hidden chamber and wove the mage-heat, illuminating the plaza and burnishing the ancient stones with a forge's glow. When she hefted her knives and cast the binding spell, their brilliance pierced the night.

She did not hesitate, not even an instant, thus denying her fear room to disturb the spell. She wove the final words into a shriek that flew with the knives, straight at the hated portal.

The knives struck, first one, then the other.

There was no sound save the furious pounding of her heart.

Instead, a spiderweb of force spread out from the two points. The portal bounced slightly, as though made from some viscous material and not wood. The overlaid webs would have been beautiful save for how they absorbed the knives' force.

Her weapons clattered to the stones. Dark. Unlovely. Useless.

The portal remained intact.

Joelle was weaving the spell again before she reached the knives. She did not chant the spell. She *screamed* it. Her cries carried such force that her breath became illuminated, weaving into the power that flooded the two blades. Again she hefted them. Again she flung them at the despised door.

Again they clattered to the stones, their force depleted, the portal undisturbed.

She was so distraught she could scarcely lift her knives, much less heft the pack from the fountain. Every step was a voluntary move back into her prison. She could not think, she could not, she could not . . .

Then a figure shifted among the shadows on the courtyard's other end. And as it did, Joelle spotted a faint shift in the night surrounding the watchtower. She had not noticed it before, because her attention had been focused exclusively on escape. But she realized now that the tower had been surrounded by a subtle wavy pattern, almost like summer heat. Now it was gone, as was the figure in the shadows. Which could only mean one thing. Trace had suspected she would act and had silenced the alarm bell. And then observed her attempted escape. And done nothing to halt her.

In such a desolate hour, she found enough solace in the Master Mage's friendship to make it back to her bed. And sleep so deeply not even her aching heart could wake her.

16

Hyam exited the kingdom gates and walked the beautiful but lonely path within the tunnel of trees. At its end, he found Dama and the destrier waiting for him. They seemed as glad as he to be reunited. Of the tinker and his wife there was no sign.

Time retook its hold upon Hyam. He camped that night and slept in a much-used clearing. The next day he arrived at the crossing and headed south. He spent one more night sheltered by the green world, and twice he awoke with the sense of being watched over by a folk who had spent ten centuries going unseen. He slept deeply and dreamed of brilliant globes that lay hidden at the joinings of fiery paths. The next morning he mounted up, well rested and ready for whatever came.

Or so he thought.

He arrived at Melcombe at noon on what appeared to be a festival day. Bunting was strung between the houses lining the route into town, and people crossing the main bridge addressed one another with determined good cheer. Hyam had stowed his Elven garb in the same satchel that held his violet Ashanta attire. He wore a farmer's simple canvas shirt and trousers. His bow and sword were sheathed by his right stirrup. The folk waiting to enter the town's stone walls gaped at him. Beneath their gaze he realized the sight he must make— dressed as a peasant, armed with bow and sword, riding a knight's steed, with a regal beast loping by his side.

The town was clearly wealthy, with royal banners fluttering from the six conical towers. Alert soldiers lined the high stone wall, and this was fronted by a moat fed from numerous streams. The road leading to the town's main portal was lined by beamed houses with lead-paned windows and roofs of slate or thatch. The closer Hyam drew to the drawbridge, the more tightly the soldiers by the guardhouse focused their attention upon him.

Hyam spied an inn on his right and pulled up. He was tempted to continue onward, for he had never seen a town and had missed his own village's spring festival. But the soldiers kept a narrow gaze on him, and he knew this was safer. He stood by the inn's kitchen window and waited.

Finally a bearded bear of a man passed by, then returned to scowl at Hyam and demand, "What manner of silliness is this? And why do you perch yourself there at my window? We have no time for beggars or brigands, do you hear me? No time!"

"Are you the innkeeper?" Hyam asked.

"Aye, that I am. The Golden Fish has been in my family for six generations. What of it?"

"Are you honest?"

"Am I—" The brutish manner was punctured by a sudden burst of laughter. "Well, that depends. Do you have money?"

"I do." Hyam leaned over so his words could be more softly spoken. "What's more, I have gold."

The man jutted his bearded jaw and spoke more softly than Hyam. "Show me."

Hyam opened the purse he had taken from the knight and extracted a gold florin. He let it flash once in the sunlight, then stowed it away.

"Well, in that case, young master, I will be more honest than the next man, and certainly more than you deserve!"

"I want a bed and a bath and a meal and a barber," Hyam said. "And a tailor. A good one."

"And you shall have it, good sir. You shall have it all!" He turned and shouted into the interior for a stable hand, then said to Hyam, "Climb off that mountain of a beast and enter."

Hyam waited until he had bathed and eaten before explaining his state. The barber worked on his head while a wizened old man measured him for clothes.

"I was attacked. I escaped and hid in the forest. A tinker rescued me and nurtured me back to life."

"A tinker!" The innkeeper was tall and burly and never still. He popped in for a few moments, delivering something or simply idling between tasks. "They've never been known as a kindly sort."

"His name was Yagel."

All three men smiled at that. "Then you were fortunate indeed, good sir," the aged tailor assured him.

The innkeeper added, "Yagel comes through here now and again. He sharpens knives, he sells what he can, I buy more than I need just because I like the look of him."

"He healed my wife of boils," the barber said. "And brought back her laugh when I feared it was lost for all time."

"He sleeps in my stable once or twice a month," the innkeeper went on. "I suspect him of healing my favorite horse, but he claims it was not his doing."

"Your wolfhound did not mind the tinker tending you?" the tailor asked.

Hyam thought of Aiyana and said, "I suspect if he had asked, my two animals would have never left his side."

"So you met Yagel, and he saved your life."

"And he refused payment." Hyam reached for his purse. "I want him to have your finest room and bath and meal. For as long as he keeps coming."

The innkeeper's smile was as huge as the rest of him. "I'd say Yagel got the better of that deal."

"I'm serious."

"I know you are, lad. And for this more than your gold, I'll call you welcome whenever you choose to return."

The tailor squatted upon a stubby-legged stool and sewed with astonishing swiftness. "Young squire has requested two sets of daytime garb."

Hyam resisted the urge to correct the tailor's manner of address. "I want to walk or ride unnoticed by soldiers and commoners in any town."

"Just so." The tailor timed his words to the rise and fall of his needle. "It is the practice among regal clans to wear their emblem upon their breast."

"Give me pen and paper and I will draw what I want."

"I am well versed in every seal of the realm, good sir," the tailor replied.

Hyam searched the three faces and decided to trust them. "I carry a charter from the House Oberon."

The tailor's movements faltered. The barber might as well have been turned to stone. The innkeeper scowled and cast a hurried glance down the hallway behind him.

"You hold a second emblem?" the tailor asked softly.

"I do."

The innkeeper departed and returned swiftly with quill and parchment and ink. "None of us heard what the lad just said. Agreed?"

"For all our lives," the barber confirmed.

Hyam dipped the quill, then asked, "Is there an Ashanta settlement near here?"

The trio's unease heightened further still. The innkeeper said, "Where do you come from?"

"Three Valleys. Beyond the forest."

"Aye, I've heard of that. An outpost region, am I right?" He did not offer Hyam a chance to respond, merely checked the hall a second time before continuing, "Mark my words if you want to keep breathing. These names you bandy about are forbidden."

"We dare not think them," the barber quavered. "Much less speak them aloud."

"Understood." He bent over his parchment and drew.

When Hyam was done, the tailor frowned over the Ashanta symbol. "This one is new to me."

"Does it matter?" the innkeeper demanded.

"Certainly not." He resumed his sewing. "Anything is better than the seal whose name I have conveniently forgotten."

The innkeeper's name was Teague, and his caution kept him from approaching Hyam again until after the evening meal. When the fire burned low and the minstrel stopped his crooning, Teague brought over two fresh mugs, seated himself across from Hyam, and said, "The tailor will deliver your goods at dawn."

"I am grateful."

"Where are you headed?"

"Havering by way of the Galwyn Hills."

The innkeeper took a long pull of his brew, swiped a sleeve across his black whiskers, and declared, "Then enjoy tomorrow's sunrise, for it will be your last."

"Why do you say that?"

"The road to Havering has been closed for these two years and more."

"By what means?"

"No one has returned to say why. Which explains the soldiers you see guarding the battlements and the bridge."

"Is there another route?"

"The merchants are taking their wares south to the port, then swinging around and coming up by way of the capital."

"How long does that take?"

"Depends upon the winds and the season. Four weeks at the minimum. Six is more likely."

"I don't have that long."

Teague planted two muscular arms on the table. "Did you not hear what I just said? The road through the Galwyn Hills promises death."

"Nonetheless, that is the road I must take." Hyam slid two gold florins across the table. "For your troubles. And your honesty."

"It's too much."

"And for Yagel to enjoy your finest for as long as he keeps coming."

"I should have done that anyway." The innkeeper pushed one coin back. "I like a man who honors his debts. If you happen to survive, know you will always be welcome here. Even if you do carry the forbidden emblem and utter names banned throughout the realm."

17

The dream took hold some time after midnight, a great thunderous assault where veins of fire opened in the earth and rose up in ferocious currents to sweep him away. Hyam seemed unable to waken himself, not even when vixens appeared and lashed him to a stone. Three of them, lovely as the dawn, until they grew fangs and talons and ripped the flesh from his bones.

It seemed as though he was kept imprisoned by the furies for eons, but it was not yet dawn when he crawled from his sweat-stained bed. He drank deep and bathed in water long gone cold. Then he heard scratchings outside his door and unsheathed his sword before unlocking the portal and discovering a parcel deposited upon the floor. He donned one set of his new clothes, fashioned from cotton and silk and supple deerskin. He slipped into the Elven boots, the one item he decided he could risk wearing.

He ate cold lamb and bread and fresh green onions, standing by the kitchen window through which he had addressed the innkeeper. Dama ate with him, and then they drank their fill from the same ladle. He packed more supplies in a canvas carryall, filled four water skins he found hanging in the pantry, then walked to the rear of the inn and slipped a second gold florin under the door of Teague's private quarters.

He saddled his horse and loaded his gear, then filled two more canvas sacks with oats from the byre and headed out. The road south was empty and quiet. At the top of the first rise, he turned and looked back at the slumbering town. The flags hung limp in the still air. Soldiers doused a pair of watch fires. It was a lovely sight, the stone wall colored a delicate rose by the dawn. Hyam wheeled his horse about and headed along the road turned yellow by dust and daylight and disuse.

The first two vales he crossed were filled with scrub pine and undergrowth. He startled a brace of quail that shot into the air, quick as arrows from a hunter's bow. Hyam met no other travelers, and all the fields he passed were empty as well. He arrived at a spring that watered a host of trees so burdened by ripe fruit their limbs almost touched the ground. Hyam held the animals back, tasted the water, waited, and decided it was both sweet and safe. He refilled the skins and drank until his belly felt distended. He ate two of the apples, cut segments from two more, and fed them to the horse. He stroked the horse's muzzle and realized aloud, "I have failed to name you."

The horse responded by searching his hand for more fruit. He cut it into segments and said, "How do you feel about the name Matu? It is the Ashanta word for defender. Does that suit you?"

The horse appeared happy enough, or perhaps merely content with the unexpected gift of apples. Hyam filled his last remaining sack with more fruit, then swung back into the saddle. "Matu, Dama, let us be off."

The change began just beyond the third rise. The cliffs to either side of the road became razor sharp. The scrub simply vanished. The rock was yellow and polished into odd-flowing designs by eons of lonely wind. The rising heat carried an arid bite. It seemed to Hyam that he could feel the excess moisture rise in shimmering waves from his own body.

By the time they halted for the night, they were parched. The salt froth had dried and caked upon Matu's flanks. Dama's constant panting formed a backdrop to their every step. Hyam selected a flat space atop another lonely ridgeline and called a halt. There was no need to pull farther from the road. He had seen no one since leaving the town. He decided against a fire, though a rock outcropping shielded his site from the moaning wind. He fed the horse another pair of apples and two handfuls of oats, then sliced a chunk of cold lamb for Dama and another for himself.

As he watered the animals from a bowl-shaped depression in the rock, Hyam found his mind returning to the questions the Mistress raised. A desert night was an excellent place for reflecting upon impossible mysteries. Such as why the Mistress of a Long Hall would interrupt her day and discuss a failed acolyte's curious heritage. As he stretched out between the dog and the horse, Hyam wondered if perhaps the old woman had been seeking forgiveness for the way he had been treated. The dog snuffled and laid her snout upon his chest, as though sharing the bitter humor. But no other reason for their conversation came to mind. Even so, not even the Elf king's command to set such ponderings aside could still his head or reseal his wounds.

When he finally slept, the dreams were more violent still, their power to hold him down seemingly endless. Had the dog not nuzzled him awake, Hyam wondered if he would have managed to survive. For the rest of the night he sat and watched the stars, rubbing the places in his flesh where the talons of three beautiful vixens had cut to the bone.

In the first light of dawn, they headed on. Hyam sent the dog loping ahead, whistling Dama back every time she slipped from view. The next ridge revealed more of the same vista, only hotter and drier.

With each rim and vale, the silence grew ever more intense. When they descended, not even the wind accompanied them. Twice Hyam stopped when Dama pointed toward some shadow and whined. It was an eerie sound, more confused than afraid, and it raised the hair on Hyam's neck.

The road itself was in fine shape. The surface was ancient brick, worn but well maintained. Whether the brick itself was cut from the yellow stone or merely coated with eons of dust, Hyam could not say. It rose up one steep incline after another in gentle curves, wide enough to hold a merchant's wagon or caravan. Every now and then the rock face was carved back, forming a space where wagons and animals could gather and allow traffic from the opposite direction to pass. To have such a road be so empty was all the warning Hyam would ever need.

Even so, the cry for help was shockingly unexpected.

Dama gave a swift woof and circled back to stand guard by his mount. The horse jerked to a halt as the cry came again.

"Help, oh please, somebody! I'm hurt, I'm hurt!"

The child's call was plaintive and piercing. Hyam knew it was a girl, probably not more than six or seven years old. "Where are you?"

"Here! Here! Are you a man or a ghoul?"

"A man."

"Oh please, please, I'm trapped on the rocks, they *hurt* me!"

Hyam dismounted and drew his sword. "Who did?"

"The witches!"

"Where are they now?"

"I don't . . . They left with the dawn. Just like they did yesterday. The light . . . Oh please, save me!"

Hyam debated bringing his bow, then decided he needed his arm free to lift the child. He tethered the horse to a rock outcropping, unsheathed his sword, then said to Dama, "Hunt, but stay close."

The dog moved forward at a crouch, ready to attack. She sniffed and searched and moved one slow step at a time. Hyam followed close behind, searching everywhere.

They rounded a stone, then another. The child's voice had reduced to a soft, panting keen. Then Dama turned another corner and tensed. For there ahead of them was the girl.

She was dressed in rags and was older than Hyam expected,

perhaps fourteen or fifteen. She was stretched spread-eagle upon a smooth rock face. She was also intensely beautiful. Her allure was almost overwhelming, a lovely girl caught at the cusp of womanhood. It was not merely her hair that was golden but her skin as well. Even her blue eyes seemed to glow with a golden light all their own.

She wept with joy at the sight of him. "You came, oh, you *came*!"

Hyam stepped around the dog and entered the sandy space in front of the rock.

The dog set up a furious racket, but only for a moment, and then went utterly still. Which should have been another call for alarm. But the woman-child's allure was so potent, Hyam found it impossible to think of anything other than his need to set her free. The closer he came, the greater the draw, until he saw nothing, *sensed* nothing, except the tugging force that pulled him forward.

Then something struck him from behind, a blow that blinded him and sent him sprawling to his knees.

A voice laughed over him and a different voice said, "I told you the young one works best."

18

When Hyam came to, powerful hands were forcing his lips apart. "Drink the potion, that's my strong fine man. No, no, don't spit it out, else we'll be forced to punish, won't we, my sweeties?"

A second voice cried, "Have him tell you why he carries a Milantian blade!"

"Questions will come later, when we've started the punishment, and he'll beg to tell us everything."

His first semi-clear thought was that he was lashed spread-eagle to a smooth rock face. Then a voice demanded, "Punish him now, save us the bother. Start with the punishment, teach them manners, that's the way!"

"Nonsense, we don't want the goods damaged before we have our fun, do we, my sweets. Drink up, that's it." When Hyam clamped his teeth shut, a hand strong as iron clenched his nose. "You will drink!"

And he did, in the end. When he opened his mouth to

gasp a breath, the hands proved quicker still and jammed the spout between his teeth. A hot gush of something both acrid and sweet spilled down his throat. He gasped and choked and spewed and snorted and struggled, but some went down.

"That's my sweet good boy. Now you'll stay with us for *all* the fun." The figure stepped back, and his eyes cleared, and he saw before him the three most beautiful women in the world. As they danced and cavorted, Hyam realized he saw the vixens from his worst dreams.

Even so, their allure was almost overpowering. One was the woman-child he had sought to save. The other was somewhat older, yet fresh and beautiful in full flower. The third was a woman of maturing years, who danced with the sweeping power of her full feminine majesty. It was she who spoke.

"You must choose, my darling boy! Which will have you first? That is the last choice you have, the last you shall ever make! So choose wisely!"

"Choose me!" The woman-child swung her hips in a lewd fashion and shrieked her laughter. "I brought him. I trapped him. He's mine!"

"Choose wisely," the older woman repeated. "The one you choose will milk you first and longest, then eat your heart when dawn returns. Between then and now we shall all have our fill of you, feasting on your flesh and your spirit both. So take what little pleasure you have left, and choose!"

He was bound to the same rock face as supposedly had held the woman-child. His limbs were lashed tight. His struggles only made the dancing women laugh more loudly still. Beyond them he spotted his dog, and farther back was his horse. Dama and Matu stood frozen. As trapped as he.

"Choose!" the women shrieked. "It's always more fun when you choose!"

The drug had set his heart to racing. Every nerve ending was buzzing, all his senses were heightened to the utmost and beyond. He felt every fleck of sand in the rock upon which he was strapped, every knot in the binding ropes.

But his senses did not stop there. He felt his mind reaching out, extending, stretching, *listening*.

And then he sensed it.

A core of power rested inside the cave he could not see. The cavern's mouth was directly behind the rock. But he was certain the power was there. Waiting. Beckoning.

The middle woman danced up close to his face and peeled back one eyelid. "He did not drink the potion."

"He drank," the older woman replied.

"He did not drink *enough*."

"Give it time. He's young, he's strong. You'll see. We haven't had one this fine in weeks. Not since those three knights who carried the king's edict." She cackled her delicious glee. "Now dance!"

Hyam's mind continued to probe until he arrived at what he realized was an orb of power. He touched it and was almost consumed by the force contained within. He drew back, but only a fraction, for he knew the women grew impatient with his silence.

"Make him drink *again*."

He tried to draw the power back with him and break his

bonds, but failed. Then the older woman jammed the spout between his teeth and held his nose until he drank again. So as he choked and the women shrieked their laughter, Hyam turned his attention to the one who might still free him.

The dog was trapped but alive. Dama fought with all her strength to free herself. Hyam knew this because as he reached forward, he sensed the world through the wolfhound's eyes.

He saw the women as the dog saw, three reptilian crones whose bodies were streaked and painted with lines of color and fire. Long yellow fangs filled their mouths. Their hands ended in curved talons that still carried the blood of their last prey.

A shadow fell on him, and a voice said, "Does he take it in?"

Only this time, the young woman spoke Milantian.

"You forget yourself," the older witch hissed.

"I forget nothing! I want him made ready! I want him to choose me *now*!"

So the three cavorting vixens were Milantians. Which meant any spell they made was designed around the same tongue. He could not break the ropes. But he could perhaps shatter their binding spell.

As he drank, Hyam reached out and tasted the force and the gemstone globe that held it. Soon as the spout was removed, he took a huge breath, drawing in the orb's power.

He cried in the witches' tongue, with all the force he had, *"Release the wolfhound!"*

The sound of the man shouting Milantian shocked the women to stillness. Which was the instant of their undoing.

Dama leapt forward with a snarl Hyam felt in his chest.

The women screamed in unison and began spouting spells, but none had a chance to finish even a single word. The wolf-hound went for their throats, biting one, clawing another, then downing the youngest with a leap that sent her crashing into the stone beside Hyam. Dama opened her mouth as wide as she could, gripped the screaming woman, and crushed her skull.

The second dose of the witches' potion left Hyam gasping hard around a wildly hammering heart. "Good dog. Thank you, Dama. Thank you."

19

The witches' potion coursed through Hyam's veins with fiery intensity. He had once held a baby bird in his hands and touched the heart as it raced within the fragile wrapping of flesh. That was how he felt as he waited for Dama to gnaw through the ropes binding him to the stone. His measly sinew and bones were scarcely enough to keep his heart from soaring away, carrying his life with it.

The dog growled as she worried the ropes, careful not to rake his exposed wrists with her fangs. Her claws scraped white streaks in the rock as she tried to dig out the metal clasps holding the lines in place.

Hyam repeated the Milantian words and released the horse from its binding spell. But Matu refused to enter the sandy expanse. The destrier pawed the trail, eager for Hyam to join him away from the bodies.

Finally his left hand came free, then his right. Hyam released his feet, then knelt and received Dama's rapturous response.

Both beasts clearly wanted to be gone from here. And he agreed. But there was one thing he needed to do first.

He slipped into his clothes and buckled on his sword. He searched frantically until he found his bow and quiver leaning against the back of his prison stone. The cavern's entrance was directly across from where he stood. Hyam fitted an arrow into place. He half drew the string and searched the dark maw. The smell was vile, but he sensed no life. Danger, however, was everywhere, or so it seemed to his addled mind. He dreaded entering that foul place, but he knew he had no choice. The orb's draw was stronger now than ever before, more powerful even than the woman-child's final plea. He shuddered at the recollection and stepped forward. Dama whined and paced about at the entrance, refusing to join him.

The gloom was sparked by whatever bizarre combination of ingredients and spells the witches had put in their brew. His eyes were able to catch and utilize the tiniest light. He moved forward, trying not to breathe more than absolutely necessary. The orb was just ahead, a dozen paces, six, four. He rounded a corner and the putrid odor became so strong he choked. A natural alcove contained an altar fashioned from human bones, upon which rested the orb. The structure was rimmed by skulls. More skulls were set within niches carved from the walls.

He hesitated an instant, then gasped the words, "May I take you?"

The orb responded with a jolt of robust impatience.

Hyam slung the bow over his shoulder and picked up the orb. The weightless globe felt smooth and cool to his grasp. He raced back outside. Dama greeted him with a delighted bark, then tracked him as he rounded the stone and jumped over the bodies and opened the drawstring to one of his canvas feed sacks. He froze for a brief instant, captured by how the orb was colored a putrid milky red. Then Dama barked a second time, and Hyam jerked back to the need to flee.

He cinched the sack shut, leapt into the saddle, took his first deep breath, then shouted with relief as strong as ecstasy, "Ride!"

20

The next valley over was broader and the slope less steep. Which was a very good thing, because the destrier attacked the road at a full gallop. Had the descent been steeper, they might have survived the witches only to plunge to their death. By the time they climbed the next ridgeline, the fear and the panic had diminished enough for Hyam to slow their pace and rise from his clenched position on Matu's neck. He searched the empty yellow reaches and saw nothing but the late afternoon heat shimmering off the lifeless rocks, and the empty blue-black sky, and the fact that he was safe. Safe and alive and able to heave another breath.

He halted at the top of the next ridge and watered both animals. This was the highest of all and revealed a creased yellow world, laid out like a giant plowed field. The sun melted upon the western horizon. Hyam could see both animals were exhausted. But he climbed back into the saddle and pressed on. The brew kept burning through him. He had no idea what would happen when it faded. But he wanted to be well clear of the hills and whatever threat they might still contain before that happened.

They rode into the night. The moon rose and transformed the vista into a world of silver and jagged edges. Hyam's heightened vision kept scanning the shadows, but he saw nothing.

He stopped again, longer this time, and held the sack of oats so Matu could eat his fill. He forced himself to eat food he did not want, sharing his meat and bread with Dama. He sliced apples taken from the sack not holding the orb, sharing with the destrier. He kept glancing at the other sack slung from the saddle. The real hunger he felt was to touch that smooth surface once more. But he fought against that desire, swung back into the saddle, and pushed on.

He was crossing the empty base of just another vale when he gasped aloud. Both animals instantly tensed. "Steady, friends. All is well."

And for the first time since entering the desert hills, he truly felt it was so.

Hyam saw nothing save the silver-clad earth. Not even his brew-sharpened eyes could pierce the rock and glimpse what he sensed was there. But as he wheeled his horse about and returned to the point in the empty vale, he was certain beyond doubt that he had found what he had not even been looking for.

He slipped from the saddle. The moment his boots touched the earth, Hyam grew more confident still. A river of power coursed below his feet, buried deep in the earth. A vein within the rock and the soil. One of many. A myriad of arteries that spanned the entire world.

He opened the sack and pulled out the orb. It pulsed gently in his hands, like a lantern whose flame was not quite ignited. The glow was enough to push the horse back two steps and cause his dog to whine. "Steady, the both of you." He balanced the orb one-handed and pointed to the earth. "Stay, Dama."

He turned and followed the flow of the unseen river. He could sense his destination up ahead, two hundred paces, perhaps a bit more. The dog barked once as he moved away. Hyam called back, "Stay!"

The orb's light grew ever stronger. There was an unclean tint to the glow, which cast the valley floor in a dismal shade of pinkish grey. Hyam wondered if he should be worried by this, how he carried a receptacle of the witches' vile intent. But there was no danger here, at least to him. Of that he was utterly confident.

He arrived at the spot where the vein he followed met a juncture with a far more powerful course. He realized that the vein he tracked was a mere creek in comparison to this unseen river, vast and deep and broad. The orb was almost blinding in its brilliance now. The light no longer pulsed, or if it did, his eyes were no longer able to discern any change. And still it grew in force.

Hyam stopped in the middle of the crossing and felt the power rise up to join with his body. There was an immense elation to the event. What he feared had been lost when he departed his oval field now surged through him with an intensity he had never imagined possible. The orb was a conduit for the force flowing beneath him, and he held the power to transform this force, redirect it, *utilize* it.

He willed this energy to cleanse him of the witches' brew. Even before the thought was fully formed, he felt the power wash over him, drenching him in a potion of undeniable force.

As it happened, he understood now that the same cleansing force could be applied to the orb itself. When he felt the final vestige of their tainted swill leave him, he reoriented the power, willing it to transform the globe itself.

Hyam could sense the change, as though the orb was connected to him through the act of cleansing. In a flash of insight he realized this was the purpose behind the witches' alcove. They sought a destructive power and linked themselves to the orb through pain and fear and destroyed lives.

Hyam felt the river flow up and through him, until he and the orb were linked as tightly as the bones of the hands that held it.

The light grew and grew, until he could see the illumination through his clenched eyes. There was neither danger nor thought in the moment, and yet there was an ability to reach beyond the place and the time and *comprehend*. And still the light grew, the intensity so great it painted every thought with brilliant clarity. Hyam opened his eyes and saw himself bathed in a radiance that defied the night, filling the entire valley with a silver-violet luminosity.

Spurred by the need to resume his journey, Hyam reluctantly stepped away from the point where the rivers joined. The light gradually faded. Yet even when he stood once more surrounded by rocky silence, Hyam's senses remained open, intensely aware.

He returned to the horse, tired yet replete. Dama danced fretfully back and forth, clearly sensing the change and uncertain whether to approach. "Here, girl. Come."

She loped forward, whining as she skipped about his legs. Matu pawed the earth as Hyam stepped to the saddle. And there he paused, examining the orb. Seeing it clearly now.

The globe was astonishingly light. It might have actually not weighed anything at all. Hyam could not quite reach his two hands completely around it. Deep in its depths were tiny flickers of light, tight sparks that came and went in regular flashes. He felt the remarkable bond, a fusion as deep as sinew.

But what held him most was the orb's color. It glowed a deep, rich violet. In certain lights it appeared almost black.

21

After the failed attempt to break through the Long Hall's portal, Joelle's days grew crowded with memories. For the first time since her arrival, she did not forcefully shove them away. There was no longer any reason. She assumed the thoughts of her parents were driven by how she would soon join them in death. It was only a matter of time.

Three things had united her parents most of all—their love for each other, Joelle, and their love of silence. Her mother could go weeks without speaking a word. And yet Joelle had loved her company, for her mother's silence had been sparked by a force as strong as any mage-heat. Joelle's mother was a telepath, and the most she ever spoke was in preparing her daughter for the gift's arrival. Which should have come during her eighteenth winter but did not. Instead, Joelle's *awareness* grew, this ability of hers to see beyond physical limits. Joelle took this to be a living sign of her tainted blood.

Her father was a hunter. He had supplied game to his

wife's clan, and thus they had met, fallen in love, and broken a thousand years of restrictions. And so her mother had been banished. Soon after, Joelle had arrived. The young woman now imprisoned for the crime of being born.

Twice more Joelle sought to break through the Long Hall's portal, weaving her spells in the moonlight and flinging her sparkling blades. She was certain now that Trace observed her. She intended to confront him, demand to know why he simply did not release the door spells and allow her to flee. But Trace had taken to avoiding her. He did not even attend his classes. As though he was waiting for something. What, she had no idea. But Joelle began spending much of her nights in the library. Several times she sensed the fleeting presence of an observer. She assumed it was Trace, who no doubt thought she searched for more powerful spells of warcraft. But he was wrong. She had another target in mind altogether.

She was only sleeping a few hours each night, between the library and the memory assaults. Joelle was therefore very surprised by how the moment came, in the breath between sleep and wakefulness. Then suddenly she was free for the first time since attacking the portal.

Free, yet not free. For as soon as she emerged, she was swept up and away. Through the tiny crack in the wall, across the moonlit expanse, up, up, and away . . .

Back to the place she had hoped she would never see again.

Joelle stood upon the desert ledge. The valley separating her from the ancient city was cast in the silver glow of a waning moon. The world was empty, silent, and yet she could sense the approach of that same dread presence.

The clarity of her vision was such that not even night could hide away the crimson mage. His arrival was marked by a bizarre cloud of metallic insects. Long before they tightened into the shape of wizard and cloak and staff and orb, she knew it was him. She wanted to flee, or at least turn away, but the same force that had brought her here gripped her with relentless strength. She saw how the buzzing insects flitted beneath the cowl, as though fashioning a face she hoped she would never see.

The hand holding the orb raised, and the crimson mage was joined by a contingent of ghostly warriors. This group held to no strict rank and made no sound as they marched. How could they, since they had neither body nor physical form. They were as vague as the moonlight, as silent as the death they wore. They drifted up and onto the distant ridge, where before, the knights had sat and drank and enjoyed the slaughter.

The wizard pointed his staff down into the valley, and at that moment a second horde rose from the valley floor. Instantly Joelle knew them to be the defeated warriors who had raced down the hillside to their doom. The new ranks of ghoulish soldiers quietly slipped down the ledge, down into the valley where their fellows waited. The wizard lifted his staff, and the army sank into the rocks and vanished in a final few wisps of fog and remorse.

Then the mage noticed her.

Joelle felt his furious perception like a fist to her soul. She fought against the force that gripped her still, knowing he was about to lift his staff and send the ghostly hordes against her . . .

In the far distance an illumination rose, a light so intense it pressed the mage back a step. For once she was not the one assaulted, because for Joelle the light carried a sense of inexpressible joy.

She knew with the certainty that such journeys carried that this was why she had come. She was meant to see *this*. The light was intended for *her*.

And with that awareness she was lifted up, up, and drawn away. But not back to her stone chamber. Instead, she flew across the vast distance to a different desert, a different valley, one filled with a light that sparked her soul in a way she could not fathom, much less name.

There at the valley's heart stood a man. At least, she thought he was both male and human, but the light was so intense all she could really see was his silhouette. He held something aloft in both hands, his arms stretched high above his head, his back arched almost painfully, and then she realized . . .

The man was in ecstasy.

He reveled in the power that gripped him. He was flooded with an elation so potent Joelle felt it as well, as though she could communicate with him not through words but through pleasure.

She wanted to reach out to him, to ask him who he was and whether he would help her . . .

The instant the thoughts took form, she was drawn away. The break was as intense as a slap to her psyche, as though she had been caught in a wrongful deed. All the way back, across meadows and valleys and forest, she argued with the force and fought its relentless grip. How could she be expected to refuse help from whatever quarter she could? How could she not strive to break free?

22

Hyam reached the city of Havering in the steamy mid-morning heat. The grand city used the arid hills as a natural barrier. As Hyam descended the final stretch, he surveyed the lush green of a cultivated world drenched in rain and wealth. Clouds blown from the distant sea met the Galwyn peaks and deposited their water upon the first ridges. On the city's far side flowed a river that shared the city's name. The River Havering was almost as wide as the Three Rivers valley. The city itself was vast and very rich. Hyam turned off the empty Galwyn trail and joined with the caravans and the merchants and the farmers who crammed the main route. He was weary in his bones. The horse was lathered and salt stained. Dama limped slightly. They pushed on because he insisted. Hyam was near collapse and needed a place where they could be genuinely safe, at least for a moment.

He selected an inn by asking a wealthy caravan master, who

pointed out a house that at first sight appeared to be a manor set within its own protective walls. But on closer inspection, Hyam saw that the walls were mostly decorative, and a small golden signpost dangled discreetly above the main gates.

Before descending the final ridge, Hyam had donned the remaining outfit made for him in Melcombe. As Hyam had hoped, his attire attracted no questioning attention. Before he had climbed down from the saddle, a young stable hand rushed forward and knuckled his forelock. "Welcome to the Three Princes, sire. May I take your steed?"

"I will want to attend to his needs."

"Certainly, sire. This way, if you please." Clearly the youth saw nothing out of the ordinary in a wellborn seeing to his mount. He led Hyam into the stable's welcome shade and pointed at an empty stall. "Will this do, your lordship?"

"Fine."

"Will your honor be staying with us?"

"Is there a private room?"

The lad hesitated with what Hyam took as a practiced delicacy, then said, "Because of the festival, a private room will be costly, sire."

"I will pay."

"How long does his honor expect to be staying?"

He had no idea, so he replied, "For the duration of the festival."

"One moment, your lordship, and I'll go ask."

Hyam unsaddled the horse and filled the byre with oats and two armfuls gathered from a pile of fresh-cut grain, then as Matu ate he brushed and curried the horse's flanks. He knew the stable hand would do a better job, for Hyam was so exhausted he could barely lift his arms. But he wanted Matu to know his gratitude in the only way that mattered. In truth, Hyam would have been happier collapsing into the straw beside his dog. But when the servant returned and announced that Hyam might have their last private chamber, he unlashed his satchel and the bundles and instructed the youth, "Treat the animal as you would your own, and I will treat you just as well."

"You can count on me, your honor, sir."

"Come, Dama."

Other guests sat or lolled about tables set around the central courtyard. They watched him with careless ease and murmured too quietly for him to catch the words. Someone laughed. A young woman scurried out the central door and hurried over. "Might I carry your satchels, sir?"

He handed over everything save his sword and the sack holding the orb. "I need a meal."

"The kitchen fire is still alight, good sir. Cook can fry you up a late breakfast."

He felt the saliva spurt at the prospect of hot food. "Tell him to hurry."

"That I shall, sir."

Another woman stood by the entry, her smile not rising to her gaze, which took the measure of him and decided that here indeed was one who could pay. "You have ridden a long way, good sir."

"Too long and too hard."

"Then you'll be pleased to know you've made it in time

for the tournament." She ushered him inside. "Welcome to the Three Princes."

"Tournament?"

She both led and followed him down a flagstone hall. "The royal joust begins at dawn."

"I am not here for such."

"Then why . . ." She went quiet as he fumbled with his purse and drew out a gold florin. Her eyes widened in greedy satisfaction. "I'm certain your honor has good reasons of his own."

"Food," Hyam ordered. "Then a bath. Hurry."

Joelle's thoughts often returned to the desert valley and the man so cloaked in bliss and power she could not make him out. She felt an uncommon yearning rise with each recollection, as though here was something she could neither comprehend nor grasp. She felt as frustrated by the sensations as she did when a spell did not form to her liking. Even so, the memories refused to be pushed away. They clouded her vision at times, even when she was most intent upon learning, or practicing with her spell-cast knives, or searching the scrolls, or trying to sleep, or rising from dreams to wakefulness . . .

These moments of liberation seldom came night after night, but for the third dawn in a row, she was drawn out of herself. Joelle hovered there for the longest moment, but she was not forced anywhere. Instead, she could go as she wished. Another breath and she was away.

Her escape point was a singular mystery, a pinprick opening

where the mortar sealing the portal to the wall's stones had fallen out. Joelle only discovered it by being drawn through it by the guiding force. Even now, after three years of such momentary freedoms, she had to hunt to find it. She poised ghostlike by the portal, feeling the force that secured it more clearly than ever, and searched for the crack. Then she slipped through the seam, flew across the meadow, and entered her home. The one place she had ever belonged.

The glade neighboring the Havering Long Hall was hardly deserving of the title *forest*. She had been raised in a realm of green so vast a traveler could spend ten days on the road and not pass from one boundary to the next. But this was enough for her, and though her lungs remained bound by stone and spell, she sensed the forest's energy and flavors. She exulted in the joy of belonging.

This time she was not so much drawn away as having her attention redirected. For a brief instant she was able to look out over an impossible distance, out to where a desert city rose upon a silent ridge.

Then she became aware of another presence. The new scent assaulted her with the force of an angry tempest. The distance between them was great, but it did not matter, for in that brief instant, shorter than the space between heartbeats, Joelle knew that she was being hunted. The crimson mage stood upon the stone citadel rising from the heart of that ancient yellow city. Searching.

And this time, the crimson mage knew she was there.

Even as the panic rose, still she was amazed at how she could be in the glade by the Long Hall meadow and peer out across a measureless distance. She saw with crystal clarity the crimson mage raise his staff and point it in her direction, as though the distance mattered less to him than it did to her. And when the orb attached to the tip of his staff began to glow, she saw the cloud of black insects fly from beneath his shadowed hood and swarm toward her.

Though she was well separated from her heart, still she could feel the surge of panic strike a frantic drumbeat in her distant chest. Joelle fled back, away from the forest and across the meadow. She arrived at the wall just as the first faint tremors of the incoming swarm drilled into her being, a sibilant rush of death and terror. She clawed at the stone, searching frantically for her way through. But in her panic she lost the place. Or perhaps it was hidden from her. Possibly she had been granted this final glimpse of her beloved woodlands before being torn apart by the metallic horde.

She risked a glance behind her and would have screamed if she had a voice. The cloud was so vast that it blocked the rising sun. The insect wings glinted bronze and russet in the dawn. Swarming. Attacking.

Then she found it. She rammed into the tight seam, her haste so great she fled across the courtyard before she was even aware she had made it through. Joelle turned back in time to see the swarm's assault.

The cloud slammed into the outer wall and the mage-force that rose above it. She had never realized until that very moment how the Long Hall's barrier was shaped like a dome, curving smooth and steady above the watchtower. She saw the insect horde strike and create the webs of power just as her knives had fashioned upon the portal.

But Trace was not there to silence the watchtower's bell. It rang now with the fierce alarm of having waited centuries for this moment. Again and again the bell struck, the sound causing the very stones to vibrate. As they did, the watchtower flamed to life, transformed from granite to fire, gathering force like a giant's wand, then shooting it out in bolts of fiery power, piercing the barrier and the cloud both.

Joelle stayed until she heard the first cries rise from the corridors leading to the mages' quarters. When she returned to her body and rose from her bed, the one thought she held was of how Trace had not merely silenced the alarm when she attacked the door but had saved her from precisely that same assault. As she began her duties, ignoring the shouts and commands and havoc about her, Joelle realized another thing. Trace had not been granting her a chance to escape. He had been allowing her to safely test the Long Hall's power. He knew she could not escape. He wanted her to find a bitter peace in remaining.

She liked him more now than ever.

But her affection for the old wizard changed nothing. Either she broke free or she died trying. And just then, it scarcely mattered to her one way or the other.

23

Hyam slept in great stretches. His slumber cut swaths from a day and a night and much of the next day. He woke to eat and stretch and check on his horse and bathe a second time and groom the dog, and then he slept again. He gorged on the inn's ample fare. His bedroom was both comfortable and luxurious, with a pair of windows opening to the field that separated the manor from the river and the city proper. He was awoken the second morning to the brassy cry of trumpets, and for a terrifying instant he was returned to the field of battle and the rise of the unearthly hordes. Then he opened his eyes, walked to the window, and watched horsemen in shining armor ride toward one another with gaily colored lances at the ready. He ignored the crash of metal, the cries, and the cheers, as one would the squalling of infants. But he knew that sleep had been taken from him, at least for a time. He went in search of more food.

When Hyam asked if there was an Ashanta banker in Havering, the innkeeper stood on the table's other side, her arms crossed over her broad girth, her hands hidden respectfully in her sleeves. "The house allied to the Ashanta stands just down the road from us. They don't care for the city crowds." She hesitated, then added, "There's word recently arrived of a dispute between the royal house and the Ashanta, good sir."

"So I have been told."

"There's others who might keep a safer hold on your gold, if you catch my meaning. I know of several whom I trust myself."

Hyam thanked her and finished eating. He returned to his room and donned his set of tailored clothes, then took Dama for a good long walk, carrying the orb sack slung from his shoulder. He kept well away from the crowds still flocking to the festival grounds. Then he left the dog guarding the sack in his room and headed out.

The banker's estate was shaped like a fortified manor, with stables and storerooms joined to a high stone wall enclosing a large forecourt in front and an even larger garden in the back. Watchtowers punctuated the four corners, with guards on constant duty. But the guards appeared more interested in the jousts than yet another well-dressed noble who sought the banker's time. Hyam was waved through the front gate. He crossed the interior courtyard, climbed the stairs, and pounded on the front door.

A serving woman opened the portal, gave him a swift glance, then said, "The banker is busy. Come back tomorrow."

He blocked her from shutting the door in his face. "I would have word with the master today."

"Release your hold!"

"I come from the Ashanta village at Eagle's Claw. I carry important news."

A voice from farther inside called, "Let him enter."

The woman had a face that was made to look sour. "His seal belongs to no great house. He's just another young squire who demands time his lordship doesn't have."

"Then you will have the pleasure of shooing him away. Now open the door." She stepped away, revealing a man in the flagstone who stood holding a feather quill and a pair of reading glasses. A man. Not Ashanta. But his manner held the imperious ease of one who had held power so long he assumed it was his by right. "State your business."

Hyam stepped through the portal. "That is for your ears alone."

One brief perusal of Hyam's royal charter was enough to cause the banker to go as pale as the parchment he held in his trembling hands. He gave back the charter, left the study where they were seated, and in the distance Hyam heard him order the housekeeper to bar the doors and refuse all entry until he said otherwise. He returned and locked the study door and closed the window shutters. In the gloomy half-light, he demanded, "What is it you want?"

"Where is the nearest Ashanta settlement?"

"I am utterly forbidden to speak of such matters." The banker's name was Vanier, and his fear was enough to send a tremor through every word he uttered. "The king has decreed that we might remain, but only because they need our gold, and only if we refuse to claim any such alliance."

"What can you tell me of this expulsion?"

He carried the document to the window and held it so the light slipping past the shutters fell directly on the parchment. He studied it carefully, then allowed, "I suppose this is genuine."

"It is."

"There hasn't been an emissary for over a century."

"I know."

He handed back the decree and dropped into his seat with a heavy sigh. "The edict of expulsion was the new king's first act."

"But . . . the king was crowned four years ago."

"Correct. For months we who serve as the Ashanta's local financiers lived in terror for our lives. The Ashanta were officially under indictment of treason and ordered to depart the empire. But why? What had they done? And were we to cease in our financial activities? We sent our own emissary to the palace and were forced to wait. Every morning for two weeks our representative presented himself, only to be turned away. Finally we were met by the new king's chief moneylender. A role which before we had always performed ourselves."

The banker's chair squeaked as he shifted his bulk forward, until mere inches separated them. "We were told that all debts held by the Ashanta financiers from the old king were erased. We protested that the treaty covering our repayment was not founded upon the Oberon line but upon the realm itself. The new king's new moneylender said, in that case, the expulsion took effect that very hour. So our representative agreed to erase the debt. What choice did we have?"

"And now?"

"Since that time, we have heard nothing. Neither that the edict has been repealed nor that we are safe. Until two months ago. Then a royal messenger arrived, and ever since we have lived upon the knife's edge."

Hyam leaned back, his mind whirling. "I don't understand."

"What is there to understand? The new king escaped from beneath a mountain of old debt. And in the process we lost a fortune. The realm owed us six tons of gold!"

Hyam pondered whether he should say anything at all about the battle. Then he decided that if the Ashanta wanted their role to be known to the outside world, or to their local representatives, they would have said it themselves. "Do you have a means of communicating with the Ashanta?"

The tension rose to where his jowls shook. "I am forbidden to speak of that as well."

"But such communications must be possible, if you are able to receive or make payments that are available anywhere in the realm, at any moment."

The banker set his jaw and did not reply.

Hyam raised the scroll to where the banker had no choice but to look. "I ask that you pass on a message."

"I am not saying that such a thing could be done. But if it were . . ."

"I need quill and parchment." When the banker supplied both, Hyam demanded, "Do you read Ashanta?"

Grudgingly the banker said, "All who serve in my role are required to learn their script."

"Excellent." Hyam bent over the parchment and wrote swiftly.

When he was done, the banker squinted and read aloud, "'Your shield was erased, but I survived. The orbs are again in the world.'"

"Correct."

"This seems hardly worth breaking a secret that has ruled my profession for centuries."

"It is what the Ashanta would wish, I assure you. They must know this now."

"To answer your question, the nearest Ashanta settlement is nine days' hard ride west and north from here, in a secret vale carved from the Galwyn Hills' trailing edge."

"Too far." Hyam rose to his feet. "One more question and I will trouble you no longer. I'm told there's a Long Hall near Havering?"

The banker worked this question with the caution of a man who had spent his lifetime guarding other people's gold. Finally he said, "Follow the river-road east and north, to where it veers away from the hills. You'll see a waterfall. At the pool by its base, you'll find a trail through the forest. The Long Hall is half a day's ride from the pool."

Hyam stowed his charter in the satchel slung from his shoulder. "I am staying at the Three Princes if you need to reach me."

The banker remained where he was. "Sir, I mean no disrespect, but I would be a happy man if I never laid eyes on you again."

24

When Hyam returned to the inn, weary knights clustered by three shaded tables. Frothy tankards of ale stood before them. One sneered as Hyam crossed the courtyard and called, "What have we here, a coward in noble garb?"

"I am here on urgent business for my liege," Hyam replied, and kept walking.

But when he tried to enter the inn, a boot rose to block his way. "What manner of emblem is that you wear? I know it not."

"I am of the Three Valleys, beyond the Galwyn Hills and the great forest."

One of the fellows said, "The Galwyn Road is blocked."

"I found it empty of life or threat," Hyam replied.

"I do not understand this." The first knight had a lazy manner of speech, which was slurred somewhat by drink and a welt rising on the side of his face. "What country lord would send his squire to the tournament and order him not to compete?"

Hyam tried to defuse the situation with humor. "One who values my services, since I have not been trained in the arts of war."

"Nonsense. Every squire is ordered by royal decree to learn a weapon. Tell me yours, I demand it."

"Leave your game," the other man complained. "We are weary and beaten."

"You may be defeated," the knight replied, his gaze burning hard. "I am resting for the morrow. Speak, country squire, or I shall be forced to show you steel."

"None of that!" The innkeeper appeared in the doorway and swatted at the boot blocking Hyam's entry. "This is a house of peace and good cheer."

"Speak," the knight snarled.

"The bow," Hyam said.

"Well then. See how easy that is?" He dropped his boot. "You shall be competing tomorrow on the field of green."

"I am called away at dawn." He started to enter, only to have the boot rise once more. "I answered your question."

"And I shall call anyone who refuses to compete a coward and expect to meet him in the courtyard!"

Hyam sighed his defeat. "I serve my liege away from Havering tomorrow, and for the next day as well. What would it take for you to release me to my duties?"

"You must accept a challenge." He glanced behind him, his head made unsteady by ale. "What say you, fellows, is that not a reasonable exchange?"

"I say you should let him go."

"Nonsense. This one must stand for his hayseed of a liege."

One of the others shrugged. "Have him shoot the target now."

"A smashing idea. What say you, Sir Hayseed? Will you shoot now rather than on the morrow?"

"Do I have a choice?"

"Most certainly." The knight took evident pleasure in laying his sword on the table.

"I'll go get my bow." Hyam returned to his room and slipped his bow from its leather cover. He slung it and a quiver over his shoulder. He then unfolded his pallet and belted on the Milantian blade. He might never have seen a tournament, but he understood the threat well enough. The knight drinking on the inn's veranda had been defeated on the tournament's first day. His pride was bruised. He was also a bully. He saw in Hyam a weaker foe, and his pride demanded a victory.

Hyam hesitated, then decided that against such numbers he needed Dama with him. But he could not leave the orb here unguarded. So he knelt and emptied his quiver.

"Bowman!" The voice came from outside his window. "This way is guarded, so don't try fleeing!"

Hyam pressed the orb down the length of the quiver. The fit was very tight, and he hoped he would not scar or shatter the thing. "Coming."

"Through the inn's gates and around to the pasture by the river, that's a good hayseed squire!"

He refilled the quiver with a score of arrows, then snapped his fingers at Dama and said, "Let's go."

Two fellows stood by the front portal waiting for Hyam and ignoring the irate innkeeper, who said when Hyam appeared, "Good sir, say the word and I'll set my guards upon them."

"And they'll perish steeped in their own blood," one snarled.

"It's fine," Hyam said, yet he sensed that it was anything but. For their grins told him they had come up with some twisted manner of ensuring he lost the contest.

But their grins vanished at the sight of Dama. "What manner of beast is this?"

"I told you it wasn't no dog," one of the others said, drawing his sword partway from its scabbard.

"This is a forbidden breed if ever I saw one," his fellow agreed.

"The king himself keeps wolfhounds," Hyam replied. "Release your blade or the contest is off."

They did not like it, but there was no disputing the fact that Hyam and his dog were already crossing the courtyard. They muttered, but they sheathed their weapons and followed.

When Hyam appeared around the corner, the waiting throng took stock of Dama and their lethal pleasure diminished. One said, "He's brought reinforcements."

"What does that matter, when we are eleven," the bully declared. He grinned and waved a mailed glove at Hyam. "This way, hayseed squire! Now then. See the post planted at the end of the festival ground? That is your target."

The post was as thick as his thigh and rose to twice the

height of a man. A red circle was painted at head height. "What is that at the target's center?"

His question drew a booming laugh from the assembly. "Why, that is the prize! Whoever strikes the center of the king's coin wins the tourney of archers!"

Hyam nodded. "Where do the archers position themselves?"

"There by the bridge, see the rope making a stall? No, no, hayseed. That is for tomorrow. You are to shoot from here."

The men found that mildly hilarious. The fact that Dama neither growled nor even looked their way caused them to ignore the dog entirely.

Hyam examined the target. Between him and the dark post was a stretch of green, the river, and the entire length of the festival grounds.

"Call it seven hundred paces," the bully offered.

Hyam looked at him. "If I hit the target, you will let me go in peace?"

The bully mocked him with, "Oh, most certainly, squire. To strike a target the king's archer could not hit. Do this and you will have our best wishes for your task tomorrow. But when you fail, you will have me to contend with."

Hyam did not respond. He had expected nothing less.

"Call it punishment for cowardice, hayseed."

Hyam looked at the beast and pointed to the space before the gathered knights. "Dama, keep them away from me."

The dog ambled over and planted herself in front of the assembly.

"Call off your pet." But the bully spoke too loudly, or perhaps he'd started toward Hyam, for Dama responded with the same roar that had preceded her attack on the witches. The bully staggered back and was only kept from going down by the grip of his fellows.

Several of the knights drew their swords, and Dama's howls grew more savage still. The traffic along the road running to Hyam's left stopped and stared. The bridge's railing became clogged with watchers.

"Dama! Silence!"

The dog stilled her roar, but the hair remained bristled over her back, and her teeth were fully bared.

"Sheath your swords!" When they hesitated, Hyam shouted louder still, "I have agreed to your contest. You have agreed to let me shoot!"

A cry rose from the inn's window. "And I stand as witness!" The innkeeper pointed to the throng now watching from the roadway. "As do they! Hold to your bargain, or I will see you banished from the festival and the city both!" A finger trembled as it took aim at the bully. "And I know you're the sheriff's son, but it won't do you no good with a hundred witnesses to your deeds!"

Reluctantly the knights sheathed their blades. Hyam turned back to the target and sought to still his trembling limbs.

"Good sir, allow me to fetch other nobles here for the tournament! They'll see these ruffians receive the treatment they deserve!"

Hyam was tempted, but he knew they would only seek another reason to challenge him. Or draw together more allies of their own. So he waved his hand to silence her and focused upon the distant pole.

When he was ready, he drew an arrow from his quiver and inspected it carefully. The shaft was straight, the point sharp and well fixed, the feathers firmly attached. He notched the shaft, took a long breath, and walked another ten paces farther from the knights.

He stood and stared at the pole. But his attention was no longer held by the target. He knew that the people lining the road and bridge had gone silent. He knew also the sheriff's son sought to distract him by flashing a plate of his armor into Hyam's eyes. None of this mattered at all.

He felt the power rise from the orb. He willed it to gather in his shoulders, his arms, his hand. Only when the force united him with bow and arrow, binding them with his gaze and his aim and his strength, did he lift the bow.

The act of pulling the string back to his chin and releasing the arrow was as fluid as falling rain. He breathed the words as he released, the Milantian spoken too softly to carry. "Fly true!"

The entire world held its breath as the arrow lifted slightly, soaring above the river's sparkling surface, then falling, falling . . .

And striking the target right in the center of the silver coin.

The roar that met him when he returned to the world of senses and form was enormous. The innkeeper was hugging herself with two brawny arms and shrieking with joyous wonder. All the knights but one gaped at Hyam as he approached them and said, "We are done here."

"Wait!" The bully's face was savage in its disappointment. Two defeats in one day had left his gaze poisonous with fury. "Who are you?"

"Come, Dama," Hyam said, and started away.

Behind him the sheriff's son shrieked, "I will have your name!"

The dog responded by leaping about and roaring with a ferocity that left the knight sprawled on the earth.

"Dama, hold." Hyam turned long enough to reply, "You will have nothing more from me. Is that clear? We are through."

25

Hyam bathed away the day's stress and replayed the contest and the cheers. As he dressed, he forced his mind to other concerns. No matter how fine the energy coursing through him might have felt, there were more important things to ponder. Such as why King Ravi had issued a surprise edict banishing the Ashanta, and if it was truly a matter of old debt, as the banker assumed, or if more was at work. And what role the crimson rider with his orb might play. Not in the battle but in the realm.

He ate in his room to avoid running into any of the defeated nobles, and was asleep before the day's final light faded from the sky.

He was awoken by a cold nose prodding his shoulder. Then he heard the scratching at his door. "Who is there?"

"The woman who wants to see you live through this night."

He recognized the innkeeper's worried voice. Hyam slipped on his trousers and opened the door. "Yes?"

She stepped inside uninvited. "The ones you vanquished sat and drank for hours. I passed by enough to know for certain they were busy hatching plans. The sheriff's son means to trap you in another challenge tomorrow. One you won't survive."

"I had planned to depart at daybreak."

"It could be too late. I suspect they're already busy gathering their mates, surrounding my place of business, cutting off your escape."

Hyam was already moving. "I am leaving now."

She watched his hasty packing with genuine regret. "Such shooting as yours should be rewarded, not form a cause for revenge."

Hyam hefted his belongings and motioned to the dog. "I need supplies for three days."

"And you'll have them." She padded quietly down the hall, through the silent great-room, and into the empty kitchen, where she hastily packed two satchels. "The sheriff's son is like many of the nobles who've risen with the new king. Too many, if you ask me." She followed him into the stable and watched him saddle his horse. "I warrant you're aligned with the house whose name I dare not utter."

"I am."

She sighed noisily and shook her head. It was all the response she would grant, and it was enough. "Where shall I say you are headed? If they ask. Which they will."

"I will take the river-road, so tell them somewhere else." He pointed to the byre holding the barn's oats. "May I fill a sack?"

"Help yourself." She watched him shovel in grain for the

horse. "Is it true what I heard you say, you came by way of the Galwyn Road?"

"I did."

"And you didn't find trouble?"

Hyam fastened the oat sack behind his satchel. "How far will this go?"

"I need attach you to nothing I say. An innkeeper knows when to forget the names of her guests. Which won't be hard in your case, since I never asked."

"There were three witches preying on travelers."

Her eyes were round and deep in the lantern's glow. "You vanquished them that bested a force of the king's own guard?"

"The witches are no more." Hyam opened his purse and extracted a florin. "For your troubles."

"The news you've just handed me is payment enough, good sir."

Hyam pressed the coin into her hands. "Then for your kindness."

Joelle had a new favorite hideaway. She had been given the responsibility of cleaning the library, partly because no one else wanted the duty, and mostly because she did a very good job. Not even the desiccated prune of a Librarian could find fault in her work. She was good because she wanted to come back. And she came back to borrow, though the Librarian would have called her a thief. Only now that was no longer necessary, for Joelle had discovered a door whose lock had become loose, and with a gentle tug she could slip inside.

And come here, to a space that was snug as a velvet cave, a place she liked to think of as made for her.

One wall actually was fashioned from velvet—long drapes that framed the lead-paned windows. The library was unique in that manner, for the Long Hall community had few windows, and none so large as these. The library windows overlooked the central fields and faced south by east, so that on clear mornings the light could be blinding. Velvet curtains fell floor to ceiling, hooked by golden ropes that could be released when the light grew fierce. The windows themselves were flanked by broad benches with rectangular horsehair pads. In the daytime, students crouched there and pondered the world they had left behind. On nights such as this, the haven was hers to claim.

She loved everything about the library except the mage who ran it. The shelves of scrolls and books ran up four times her own height. The vast chamber was wrapped on three sides by a balcony whose bronze railing she carefully polished. She loved walking the narrow way, dusting the shelves, deciding which of the tomes she would dive into next.

Since being defeated by the portal, all her nights had been given over to finding a means of unlocking the binding spells that sealed the Long Hall's only exit. Failing that, she sought a way into the chamber at the Long Hall's heart. So far, both goals had eluded her. The library held two locked side alcoves, and she suspected the answer might rest there. Both were surrounded by fierce mage-heat. A senior mage might request entry, but the Librarian alone held access. Even so, Joelle was determined to find a way inside. It was only a matter of time.

She settled into her niche and tugged the curtains closed,

then fashioned a candle to illuminate her space. She loved practicing these small bits of magic, especially when she heard acolytes complain they could never make the light stable. Her own candle glowed a foot or so above her head, steady as her breathing. She unrolled the scroll, then froze as a door creaked.

"See there, it's just as I said. She's magicking, she is!"

The voice belonged to the Librarian and rang with the triumph of one who lived to forbid, to punish, to wreak havoc on those within reach. Joelle set the scroll aside and gripped for the knives she always carried. To attack now would mean certain defeat. She was not ready. But attack she would. And to take this one down with her would offer a small portion—

"I've noted your complaint," Trace replied. "Now let's be—"

"Complaint, you say? Complaint?" The Doorkeeper sounded outraged. Of course the Librarian would not come alone. Not when accusing her before the Master Wizard. "What she's doing there is *forbidden*!"

"Duly noted." The voice rang clearly from the gallery across from her alcove. Trace sounded wearily defeated. "It's late, and I'm tired from a long—"

"She must be made to bleed, I tell you. *Bleed!*" the Doorkeeper snarled.

Trace underwent a remarkable transformation, one so potent it ruffled the velvet drape by her cheek. "There's a hermitage high in the western badlands that's awaiting your arrival. I could send you both there tonight. Announce your retirements after you're gone. Perhaps I should."

The Librarian's indignation rang through the chamber. "She's the one doing wrong! Not us!"

"She's the most innocent person who's ever graced this Long Hall," Trace replied.

"She's *imprisoned*!" The Doorkeeper sounded as if he gargled with lava. "She's to be held here for *life*!"

"But the pair of you have no idea why, do you. So you feed those shriveled, wretched excuses you have for souls with rumors."

"This is an *outrage*!"

"I couldn't agree more. If either of you speak a word of this to anyone, you'll be off to the windswept reaches that same day. And *you'll* be the ones banished for life."

"And you dare call yourself a Master Mage!"

"And you, the both of you, dare call yourselves human!"

"I knew you were a fraud!" The Librarian revealed a stutter in his fury. "First time I ever set eyes on you!"

"You disgrace the Long Hall," the Doorkeeper agreed.

"Get out of my sight while you still have posts to claim," Trace snapped. "Go on. *Move!*"

When the door slammed shut and the voices rang ever more faintly, Joelle finally released her breath and tremors both. She used a shaky finger to repair the tear in the scroll, then rose from the place that was her haven no longer. It was only a matter of time before the Librarian, the Doorkeeper, and their venomous allies shut her away. And when that happened, she would fight.

She set the scroll back in its place, crossed the library, and headed back for her room. She would spend the rest of this empty night with her knives as companions. Fighting away the tragic knowledge that she had already lost. But fight she would.

26

The rain set in soon after Hyam left the main road. It began as a gentle apology, a soft mist that drifted and coalesced into gradually larger drops. By the start of his second hour upon the road, Hyam could scarcely see the horse's head, the rain was so hard. What was more, the trail he followed was hardly ever used. The earthen track was turned into a rivulet, then a stream. They were well into the forest now, and the trees became sentries guarding a myriad of what might have been paths, all of them inviting Hyam to become extremely lost.

He halted beneath a giant hardwood whose boughs melted into the dark and the rain. He stood for a time, then squatted, and finally sat. The rain washed away the day's heat and replaced it with a chilling edge. Dama's thick pelt protected her from the wet cold, but Matu's flanks began trembling. Hyam knew the destrier would survive the night, but the question was, did they have to do so in such sightless misery.

He drew the orb from the bottom of his quiver. As soon as his hands fastened upon the globe, a light gleamed through the mouth and the canvas fabric. He pulled it out and stood holding it, marveling at the immediate sense of force at his disposal. Once again the bond was forged with the earth beneath his sodden feet. He lifted the globe, holding its smooth surface with both hands, and willed the light not just to strengthen but to shield.

Instantly the rain stopped falling. Or rather, it stopped touching them.

The rushing drumbeat of raindrops surrounded them. But where they stood, an island had been formed, a refuge illuminated by a brilliant purple glow.

He set the globe on a stump, then unsaddled the destrier and tethered him to a nearby sapling. He stared at the globe for a time, then decided he wanted to see how far this mystery could be taken. Hyam lifted the orb and instructed the light to vanish but the protection to remain.

Immediately the darkness returned, and yet they remained shielded from the storm.

Hyam pressed his hands down more tightly and clenched his eyes shut, as if he needed a stronger grip to try the next step.

Slowly, steadily, the moisture evaporated from his clothes.

Hyam opened his eyes to discover Matu and Dama both watching him. He set the globe back on the stump and stroked first the horse, then the dog. Both were dry. As was the earth at their feet. The torrent ran in a steady course around their haven.

Hyam slipped the globe back into the quiver and replaced the arrows by touch alone. Then he lay down on the springy dry earth. And slept.

The night was almost over when the dream carried Hyam away. He knew this because the first image he had when he rose from his body was of a faint light growing in the east. The clouds made for a beautiful and subtle dawn. Hyam had no chance to pause over the glory, however. For he was drawn as he had been before, following a current not of his own making.

He swept over forest, he passed high above the waterfall and the pool, he flew across a trio of hidden vales, and then he arrived at the wide emerald pasture that framed the Havering Long Hall. Before his repulsion could rise strong enough to halt him, he passed through a tiny crack in the stone alongside the main portal. The spells that protected the mages from unwanted visitors were mere spiderwebs, tiny fragments of force that could not hold him. He wondered idly if they were alerted to his passage, but he had no space for concern. As before, his focus remained not just intent but single-minded. All he could see clearly was the next portion of his path, leading to his unseen destination.

Then he heard the weeping.

A woman sobbed deep within her broken heart. The silent lament was one she had fashioned over years. He knew this without question, just as Hyam knew she was three years younger than he. The same awareness he had known within the Assembly filled him now, directed like a compass to this young woman's heart. But when he entered her windowless cell, much like the one that had held him for five long years, the woman revealed no tears. Instead, she raged in a tightly controlled manner.

The furniture was crammed to one side, the battered table and chair piled atop her bed. Hyam's awareness was such that he knew she did this every morning. It was her ritual method of meeting each new day. Neither bowed nor beaten. She was a fighter. She prepared. She was going to war.

A book lay open on the bed, one detailing stances for a knife fighter. Her hands held two implements she had fashioned herself. She had spent months honing and balancing four kitchen knives until they were instruments of combat. Two were for throwing, two for wielding. Her movements were a dance of fierce coordination and vicious intent. Hyam realized she intended to break out of the Long Hall. Her sweeping stabs and high kicks were aimed straight at the Doorkeeper and the Librarian and their aides. To take on an entire bevy of wizards armed only with knives suggested a courage and ferocity that left him in awe.

She was also breathtakingly beautiful.

Hyam watched her spin and stab and slice and parry, and wondered if anyone else had managed to pierce her armor and perceive her heart's tears.

She remained lost in her routine for a few moments longer, then stopped and breathed hard. And realized she was no longer alone. She cried aloud, "Who is there?"

Hyam had no idea how to respond, except, "It is I."

"You are a Long Hall mage?"

"I have nothing to do with the Long Hall."

His disgust must have resonated, for her panic eased. "Who are you, then?"

"My name is Hyam. And you are . . ."

"Joelle."

But that was not what he intended to say. "You are Ashanta."

The heart's dirge rose up once more, so potent it masked the rage in her words. "I am *nothing*! I am *no one*!"

"I don't understand. The only other time this has happened to me was when I traveled to an Ashanta Assembly."

Her anger became matched by a desperate hunger. "They let you in?"

"My arrival was unexpected. I caught them all by surprise. But they let me stay. Reluctantly."

"I visited their settlement once. They forbade me from ever returning." She used both hands to clear her face of more than just sweat. "I still dream of them sometimes. Those are the harshest dreams of all."

"Why are you here?"

"Because the Ashanta ordered the mages to hold me." Her lovely face twisted with bitter ire. "I am the girl who should never have been born."

He realized, "You are half human."

Hyam hated how this flooded her with shame. Joelle swiped the air in front of her face with one of the knives. "I am leaving. The mages say I will perish if I depart and have vowed to keep me here all my days." She glared at where he would have been, had he actually been in the chamber at all.

"But I am through heeding their words. Either I leave or I die in the process."

Hyam felt the gentle tug drawing him away. He called back while he could still be heard, "Stay where you are. Be patient. Let me help."

She sensed his departure and cried after him, "Don't leave me here!"

But he was already gone. He swept back into his body and awoke.

Hyam opened his eyes and leapt to his feet, calling out to the forest that surrounded him, "I am coming!"

27

The orb was utterly blank when Hyam awoke. He stared into its dull depths as he walked the forest trail and listened to the remnants of last night's storm drip from every leaf and limb. There was clearly some limit to the orb's potency, but how it returned, he had no idea. Unless, of course, he happened upon a river of power coursing here as it had in the desert. And if he was able to sense the current and draw it up. Otherwise he might as well be carrying an oversized glass bauble. Hyam slipped the orb back inside his saddlebag and did his best to plan. Though pondering on how he might manage to rescue a lovely young woman trapped inside a Long Hall only drew up outraged memories of his own treatment at the mages' hands.

Dawn's beauty was soon replaced by a sullen, steamy heat. The rising sun chased away the few remaining clouds and bore down hard. By the time Hyam passed the waterfall and the glade's green pool, he and his animals were panting from the simple exertion of drawing a decent breath. The forest trail was empty and airless. Hyam let the animals drink, then rounded the lake and continued through the glade. The two vales trapped the heat and the humidity both and fought him for every inch of forward movement. He had no idea if the globe might have cooled them, had there been any force remaining. Still, he decided it was not altogether bad that he could not form another spell as he approached the Long Hall. If the mages had not detected his nighttime passage, he had no interest in alerting them to his approach. They would find out soon enough.

Perhaps his rage granted him the same heightened senses as the witches' brew. Or perhaps the orb's hold had grown on him after a night of resting under its protection. Hyam had no idea, nor did he want to take time for such ruminations. What he could say, however, was that when he entered the meadows surrounding the Long Hall, he found himself anchored to one particular spot.

He slipped from his horse and stood listening. Not to the rising wind, not to the rustling grass, not to the birdsong from the trees behind him. But rather to what flowed beneath his feet.

Deep down, buried far in the earth, ran another huge river. The currents were as broad and strong as in the desert vale. Here he stood upon the emerald edge of the knob that held the Long Hall. The hill's height made no difference, like the crest or trough of a wave observed from the seabed. The power was far, far below where he stood. As immense as it was unmistakable.

Coursing out from this was a tiny trickle, scarcely more than a breath of force. And it was upon this minor stream that the Long Hall rested.

Hyam laughed out loud. He yelled at the hated stone walls, "You chose the wrong spot!"

He dropped the saddle to the ground and removed the bit from Matu's mouth. He tethered the horse to a young tree, then fed both animals. He was in no hurry. The wind heightened as the sun reached its zenith, amplifying the heat he carried.

He left his sword and bow on the ground beside his beasts and placed the sack holding the orb directly above the power's center. He approached the Long Hall with empty hands.

He pounded the door with his fist. When there was no response, he took out his knife and hammered with his hilt. He struck hard enough to dent the ancient oak. And took great pleasure from the act.

The door swung inward, drawn by the type of mage Hyam had despised most. Narrow in face, disapproving in manner. Mean and tight, his only pleasure in tormenting the helpless. "What is the meaning of this?"

"I wish to have a word with your Master Trace."

The mage stared aghast at the damage Hyam's knife had done. "This will not go unpunished!"

Hyam closed the distance between them and roared in the man's face, "Trace! Now!"

The mage jerked back in genuine disgust. "You carry the stench of expulsion! You are forbidden to enter these hallowed grounds!"

Then a voice rose from behind the mage, merry as the Doorkeeper was grim. "The one you seek is here!"

The wizard known as Trace was a sprightly greybeard who moved with the energy of someone a third his age. He almost danced across the green expanse to the inevitable bench that sat looking out over the world. "What a delight to greet a man who dares to pull the Doorkeeper's beard!"

"Your watchman is clean shaven," Hyam pointed out.

"And more's the pity! If he had a beard, you'd have plucked it!" The mage cackled. "I would pay good gold florins to see his expression right now."

"All you need to do is turn around."

"Oh, I dare not. Because if I did, he would know I laugh at him. Then that sourpuss would make my life pure misery!"

Hyam felt no such qualms over glancing back. "He is examining his door and looking like he is eating unripe lemons."

The historian's merry laugh raced about the fields. "Wonderful! I am in your debt! Do you know, he actually questions my right to walk out here and enjoy the view!"

"Acolytes were forbidden to pass beyond the door."

"Yes, I know a bit of your former plight, and how you never knew the purposes behind the discipline and the lessons. Only the agony." He bowed in a courtly manner. "I apologize on behalf of all my brethren and sisters."

Hyam found himself resisting a strong desire to like this man. "If you really meant it, you would change the regime by which those poor children are kept."

"If only I could!" The sweep of his arm took in the stern stone walls and the roofs rising within. "But who am I, a lone Master at the edge of the realm, to take on the might and tradition of a hundred Long Halls?"

Hyam settled upon the bench. Their perch looked out over a green vale and a small river. Far into the distance stretched more meadows and flocks of woolly sheep. The Long Hall's myth of idyllic calm was complete. "I was sent here by the Mistress of the Three Valleys Long Hall."

"Yes, she said you might appear. What can I do for you?"

Hyam had not expected to like this wizard, or any mage, for that matter. He had planned to come and ask his questions, then deliver his ultimatum for them to release Joelle, and then prepare for the battle that would ensue. He had no idea how he might breach these magically strengthened walls. Only that he would rescue Joelle or die in the attempt.

Hyam studied the mage's cheerful visage and asked, "What can you tell me of the Elves' demise?"

"What an astonishing man you are!" Trace clapped his hands in pure delight. "And here I thought I was the only person on earth who gave a fig over such long-dead matters. Might I be so bold as to ask your name?"

"Hyam."

"Well, Hyam, the answer is quite simple. The Ashanta entered the battle too late. They were too slow to act! Those remarkable folk love nothing more than deliberation. Well, they love secrecy most of all. But within those great, silent halls of theirs, they gather in what are known as Assemblies. But you know this, of course. Your former Mistress claimed you are fluent in their tongue and have read all the scrolls your Long Hall possesses. And that particular Long Hall contains the finest collection of Ashanta documents anywhere!" He sighed with longing. "What I would give for a chance to delve into those scrolls. But my own Long Hall refuses me the right to travel! Can you imagine such a travesty?"

"I thought all senior mages were required to spend a year in the outer world."

The mage looked genuinely shocked. "Where on earth did you hear that?"

"I can't say."

"Such information is counted as one of our most closely guarded secrets." He dropped his voice to a conspiratorial whisper. "Tell me. I beg you. It will go no further."

"No."

"A mage at your Long Hall dared share our mysteries?"

"They did not."

"What if I refuse to answer your question unless you speak?"

"Then our conversation is over."

He poked Hyam's ribs with a bony finger. "You really are a wretched boy. No wonder they kicked you out."

Hyam stifled a smile. "The Elves."

"Those violet-eyed Ashanta sat within their white walls and . . . Do you know where they get that remarkable stone from? No? Neither do I! But I came across a scroll once, oh my, it was back when I was no older than you are now. How old did you say you were? Never mind. The scroll claimed they brought all that stone from a secret mine far, far in the north. And do you know how they accomplished this marvel?"

"By the strength of their combined mental powers," Hyam replied.

The mage's curiosity was a burning ember now. "You read the same scroll?"

"No. But I know a little about the Ashanta. Enough to suppose they could accomplish anything they set their collective mind to."

"True enough!" He sighed delightedly. "What astonishing conversations you and I might have. Can you stay awhile?"

"Not a chance."

"No, I thought not. Where was I?"

"The Ashanta were too late."

"Oh, they probably never intended to do anything at all. That is what some of our own generals and mages of the time suspected. But after the Elves were decimated, the Ashanta realized that once the humans were defeated and enslaved, the Milantians would come after them next. So the Ashanta approached the first King Oberon and offered their help." He shuddered from his sandals to his long grey beard. "I hate to think what would have befallen humankind if they had not!"

Hyam pondered that a long moment, surprised by the temptation to share his own secret. Instead, he changed the subject and asked, "What can you tell me of the realm's new ruler?"

"King Ravi?" The mage frowned. "Very little, and none of it good. What does this have to do with the Elves?"

"You know of the edict expelling the Ashanta from the realm?"

"A testimony to the idiocy of our new dunderheaded king. The old king, the last of the Oberon line, was hardly better. He ran up a king's ransom in debts. Which was the purpose behind the edict, of course. Force the Ashanta to write off the crippling arrears." He clapped his hands delightedly. "A king's ransom. Clever, what?"

"What if the edict wasn't about the debt at all?"

"I don't understand."

Hyam stared into the distance, then decided, "I need to tell you something to be passed on to the other Long Halls." He swiftly recounted the army's arrival, the battle, and the crimson rider. By the time he finished, the mage's good humor had utterly vanished.

"What you tell me is a calamity!"

"Which is why you needed to know."

"A crimson orb traveled with the king's own brother? Worse than calamity! This has been forbidden for a thousand years! It has ensured our peace!" He rose and started back. "I must alert the others."

"Wait! We are not done!"

"Eh?" The mage forced himself to focus on Hyam. "What is it that has you so riled, lad? Have I said something to offend you?"

"Not you. Your kind."

"My kind?" As distressed as he was, the mage still found the strength to offer a wry smile. "You speak as though we were a breed apart."

"You hold a woman prisoner."

Nothing he had said that day caused the mage more consternation. "What . . . How do you know?"

Hyam's rage surged up. "Is it not enough that the Long Halls imprison their acolytes? Now you take slaves?"

"I . . . That is, we—"

"Release the woman."

"The Ashanta have vowed to kill her if she leaves."

"Hand her into my protection. I will keep her safe."

"You? Against the Ashanta? I think not, lad."

"Release her!"

"Even if I wanted to, the other elders will not agree."

"They will have no choice," Hyam snarled.

"Lad, I beg you, don't do anything rash!"

Hyam started back across the meadow. "This conversation is over."

28

Hyam did not move toward where the Doorkeeper still moaned over his damaged portal. Instead, he strode back to where the horse calmly cropped grass and Dama sprawled, panting softly. Back to where the power surged deep in the earth. A power he needed to tap in order to survive. A power that seemed to have been waiting for his return. For as soon as he gripped the canvas satchel, the energy rose to link with his orb and then fill him, a heaving invisible fount, granting him a sense of magnificent ire.

The old mage glanced in his direction and raised a hesitant arm in farewell. Then Trace gathered his robe and started back toward the Long Hall.

Hyam yelled, "Stay where you are!"

The power of his voice was amplified to where it froze not just the mage but the Doorkeeper as well. Hyam's awareness extended outward with his voice, and he saw how wizards throughout the Long Hall paused in their magery and their studies. Called to alert by the strength behind his words. Hyam had no idea what he was about to do. Only that he needed to act, and now.

He felt the mages gather their force in response to the threat beyond their portal. He cast a desperate plea in the only direction from which help might come. He gripped the satchel more tightly and actually said the words aloud. "Help me!"

The idea came to him with such immediacy it seemed as though it had been waiting for him to make ready.

He drew upon the coursing power, sucking more and more into his being, like he was expanding a giant's lung, taking an impossibly huge breath of energy. His awareness expanded and crystallized to where he could trace his way through the Long Hall, down the forbidden ways, into the secret reaches that had been barred to him as a despised acolyte.

As he moved, he raised the alarm. He actually heard with his sharpened ears the cries of real panic rising from inside. He knew they were searching for their wands and drawing on their secret spells.

With a flick of his mental hands, he stripped away the spells encasing the most private chamber of all. The very heart of the Long Hall. The cavernous room that held their orb.

He reached across the distance and gripped the globe.

The one in his canvas sack reached with him. The two orbs began vibrating in a harmony that resonated in his bones, humming in timbre to the power that flowed back and forth between the globes.

He sensed a senior mage reach down and grip the orb, calling upon the power. Hyam flicked him away. The wizard crashed against the cavern's wall. Now the screams were turning wild, rising like shrieks of a storm wind. Calling out spell after spell. Binding the orb, the Long Hall, the meadow, and him.

Hyam reached out with both hands and saw with a vision beyond mere sight how tendrils of power extended from his fingers, streaming across the meadow. The Doorkeeper sensed the assault and leapt inside, slamming the portal shut.

Hyam flicked his hand and blasted away the Long Hall portal and the spells wrapped about the stone frame. The door and rocks were shattered into dust and splinters.

The watchtower bell rang with a frenzy to match the wizards inside. Lightning ripped across the meadow, a furious attack upon where he stood. And yet it was no more effective than the summer breeze. Hyam did not even need to deflect the barrage. He simply fed upon the power and reached farther still.

He stripped away the wizards' half-formed spells. He felt only scorn for the mages and their complacent ways, the crusty conservatism, the smug sense that they had generations at their disposal. They had lost their edge. If they had ever had one at all.

He wrenched the Long Hall orb from its stanchion and drew it back toward him. He detonated every wall he met. Firing a continuous line of holes through whatever barrier that separated him from the wizards' globe.

As it approached the outer portal, Hyam strode across the meadow, coming to meet it.

The globe arrived at the destroyed portal and passed

through. The ball carried a dazzling luminescence, the color of an emerald dawn, green and gold and mesmerizing. If Hyam only had time, he would have willingly lost himself in its depths.

Instead, he brought the orb to a halt directly over his head. He stopped before the smashed portal, looked at the terrified Doorkeeper sprawled on the interior cobblestones, and said, "Invite me to enter."

The mage waved a frantic hand in a feeble attempt to bind the orb and draw it back. In reply, Hyam wrenched the man from the ground, flung him across the courtyard, and slammed him against the rear wall. This time his voice was powerful enough to shatter doors and windows both. *"Invite me inside!"*

Master Trace spoke from behind him. "Please, honored sir. Enter. You are most welcome."

Hyam stepped over the demolished entry. He did not run. He was invading. He conquered. The Elven words he had spoken to the fallen knight returned in a blaze of fury to his mind. *I am vengeance. I am the protector of my people. I am wrath unleashed.*

Anyone so foolish as to come within reach, or even suggest a movement of defiance, was met with dreadful force. Hyam pinned them to the walls as he passed, binding them to the stone. He veered slightly from the most direct route to his destination in order to pass down the hall lined with the acolytes' cells. The windowless cages drew from him the strongest wrath of all. He blasted out the doors. He wreaked havoc on the exterior walls blocking them from the meadow

192

and freedom. At the hall's far end he turned and shouted, "If you want, leave! You are prisoners no longer!"

He turned back to the wall before him and tore it apart.

He stepped over the rubble in time to see the kitchen staff and the acolytes assigned to scrub the pots and knead the bread flee in a shrieking mob. Only one person remained. She rose from her knees, the wire brush she had used to scrub the flagstones dripping unnoticed in her hand.

Joelle greeted him as one who had managed to hold on to her pride and strength both. She was, Hyam knew, stronger than he would ever become. No amount of magery or earth-bound force could compare with her ability to greet him with the calmly stated words, "You came."

Hyam looked into the most beautiful eyes he had ever seen. A broad circle of purest violet rimmed pale grey irises. Their gemstone beauty matched the woman, for she was lovely indeed. "Joelle, it is time for us to depart."

She dropped her brush. "Will you give me new weapons?"

"I will."

"Knives and sword and shield?"

"That and perhaps even more."

"More?"

"Maybe I can give you a reason to fight."

She stepped toward him. "I am ready."

29

Hyam led her to where his packs lay upon the grass, then walked back to where the old wizard waited by the demolished front portal.

Trace demanded, "Was it absolutely necessary for you to make enemies of every wizard throughout the realm?"

"All Long Halls have been my foe since I was ten years old. And they knew it." Hyam surveyed his havoc with bone-deep satisfaction. "Only up to now, they didn't care."

The wizard stroked his beard and gave a scholar's studied examination to the orb still hovering above Hyam's head. "Must you keep my kindred wizards bound any longer?"

The outer wall was a smoldering ruin where it ran closest to the acolytes' shattered cells. Two youths scrambled over the remains and ran for the forest trail. Hyam waited for more to flee, but the other acolytes merely showed fearful faces through the holes he had made. Hyam extended his arms, and the youths vanished back inside. He reached with his

194

extended power-senses back into the Long Hall and released every spell he had made.

"Thank you," the greybeard said quietly.

Hyam heard the soft rush of many feet, and mages swarmed into the courtyard. They scurried toward him, their sandals slapping frantically upon the cobblestones. But they did not come to attack. Instead, they clustered and clutched at the ragged opening, their gazes locked on the orb hovering above Hyam's head. Hyam could well understand why. Without the globe, they were not merely stripped of power. Their entire existence was rendered futile. If it ever had any point at all.

Hyam reached above his head and took hold of the still-glowing orb. He offered it to the wizard. "This is yours."

"Yes," Trace solemnly agreed. "It is."

"Promise me you will never hold another prisoner within your walls. Including your acolytes. Each year, all who live here shall be granted the right to depart."

"This do I vow."

"You will do your utmost to see this becomes the rule in every Long Hall."

"Agreed. I and my successors."

"Then take it."

The greybeard gravely accepted hold of the orb, and instantly the light diminished. This was not lost on the mage or on the other wizards who clustered in the front courtyard.

Hyam turned away, only to be drawn back by the mage saying, "May I ask a boon of you? I know I hardly hold any right. But . . ."

"Speak."

The mage leaned in close enough to reveal the desperation in his bright blue eyes. "Take me with you!"

Their departure from the Long Hall meadows was delayed until well after dark. Three times one of the remaining acolytes came out to beg Hyam's patience. The last youth's gaze lingered overlong on Joelle, then he caught Hyam's glare, blanched in the torchlight, and tried to slip through the ruined wall.

"Come back here!" When the youth stood tremblingly before him again, Hyam demanded, "You were her friend?"

"She was kind to me, after a fashion. The first months were hard, they were."

"And yet you stayed. Not then. Now. When I gave you release." Hyam studied the acolyte and realized, "You like it here."

"Ever so much, your lordship."

"Why?"

"I am hungry for learning. They feed me. Master Trace most of all."

"I was hungry too, once," Hyam replied. "But the mages beat it out of me."

"I was beaten at home," the youth said. "But not here."

"Never?"

"Not once. Master Trace won't allow it." He twisted his hands nervously. "You'll keep him safe, won't you, your lordship? We're ever so fond of him."

Hyam moved Joelle and his animals back to where the

meadow met the forest. Joelle spoke little and cast furtive glances toward her former prison. When he offered her food, she refused to eat until he assured her it had not come from the Long Hall. The young woman's silent burdens made Hyam steam.

He had trouble not staring at her, for she was truly lovely. But he could feel a fearful tension radiating from her. So Hyam moved back to where he stood between her and the Long Hall. Torchlight and candles and magical illumination poured through the gaping holes. Perhaps he should have felt satisfaction over the evidence of his vengeance. But the young acolyte's shining gaze and the words he had spoken left Hyam feeling vaguely ashamed.

He walked back to where Joelle sat watching him with her unblinking gaze. Hyam hefted the saddlebag and moved down to where the meadow joined with the ruined outer wall. He stood quietly, feeling his exhaustion, and wondered if this sensation of being so utterly drained was the price one paid for using the orb. If so, he would soon be in even worse shape.

The trickle of power flowed directly beneath his feet before passing beneath the Long Hall. Hyam's ability to reach out was weakened by his fatigue. But the connection was still there, the orb filled with a force he could draw upon. His exhaustion did not vanish as the power surged through him. It simply no longer mattered. He extended his arms toward the broken wall, and farther still. Out to the hidden chamber where the orb had been replaced and where all the mages now gathered. He resealed the chamber, repairing the walls, drawing the stones together in a flow as constant and steady as the power upon which he drew.

The old mage found Hyam returning the outer wall's stones to their proper order. Trace watched in silence as Hyam completed his work. The wizard then stepped forward and ran his hand over the restored wall. Lines of fire glimmered between the stones, fading gradually.

Hyam walked back to where the Doorkeeper and several of the other mages observed him cautiously through the ruined portal. They stepped well back as he began the process of healing the door frame. He reached into the forest behind him and hefted a massive felled trunk. He drew it to him, held it in midair, stripped away the branches, then sectioned it into planks and spliced them together with the same veins of fire that had sealed the walls. Then he shut the portal and blocked his view of the mages' burning gazes. Sealing him outside. Beyond the hallowed walls. Where he belonged.

"They won't thank you, you know," Master Trace said.

"I want nothing from them."

"Well, on that point they will most certainly satisfy you. For that is precisely what you will get for your trouble. Nothing." The old mage fell into step beside him as Hyam started back across the night-clad meadow. "You shoved them off their self-righteous throne. You shattered their sense of worth and power. You terrified them."

"I'm glad."

A wide swath of gleaming teeth appeared amid his beard. "So am I."

"Strange attitude for the Master to take. As strange as hearing the acolytes liked you."

The mage flicked his hand, and a light the size and strength of a lantern's glow appeared above his right shoulder. "It is such a pity they treated you so harshly."

Hyam's fatigue robbed his words of ire. Still, he spoke because he wanted Joelle to hear. "They beat me until I bled."

"We do not beat our protégés. It is forbidden."

"I'll wager that won't last with you gone."

"Forbidden," the mage repeated, raising an arm in greeting to the slit-eyed woman. "That was why I tarried so long. Ensuring that my chosen successor was set in place and that she acknowledged my goals and my vows as her own."

Hyam bent over his gear, then paused, doubting he had the strength to lift the saddle.

The old man touched his shoulder. "Let me do that, lad."

Hyam stepped back because he had to and watched the old man huff and heave the saddle into place.

"Just because my fellow wizards are too shaken to do what is right and proper does not mean it must be left undone." Master Trace straightened into the formal stance of a senior mage and said, "Thank you for restoring our orb and healing our home."

They traveled less than an hour, which was good, because Hyam's feet became increasingly reluctant to rise from the trail. Joelle rode. The Master walked ahead of them with his soft light revealing the path. Hyam walked behind, using his bow stave for support. Dama took up the rear, glancing back so often Hyam wondered if perhaps the mages were trailing along behind. Then he decided he did not care what the wizards did.

He had reached the limits of his endurance when they arrived at the base of the second narrow valley. Hyam sensed a distant coursing flow of power rising through his exhausted legs and declared, "We stop here."

"There is a pool just beyond the next ridge," the mage responded. "With a cave that offers a fine shelter."

"Here," Hyam insisted. When Joelle descended from the saddle, he told her, "I brought only the one bedroll."

"I do not care." Her eyes gleamed in the light. "I am far too excited to sleep."

"Then you can stand guard." Hyam tossed Trace the pallet, threw himself onto the earth, and was gone.

He awoke in the depths of night. The wizard slumbered off to his right, the magical light nestled in the boughs of a sapling that rose by his head. Joelle sat with her back against a tree on the trail's other side. Someone had dragged the saddle off the horse. Dama rose from her position beside Hyam and nuzzled him as he groaned softly and forced himself erect. He walked to the pile of gear and hefted a water skin and a sack of food from the inn. He eased himself down beside the woman and offered her the skin. She drank briefly, accepted bread and cheese and a plum. While she ate and drank, Joelle's gaze never left his face.

"Are you tired?" Hyam asked.

"For three years and seventeen days, I have lain in my chamber and dreamed of this night. When I could taste the wind and smell the forest and watch the stars. I will sleep later."

"How old were you when you entered the Long Hall?"

"Fifteen. My parents died from a fever that swept through the forest where we had our cottage. I lived alone for a year. Then the sickness returned, and I thought I was going to die. Then someone rescued me. I thought . . ."

"Tell me. Please."

"I thought the person had green skin." She looked ashamed by the admission. "I was very sick."

"What happened then?"

"I was taken to another place where someone else cared for me. I remember a home made from white stone where they fed me a potion that tasted dreadful."

"The Ashanta took you in," he realized. In the mage's light, her features were smooth as carved alabaster. Her pain was an alien presence and did not belong.

"Those people were not kind. They treated me without feeling. Everything they did for me was a chore. They kept me until they were certain I would survive, and not a moment longer, then they brought me to the Long Hall." She smeared streaks of wet across her cheeks. "Tonight is the first time I have been back in my beloved forest. I never thought this night would come."

He set the water skin aside and retied the food sack. "I need to ask you to do something."

Her gaze was steady, her voice flat and hard as the blade beside her hand. "I will do whatever you ask."

Hyam realized with a start what she expected him to say.

He blushed furiously. "No, it's not . . . I don't . . . Well, I do, but . . ."

She sat and watched him, her gaze like lavender stone.

Hyam took a deep breath and tried again. "I need to contact the Ashanta."

She started. "What does that have to do with me?"

"When I came to you in the night, you realized I was there. How?"

"I saw you with my other eyes."

"What do you mean?"

"The Master instructed me never to speak of these things." She glanced over to where the wizard slept. "He was my best friend among the mages. He tried to teach me. He tried . . ."

Hyam recalled the narrow-faced Doorkeeper and finished for her, "Some of the mages forbade it. And took pleasure in doing so."

Her gaze returned to the slumbering magician. "Trace spent time with me. He instructed me, even when others said it was forbidden."

Hyam heard the unspoken. "He taught you magic?"

"Some. A little. He seemed thrilled when I showed talent. Some of the others were . . . not pleased."

Hyam resisted the urge to tell her of his own experiences at the hands of narrow-minded wizards. "You don't have to do what the mages said, not ever again."

Joelle nodded slowly. "What do you want?"

"This second vision of yours. Tell me how it works."

"You came to me, and you do not know this?"

"I have only been able to do it in dreams, and never by my

own will. I am drawn forward." He lifted his hands. "I don't know any other way to describe it."

"That happens to me sometimes as well. Other times I am free. For a moment or so."

"When did this process begin?"

"A few months ago." She smiled at the memory. "The first time, I thought I had truly escaped. Waking up was dreadful."

"And this second sight?"

"That came the year after my parents died. Gradually, slowly."

"How do you travel?"

"It always happens upon awakening. I have often wondered if I might learn to control it. Go when I want, rather than wait for it to happen." She extended her arms. "Just reach out and fly."

"Will you try now?"

"If it is important to you. But . . ." She turned away from him and the mage's light and stared into the darkness. "I went once to the Ashanta. They punished me for coming and told me never to return. They called me a woman of tainted blood. They said I was forbidden from ever approaching them again."

Her angry pain clenched his chest. "You miss them."

Again she swiped at her cheeks. "I have done *nothing* to them. They had me locked away. And now . . ."

The tightness compressed his own rage into a tightly controlled flame. "If I can, I am going to change all that."

She seemed to have difficulty even hearing his words. "But how?"

"That's why I need your help," Hyam replied. "To do this very thing."

30

Hyam found a softly padded section of ground where moss grew thick beneath a massive oak. He used the sack holding the orb for a headrest. He watched as Joelle hesitated, then lay down not two full paces away from him. "I don't know if this will work."

"Thank you for trying." The words seemed feeble, given all her reasons for denying his request. "I mean that."

"I know you do, Hyam." She spoke his name for the first time. "And it amazes me that you should find it necessary to thank me for anything. Ever."

Again he felt the flush rise from his collar, for he heard the clear invitation in her voice. As well as the bitter resignation. This time, he could not draw his gaze away. Her hair was shaded somewhere between russet and blonde. That and her eyes were the clearest signs of her human blood. There were many beautiful women among the Ashanta, who were known as a handsome race. But none that Hyam had ever met carried her sorrow.

"There is an energy far below us."

She blinked, clearly expecting him to say something else. "Inside the earth?"

"Very deep." He poked the moss at his side. "Do you feel it?"

"I don't . . ." She was silent for a time. "No. I sense no such thing."

"It's very faint here. We'll try this again elsewhere." He settled into a prone position and shut his eyes. "I will connect with this energy, then encircle us both. Perhaps that will make the transition easier for you."

He sensed as much as heard her lie back. "All right."

He bonded with the orb and reached down, down. His awareness of the streaming force grew with each exercise. The current here was a minuscule stream. Hyam saw how the orb was both a receptacle and conduit, that in fact he could connect with the coursing energy precisely because of the orb's presence. He breathed in the growing force, then out, encircling them both. When the mage-force fully enveloped them, he heard Joelle whisper, "I feel it."

"Try to go now."

Hyam waited, and when Joelle did not speak again, he assumed she had been successful. The question was how to join her.

He did not so much speak the command as visualize what he wanted. Then mentally he reached out, searching for a woman who was disconnected from the body laying beside him. Instantly he rose from his body, smooth and precise. He hovered long enough to focus his awareness and found Joelle there waiting for him.

She remained where she was for a time, studying this unformed component of him. Then she turned her awareness away and extended.

He sensed clearly that Joelle was seeing, searching, and then once she located her destination, she moved. And as she sped away from where they both lay, he journeyed with her.

Farther and farther they went, until she arrived at a pristine meadow. The fields were far greater than the ones surrounding the Three Valleys settlement. And the Ashanta city rising from its heart was far grander.

Joelle stopped by the nearest boundary stone and said, "I dare go no farther."

"Will you wait here?"

He did not know how it was possible for him to hear her so clearly. Not merely the words, but the timbre of her speech and the pungent fear. "If you command, then yes. But I'd rather . . ."

"Don't go."

"When I last came, they hurt me."

"They won't do that again." His vision blurred slightly beneath the sudden wash of rage. "I promise you."

"All right. I'll wait."

He swept through the boundary stones, and this time the sentries in the watchtowers were alerted to his arrival. Ahead of him rose an abrupt heaving alarm. Which meant his next move was redundant. But his anger over the way they had treated Joelle needed venting.

Hyam drew in all the power he could muster, then released it in a bellow that shook the watchtowers on their foundations.

"WAKE UP!"

The hastily gathered Assembly might have held a comic edge, had the intent not been so serious. Many of the Ashanta arrived directly from a disturbed sleep. More still were aghast at the fact that they had been called by the presence of an interloper. An outsider. One who was not of them. The fact that he bore the title of emissary changed none of this.

Had he not still been so irate over their treatment of Joelle, Hyam might have been more respectful. As it was, he waited impatiently while the leader mounted the platform and gathered his robes of office. The number of people there in bodily form was much reduced from the last time. Yet the unseen host that surrounded him was as numerous as before. And far more alarmed. Clearly these secretive folk disliked being hauled from their complacent isolation as much as the Long Hall mages.

The leader called the Assembly to order and addressed Hyam in arched formality. "It is good to know that you survived the assault."

Hyam located the Seer far back in the multitude, hiding away, or trying to. "No thanks to you."

The leader coughed discreetly. "You have a report to make?"

207

He had intended to discuss the attack, but as he started to speak, he felt a rising compunction. "Actually, I must deliver two statements. The first is out of order but is quickest. The Elves are aware of the threat. They wish you to know that they stand ready to join with you, if help is required."

The consternation at his arrival was nothing compared to what erupted now. The leader had to actually shout for silence. Hyam gave the briefest of accounts, then said, "More will have to wait for another time."

"I have questions."

"I'm sure you do. So do I. But we will both have to be patient. The other portion of my message is too vital." Swiftly he related his experience at the attack. And his sighting of the crimson rider, first in the company of the king's own brother, then before the Ashanta raised their ghoulish army.

When he finished, the appalled Assembly met him with silence. Finally, the leader said hoarsely, "You have had time to ponder this."

"I have."

"What is your assessment?"

"The attack was a feint," Hyam replied. "The army was always intended to perish at your hands."

The leader wanted to argue. Hyam was certain of this. But he merely said, "The purpose of this feint?"

"Perhaps there was some political intent behind the prince's demise. But I think the real reason was for the crimson rider to gauge your strength. See if you still possessed the power to wreak havoc among your foes."

"Though I despair of saying it, I agree with your conclusion. They sought to test our mettle. See if the legends still lived." The leader lifted his gaze. "Discussion? Anyone?"

"We were duped," a voice replied. "We were forced to show our hand."

"We acted rightly," another said. "Our treaty lands were invaded."

"That has nothing to do with our discussion."

"It has everything to do with all of this."

The leader remained untouched by the swirl of emotions and words. Hyam waited with him. Finally silence was restored, restive, anxious, and the leader said, "Your conclusion?"

"The wizard showed his own hand in the process," Hyam replied. "The crimson mage revealed himself. And the orb."

"He did not expect you to survive," the leader realized.

"He must have known this was a risk. He acted anyway."

"Which means . . ."

"This was only the beginning," Hyam said. "He is planning something far greater."

A collective shudder raced through the Assembly when the leader replied, "Again, I concur."

"I have an idea," Hyam said. "But to succeed, I need three things. First, we must locate the crimson rider."

"Orbs are hidden and always have been. How, we do not know. But this is part of their power. Word will be sent throughout the realm."

"Today," Hyam said. "Immediately."

"It will be done. Next?"

"I need gold."

"That we have."

"I will need so much you will feel its loss," Hyam warned. "More."

The leader showed a moment's genuine concern. "It is so important?"

"Vital," Hyam replied.

"Tell us why."

He did so as swiftly as possible. When he was done, the leader lifted his gaze and asked the Assembly, "Objections?" There were none. "It will be done. And your third request?"

In response, Hyam turned around and demanded, "Where is the Seer who promised I would remain safe during and after the attack?"

The ancient crone's voice quaked out, "Here."

"You vowed to protect me!" Hyam roared with remembered fear and agony. "You broke your vow!"

"I did not know a mage rode with them! You heard our leader. I am unable to detect an orb. Their power is masked!"

"You are a Seer! It is your business to know!"

"You are right. I failed. I apolo—"

"I do not want your apology. I *reject* it. A vow is a vow!"

"Yes . . . Yes."

"Say it!"

"A vow is a vow."

Hyam turned back to the leader on the high podium. "What happens when a vow is broken?"

The leader showed uncertainty but replied, "Compensation is determined by the one disabused."

Which was precisely what Hyam had hoped. "In that case,

here is my demand." He extended back to where Joelle cowered beyond the boundary stones. "This one is to be made welcome."

A horrified roar rose from the Assembly. "No!"

He shouted louder still. "She will take her place among you!"

"It is forbidden!"

In reply he called, "Joelle! Come now!" When she backed away, he gripped her with a clutch so powerful she had no choice but to obey, though she fought him every inch of the way.

When they were inside the hall, he took yet another great heaving breath from the underground force, then shouted, *"I am the emissary! I have been wronged! This is my demand!"*

The power of his outburst shattered one of the high windows. A shower of glass fell upon the hall, the sound almost musical in the stunned silence.

Instantly he was flooded with shame. As soon as the final shards clinked upon the tiles, Hyam remade the window. It was hard to tell what shocked the Assembly more. His ability to destroy a window or restore it.

When he was done, and the murmuring died with the fragile veins of light that knit the glass together, the leader allowed, "We will discuss this."

"No." Hyam knew he had to convince them, else they would take their revenge on her when he was gone. "No. You will *decide*. You will do so *now*." When the leader looked ready to argue, Hyam stopped him with, "Have you learned nothing from the past? Must you always be forced by outside events to do the right thing?"

"We do not know this is right."

"You do. And I suspect you always have. You just refuse to accept it. Instead, you pretended the issue was gone. You hid her away in a Long Hall and played as though she did not exist. As a result—" He had to stop and breathe away his rage, pushing it down, clamping a fierce hold over the recollection of the woman's endless weeping. "You threatened a beautiful life. You consigned an innocent to imprisonment."

"But the blood of this one—"

The leader's response was cut off by Joelle declaring, "I don't want to stay here."

Hyam turned to her. "This is your home."

"My *home*?" Her bitter laugh echoed through him. "If they don't want me, I would only be trading one prison for another."

"We may accept you," the leader said. "Though it will mean breaking a vow we made to ourselves over fifteen centuries ago and has lasted for as long as we have had contact with humans."

"You will do so reluctantly. Many will resent my presence. I have had my fill of such welcomes." She drew closer to Hyam. "Can't I stay with you?"

"I have no home," he said, shamed by the hundred thousand listening ears. "No place. No one."

"Then we will wander alone, together," she replied. "If you agree."

31

It was well past noon when Hyam and Joelle rose from their
pallets. His back ached from lumps in the mossy earth
that he had not noticed when settling down. His head
thundered. His body felt pummeled. He helped Joelle to her
feet and then staggered about. Some unnamed component
of his body felt assaulted by his expedition to the Ashanta.

The mage said nothing as they brewed tea and ate a cold
meal and saddled up and set off. Joelle insisted that she wanted
to walk, and Hyam did not object, for he was glad to let the
horse walk for him. Even so, the saddle fit uncomfortably
between his legs and the rocking motions disagreed with his
bruised state. He finally gave up and walked alongside the
horse. Joelle looked a bit better than he felt, but not much.
After a time, she climbed into the empty saddle.

The mage could not have appeared more different. He
took delight in the road and the day. "I have not slept so fine
in years!"

Hyam winced. "Quieter, please. You are in the company of the ill-treated."

Master Trace responded by taking in a massive breath of the steamy air. "Joelle is not the only one who has felt captured by the Long Hall. I cannot recall the last time I was not woken by one crisis or another. No clanging bells, no moaning elders. How they droned! An old wizard loves nothing more than the sound of his own voice!"

"You are a wizard," Hyam pointed out. "And you are old."

"There are always exceptions," Trace replied breezily. "When I awoke this morning, I thought I was still dreaming. No stone, no cell, no door! No bevy of acolytes clutching at the hem of my robe, begging for another book, another lesson. My only company was a young couple who were still as death."

They traversed the forested ridgeline, a trivial lump compared to the crests Hyam had crossed in the Galwyn Hills. Even so, it was enough to settle him wearily onto a stump. He panted and drank and panted some more. In the distance shimmered a ribbon of water, falling, falling, down into a glistening pool. "You say there is a cavern?"

"It is a well-known resting place for the folk who visit us in festival season."

"We'll stop there." The decision was enough to straighten Joelle's shoulders and lift him to his feet. They began the descent, and Matu's steady plodding carried the horse ahead of them. Hyam sent the dog on to lope alongside the destrier.

Master Trace stepped off the trail and disappeared into the undergrowth. He returned carrying a narrow branch that served him as a staff. He offered it to Hyam. "This might assist."

"Keep it. I could use my bow. But it wouldn't help." Hyam gestured to the small burlap sack strung over the mage's shoulder. "You travel light."

"It is how the mages depart for their year in the outer world. Stripped of comfort and safety, carrying a few coins, a single change of clothes, a bit of food and water. They must forage, they must work, they must join in the tumult and chaos of daily life."

"What did you do?"

"I worked as a nobleman's private secretary. The count is now disgraced, I fear, as he was loyal to House Oberon. Which is a pity, for he was a good man, one of the finest I ever knew. It was a pleasure to work in his service. I came from such a family, the younger son of a minor squire. I wanted to see the life I had forsaken." He walked on for a time, then confessed, "When my year was over, I did not want to return to Long Hall."

"Why did you?"

"I almost remained. The count offered me a permanent position. I liked him, I liked his family. There was a young lass . . ." He smiled and let his gaze drift away. "Eh. She's old and fat and shrewish by now. I don't even remember her name."

"Yes you do."

"Well, perhaps." The mage cast Hyam a shrewd glance. "Might a simple traveler ask a question of his own?"

"I suppose."

"Do you know why I chose not to approach the two of you, even when I feared you had been captured by some forbidden spell work that had robbed you of breath and life both? I shall tell you why. Because the sack beneath your head was glowing."

Hyam shook his head. "Some questions you must not ask."

"The most brilliant purple, that light," Master Trace persisted. "And so fierce it shone through the canvas and illuminated each thread hole."

"Don't."

"What must I do for you to trust me?" When Hyam did not reply, he went on, "A mage who becomes Master of a Long Hall takes vows that bind him for all his life. I forsook those oaths, lad. For you. And do you know why?"

Hyam continued walking. Slowly. Down the descending trail.

"I am here because of the news you carried and the power you revealed. These defy a thousand years of Long Hall wisdom! How can we burrow down in our safe little huts and hide away from these facts?"

"So you believed what I said about the crimson mage."

"Yes, and I'll tell you why. First, because for some time now, shadowy tidings have reached my ears. Of dark forces moving in secret through our realm. And second, because the other night our refuge was attacked. By what, I can't say. I suspect our young companion might know something, but I need to gain her trust as well. So I begged and pleaded and implored my fellow elders until they finally released me from my vows and sent me on my way. With you." He sputtered

216

a moment, then added at a shout, "At my age! Doesn't that count for something?"

Hyam spotted the pool up ahead, the green waters shimmering through the last line of trees. "I don't know what to tell you, except that I must rest."

The cavern's mouth was just high enough to permit Hyam to enter without bending down. Inside, the ceiling rose to an immense height. The cave contained three great chambers. The third held a pool, fed from a stream that fell through an opening in the roof. The light turned the pool a milky white. They took turns bathing in the cool waters, then gathered in the front chamber and ate the rest of their provisions, sharing what little they had with the dog. Hyam tethered the horse so it could crop the grass growing around the lake's perimeter. The second chamber was floored in a loamy soil that felt cool and welcoming when Hyam lay down.

He slept well and woke up refreshed. He rolled over and looked out the wide opening that separated them from the front chamber. The light spilling through the cavern's mouth was angled from the east. Which meant he had slept through the afternoon and evening and night.

Joelle lay on the cavern's far side, but he had the impression she was both awake and watching him. When he rose, she sat up and looked at him. The mage was nowhere to be seen.

He walked over and squatted down beside her. "How did you sleep?"

She responded by merely sitting there. Waiting. Her eyes

looked huge in the dim light. Bold and luminescent and inviting.

A fleck of earth had become attached to her cheek. He reached over to brush it off. She caught his hand and held it. The invitation was there in her gaze and her grip.

When he made no move, she spoke in a rasping whisper, almost a moan. "Why do you make me say it?"

Hyam had no idea how to respond. Or why this woman was so capable of robbing him of speech.

"Don't you want me?"

"So much," he managed.

"Then why?"

"Because." He knew it was not enough. But the words came with such a struggle he needed half a dozen breaths to go on. "You are sad."

She jerked slightly, the motion enough to rock their bodies together. Her heat was electric. "What does that have to do with this?"

He rose to his feet. He had no choice. If he remained, he would be lost. Lost.

He staggered into the first cavern and discovered the mage seated on a rock by the entry, feeding branches to a merry fire.

He heard Joelle rush up behind him. But he did not turn around. Not even when she cried, "Don't I even deserve an answer? Tell me why!"

But it was the mage who answered, "That's simple enough, lass. He doesn't want you."

Hyam sank onto a rock by the entrance and sat staring at the fire.

"But he said . . ."

"He doesn't want you," the wizard repeated. His voice held the gentle cadence of a tutor instructing a favorite child. "Not as all the others have wanted and lusted and pressed and threatened. It's not enough for this one to *take* you. He's not after a momentary possession."

"I-I don't understand."

"No, and you won't until and unless you take the time to discover who you are, and what *you* want."

"I know what I want!"

"No, lass, you don't. You think you must offer yourself in order to, what, pay for your keep? Ensure your safety? Make him promise to let you stay?" Trace used a stick to push hot coals atop the flat stones surrounding the fire pit. "He gives all this to you freely. Is that not so, lad."

Hyam took up a second branch, cracked it across his knee, and began scooping out more coals. Heating the stones.

"The two of you will make a powerful union." The mage pointed his burning stick at her. "But only if you first give yourself time to heal. And trust him to wait until you are ready. But in the meantime, you mustn't tempt him anymore. He is, after all, only human."

She stood there, her silent tension radiating over them. Then she turned and stomped back into the cavern's depths.

Trace murmured, "Give her time, lad. She'll come around."

By the time Joelle finally rejoined them, Trace had caught five large trout. He used nothing but his hands and his voice, and cackled each time he drew a wiggling fish from the waters. He cleaned the fish and set the fillets on the hot stones, then surrounded them with roots and leaves he had found in the neighboring woods. The mage let Hyam do nothing but feed the fire.

When Joelle returned, her hair still damp from the pool, the mage greeted her with a delighted, "Just in time! You look divine, my dear, and for that you earn the first portion."

Her voice carried a sullen edge. "I'm not hungry."

"Nonsense. We have a big day ahead of us, I warrant. A big day! And for that you must be fed as well as washed and rested!" He covered the strain with a merry chatter as he ladled the grilled trout onto broad leaves. They ate with their fingers.

When they were done, and they had washed their hands and faces in the pool and drunk their fill from the waterfall, Joelle had still not looked in Hyam's direction. He felt the loss as keenly as a wound to his flesh, but he was powerless to do anything more than say, "We should be going."

"Could we stay a bit longer, lad? There's something I'd like to address." But when they had resettled on their rock perches, all the wizard said was, "I don't know if I've ever enjoyed anything quite so much as catching those fish. It is perhaps the first time in a thousand years that a Long Hall mage has practiced real magic beyond the safety of his confines."

"You made a light for our departure," Hyam pointed out.

"That I did, and it was as much for the wizards who watched as for us. They needed to understand the time has come to set the old ways aside." He settled back upon the ledge. "All humankind faces a grave peril. One we do not yet understand. There are records, ten centuries old and forgotten by all save a handful of dusty old scholars like myself. They speak of the coming of the crimson foes. That was how we first observed the dreaded Milantian mages. As cloaked riders upon roan-colored steeds."

Hyam felt his gorge rise, threatening to bring back up his meal. "I may have a plan," he said, but the confidence he had felt within the Ashanta assembly was replaced by a cold and empty uncertainty.

"I'm counting on just that, lad." The mage stroked his beard for a time, then asked, "Perhaps I should offer you fealty?"

"What?"

"I'm freed from my vows as Master. I need to earn your trust. It is a crucial step, and not just to feed my voracious curiosity. I am certain you need my help. I feel it in my bones. But first you must come to rely on me, as we must on you." The mage's eyes glowed bright. "So I am offering you my fealty. If you will have me."

Joelle spoke from the fire's opposite side. "I want to do this too."

32

I, the wizard known as Trace, formerly Master of the Havering Long Hall, do hereby swear fealty to Hyam, Emissary to the Ashanta."

The wizard had worked out the wording, pausing now and then for Hyam to offer corrections, but he had none. They had all been moved by the simple preparations, though done in haste. The words' authority left Hyam awestruck.

The mage knelt in the loam in the cavern's mouth. His words were smooth, his delivery fervent. "I pledge my allegiance, my life, my talents, my powers, and my wisdom to his safety and the accomplishment of his aims. What he commands, I shall do. To the utmost of my ability, to the very limits of my strength. With my dying breath, if it is required of me. From this day forward."

The glade was filled with birdsong and the waterfall's melody and the sun's midmorning heat. Hyam gripped the sword given to him by the Ashanta. He tapped the kneeling wizard first on the right shoulder, then the left, then the right again. "Arise, Master Trace."

The old man did so, bowed deeply, and said, "My liege."

Hyam found his vision had grown unclear as he turned to where Joelle knelt. He stood and listened to her intone the same words. When she hesitated once, the old man kindly assisted her.

Hyam tapped her shoulders as well, settling the pale blade to either side of where her hair fell. "Arise, Lady Joelle."

She started to object to his granting her a title, but the mage shushed her gently. She stood and bowed and said, "My liege."

They stood there, the three of them joined by more than a few quietly uttered words. And then Joelle smiled at him. It was a small thing, scarcely a trace of change to her features. But the day and the events all shone brighter still. Hyam wished he knew some grand words to offer, but nothing came to mind except, "Thank you."

Their response was cut off by a gasp from Joelle, who took a step back and said, "Someone is coming."

Hyam whipped about, sword at the ready. "Where?"

She pointed at the empty sand beside the pool. "Someone is here."

"I don't want to go up again," Hyam decided. "We need to head into the city, and the magic leaves me drained."

"You want me to speak for her?" Joelle asked.

"It's a woman?"

She settled upon the rock at the cavern's mouth and studied the sunlit air above the pond. "She says she is your childhood friend."

"Bryna."

Joelle nodded. "The entire Assembly talks of little besides your growing power. She asks if you will speak about this."

In response, Hyam walked into the cavern and returned with his satchel. He released the catches and pulled out the orb. It glowed soft in the daylight, the light pulsing, the bond unmistakable.

The awestruck wizard reached out one tentative hand. "May I?"

Hyam saw no reason not to pass it over. The wizard cradled the globe, then raised his rapt gaze to Hyam and said, "Thank you, my liege."

Hyam nodded, glad he had done the right thing. He related how the witches had attacked, leaving nothing out, not even the shameful error of his being drawn blindly into their trap. The dog heard Hyam speak her name and came over to nestle by his side.

When he was done, Bryna said through Joelle, "All the Assembly thanks you for this gift of trust. They would like to ask another question."

"Anything."

"You say you can sense the lines of fire. Would you describe this?"

"I thought all Ashanta could do this thing."

"Some can. A very few. After much training." There was

a pause, then, "They seek confirmation of your ability but mean no offense."

"None taken." He described the sensation, the depth of the river, the drawing up of power, the orb's ability to transform and focus and emit.

When he was done, Trace breathed, "The legends come alive before my very eyes."

"What do you mean?"

"Occasionally one of our mages claims to detect the river of force beneath our Long Hall. But not many, and fewer still are believed. It is one reason why wizards do not travel. The Long Halls were planted upon these living currents and spaced about the realm so that their protection was everywhere in case the threat returned. The orbs serve as conduits to this power. Certain simple acts of magic are possible without the orb to those gifted in mage-work. To hold our talent means the acolyte can tap into the inherent force that comes with life. But what you are saying . . ." Trace continued to stare at the orb. "Never in my life have I met another wizard capable of identifying the location of these earth currents."

Hyam resisted the urge to correct the old man and declaim the title of wizard. Then Joelle intoned, "The Ashanta offer you trust for trust. Our treaty lands are placed where they are for the very same reason. Our Guardians hold the ability to draw upon this same force and cast certain spells. But it takes a number of them acting together, and never for very long. And very few of us can actually detect the rivers of power. One of our oldest legacies was this ability of the Ancients. That and the orbs are our only clear sign that they ever existed at all."

Hyam asked, "You're saying I'm somehow tied to them?"

"We do not know. Only that your heritage is hidden from us." Joelle went silent for a time, then said, "They are all gone but the woman."

"I say," the wizard groused, "that's rather abrupt."

"It's their way," Hyam replied. "They speak no words of greeting nor leave-taking."

Joelle went on, "Bryna wishes to tell you that the child you loved is fading. With the next full moon she begins her training, first as Sentry, then as Seer. At that time, the one you knew will vanish entirely."

He had no reason to feel such a keen loss at the news. "I understand."

"She desires to forge a new bond. One between the man known as the Ashanta emissary and the woman she will soon become, and through her with—" Joelle covered her face with her hands.

Hyam said as gently as he could, "Tell me the rest."

"With me." Joelle raised her tear-streaked face. "Bryna asks if she might become my friend."

33

They set off again, only this time with the ease of close companions. Hyam's distrust of everything to do with the Long Hall was not erased. He simply no longer counted Trace as belonging to that group. The mage was right. He had never been more in need of allies.

When the trail widened and the main road came into view, Hyam asked, "What can you tell me of the nobles allied to House Oberon?"

"They are disgraced, one and all. Those who were not defeated in the wars against the new king."

"What about your family?"

"Oh, they're well enough. The clan's fiefdom is too small and poor to be of notice. Besides that, my oldest brother is a ditherer. He has always found it easiest to postpone all decisions. For once, his inaction served the family well. The Oberons lost power before my brother answered the call to arms. He swore fealty to the new king and saw his holdings increase as a result. I keep in touch with my sister, who is wed to the former chief man-at-arms. A lovely lady with a fair hand at her letters."

"How many Oberon allies survived the battles?"

"I have no idea." Trace glanced down from the horse. He had been riding since they arrived at the forest's verge. "Do you have a plan?"

"Maybe," Hyam replied. "The tiniest fragments of one."

They rode and walked and joined the flow. Master Trace slipped from the horse and waited while Hyam helped Joelle into the saddle. The dog was sufficient to keep other travelers well away.

The mage asked, "This sensing of the flow, it comes easy to you?"

"More than easy," Hyam replied. "It feels natural."

"Wonder upon wonder." The mage tugged on his beard. "Those mages who can detect the power require much fasting and purges and trials. The practice is considered so difficult and so unprofitable, few accept the challenge. Why should anyone bother? It's not like we're going anywhere or establishing more Long Halls. After all, we possess all the surviving orbs." He shook his head. "What utter buffoons we've been."

"Which explains why your Long Hall was built on the wrong spot," Hyam said.

"What?"

"There is a tiny rivulet of power beneath the settlement. A narrow creek." Hyam could not suppress his grin. Nor did he try very hard. "And on the meadow's other side, over where the forest begins, there is one of the strongest currents

I have ever felt. That's what I drew on when I captured your orb. And that is why I overpowered your mages."

To his surprise, the old man cackled. "I hope you don't feel any need to share this news with my fellow wizards."

"Not particularly."

"Oh, good. Let me."

"You have a particularly nasty laugh, old man."

The wizard cackled his reply.

The innkeeper was so relieved to see Hyam alive and safe that she actually wept a few tears. "Them nobles kept sniffing about, then they drifted off quiet-like. I was ever so afraid they'd caught up with your honor."

"I'm here," Hyam replied. "And I need your help."

"Anything, your lordship. Long as it's legal." She revealed a surprisingly girlish smile. "And maybe even if it's not."

He waved Joelle and Trace over and introduced them as his trusted associates. "Whatever their request, whatever they need, I ask that you treat it as coming from me."

"That's certainly within my doing, good sir." She glanced about. "But if you'll excuse me for saying, these two won't be enough to keep you safe."

"I'm coming to that. But first I want to take over one entire wing of your good establishment."

"That's doable as well." She gave a delicate hesitation. "Though the private wing holds five rooms on two floors."

"I'll take them. Strip two of beds and replace them with tables from your front room and some chairs. Next, and more importantly, do you have any connection with officers who once served in the company of disgraced houses?"

"You mean . . ."

"I'm after professional soldiers who have lost their postings and are looking for service. And I can pay."

"You'll trust men whose loyalty you can buy?" the mage asked.

"No," Hyam replied. "I'll trust soldiers who may never have another chance."

There was no attempting to bar the banker's door in Hyam's face. This time, when he presented himself at the main portal, the financier himself scurried forward to usher him and his associates inside. He was mighty reluctant to discuss the matters at hand in the company of others. But this diminished when Hyam introduced the old man as his personal aide and secretary. When the banker's gaze switched to Joelle, Hyam explained, "The Lady Joelle has been assigned as my attaché."

The banker took in the purple cast to her eyes, and his aplomb vanished. "But . . . the Ashanta never travel."

"That is all I will say on the matter," Hyam replied. "Except that whatever these two ask of you, please treat it as coming from me personally."

He looked from one to the other. "I shall need that in writing."

"Give me parchment and quill and you'll have it."

When Hyam completed his task, the banker inspected

the document, stowed it away, and declared, "I've received the most remarkable set of instructions. As has every other Ashanta financier in the realm, or so I'm led to believe." He lifted a paper from his desk, adjusted his reading spectacles, and read, "'Any and all requests for funds by the emissary Hyam shall be granted without delay or question. Any request for assistance will be treated in the same manner.'"

Hyam had no idea what was expected, so he simply said, "Excellent."

The banker dropped the paper. "I suppose you realize this will make you the wealthiest individual in the realm. If that's what you want."

It wasn't, but Hyam knew the man counted money as a measure of a man's worth. "How much gold do you hold here?"

"Quite a lot, actually." The words were accompanied by a hint of mocking humor. Clearly the financier felt a faint disdain for this rough-hewn lad with his two associates in peasant garb. None of whom had any idea of money. "How much do you need?"

"I'll take two purses now. And either I or one of my associates will be by shortly for more. Now please shut the door." When the banker had done so, Hyam said, "Tell me everything you can about this new king."

Late spring rains set in that night and washed over them for the next three days. Hyam welcomed the rain like a farmer, knowing the season's uncommon heat had parched the earth, even in a land as well-watered as this. He stood for hours in the inn's gateway, sheltered beneath the stone arch. These were the first easy moments he had known since traveling to the Long Hall. It left him feeling almost guilty.

The innkeeper proved a strong and capable ally. The message he gave her was sent out quietly through the city, passed from one trusted friend to another. While they waited, Hyam ordered a tailor to fit them all out in a noble's idea of traveling garb. All their outfits were to be trimmed in violet and bear the Ashanta seal sewn onto the breast.

Hyam asked Trace to continue instructing Joelle in the mage's arts. "Our survival might depend upon it," he declared. There was a moment's silence, then to his relief both agreed.

They took their meals in the room they had turned into Hyam's office. A fire burned in the grate, and their isolation was a comfort. Over dinner that night, Trace said, "It wouldn't hurt for you to train some yourself, lad."

He had a hundred reasons for declining, most especially how he reveled in these few quiet hours. And said so.

But Trace was insistent. "There are any number of reasons why you should heed my advice. Spells are shaped around a certain form, and the first aim of each is to keep the mage alive. The orb carries sufficient force to burn a wizard to a crisp. Your actions are astonishing because you do what has not been done before."

"And survived," Hyam pointed out.

"But for how long? And to what point? Would it not be better to understand the structure behind shaping spells?"

Hyam disliked this invasion into his idle moment, but he said, "All right."

The next morning, Trace started them on simple exercises used to train young wizards. For Hyam it was as senseless a task as watching the rain, but he did not mind, especially after Joelle lit up with unbridled delight at her every success. All that day she continually bathed them with her joy.

Twice the orb's power faded to a dull hue, so Hyam walked away from the inn, along the riverbank to where he detected an underground current. Any onlookers would have merely seen a traveler out walking his wolfhound and tossing stones into the River Havering's rain-dappled waters. The satchel Hyam carried was made bulky by the blanket he'd wrapped about the orb so that none of its gleam might be detected.

On the third night he dreamed of his mother. Not as she was in those final hard months, when all her attention was focused upon the unseen door. He dreamed of how she had been during his childhood. Calm and intent upon each chore in turn. A mage in her own way at the loom. Turning threads she dyed herself into fields of magical beasts that almost danced off the cloth, and often did in his mind. She was never one to scold, not even when he deserved it, which was often, for as a boy he had loved nothing more than testing his own limits.

The dream revealed her working upon the last of her tapestries. Only in this night, the horse cantered with rippling muscles across a field turned violet by the orb's light. Hyam wore what he now recognized as the emissary's garb. The orb rested atop a tall wooden lance, one fashioned so that it gripped the globe in a tight wooden fist.

His mother stopped in her work and turned to him, and said his name. *Hyam*. And in that single utterance he was returned to the joy he had known every time he had stepped through their cottage door. Knowing that here was a place where he would always belong.

Though he woke to sunlight and birdsong beyond his bedroom's open window, Hyam rose with a deep bitterness in his heart. It was not enough that he searched for an enemy whose name he did not know. He had been stripped of home and heritage. The fact that he belonged nowhere weighed on him like an open wound.

Their sleeping chambers were on the wing's upper floor and thus somewhat protected. The two larger rooms downstairs had been turned into offices. As Hyam descended the stairs, he glanced down the hall that connected them to the inn's main chamber and saw it was filled with men and weapons and chatter.

Trace greeted him with, "Your news has reached interested ears. The question remains—are these the ones we need?"

"I want you to interview them first. Only send those to me who you feel are trustworthy."

The old man nodded. "I can do that."

"Where is Joelle?"

"Still sleeping, I expect. We practiced with your orb into the wee hours."

"Why are you awake, then?"

"Elders require less sleep. Or perhaps it is that sleep comes more reluctantly." He smiled through his beard. "She is a thrilling lass to instruct. She laps it up like a kitten would fresh cream."

"It is good of you to teach her."

Trace shrugged. "It is a squire's duty to serve."

"Despite the Long Hall code?"

"My one remaining oath is that which I swore to you." His eyes showed a guileless humor. "Of course, the fact that she is lovely as the dawn doesn't hurt."

"Go and wake her. Ask if she will assist in these interviews. I want all who join with us to recognize her authority."

By noontime fourteen former officers had been chosen and assembled in his study. Another forty male foot soldiers patrolled around the inn or erected tents in the forecourt.

Joining the male officers in his study were six women, hard-faced and formed into a tight unit by the window. Their leader was a former captain named Meda, a handsome woman in her late twenties or early thirties with a suspicious, knowing gaze. The senior officer among the men was a former colonel named Adler. He lounged with counterfeit ease by the opposite wall. He was older than most, with a savage cast to his features and a scar that clipped off the top of his left ear and ran above his eye and disappeared into his hairline.

Hyam's first act was to loose the knot on a heavy leather purse and upend the contents on his table. The gold florins glinted in the light and in the assembled warriors' gazes. Their clothes were tattered, their features gnawed by hardship and hunger.

He then unfurled the royal charter and anchored it with two

candlesticks. "This decree is a thousand years old. It assigns me, the appointed emissary of the Ashanta, the rights and powers of a knight of the realm. The seal at its base is that of the Oberons, and the original charter was signed by the first king to bear that name. Some say that with the ending of the Oberons' reign, the decree no longer holds power. Any who agree with this should now leave."

No one moved.

"Let us be perfectly clear. The new king is not my enemy. I will not have these ranks become a haven for rehashing old quarrels or fighting old battles. Our enemy is real, he is out there, and I need your help in taking him down."

The leader of the women demanded, "Who is he?"

"I have no idea. Nor do I know where he is."

The one known as Adler said, "If it wasn't for the pile of gold there, I'd say you were the closest I've come to a crazy person."

"The enemy is real," Hyam repeated. "Answer me one question. Who among you participated in the battle that brought down the Oberons?"

"That's easy enough," Meda replied. "None of us."

"Not a single solitary soldier survived that encounter," Adler agreed. "Not a camp follower, not a squire, not a blacksmith, not a healer. Every member of the army and its supply train were wiped out."

"How long did the battle last?"

"No one knows," Meda replied. "I led my liege's forces on a hard march and still arrived at the battlefield after it was over and the Oberon king had surrendered."

"The king perished with his troops," Adler pointed out.

"Not him. The nephew, Bayard. The one who sued for peace." To Hyam, Meda went on, "I'll never forget that day, climbing the ridge and seeing there before me a sea of black ash and wasted bodies."

"That's where I saw you before," Adler said. "You were with House Rideau."

"I was. And you?"

"Count Grafton."

"A good man, by all accounts. How is he faring?"

"Not well. The taxes, the oppression." Adler shrugged. "We are here. That says it all."

Hyam asked, "What if I were to tell you that it was not the army of Ravi your king that defeated the Oberon forces?"

The room had been quiet before. Now it was clenched in the alert stillness of warriors who had known the closeness of death.

He went on, "What if I said that the forbidden forces of magic were once again released into this realm?"

"There have been rumors," Adler allowed.

"The rumors," Hyam said, "are true."

"If that's so, what do you want us for?" Meda gestured toward her group. "I'll not have my troops become your sacrificial lamb."

"Let him speak first," Adler suggested. "We can walk away after."

Hyam described his encounter with the prince's forces on the Ashanta field, the crimson rider, the Ashanta's response.

There was a lingering silence, then Meda said, "My question still stands."

"I do not expect you to go up against the crimson one," Hyam replied. "That's my job."

"Who are you?"

"The Ashanta's appointed emissary," Adler replied. "He's already told you that."

"So their power of battle is assigned to him?"

"If it wasn't, he'd be a fool to go after a crimson mage." Adler revealed a warrior's grin, steel and teeth and no humor at all. "And I'm beginning to think the lad here is no fool."

"I need two things from you," Hyam went on. "First, I need scouts to locate this mage. And second, I want to draw together a force of trained soldiers to take on whoever accompanies him."

34

Hyam spent the afternoon and evening paying his new soldiers and forming them into units. In truth, what he really wanted was a chance to know them a little. He had never been around soldiers before and never been in a position to hire a farmhand, much less a trained warrior. So he took a page from Norvin's book.

The mayor had always insisted upon paying the harvest workers half in advance. Too often these landless workers carried hostility from landowners who had cheated them in the past. Norvin wanted them to know he could be trusted. The mayor also sought to identify those he could trust in return. So Norvin paid half, then he gave them the night off. Those who were too drunk to rise the next dawn were assigned the worst duties, out where there was nothing for them to steal, and they were never offered work again.

The standard pay for a foot soldier was a gold florin per year. Those who supplied their own mounts received two.

Officers, four. Senior officers, eight. Booty was at the discretion of the master, though the tradition during the long Oberon reign was for the house to receive half and the rest to be distributed in accordance with pay. Hyam paid each man half a year's salary in advance, accepted their oaths of allegiance, told them to report in the morning, then sat and observed and learned.

The troops gathered around tables that filled the forecourt, while the innkeeper opened barrels and hired a roving band of minstrels. An entire hog was spitted and roasted. The innkeeper was kept both busy and happy, for her establishment was filled with paying customers and officers to keep them in line.

As darkness cast its cloak over the clear night, the men spoke in easy longing for the Oberons. The last king was a massively fat wastrel and roundly despised. But these were soldiers, and most had endured any number of bad officers. Their respect for the lineage and their history of the realm was instructive. The new Oberon, Bayard, was by all accounts a good man. Though he had been reduced to ruling a fiefdom at the border of the realm.

The women drank little and spoke less. Meda and her sergeant sat at Hyam's table and studied him hard. The one time she spoke was when Joelle slipped onto the bench beside her and asked, "Would you teach me to fight?"

Meda studied her as she would a rank recruit. "What do you know?"

"Almost nothing."

Meda sipped from a tankard that Hyam knew held only water. And waited in silence.

Finally Joelle said, "I have studied books. I have taught myself the knives."

"Throwing or combat?"

"Both. But it's from books. I know nothing of real combat."

"I'll be the judge of that." Her gaze was tight, measuring. "On the training ground, I am the only authority. The man seated across from you there holds no sway."

"Agreed."

She nodded slowly. "Then you're welcome."

Meda turned away, pretending to ignore the taut excitement that pulled at Joelle's features. All save Adler and his aide had left to dance with the barmaids and carouse around the central fire pit. Meda set her elbows on the table and asked Hyam, "Why am I here?"

Their table held space for twenty. Now there were just seven—Adler and his aide, Meda and her subaltern, Trace, Joelle, and himself. When one of the other sergeants brought over a fresh mug for Adler, the senior officer waved him away. And waited with the women.

"I don't understand," Hyam replied.

"Women are forbidden to bear arms," she said.

"I have no idea what you're talking about."

"How could a royal emissary not know about the king's edicts?"

"I am not a royal anything," Hyam said. "Until a few weeks ago, I had never been outside my home region."

"Which is where, exactly?"

"Three Valleys. Beyond the Galwyn Hills. East and south of

the great forest." He pointed in the direction of the Havering walls. "I have never been inside a city, including that one. I heard there was a new king. But it mattered little. We in the Three Valleys pay our taxes. Otherwise we are left alone. The world passes us by. For most villagers, that is how they want it."

She examined him with the cold gaze of a seasoned warrior. "My question still stands."

"How I came to be here is a story for another time. For now, all I can tell you is this. I don't care what the king makes for edicts. Everything about my duty is probably illegal in his eyes. If the crimson rider is allied to him, as I suspect he is, then the king is my enemy."

Hyam had not expected to say aloud what he had been thinking. But the truth sounded good to his own ears and seemed to settle well upon the table.

"But you told us that you were not attacking the monarchy," Adler said.

"That is correct. I am going after the crimson rider. Once he is vanquished, I want to go home." But even before the words emerged, they sounded hollow. Vacant. "Now I have a question for you. Why did they ban women from the ranks?"

"It is a question," Adler replied, "that has been argued over for three and a half years."

"It's simple enough," Meda countered. "He wanted to strip away his enemies' best warriors."

"Well, now," Adler said, and displayed a smile that did not touch his eyes.

Meda went on, "The Ravis have taxed to death the houses once loyal to the Oberons. The king has pared away their warriors. He reduces female combatants to the ranks of weavers and healers and courtesans." Her boiling ire gave her the confidence to turn and demand of the silent figures across from her, "And now is the time to know exactly who these three are, and what role they play in it all."

Adler cautioned, "Steady, lass."

"It's a fair question," Meda insisted, "and the night is made for answers."

"She's right," Hyam said. "Can I count on your silence?"

"You give us the chance to bear arms with honor once again, I'll offer you a blood oath," Adler replied.

Hyam gestured down the table. "The gentleman is Master Trace, the former head of the Havering Long Hall."

A soft gasp was shared around the table. "A mage? For truth?"

"You heard what the emissary said," Trace replied. "Wizardry has been unleashed into the world. It feeds upon death and destruction. We who have preserved the hidden mysteries for a thousand years are now forced to respond."

Hyam felt a subtle shift in the air, a hidden whisper that he could not detect. Yet Trace's words left him certain he was missing something vital.

He pondered on this until Meda pointed to Joelle. "And this one?"

Hyam caught the desperate plea in her grey and violet eyes and said simply, "The Lady Joelle comes from the Long Hall as well."

"Two mages," Adler murmured.

"Three," Trace countered, gesturing at Hyam. "For there sits the strongest of us all."

Meda squinted at him, a warrior taking aim. "You said you were a simple farmer."

"I am. I was. Now . . ." He shrugged, then found himself pushed to his feet by the unheard warning in Trace's words. "I don't know what I am."

He bid the group a good night and started away, only to be snagged by Trace, who called after him, "You know exactly who you are, lad. And it's time you accepted it. For all our sakes."

Hyam carried the mage's words to bed that night. He tossed and turned for hours, while below his open window patrolled his only sober troops. He had no idea why Trace's comments gripped him so. He knew wizardry had been released. There was neither surprise nor new alarm to the warning. But the talons of worry and dread did not release him. He slept in the end, dreaming of a crimson orb and wasted valleys filled with ashes and charred bones.

He felt sore and mishandled the next morning, which meant he fit in well with the courtyard's atmosphere. The kitchen fire was still cold, and the inn's maids were nowhere to be found. He breakfasted on bread and cheese and pickles, and fed Dama with strips of meat cut from a smoked ham. He washed like a farmhand, dousing himself in the stable trough and rubbing himself dry with a strip of burlap. Which was where Adler found him, drinking a ladle of well water and watching the light rise in the east.

"The question," Hyam said, hanging the ladle beside the bucket, "is where to look."

Adler took his time around the dog, giving her a chance to sniff his hand and decide whether she wished to be stroked. He then drank his fill and declared, "Maps."

"Yes?"

"Lay out what evidence you have in a pattern you can see," Adler said. "Maps are the key to any good campaign."

"I don't have evidence," Hyam said, nodding a greeting to Meda and her silent aide.

"You mentioned a chest of booty. You're certain it came from battle?"

"The gold was bloodstained, and some rings still held parts of their former owners."

Adler asked Meda, "You heard of such raids?"

"Nothing."

Adler mused aloud, "A single officer on patrol carries a chest of gold. Behind him rides an army led by the king's brother. Which means two things. First, the prince will be carrying the richest treasures of all, and second, other knights in the force will have gained their own booty."

"Most knights will hold the booty of their soldiers, which guarantees they watch for his safety," Meda explained.

"This wasn't a single raid on one lone Ashanta settlement," Adler went on. "And wherever they were attacking had to be far enough removed for word not to carry."

Once again Hyam felt the rise of dread. The certainty that

he was missing a vital clue turned his belly into a lava-filled vessel. "I don't . . ."

"The army came from these raids, following new orders," Adler explained. "They were commanded to attack an Ashanta settlement. Which means wherever they were before then had no Ashanta. Otherwise why go to Three Valleys?"

"We're a wealthy region," Hyam pointed out. "Good land, prosperous holdings."

"Farming hamlets don't interest the likes of these, not when they're carrying gold." Adler looked from one to the other. "A region rich and yet cut off from the realm. Whose closest Ashanta town is Three Valleys. They ride in through the great forest . . ."

"The badlands," Meda said, nodding slowly.

"That's my thinking as well. Where do the badlands lie closest to the Three Valleys?" Adler squinted into the distance. "Twelve days' hard ride?"

"More like twenty. They run north to south far to the east. Where the Iron Cliffs meet the sea."

"I never served in those parts."

"I did. I was just a lass when I entered the badlands." Her countenance melted with grim recollections. "I wasn't when I left."

"Hard duty, was it."

"They earn their name, the badlands do."

"Did you ever visit the fiefdom now assigned to the Oberons?"

"Falmouth Port. I did." Her gaze went distant. "Clannish, they were, but held in check by loyalty to their earl. A dire region of black rock and terrible seas and worse winters."

"Those loyal to the Oberons who survived often wondered why Bayard accepted Falmouth without more of a struggle."

"He was not sent," Meda replied. "He asked for Falmouth as his holding."

"I had heard that," Adler said, nodding slowly. "And discounted it as myth."

"He asked, he was granted, he went," Meda confirmed. "My liege was there when it happened. Why, no one knows but Bayard. And he's not saying. Since his arrival in Falmouth, no one has heard a word from him."

"I have no idea what you two are discussing," Hyam said.

"Maps," Adler declared. "Maps are the key."

35

As they readied to depart for Havering, a clutch of foot soldiers and officers came forward together. Hyam liked how they were mostly clear-eyed and erect, though a few winced at the sound of a blacksmith shoeing a horse in the stables. There were only a few inert forms sprawled by the tents set up along the far wall. Hyam saw how Adler marked them with a frown.

The soldiers' spokesman asked permission to pay the Ashanta banker a visit. Adler explained, "Most of these men were drawn here by desperation and the hopes of winning the tournament purse. Some of their families face grave hardship."

Hyam asked the women, "Is that why you came as well?"

"We are forbidden to fight in the tournaments," Meda replied bitterly. "But give a man a few ales, and he likes the idea of besting some woman foolish enough to challenge him to a duel with steel."

Hyam saw Joelle appear on the top step and waved her

over. "I want you to go with these men to the banker Vanier. Fetch another sack of gold and pay everyone the second portion owed for this year."

Adler showed astonishment. "That's too much!"

"I've known hardship, and I've lived with hunger," Hyam replied. "None of my troops should ever worry about either."

"I will go," Joelle agreed.

"Ask the banker if he knows of any Ashanta financier in the badlands, especially around . . ." He asked Adler, "What was the name of that Oberon city?"

"Falmouth Port."

"Ask if any have gone missing or can't be accounted for. Tell him it's urgent."

"The Ashanta financiers spend their words as carefully as they do their gold," Meda warned.

"He will answer me," Joelle assured the officer.

Meda responded with a tight grin. "Something tells me you're going to make a fine soldier."

Hyam entered Havering in the company of Adler, Meda, their two aides, and four foot soldiers who had served a disgraced count. Clearly they still held their former leader in affection and despised the rulers of this prospering town. Their taut gazes scanned the walls and barbican and portcullis for threats, and were never still. The two women walked with hands resting upon the hilts of their long knives. They shared the troopers' sour expression. Hyam had never felt safer.

It was not the first time he had been proven wrong.

Adler saluted the portcullis guards, then led them across the bridge and beneath the raised gate. They entered the tumult of a thriving market town. Tournament banners still hung from the main walls, while the winners' pennants flew atop the main keep. Between the palace's inner walls and the city's outer barricades stretched a warren of cobblestone streets. The lanes were packed with people and beasts and hawkers and stalls. The noise and the smells assaulted Hyam from every side. He followed Adler down one crowded lane after another and wondered if he would ever become comfortable with a city's chaotic din.

The mapmaker was hardly into his thirties and already bald. His hands were yellowish and his fingers as scrawny as a chicken's claws. He punctuated each response with a nervous bow. Adler demanded his most complete maps of the realm, but when they were unrolled, the officer frowned and declared, "These won't do. They won't do at all!"

"They are our finest, good sir. I drew them myself. The hide is deerskin vellum stretched and—"

"Swallow your lecture on parchment and ink," Adler said, stabbing the border regions with an outraged finger. "The badlands are empty!"

The man's Adam's apple bobbed as nervously as his spine. "Of course, good sir."

"He hasn't even drawn in Falmouth Port!" Meda exclaimed.

"Of course not, madam."

"Stand straight, man," Adler commanded. "What's the meaning of this? You can't just erase five dozen fiefs with the swipe of your pen and expect me to call you a mapmaker."

The narrow man bridled. "The edict expressly forbids any mention of badlands."

"What edict is that?"

Hyam stepped forward. "Never mind."

"What nonsense is this? The man has left out everything—" Adler jerked when Meda poked him in the ribs. Then the light dawned. "Oh. Yes."

Hyam asked the mapmaker, "Can we see your earlier maps?"

The man blanched whiter than he already was. "I was ordered to burn them."

"But you didn't destroy your own work, did you. You hid them and hoped someone would come offering gold." Hyam opened his purse. "That day has arrived."

The sight of florins brought a greedy glint to the mapmaker's gaze. "Such maps would carry a heavy price, good sir."

"No doubt," Hyam said, satisfied. "Show us what you have."

They were led through a peaked oak door and up narrow stairs to where a score of men and women of all ages labored at long desks. The rear windows and two skylights were open, admitting a stronger hint of the odor Hyam had detected downstairs. He glanced out the back and found another team curing hides and grinding ink.

The mapmaker led them into a side office, where an old man hastily scooped a pile of silver coins into a sack and demanded, "What's the meaning of this?"

"Go watch the store, Uncle."

"You dare bring customers into my office and then order me

away?" The old man showed remarkable agility as he sprang up and rushed around his desk, waving his arms. "Your place is downstairs, not here! Not here!"

"They bring gold, Uncle."

"Eh?"

The younger mapmaker shut the door and whispered, "They seek Oberon maps."

The uncle blanched, then hissed, "I ordered you to burn them as the king commanded!"

"Then you would not have my gold," Hyam said, extracting a pair of florins.

"Go watch the store," the young man said, opening the door and shoving his uncle out.

"Make sure the coins are real!"

The young man shut the door again, sighed, and said, "Wait here." He unlocked a rear cupboard, inspected the hoard, and asked, "How many do you need?"

"Several."

"I have that many." He extracted an armful. "Come to think of it, perhaps you should take them all."

They unfurled them one by one, making a substantial pile on the desk. They were studying them intently when the uncle burst back in, recoiled at the maps arrayed across his desk, and hissed, "The sheriff's men are here!"

"What do they want?"

"The squire of the Three Valleys." The uncle pointed a trembling finger at Hyam. "He described you down to a bow you do not carry."

"Old trouble?" Adler asked.

"The squire's son was bested in the tournament," Hyam replied. "He tried to take it out on me. He failed."

"No bloodshed," the younger mapmaker said. "Vellum never gives up fresh blood."

Meda checked out the rear window, then drew back and hissed, "The place is ringed by crossbows."

"This looks far more serious than a matter of wounded pride," Adler said.

Hyam tried to find the orb and forge a mental connection, but the distance was too great. He regretted coming into town. What was more, he regretted not thinking before now to try to extend his connection to the globe.

A voice from beyond the house called, "Squire Hayseed! Must I come and drag you out?"

Hyam handed the senior officer his purse. "Adler, stay and acquire the maps. Meda, come with me."

Adler clearly did not like this. "Sire—"

"If they're after trouble, your men will not help. We're outnumbered and trapped. Get the maps back to the inn. If I am arrested, tell Trace."

He halted further argument by slipping by the garrulous uncle and descending the stairs. As expected, the first face he spotted when entering the main chamber was the knight who had challenged him in the inn's forecourt. The sheriff's son declared, "When they told me you had shown up again at the inn, I said to my aide, no man could be that stupid. Wasn't that what I said?"

"That is what you said, my lord." The man was massive and scarred and responded with a bored voice. Hyam recognized him as one of the group that had shared the squire's table.

A dozen men armed with crossbows took aim through the house's windows. Four more men-at-arms crowded around the map tables, their swords at the ready.

"My aide is a hothead," the sheriff's son went on. "He wanted to run out and arrest you. But I said no, did I not."

"You did, my lord," the warrior agreed, his voice as flat as his gaze.

"We must wait," the young knight said. The map room did not grant him much space to swagger, but he did his best. "Wait and let the fool enter our lair. Which you have. Didn't he walk straight into our clutches."

"He did indeed, my lord."

Meda demanded, "What right do you have to waylay my liege as he goes about his lawful affairs?"

"But they're not lawful at all, are they." The sheriff's son sneered at the guards' captain. "Not when he's guarded by women the king himself has ordered be made toothless. Is that not so."

"Toothless it is, my lord. Every one."

"So our Squire Hayseed must now be brought up before my father the sheriff."

"And the lass, my lord?"

He stripped Meda with a careless gaze. "She's hardly worth the trouble. You're free to go, woman. No doubt the inn's scullery wench could use your help." He smiled at Hyam's defenselessness. "I failed to gain your name the last time we met."

"Hyam."

"An odd name for a squire. But never mind." He gestured to the hulking brute. "Bind him. Bring him."

36

They dragged Hyam through Havering and into the central keep. Beyond the palace stables, a narrow portal opened into the keep's wall, and circular stairs emitted a stench that was laced with pain and terror. Hyam had tried repeatedly to connect with the orb on his way along the city's lanes. As they approached the dungeon portal, he desperately strived to bridge the distance and failed yet again.

The city dungeons were a vast underground arena whose peaked ceiling was supported by massive stone pillars. The aide of the sheriff's son was careless and unemotional in his violence, cuffing Hyam when ordered with an almost bored casualness. The sheriff's son, however, took pleasure in leading Hyam through the central chambers, introducing him to the various implements of torture and assuring Hyam that he would soon become familiar with them all.

The sheriff's son stood pretending to debate over which

tool to apply first, when footsteps echoed upon the stone stairs and a voice called, "Where is the prisoner?"

The sheriff's son blanched. "Here, my lord."

"Did I not say I wished to meet him?" A portly man accompanied by two guards with torches appeared at the stairwell. "Is this the one?"

"He is, my lord."

"Are you certain?" The older man wore his remaining hair like a froth encircling his bald pate. His breastplate had been scrubbed and polished until it shone like silver. It was the only military aspect about him. He was peevish and flaccid and chinless. "He certainly has the build. And the hair. You there, what is your name?"

"Hyam, my lord."

The sheriff's son offered, "I could apply the screws and make sure he speaks the truth."

"Certainly not. I told you, our instructions from the palace were most precise. This man was to be delivered unharmed. What's more, a second message has just arrived. Every last iota of his gear must be delivered untouched and unsearched."

The young man turned sour. "By what right does some palace lackey order us about like serfs?"

The newcomer eyed the sheriff's son with distaste. "If you knew who made the request, you would not open your vile little mouth. Chain him, post a guard, and see he remains unharmed. Where was he staying?"

He went as sullen as a disciplined child. "Three Princes Inn, my lord."

"Send someone we can trust for his belongings. Then join

me in the hall. I must alert the palace. We have matters to discuss."

Hyam was heaved into a cell that contained one other unfortunate guest. The sheriff's son kicked Hyam hard in the ribs, then again. He watched as the brute locked a chain to his ankle and kicked Hyam a third time. He leaned tight into Hyam's moaning face and promised, "We shall meet again."

Hyam thought he was too sore and too worried to sleep. He was also hungry and he was afraid. His cell mate was a man he could scarcely see in the gloom, with matted hair and beard, and dressed in rags. The man's age was impossible to guess. Hyam heard one of the passing guards call the man Warbler. The prisoner crooned a single wavering note. He did not even seem to draw breath. The sound worked on Hyam's brain like a spike.

Even so, he slept.

Instantly the dream gripped him in claws as desperate as the dungeon's air. He was again trapped within the ash-covered valley. The glowing red orb hovered at the valley's other side, held in place by a rider whose crimson robes ran and flowed like spilled blood.

Slowly the rider lifted his free hand and drew back his hood.

There was no face to the figure that was revealed. Only a skull that seemed woven from the same metallic insects that formed a vile cloud about him. The mage grinned at Hyam and said, "Hello, cousin."

Hyam woke up gasping. One of the squire's kicks had cracked a rib, for the breath that woke him also stabbed his side. He levered himself off the damp stone floor in gradual stages. Across from him, the prisoner continued his crooning. Hyam stared out the crossed metal bars that stood between him and the various implements that filled the central chambers, positioned so the prisoners never lost sight of the fate that would soon consume them. Only he did not see them now. His vision remained trapped by the skull and the glowing red orb, and the fact that he had missed something vital.

"I've been a fool," he said to no one in particular.

The guard outside his portal chuckled. "Little late to be noticing that."

Hyam shook his head in the darkness. The dream had carried a message, one he should have realized long before now. He had been blind to a crucial element. If he had seen it earlier, he might well have managed to avoid his fate.

As if the guard could read his thoughts, he said, "Nothing like a night in the dungeon to force a man to drink the potion of regret."

Gingerly Hyam crawled toward the portal, until his chain clinked tight. "What time is it?"

"Doesn't really matter, does it. Few more hours, I go off duty. Not long after that, you'll be missing one of your last dawns."

"I don't even know why I'm here."

"Nor do I. But I know enough about the message to be

glad I'm not the one bound in that cell." The guard shifted around to where he could look through the bars. "What's your name?"

"Hyam."

"Rumor has it you're practicing the dark arts."

"That is absolutely not true."

"Maybe it is, maybe it isn't. But there's one coming from the king's palace who will be asking you questions. And whatever you say in reply, two things are for certain. You won't like the questions, and you won't survive the conversation."

"Who is coming?"

"All I know are rumors. Most of which can't be true."

"Will you tell me?"

Curiosity showed in the guard's gaze. "You'll tell me what you've done?"

"My only crime was to best the sheriff's son."

"I heard about that. You truly shot the arrow across the river and hit the earl's coin?"

"I did."

"Wish I'd seen that. Though the squire is not a man to cross."

"So I've learned."

"Yeah, pity, that." He scratched his back by rubbing up and down the foul stones.

Hyam repeated softly, "Who is coming?"

"The king's own adviser is who I've heard."

"Does this adviser have a name?"

The guard turned and showed him a stony expression. "No."

"All right."

"If you knew anything, you'd know not to ask such a thing. Not even here."

Hyam clenched his eyes and reached out, hunting anxiously. But the walls and the stench and the dark all mocked him. And behind his closed eyelids loomed the dream's image of a valley filled with charred remnants and a faceless rider. Coming. Coming.

He sighed his defeat and opened his eyes. "How long do I have?"

"The capital is six days' hard ride. Though my mates are taking bets on whether the sheriff's son can be forced to wait that long before starting on questions of his own." His battle-hardened features carried a hint of sympathy. "I'd find what peace I could if I were you. While you still have time."

37

Hyam must have drifted off again, for when he opened his eyes, there was a different guard on duty outside his barred door. He started to speak, but his mouth was gummed and his jaw ached from the brute's casual cuffs. His chest had tightened to where each breath was a grunt against the pain.

Hyam noticed none of this.

In the far distance he sensed a faint glimmer of power. It was so unexpected and so out of place he had difficulty believing it was real. He wondered if he was still dreaming. But the force gained strength until he was almost ready, when he heard a familiar voice say, "I hope you have the lout chained up."

"We do, my lord." The squire's voice boomed cheerfully from the curved stairwell. "We do indeed."

"Is he in pain?" Trace's voice sounded older than Hyam recalled, as though the mage had aged decades since Hyam's capture. Which made two of them. "Does he bleed? Does he moan with agony?"

"Soon, my lord. Very soon." The sheriff's son did not quite hide his laughter. "Watch your step here."

"Eh, what difference does it make, a turned ankle or a bruised shin, when the rogue has already injured what is most precious to me?"

"I'm sure he'll appreciate hearing this from your own lips." A lantern appeared in the distance, and the guard beyond his door snapped to attention. "If he doesn't, I certainly will."

Trace followed the sheriff's son and the massive retainer into the dungeon. Beside him walked a woman in a long, flowing robe. Trace demanded, "Where is he? Where is the hoodlum who stole my daughter's honor?"

The squire grinned as he approached Hyam's cell and pointed through the iron bars. "In there."

"Where? Where? My eyes aren't nearly as they once were. Give me light."

"There is the matter of your promised payment, my lord."

"Eh, oh. Yes. Of course. Of course." The old man fumbled at his purse. "I for one live up to my oaths. Unlike the ruffian you have chained in there. Death is too good for that one, do you hear me?"

"I do indeed, my lord." He pocketed the gold, then ordered the guard, "Draw the lantern closer."

The old mage was dressed in fine robes that clearly were intended for a far larger man. The collar would have slipped off Trace's scrawny shoulders had it not been for the gold chain of office that clasped the opening's two sides. Trace's beard trembled with what appeared to be genuine outrage as he pushed the woman ahead of him. "Look! Look at the ruin you have caused. My daughter! My house's good name! I trusted you!"

Joelle was draped in a penitent's cloak of grey burlap, but beneath she wore a frock as refined as the mage's clothes. Her belly was huge, a great swelling that poked out the front of her dress and shoved aside the cloak's borders. She cradled her middle with both hands as she moved toward the portal, then spoke for the first time. "May I approach him?"

"What did you just say?" the old man sputtered.

"I would like him to touch"—Joelle caressed her swollen middle—"what he has wrought."

"My apologies, my lady. But I can't permit you inside. Take comfort that he'll never touch anyone again." The squire grinned through the bars and announced happily, "We'll start with his hands."

Joelle lunged for the portal and thrust one hand through the bars. "Hyam!"

He was ready, and extended his body and arm and hand as far as the chain permitted.

The squire sneered, "This really is all very . . ."

His scorn faded into horror-stricken astonishment as a spark leapt from Joelle's hand to Hyam's. The crack lashed the air and filled the chamber with an acrid burning. The spark grew into a river of light so brilliant it branded Hyam's gaze. But he did not turn away. He drew it in with the desperate need of a drowning man.

Trace moved forward, rested his hand on Joelle's shoulder,

and weaved his other hand in an intricate design. He cried, "*Open!*"

Every lock in the dungeon splintered apart.

Joelle withdrew her arm from the bars, the light still blazing from her fingers. She flung out an arc of fiery power, sending the squire and the two guards crashing against the wall. She held them there, her face filled with a wrath as powerful as the light coursing from her hand.

"That is enough, my dear," Trace said. "We don't want to kill them."

"We don't?" The force still streamed from her. The orb glowed fiercely, the violet light streaming through her dress and cloak both, turning her into a beacon. "Why ever not?"

"Joelle," the wizard pressed. "Enough."

Reluctantly she dropped her hand. The power dimmed, then vanished entirely. The guards and the sheriff's son slumped to the floor. The chamber was silent save for the sputtering torches and the squeak of prison doors being pushed open.

Hyam felt the energy course through him, healing as it went.

Only then did he notice that his cell mate had stopped humming. Hyam knelt beside the man and realized the prisoner had breathed his last.

Hyam stepped through the cell doorway and into Joelle's embrace. It was the first time he had held her. Her strength was an elixir to his soul. Despite the orb pressing into his belly, he did not want to let go. But she released him and asked, "They hurt you?"

"I'm fine, thanks to you two."

"We must be off. The palace is swarming with armed men," Trace said.

"One moment." He gripped Joelle's hand, then turned and extended his other arm, flattening each of the dungeon's dire instruments in turn. He wrenched each of the cell doors off their hinges so they could not be locked again, all but the one where he had been held. As fearful faces appeared in the central hold, Hyam called, "Wait until we have departed! Then you all are free to go!"

Hyam turned his attention back to the sheriff's son. The squire watched Hyam's approach with very real dread.

"You notice I never asked your name," Hyam said. "It's because I don't care."

"I . . . You . . . The realm will know of this!"

"They probably will. But that's not your concern, is it."

"I knew you used magic—no one could have shot that arrow without it!"

"And yet you still hunted me. Does that seem the least bit sensible to you now?"

"We must be off," Trace insisted.

Hyam drew in sufficient power to lift the sheriff's son and slam him into the cell holding the silent body. He then sealed the portal in place, welding it to the stone.

A desperate hand reached through the bars. "You can't leave me in here!"

Hyam ignored the panic-stricken shrieks and said to the hulking man-at-arms, "Tell me you want to live."

"I want to live, sire." For once the man sounded genuinely sincere.

Hyam turned to the cowering guard. "Get into one of the unoccupied cells. Don't move. Don't even breathe."

The man vanished.

Hyam said to the squire's aide, "Now you lead us out of here." But as they crossed the central space toward the winding stone stairs, Hyam said, "No, wait."

"The hounds will soon be loosed," Trace urged.

Hyam lifted his hand, halting both the mage's protest and the flow of bedraggled prisoners. He asked the brute, "How does the earl communicate with the king?" When the soldier hesitated, Hyam went on, "Someone at the palace sent the earl my description and the order to seize me. When the earl sent word that I was captured, a response came saying someone was coming to question me. All within a matter of hours, perhaps less. This is no mere exchange of carrier pigeons."

"I am forbidden to speak of it, sire."

Hyam started to threaten when the wizard replied, "I can answer that. The healing arts are not the only magic that still exists within the realm. There is another. All senior nobles are granted a mirror and a password. It is handed down from generation to generation and fiercely guarded."

Joelle asked, "Shouldn't we—"

"Soon." Hyam reached out and touched the globe through her dress. He shut his eyes and drew on the power, extending his awareness, searching, searching, until he found it. "A small frame of gold, no broader than three hands, in a tower chamber without windows. The door is always guarded." He opened his eyes. "Is that the one?"

The soldier's astonished expression was all the reply Hyam

needed. He shut his eyes again, reached out, and shattered the mirror.

The stone vault shook from the blast. Beyond the stairs and the dungeon portal, shouts and pandemonium filled the air.

Hyam opened his eyes. "Now we can leave."

The keep's forecourt was a chaotic din. Hyam could have walked through leading the earl's own steed and no one would have noticed. The castle's highest tower was reduced to a stubby pile of smoldering rubble. A score of fires blazed about the inner keep. To Hyam's hasty eye it seemed as though the fallen stones themselves were alight. Men swarmed and yelled and pointed and ran.

They passed through the main portcullis, and before Hyam could release the man-at-arms, the brute said, "Allow me to offer you my fealty, sire."

Hyam had no idea what to say. The mage responded for him. "You wish to shift your loyalties? Why?"

"I have witnessed a change to the realm." The hulking soldier showed genuine pain. "The wrong people lead us now, and for the wrong reasons."

Trace was not convinced. "How can we trust you to remain true to your new oath?"

He glanced back at the keep. "Evil is about, sire. Unnatural forces rule because the rulers let them."

"You are right," the mage confirmed. "And we oppose these forces."

Though it was the mage who spoke, the brute continued to address Hyam. "Let us oppose them with you, sire."

"You speak for others?" Trace asked.

"I am not alone in wishing for a leader who will show us the proper path."

Hyam nodded to the mage, who said, "Gather only those you would trust with your life and ours. Meet us at the river port. Hurry."

38

Hyam's troops had seized three riverboats and ordered them ready for immediate departure. They had also promised their captain full payment. But the man insisted upon hearing it straight from Hyam. When they crossed the gangplank, they heard the skipper shout, "Gold! I'll take you to the gates of doom for gold! But you try and steal from me and I'll ram the banks and set my vessels alight. You see if I don't!"

The man was short and stumpy and bearded, and he smelled. Hyam liked him on sight. "I have gold. But I need to know the price is fair and the vessels seaworthy."

"River worthy, you mean. Take this sow into the open waves, and you'll die screaming about the fool the ocean has shown you to be." He planted small fists on his hips and demanded, "You lead this band of pirates?"

"I direct this honorable company, yes."

"Wastrels, the lot of them. They spill uninvited onto my

vessels and tell me I'm headed for Port Sutton. Why should I, I ask this one. And how does he respond but offer to show me the edge of his blade."

"We are under pressure, you see. But I assure you the good man meant nothing by it. Adler, apologize to the captain."

The officer's response was decidedly something else. Even so, the skipper grinned his approval. "I suppose you're the lot who tweaked the dragon's nose and burned the earl out of house and home."

"We did."

The captain turned and eyed the smoldering castle with evident approval. "Never did like the man. All right. Show me your gold and let's bid this burning city a swift farewell."

The captain's name was Gimmit and he had nothing good to say about anyone or anything. He saved his harshest comments for his five sons, all of whom could have lifted their father one-handed and flung him far across the river's silken waters. The youngest did not yet shave and already towered a full head above Hyam. They shared the same ready smile filled with teeth the size of paving stones, which had to have been a gift from their mother, for Gimmit's teeth were ground down to yellow nubs.

The only man taller than the largest of Gimmit's sons was Gault, the Havering soldier. The squire's former man-at-arms arrived just as the second boat was pushing off. Gault led twenty-seven other troopers, a full company minus two who were too sick to travel. Adler did not want them, but the desperation in their voices swayed even him.

The three vessels were each eighty paces long and broad at the beam and stable enough to keep calm the dozen horses Hyam's troops had brought along. They were also very slow. The boats were equipped with lateen sails that the captain refused to raise at night. The riverbank drifted by at a walking pace, and Hyam knew they had to move faster. But the skipper was adamant. "If your goal is to plant your sorry hide on the shoals and gut my ladies, then yes, I'll raise my sails. But only after you hand me their weight in gold."

Hyam knew he had no choice but to show his hand. "What would you require to speed up and remain in total safety?"

The skipper had a vicious laugh. "To see the sun rise in the west!"

"I'm serious."

"As am I!" He pointed downriver. "Ten leagues and three bends from now, rocks rise like jagged teeth. They are black and they are hungry. In the daylight you'll see the wreckage of vessels skippered by fools who dared ride a rushing spring flood like this, thinking it would keep them safe."

"There is no rush to our pace," Hyam protested.

"Wait until you must travel against the stream, and you'll understand how slow a river journey can be." The skipper spat over the gunnel. "The worst of the river's teeth are hidden just below the surface. They'll gnaw at our belly and gut my ladies. If I let them. Which I won't."

"My question still stands. What would you need—"

"A thousand torches, which we don't have. And a wind blowing straight from our stern, one that twists and turns in line with the river." The skipper settled one hand on the tiller, testing the river's currents through his fingers. "Go to sleep, lad. The river has its own . . ."

He stopped talking as Hyam took the sack off Trace's shoulder, the one where Joelle had slipped the orb. Hyam clambered atop the central hold. And he searched.

Reconnecting with the orb carried an exultant joy so fierce he reveled a moment before extending his awareness outward. What he had sensed upon setting off became clearer still. Far beneath the earth's surface, a current of power ran in line with the river's course.

He lifted his hands over his head, drawing the power up and into the orb. Once this bond was forged, he fashioned the energy into three brilliant lights. One for each of the bows. The light transformed the surrounding fields and dressed the rocky shoreline in a violet glow. He turned to the astounded captain and said, "Raise your sails. I will give you your wind."

39

Hyam remained on duty for another hour, until Trace insisted he could keep the winds and the vessels on course, and then showed himself capable of the task. Hyam used an extra sail to fashion a bed in the bow, out where he could rise and check both the lights and the wind. His sleep was punctuated every hour or so by an image of the crimson rider, who chased through clouds of ash, hunting, searching. Every time the sightless skull turned toward him, Hyam jerked awake and counted himself fortunate not to have been captured, not even in dreams. For he was certain he had learned the rider's secret, and it filled him with terror.

Finally toward dawn he slipped into a deeper sleep and awoke somewhat refreshed. He breakfasted on plums and cheese and hardtack, and watched Joelle train as he ate. Meda had taken over the foredeck and worked her soldiers hard. The women could not match the men for brute strength, Meda repeated time and again. But they possessed the supple swiftness of an assassin's blade and, with practice, could overcome the strongest man by unbalancing him and striking harder than he expected. Meda's aide fought against Joelle, and the two women danced at death with such unbridled ferocity that it silenced the entire ship. Even Gimmit and his sons gaped at the two women as their sweat formed silver arcs in the sunlight and their blades whispered a lethal tune.

When they were done, Meda drew Joelle apart and spoke too softly for Hyam to overhear. The officer patted Joelle's arm, spoke again, and turned away. Joelle's smile competed with the sun for brilliance.

Joelle treated herself to a seaman's bath, dunking herself in the river, then ladling fresh water from the rain cistern tied to the lee gunnel. Hyam observed how Joelle greeted every word cast her way with the same vestige of a smile. He could not stop looking, for in this brief instant of hard-earned joy, he saw a hope that they both might leave the unfair past behind.

Meda returned on deck with a bundle and called to Joelle, who unfolded the coverlet to reveal a set of fighting clothes like those worn by Meda's troops. From his place in the bow, Trace said, "It is good to see her rewarded as she deserves."

"It's more than that," Hyam replied. He felt uneasy declaring that such was another person's destiny, when he had little idea of his own. But when she returned on deck and stood glowing with pride over her fighting gear, Hyam wished for some way to not only confirm the moment but add to it himself.

But for the moment he could do nothing save walk over and declare, "It was thrilling to watch you train."

"This lass has the makings of a fine warrior," Meda declared. "And the speed of one who has trained for years."

"I have," Joelle replied. "But only against imaginary foes. The first time I fought with another was today."

"The clothes suit you as well." Hyam gazed into those remarkable grey-violet eyes and wished for a private hour. But the unknown awaited them around the next bend, and his planning could not wait. "I need to speak with Bryna."

It was difficult to watch her joy fade and know his words were the cause. Joelle replied, "The Ashanta were frantic when they learned of your capture. Bryna wanted the Ashanta to reveal their armies. Trace urged her to wait."

"I'm glad he did." He pointed to the bow. "Trace needs to hear this as well."

The mage was maintaining his wind spell with one-handed ease while chatting happily with Gimmit's oldest boy, who frowned over what he heard. The lad saluted Hyam with a knuckle to his forehead and slipped away.

"Why does he run from me?" Hyam asked.

"He asked about our quest. I told him. There's no secret, is there?"

"I suppose not." He turned to Joelle. "Have you summoned her?"

"Bryna is coming." A pause, then, "She is here."

"Tell her I was wrong about why the army assaulted the Ashanta settlement."

"She can hear you, Hyam. Speak to her directly. I will repeat her answers."

He liked how his name fit so comfortably in Joelle's mouth,

but now was not the time for such simple pleasures. He related his dream, then waited.

"Bryna hears your concern but does not understand the cause."

"Remember the witches. They fed their globe with pickings from the desert road. They built an altar of bones. And the globe was turning pinkish."

"So this crimson rider . . ."

"The army has assaulted one badlands outpost after another. The rider feeds on this. Growing ever stronger. Until the moment arrives when they attack the Ashanta settlement."

Joelle's features reflected the concern of listening multitudes. "You are suggesting the crimson mage brought the king's brother and his army to their doom?"

Trace looked down from his position in the bow. "He *meant* for them to lose."

"That is my thinking," Hyam confirmed. "I assumed the crimson one fled into the forest. Now I believe I was wrong. He retreated to a safe position, from where he might feed upon their deaths."

"This is horrible."

"It is. And there is more."

Trace said, "More?"

"The crimson rider feeds on death. Think on what this means."

Joelle's features creased in worry. "They don't understand what you are saying."

"The Ashanta form of attack was to raise up a ghoulish horde. What if the rider now controls them?"

Both faces showed genuine terror. The boat's progress slowed as the magical wind faded. Trace demanded, "The rider has stolen the Ashanta army?"

"I have no idea. But I think, yes." Hyam pointed to the sails and waited until Trace had resumed his magical task to add, "I fear it in my bones."

For much of the day Trace remained alone in the bow of the first boat, with Dama and the orb for company. Hyam had one of the middle sons row him and Joelle to the middle boat. The young man was Hyam's age, perhaps a year or so older, but he remained silent and cowed by whatever Trace had shared with his brother. Hyam suspected it would be the response of most people to him, if he survived.

He and Joelle stationed themselves in the bow of the second boat and worked at extending their reach, connecting to the orb, drawing the power. Joelle found it both difficult and exhausting, but for Hyam the distance was not great enough to challenge. So he left her there and moved to the rearmost vessel. Adler sailed upon this vessel, along with the Havering contingent. Hyam waved them off and focused on the orb. The hold was more tenuous now, but over time it grew to where he was certain he could connect at will with the orb.

He lowered himself into the rowboat and ordered the son to stay away. He loosed the rope and let himself drift back. He ignored the worried faces that gathered at the vessel's stern, focusing instead on the orb that grew ever more distant. He could not risk loosening his grip, not even for an instant, not without forcing Trace to turn the lead vessel around. And speed was everything. The closer they drew to the river mouth and Port Sutton, the more certain Hyam grew that they were racing death itself.

Which granted his exercise a vital importance. He focused on the unseen orb, strengthening his grip, extending his reach. As soon as he grew comfortable with the distance, he extended it farther still, until the first vessel's sail was a distant fleck of white, smaller than his little fingernail. By now the third vessel's stern was crowded with gesticulating figures. Hyam powered his little vessel forward until it drew close enough for him to shout up, "I am fine. And this is important."

Adler called back, "We are drawing into the fishing lanes, sire."

He resisted the urge to correct his manner of address. "So?"

"One vessel talking of how a rowboat without oars keeps up with a sail-driven vessel might be discounted. But if a fishing fleet were all to carry home the same message?"

"You're right." Hyam pulled over to the side where a rope ladder traced a line in the green waters.

None of the sailors moved forward to tie him up, however. Finally Adler stepped down himself and made fast the vessel. "Was there a purpose to this?"

"There was."

"Oh, good. I would hate to think our leader caused such alarm simply because he needed a few hours of solitude."

"There may come a time when I need to appear empty-handed," Hyam replied. Now that he was done with the exercise, fatigue lapped over him like the waves rocking his little vessel. "If I had done this earlier, I could have drawn on the orb when we were assaulted at the mapmaker's. Now help me up."

Adler offered a warrior's grin along with his aid. "You think like an officer."

"I don't see how. I have never been in battle," Hyam confessed. "Except the one time I ran away."

Hyam retrieved Joelle from the middle boat and returned to the first vessel. As they clambered on board, an idea struck him. The thought was so outrageous he took it first to Trace. The old mage heard him out in silence, his only response a slight furrowing of his brow.

When Hyam finished, the wizard said kindly, "You realize what you are suggesting is not new."

"Is that bad?"

"Of course not. But your idea carries powerful implications."

"My question stands," Hyam said. "Should I do this?"

"Your idea is a good one. Excellent, in fact."

Hyam found himself slightly giddy with relief. "Should I wait?"

"Whatever for?"

But now that his thought was approaching action, he found himself vaguely embarrassed. As if by carrying out the deed, he was binding himself not just more closely to Joelle but also to a future he dreaded.

Trace must have sensed his hesitation, for he said, "The time is right, the deed a good one. Go."

Hyam clambered down the stairs to the main deck, where Meda and her aide were wielding swords in slow motion, the officer talking through every motion. Joelle watched in rapt attention.

At Hyam's approach, Meda stopped and said, "You need something?"

"Could all of you join me on the foredeck, please." He led them back up the bow stairs, searched beneath the sailcloth, and came up with his pack. Only as he drew the sword and scabbard from his belongings did he realize he had no idea what to say. "Trace, help me."

"It is your idea, my liege. Your decision. Your deed."

"I don't know the proper words."

"The act is what matters, my liege." The old mage could not quite keep the smile from his voice.

Hyam fought down his nerves and faced an uncertain Joelle. "Back at the Long Hall, you asked if I would arm you. I agreed."

Joelle swept a hand over the clustered troop. "They are doing that and more."

"Lass," Trace said gently. "Let him speak."

Hyam drew his sword. As the milky blade appeared, the women gasped. Meda breathed, "Is that . . ."

"Milantian steel," Trace confirmed. "Yet another legend comes to life."

"I want you to carry this," Hyam said.

Joelle did not move. "I-I don't understand."

Trace's tone became formal. "My lady, you are being asked to serve as sword bearer to the Ashanta emissary."

"If you will," Hyam added.

Joelle stared at the blade for a very long time. Finally Meda asked, "Do you agree?"

"I . . . Yes."

Meda gave a hand sign to her troops, who came to attention. She said, "Do you pledge to bear this weapon in defense of your liege? Make his enemies your own, his battles yours as well?"

"I do," she whispered.

Hyam sheathed the blade and handed her the sword. "It's yours."

40

The river broadened until both banks disappeared beyond the horizon. Sails of all shapes and sizes filled the water. Fishing vessels dipped great booms from either side, their nets spread like tawdry wings. They emerged filled with fish that sparkled in the afternoon light.

Hyam took over the wind spell, allowing Trace and Joelle to doze for a time. Then Adler arrived from the third vessel, drawn by the news that Joelle now possessed a Milantian sword. He and Meda and Gimmit and the other officers inspected the milky steel with the astonishment of seeing ancient fables arise before their very eyes. Adler fashioned a shoulder harness, fitted it to Joelle's back, then used his own blade to show her how to draw and sweep and attack, all in one fluid motion. Joelle proved adept at this as well, so Adler challenged her to fight. The mock battle lasted all of two seconds, for at her first parry Joelle sliced Adler's blade off an inch above the pommel. Crew and warriors all gaped as the metal clattered to the deck.

Later Hyam, Trace, and Joelle ate a ship's feast of hardtack, plums, cherries, and cheese that crumbled at the touch. And they talked. Hyam wondered aloud how their one orb served an entire Long Hall of mages.

"The orb has a master," Trace replied. "Whether the master takes on the orb or is himself chosen has been debated for a thousand years."

Hyam recalled his moment of connection, a visceral bond that defied even the witches' brew. "You were Master of the orb as well as the Long Hall?"

"Until you stripped away my power and my comfort," Trace replied, poking him in the ribs. "You scoundrel."

"You can't call our surroundings unpleasant," Hyam replied.

"Not for an instant." Trace tossed a fragment of hardtack to a patrolling seagull. He leaned against the forward gunnel with a bundled sailcloth for a cushion. "Still, there were many grand aspects to my former life. We numbered four hundred wizards and half again as many acolytes. All I need do was speak a wish, and if it was within power of mage or man, it was done. Which only made my foes among their ranks all the more sour."

Joelle spoke softly. "Except for those items where they could block you."

"True enough, my dear. True enough." Trace spent a long time staring out over the water, then said, "Many are the comforts that can blind a man to his imprisonment."

"We were speaking," Hyam said, "of one orb and many users."

"All mages whom the Master welcomes may use the orb. There is no limit to the number. The Master may require oaths, he may also deny access. In some Long Halls, this is where the greatest abuse of power arose. The threat of exclusion is used to bind the wrong mages, and for all the wrong reasons. When I was named Master, I promised that no wizard would ever be denied access to the orb." He smiled sadly at Joelle. "There were times when I immensely regretted this vow. One of the few important losses my opponents dealt me was over my right to teach you openly."

The sour taste of Hyam's unwanted memories joined with those that stained Joelle's face. "The Three Valleys Mistress claims I'm not human either. Why did the mages teach me?"

"Ah. The question for which there is no answer but one. And none knows that answer save the Mistress of that Long Hall. And she is not saying."

"I thought you said you talked."

"We did. And I asked. As did others. The Mistress would only say that she was told to do this. Not asked. Told. Who might be in a position to give orders to a Long Hall Mistress is a mystery wrapped in an enigma." Trace sighed contentedly to the sky overhead. "When you uncover the answer, lad, be sure and let me know."

Hyam's response was cut off by the signalman atop the mast crying, "Port Sutton to starboard!"

284

The seaman's eyes were far keener than Hyam's, which only saw a stain upon the horizon. The sky was the color of an infant's eyes, pale and milky blue, except in the direction where the watcher pointed. A yellow cloud hovered like a blemish.

The skipper climbed the wooden steps and entered the bow station. "The wind is against us."

"So it is," Hyam agreed.

"If I tack into the harbor, it will take us the better part of the day."

"Which we do not have."

"But if three crowded river vessels are seen sailing with a wind that is theirs alone, people will talk."

"Which we don't want," Hyam said, and shut his eyes.

A moment later, the nearest son called, "Ho, the wind!"

"Don't just stand there like a buffoon! Come about!" Gimmit roared. But he remained planted upon his stubby legs, glaring up at Hyam.

"Was there something else?"

"Aye, there might be." Gimmit turned and gestured. Three of his sons approached with nervous smiles and offered a forelock to Hyam and Trace and Joelle. The skipper declared, "My sons are determined to see me planted in a watery grave."

"We've heard your company talking, sire," the youngest said. "We want to sign on."

Gimmit stomped to the lee gunnel and spat over the railing.

"Sailors are born spying things others don't," the older lad said. "Rocks and shoals aren't the only hazards we have to see well before they're trouble."

"We know something is amiss in this realm," the eldest said. "A shadow of doom is about."

"If it's true you're headed off to battle the bringers of woe and ruin, we want to help," the youngest said.

Hyam turned to where the skipper stared out over the waters, beyond the city rising within the harbor walls, into the unseen. "What say you, Captain?"

"My sons are scamps and ne'er-do-wells. But on this they're right." He wheeled about. "Is Port Sutton your destination?"

"It is not."

"Where are you headed?" When Hyam hesitated, the skipper barked, "You've had time to take your measure of me and my sailors. As I have of you."

"We must find passage to Falmouth Port. From there we head into the badlands."

The sons were turned grim by the news. The skipper kicked at a wooden cleat, then declared, "You won't find passage. And do you know why? Because all vessels are forbidden from traveling to the Oberon fiefdom."

"Then what—"

"You'll need to trust me, is what! I'll buy us a ship and I'll sail us!" He glowered at the three grinning youths. "See what your pestering has brought us? Misery and unlawful deeds and doom beyond the horizon! Up in the rigging, the lot of you! Make ready for docking and the calamity to come!"

41

Arriving at a port city and acquiring a seagoing vessel was not like buying a loaf of bread, according to Gimmit. Not if the skipper ever intended to show his face in the town again, which Gimmit most certainly did. When the third river barge was drawn up at the stone quayside, he ordered Hyam and his team to seek refuge in a sailors' tavern. And wait.

The inn was clean enough, crowded and noisy and filled with good cheer. Hyam left his gear with the others and ordered up a bath. The bustling innkeeper was accustomed to travelers demanding anything at every hour of the day or night. Hyam was soon led out the rear door and into a windowless hut of stone and heavy beams. A great copper tub steamed in fragrant welcome. He eased himself down in stages, sighing contentedly. He must have fallen asleep, for the next thing he knew Gimmit was pounding on his door and demanding, "Five minutes more and you'll miss your own boat!"

Hyam dressed hastily, only to discover the skipper had no intention of leaving before he enjoyed a well-deserved meal. Together they feasted on roast lamb and white beans and fresh-baked bread. Joelle emerged from the baths with her hair still wet, dressed in Meda's idea of a uniform. The hilt of Hyam's sword rose by her left shoulder, and four knives rested snug in her belt. Hyam was not the only one to nod his approval, but he was the one who was rewarded with Joelle's rare smile.

He ate until his belly stretched tight as a drum, reveling in the simple pleasures of good food and firelight and friends. When they left the inn, he cast a longing glance in the direction of the night-clad city.

Gimmit asked, "Never been to Port Sutton before?"

"I've never seen a town. I entered Havering and five minutes later I was arrested."

"And I've never been anywhere at all," Joelle added.

"I suppose we can spare you time for a bit of a wander." The captain glowered. "Long as you don't waltz around blowing things up."

The night market was a whimsical fairyland. Adler and two of his men and the skipper's youngest son accompanied them. The officer had traveled by ship before and urged them to buy fresh victuals for the journey. They purchased fruits and cheese and a variety of other items that Hyam scarcely saw. Port Sutton was a major trading hub, and the harbor market traded in goods from every corner of the realm. Hyam could have spent days wandering the crowded lanes. Weeks. Instead, it seemed as though they had scarcely entered before the youth declared, "We must be away, sire."

Hyam smelled the vessels long before he spied them. They were the ugliest ships tied up to the harbor wall, two great hulking vessels that stank of pig. But for once, the skipper was smiling. Gimmit stumped down the gangplank, his yellow teeth glinting in the torchlight. "They're old, they're ugly, and they came cheap."

Adler snorted. "You should have spent more money."

"No, no, that's where you're wrong. We could have spent days dickering over finer ladies. But the skipper of these is a mate, and he was only too happy to hire them out. As far as their owner is concerned, I'm transporting soldiers to the Lacombe tourneys. My clients are nobles, but they're poor, and they are willing to show up smelling of porkers." Gimmit studied the two hulking shapes with genuine satisfaction. "They leak like sieves. I assured the owner my poor nobles could be taught to bail."

"I can seal the hulls," Hyam said, hoping it was true.

"That's what I'm counting on."

His eldest son trotted up. "The last of the water barrels is loaded, Pa."

"Call up the first watch." Gimmit gave a mock bow and ushered them on board. "Now let's be off while the dark still hides us."

Hyam joined Trace and Joelle on the first vessel's forward deck. It had clearly been used by the crew, for it stank a bit less. As they cast off, Hyam held the sack containing the orb and called up a gentle wind. The vessel creaked and lumbered and came about, followed a long moment afterward by her mate. The two boats were both high-decked and twin-masted. They were also very slow. Hyam resisted the urge to speed them onward.

Finally the fires burning in the stone towers atop the harbor's twin arms drifted past, and they entered open waters. Hyam took that as his sign and pressed the two boats to greater speed. Then more, and more still, until the wind that was supposedly blowing from behind them pushed the sails into a backward position. When Gimmit came forward to protest, Hyam cut him off with, "Lower the sails."

"Lower—"

"We are sailing in the forbidden direction. It's a moonless night. We must make all possible haste. Lower the sails."

Gimmit stared at him a long moment, then turned and called softly to his sailors. He used a signal lamp to direct the second vessel.

Hyam moved apart from the others and shut his eyes. He centered upon the orb, then willed his attention down, down through the ocean depths and farther still, out to where he sensed the flow of power. He opened his eyes and said to Joelle, "Have the helmsman steer us in that direction."

But Gimmit himself came forward to protest, "You're asking us to steer farther from shore and our destination."

Hyam had no choice but relinquish his bond to the orb and the distant source. "I am."

"In case you hadn't noticed, these sows are just begging to founder and sink with the loss of all hands."

Trace saved him from needing to explain. "Do as he says."

"But—"

"And fast," Hyam said. He could feel the orb's power waning.

Gimmit sputtered, but in the end stamped back and roared his opposition in the form of angry commands. Hyam shut his eyes once more, searching down, down, and out.

Finally the orb began humming in harmony with the power deep below, and the light spilled over Hyam's clenched lids. "Tell Gimmit to steer a bit farther to port."

"You've found a river of power?" Trace asked.

"A big one," Hyam confirmed, and filled himself with the orb's force, then extended it out. First to their vessel, then the other. Sealing the hull, cleansing the deck, scrubbing away the filth, scraping off the burdens of barnacles and seaweed. The vessels sliced through the water more easily after that and rode higher. The stench of caged animals was replaced by the fresh sea breeze.

His work completed, Hyam sighed against the flood of weariness and asked Trace and Joelle, "Can you keep us moving? I must rest."

As he fashioned a pallet of sailcloth and sacking, Trace asked, "Why are we hurrying?"

"Tomorrow," Hyam replied, and was gone.

The dream followed him out into the open waters, and his sleeping senses were soon filled with the reek of old ashes. A roan trotted above the cinders and the residue of death. Upon its back rode the crimson one. The sightless eyes searched the distance. Hunting.

When Hyam shifted and jerked, he felt a gentle hand settle upon his cheek. The woman's heart spoke through the touch, quieting him and easing him and forcing away the rider and sending his dreams into a calm and welcoming mist.

Joelle left her hand in place, though Trace watched her, as did two of Gimmit's sons. She knew they thought it was an act of growing affection, and perhaps it was, at some deep and mysterious level. But in truth Joelle used the moment mostly to accustom herself to this man she was only now coming to truly see. Not as the one who broke her free from her prison and made fast the friendship with Trace. Not the one of power. But the man whom she could trust.

Hyam defied her every expectation. He gave because it was his nature. He wanted, but discounted his own desires. He was lonely. He hurt. And he masked it all very well. She wondered if she was the only person who saw the inner fragility, the aching wound where his home should have been. She had heard fragments of talk between him and Trace and Adler, about an orphan who had only recently learned he was in fact not sired by those he had called parents. She understood his fear over the unanswered questions. She saw how others expected him to push all this aside and do what needed doing. For what they called the greater good. And he accepted this. Because this was who he was.

Her emotions were as confused as her own internal state. Touching his face was enough to create a hurricane of conflict within her heart and mind. She had survived by showing the world an iron-hard determination. Without speaking a word, he asked her to set down her barriers.

Hyam terrified her.

The next morning they breakfasted with the maps that had almost spelled Hyam's doom. The mapmakers had felt guilty over seeing Hyam captured. So they had charged a fair price and gifted Adler a gilded compass. Hyam and the others admired the instrument over tea and bread and cheese and chutney in the first vessel's stern cabin. It smelled far better now, but the walls were scarred and the furniture decrepit. Gimmit urged Hyam to leave things as they were, since nobles might be made to holystone decks but not be transformed into skilled carpenters.

Gimmit traced their way along the course Hyam insisted upon, though it took them far out to sea. Ahead and to port rose the Great Headlands, a massive spit of land that marked the realm's official end.

"When we round the headlands, what then?" he asked.

"I will find a new course," Hyam said.

When Gimmit looked ready to argue, Trace said mildly, "I trust the lad to do as he says, and so should you."

Gimmit ground his teeth for a moment, then said, "Two hundred leagues beyond the headlands lies Falmouth Port and the entry to the badlands. I visited Falmouth once as a lad. The approach gives me nightmares to this day. The port's entry is narrow and guarded by black spears that rise high as the castle towers. You wait for the quiet between tides, and you beg the winds to give you just that one nudge to see you safely inside." The squat sailor did not actually shiver, but his hands quivered as though still gripping the tiller. "You are allowed one chance. And for what? In the harbor there is only hardship and gloom, for all of Falmouth is built from that same dark stone. The castle is called Dragon's Tooth, and for good reason."

"I wonder why the Oberons chose to reside there," Trace said.

"It is as I have said," Meda replied. "The Oberons handed Ravi the crown and offered fealty, if Ravi would grant them Falmouth in perpetuity."

"But why?"

"That has been argued over for four years. And the answer is, no one knows."

Gimmit set his mug aside and glowered at the map. "I can tell you about the port and the approach. But what lies beyond Falmouth itself, I have no idea."

"I served there," Meda offered, and sketched out a swift overview of fiefdoms and feuds that filled the craggy land. "The clans are all related, and this only makes their feuds more vicious. They fight over everything. Water, sheep, gold, a gemstone that is as black as the rock from which it is drawn. Some say the badland clans could conquer the realm if only they were somehow forced to make peace among themselves. For they love nothing better than a good fight. And loathe nothing more than an outsider."

"A surly lot who shun the realm," Trace mused. "It would be an easy place for chaos and destruction to go unnoticed."

"The Havering banker said there is only the Ashanta financier in Falmouth, and not another until Emporis," Joelle said.

"Emporis." Gimmit shook his head. "There's a name from childhood fables."

Hyam felt a vague unease, like a dark flower opening in his gut. "What is Emporis?"

"A caravan city," Meda replied, pointing to the unshaded region beyond the badland borders, right on the edge of the parchment. "I never visited there."

"If it exists at all," Gimmit said.

"Oh, it's real," Meda assured him. "I have met caravans headed there. They claimed it was the last remaining city of the ancients. A place beyond time, built of brick and stone as yellow as the surrounding mountains."

Joelle's quiet intake of breath turned them all around. Trace demanded, "What is it?"

"Dreams. Perhaps nothing but imaginings and . . ."

"I see in your face that it is far more," Trace replied. When Joelle remained silent, he softly pressed, "Lass, look around you. You are surrounded on all sides by friends. Now tell us what you think might help us."

Her breath became unsteady as she said, "I have been traveling beyond my physical form."

Trace halted Gimmit's outburst before it formed. "It is a common enough trait of the Ashanta. You did this while residing at the Long Hall?"

"For a few months. It was often not under my control. Sometimes I went where I wished. Other times . . ."

"You were taken," Hyam offered.

"I saw you once, or at least, I think it was you. In a desert valley. Not the one above the badlands, a different place. You held the orb. You were lost to a light that blinded me."

Hyam liked that enough to smile. Their eyes met for a time, then he pressed, "What does this have to do with Emporis?"

"I have been taken to a city beyond time. Yellow and surrounded by desert ridges sharp as razors. A round citadel rises from the city's heart, built from yellow stone."

"A vast tower that dominates the city," Meda said. "I have heard Emporis has such a keep."

Joelle nodded slowly. "I have seen the crimson mage walk the battlements. And ride out through the city gates. And gather a ghoulish army in the valley below. Just as Hyam warned."

The grip upon Hyam's core grew so fierce he could scarcely draw breath, much less ask Meda, "Tell me what else you know of this place."

Something in the way he spoke lifted all the other gazes in the cabin. Meda said, "Beyond the badlands is a great arid plain. No water for days. Where the badlands end and the desert begins rises a last lone mountain. The peak has been carved away, and in its place stands a walled city."

"Emporis," he breathed, and felt a sense of locking down. Taking aim.

"It has stood for so long, the caravan masters say it was a city before mankind ever laid claim to the realm."

"That is our destination," Hyam said, his breath almost choked off by the turbulent power that gripped him.

The room went quiet, save for the creaking timbers and

the rush of water beyond the hull. Finally Trace said, "You're sure?"

"He is there," Hyam said. "The crimson one has taken over the city."

Hyam turned and walked to the stern window. Behind him, the others began making plans. He knew he should join them, but just then he was too consumed by one other certainty.

The crimson one had found him as well.

42

Hyam left them peering over the unfurled parchments and clambered back on deck. The sunlight did not dispel the tension that gripped him. Instead, he found it hard not to wince as he scanned the sparkling waters. A few clouds sailed along overhead. The sea was empty, the ships moving steady.

Joelle climbed the stairs to stand on the bow deck beside him. "Something is wrong," she declared. When Hyam hesitated, wondering whether he should worry someone else, Joelle pressed, "Tell me. I can't help you unless you speak."

"The crimson rider knows we are coming."

"How can you be certain?"

He struggled to describe the sensation he had felt when hearing the city named. He thought he had failed, but she cut him off and said, "Wait here."

"Where are you going?"

"The others need to hear this."

She returned with Adler and Meda and Trace and Gimmit and three of the sons. She made Hyam repeat what he had tried to explain. The words came no easier the second time.

And yet, when he was done, they all shared the same worried scowl. Joelle finally said, "In my travels, I sensed he was hunting me. And perhaps . . ."

"Tell us," Trace pressed.

"Sometimes I wondered if perhaps I was hunting him as well."

Gimmit scanned the horizon, then told his oldest boy, "You've got the sharpest eyes. Scale that pole and plant yourself in the crow's nest. Anything that don't fit, be it spouts or clouds or the ruffle of a wrong wind, you sing out."

"Aye, Pa." He scampered up.

"What do we do?" Adler demanded.

There was an uncommon comfort in these seasoned few trusting him. Hyam hefted the sack that held the orb, cinching it tight to his chest. "I need to push us as hard as I possibly can."

"If any see us, we might as well fly a wizard's flag," Gimmit warned.

"The sea is empty, and speed our only friend," Hyam replied. "Give me the compass heading for our destination."

Gimmit pointed ahead and to his left. "Five points off the port bow."

"Tell your helmsman to be ready to turn on my word." Hyam walked to the bowsprit and shut his eyes. Gathering his forces, he extended his arms and senses both. Behind him the roar of commands and the swift padding of bare feet on planks faded away. He searched down, connected with the distant coursing power, and extended out and ahead, hunting.

A vein opened not far from where they traveled, not as great as he would like, but coursing toward their destination. Hyam lifted his left hand higher still.

"Ready about!" Gimmit roared. "And signal the other vessel!"

Hyam pointed, the vessels turned, and he focused more intently still. He faced three tasks. First, the sea ahead must be flattened to a glassy expanse, smooth and slick and safe. Second, the two ships had to be linked so that the pace of one was matched by the other.

And finally, they had to speed up. Hyam had no idea what the crimson one would throw their way, but he was certain the enemy was coming. Winning the race was their only chance of survival.

There were shouts of alarm as the two ships drew ever closer. Hyam did not move.

Gimmit called from somewhere, "Hyam?"

Joelle answered for him. "Leave him be."

He could not actually lift the ships from the water. He tried, but because of either their size and weight or some force linking them to the ocean, they would not come completely free. Yet he could lift them higher, reducing the sea's drag. And he could certainly increase their pace.

The sound of rushing water grew steadily, and with it the crews' alarm. Finally Gimmit roared loud enough to be heard on the second vessel's deck, commanding them to be silent and hold steady to their new course. Hyam took this as a sign that the skipper was with him. He gripped the ships in his energy and pushed them as hard as he was able.

The rushing sound grew to a crescendo, a sibilant tide of liquid cymbals. He knew the ships could go no faster when water began cresting up over the bow, splashing him in the face. Hyam opened his eyes to the sight of a long silver ribbon of calm water extending out before them, while to either side clamored both wind and waves. Their vessel plowed a great furrow down the center of the glassy lane. Their speed was astonishing. Hyam turned and saw the second vessel was following in their wake, so close a sailor could have leapt from their tiller to the other ship's bowsprit. The men on both vessels watched him now in wide-eyed silence. The only sound came from the constant rushing seas.

Hyam asked Joelle, "Can you do this?"

Trace climbed the bow stairs. "We can and will, lad. You rest."

"If there is any sign—"

"Rest," Joelle agreed.

He threw himself down and shut his eyes. But he did not sleep. The sound of rushing water formed a comforting backdrop, however, offering the faint hope that they still might outrun this threat.

Hyam was up and eating a late lunch in the shade of the lee railing. He had twice tried to retake control of their progress, but Trace had sternly ordered him to hold off and stay rested for whatever loomed beyond the horizon. Hyam liked how the old mage spoke quietly with Joelle, extending his arms and inviting her to copy his example by shutting her beautiful eyes and facing the ribbon ahead, sensing the dominions beyond human sight and reach. Trace spoke words too soft to carry, and Joelle opened her eyes to smile her thanks.

The day was warm and the air sea-sweet. Hyam tried to tell himself the empty sea held no threat. But his gut said otherwise. Every now and then he lifted his head above the railing and checked their surroundings. But mostly he trusted the youth in the crow's nest. And the skipper, who made sure his son remained alert by calling up, "Anything?"

"Nothing, Pa."

"You better not be dozing up there!"

"I've never been more awake. Though there's nary a thing to see, not even a gull."

"Keep a tight eye on the horizon, boy!"

His son sat with his back on the mast, his feet dangling over the roost's narrow ledge. "I am, Pa. Don't fuss so."

Gimmit had scarcely turned away when the lad called down, "Pa!"

"What is it?"

The entire vessel watched as the boy rose to his feet. He squinted into the distance beyond the second vessel, followed by a hundred and more pairs of eyes.

"Speak to me, lad!"

"I thought I saw . . ."

"Where away?"

"Dead astern. But now I can't . . ." He jerked and pointed. "There it is again!"

Hyam still saw nothing. But he no longer needed to. He turned to Trace and said, "It's him."

"You're certain?"

Hyam gave a grim nod. "I can feel it."

Gimmit heard the exchange and called over, "The crimson rider?"

"Yes. He's coming."

Soon, too soon, their foe arrived. The sight was so incongruous it was hard to take in. At first it appeared as merely a great lump drawn skyward from the sea. But the nearer it drew, the more ferocious became the spectacle. For this was no mere wave. No rush of water they might seek to ride over and escape.

It was alive. A great heaving mass pounded upon hooves of sea and froth. These liquid fiends raced toward them, driven by a single unified purpose. To attack, to devour, to destroy.

Hyam lifted the orb high. "Trace, Joelle, keep us moving forward."

In response, the mage said, "Joelle, grip his other side. No, lass, don't touch his arms. Hold his body. All right, lad. We'll maintain our forward progress. You do what must be done."

"Fast as we can go," Hyam said, and shut his eyes.

He did not need to see the horde of fluid foes. He could sense them. He could also hear the screams of pure terror rising from the rear vessel.

And he could sense the crimson one.

Their enemy rode with the horde. His sightless eyes were fastened upon Hyam as he lifted the phantom staff over his head and cried, "Join me, cousin, and I will spare your friends!"

"You lie!" Hyam cried, and only realized he had spoken aloud when Joelle said, "Hyam?"

"Focus, lass!" Trace called. "Speed! For all our sakes!"

The crimson one laughed, a spectral sound of dust from open graves. "You're right, cousin! But bond with me and I will give you the lass to do with as you will!"

Joelle must have caught some whiff of the real threat, for she faltered and the ships slowed, until Trace shrilled with all his might, *"Focus!"*

The vessels sped back up, lifting almost clear of the water. But still they could not outrun the thundering mass of liquid fiends.

From the crow's nest came a cry so high-pitched it might have belonged to a young girl. "Land, Pa! *Land!*"

"Where away?"

"Falmouth rocks, two points off dead ahead!"

"Trace!"

"Focus, lass. Power, focus, *speed*!"

And still it was not enough. Hyam did not need to open his eyes to know they would not make it. He could not halt the tide of fury. He strained, he fought with every sinew of his being. The crimson rider deflected his strongest push with terrifying ease. The skull *laughed* at him.

The screams from the rear vessel rose to a crescendo.

Hyam opened his eyes. He was defeated long before he saw the foe.

The wave towered a thousand paces straight up, curved slightly at the crest. The wave was rimmed by fangs long as oars, and upon the highest peak rode a pale version of the crimson roan. Within the liquid wall sped an army of unworldly beings. Specters without name or true form, as they shifted and grew and reached out with swords and spears and then with nothing more than claws the size of sails. Sailors and warriors in the rear vessel had crowded to the bow deck and wailed in helpless terror.

Hyam would gladly have thrown himself overboard, given himself as a sacrifice, but it would have achieved nothing. He had never known what it meant to be totally powerless before, not even at his weakest in the empty Long Hall nights. Nothing compared to having people who trusted him pay the ultimate price.

He screamed his futile fury and lifted the orb higher still, pushing back against the onslaught with all his might.

When from behind him, out beyond the rocks he had never even seen, a dark castle emitted its own light. It linked with his orb, a joining so simple and uniquely powerful his scream was instantly silenced.

A brilliance spread out over the sea, a pearl-white luminescence shot with violet. The joined lights dwarfed even the sun. The combined force stilled the vessels' frantic rush for safety, then passed over them and left them limp and stalled. But speed was no longer required. For behind them the wave was gone. The beasts were mashed back into the ocean's depths.

Of the crimson rider there was no sign.

43

Hyam spent his first four days at Falmouth Port buried in stone. He found a particular irony at being kept inside a windowless cell of ancient black rock, while all his efforts were focused upon the same activities that formed the core of every Long Hall.

The same, and yet utterly different.

The only time he left the castle cellars was to visit the stables once each day. Dama had fretted terribly over being taken underground, so Hyam left the dog with Matu. The destrier occupied one of a long line of stables meant for warhorses. The dog and steed were content.

"Falmouth Port has no Long Hall!" Master Trace said the words so often he might as well have adopted it as his new litany. But there was no ire to his words, only wonder. The answers he sought came on the fourth morning, when they were visited by Bayard, the leader of Falmouth, the reigning Earl of Oberon.

Bayard had been out on patrol when they had presented the city with a quandary. The wizards of Falmouth had kept their prowess a secret for a thousand years. As they had the fact that the Oberons had established the port for the explicit purpose of hiding their orb. Protecting their powers. Just in case. That was how the senior mage responded to every one of Trace's questions. Just in case. More the mage would not say until the earl returned.

Now the earl was here. And he greeted his senior wizard with an embrace that mashed the old woman to his dusty armor. She protested, "Unhand me, good sir!"

"You did well, Edlyn."

"Of course I did. I always have. I always will. But that does not grant you the right to paw me!"

"It is your magnetic quality," the earl replied, his face grave, his eyes sparkling. "It is your immense beauty. Your winsome ways."

"And you are a liar and a scurrilous lout." Edlyn was as old as Trace and made the former Master of Havering Long Hall look positively fat. Hyam doubted she weighed as much as her robes. "I should have spanked you as a child."

"You did. Many times."

"Not hard enough." She motioned to where Hyam stood by the central slab. "My lord, may I have the pleasure of introducing Hyam of the Three Valleys, Emissary to the Ashanta. And these are his company, Master Trace and Lady Joelle. This is Bayard, Earl of Oberon and the seventy-first of his line."

"Three mages whose approach forced the crimson rider

to show his hand." The Earl of Oberon studied them with frank intent. "Were the reports true?"

"They were indeed." Mistress Edlyn placed a protective hand upon the hidden orb of Falmouth. "Had I not been safe down here, without a window to look through, I would have been frightened out of my skin."

Bayard, Earl of Oberon, was a tall man with long dark hair that spilled over his mail. He bore the face of a fighter, which meant he was aged far beyond his thirty-some years. "The reports made much of a wave tall as the castle keep and beasts fashioned from the ocean depths."

"And the crimson one rode atop the crest," Trace confirmed. "I saw it, and I shall continue to do so in my dreams."

"Your Mistress saved our lives," Hyam said.

"Which means you are in my debt," the earl said.

"We are," Hyam agreed.

"So may I count upon your support in our quest?"

"Only if your aim is to bring down the dread foe."

The earl revealed a remarkably sunny smile, which contrasted sharply with the grave cast to his features. "I think this calls for a banquet."

They assembled in a great hall that dated back to the dawn of the current age. The shadow of dread and hardship was left beyond the portals, for within was good cheer and warmth from six fireplaces and excellent food. There was goose roasted with a honey glaze and venison and a stew of lamb and plums. There were six different platters of steaks carved from some great fish—Hyam doubted the stories told by those who served him—of sea creatures as massive as their ships. But Gimmit assured him they were true.

The earl had wanted Hyam to join him at the head table. But Hyam had not seen his company since the first morning after his arrival, and besides that, he was made uncomfortable by the regal nature of the hall and the gathering. Hyam and his crew occupied three tables down the hall's right side, with him seated closest to the earl's throne.

He was glad for the chance to set down his burdens and his work. For since his arrival he had done little save struggle to fashion a way to bring down his foe. But all was not adversity and worry. Hyam had been given a cell carved deep in the rock upon which the Falmouth castle rested, and the stone and the two orbs had sheltered his dreams, and he had been well fed, and he had been surrounded by allies. The Mistress of the hidden orb was a capable teacher, and her fifty mages welcomed the strangers because she ordered them to do so.

The company of mages enjoyed the banquet from their table along the opposite wall. Their grey robes and their magical abilities were the only two things they shared with their Long Hall cousins, as far as Hyam was concerned.

The hall was larger than Hyam's village square and lined on either side by pillars the size of forest trees. The distant ceiling was painted with scenes from the Milantian war. One of the mages' duties was to keep the images fresh and the colors pure. The illustrations carried such vibrancy Hyam could almost hear the sounds of battle, feel the impact of warring magic. Dangling from each pillar was a giant standard, each representing one of the fiefs that had come when the first King Oberon had raised the war banner, the colors as vivid as they had been a thousand years before. The message was clear enough. Here in this place, the past remained alive. The sacrifices that had resulted in the realm's survival were held close. The watch remained on duty. The foes would not vanquish mankind. Not so long as Falmouth survived.

When he was done eating, Bayard carried his goblet to each long table in turn, toasting those seated there. His salutes were formal and courteous, as were his guests' responses. When the earl arrived at their table, Hyam and his company were ready. They rose to their feet and saluted the earl and responded with the same formal words as had been spoken by all the other clans. They thanked him for his hospitality and stood ready for his call.

But instead of returning to the main table where his wife sat with their only child, Bayard gestured to an aide, who brought over a high-backed chair. The earl seated himself between Hyam and Trace. "Now you may ask your question again."

"How on heaven and earth," Trace replied, "did your ancestor manage to hide an orb here?"

"My forebear, the first king, was by all accounts a remarkable individual. I have studied all I can and tried to cut away ten centuries of lore to find the heart of the man himself." Bayard drained his goblet and held it out for the aide to refill. "I had little choice, given my immediate predecessors."

Hyam ventured, "My home was so isolated I did not even know the old king had been a poor ruler."

"My uncle was a drunkard who saw the throne as little

more than a chance to indulge his every whim. Most of which had to do with either wine or serving wenches. He learned all those lessons at his father's knee, who was himself a lecher with a violent temper. My uncle grew so fat he could not climb into the saddle unaided. Every year they had to make new armor." Bayard drained his goblet and held it out once more. "My parents died in the fevers. My uncle accepted me as his heir because he had no choice. That is all I care to say about the man whose excesses and blindness cost us the empire."

"The orb," Trace repeated.

"What did Mistress Edlyn tell you?"

"She said to ask you," Trace replied. "Nothing more."

"The first king found it upon the battlefield. I assume it belonged to one of the vanquished Milantians, but I can find no record of it. When the orbs were destroyed, the king kept this one in secret. He chose Falmouth as its hiding place for two reasons. First, because of its location. It is forbidding and dangerous and far from prying eyes, with mountains to its back and storm-tossed seas to its face, and the badlands leading down to the desert."

"After Ravi defeated your uncle and you asked for this as your fief, we thought you were hiding away in shame," Trace recalled.

"And so we wanted everyone to assume. But the crimson mage must have suspected we held a secret power, or sensed it. Because when he started wreaking havoc among the badland clans, he never approached us. Until you came." The jewels rimming the goblet sparkled in the torchlight as he drank. "The first king worried over the Ashanta's insistence that all the remaining orbs be kept in what came to be known as Long Halls. The risk was too great that the wizards would grow lazy."

"Not to mention self-righteous and complacent," Hyam added.

"And smug and petty and bitter and spiteful," Joelle finished.

Bayard smiled at them. "Well, now."

"The hidden orb," Trace pressed.

"My forebear ordered the formation of a secret clan of wizards, one based here. And that brings us to the second reason why Falmouth was chosen. He wanted a place close enough to the edge of civilization to always know risk and hazard and a need for vigilance. A place unable to forget that danger does not die away. Peril does not vanish. It merely slumbers for a time, then rises up once more and seeks a weakness. A vulnerability that can be utilized. A failing where it can strike."

The earl then turned to Hyam. He drank from his goblet. And he watched the younger man over the rim. Waiting.

"There is a third reason," Hyam said.

The earl set down his chalice. "Is there."

"There is a river of power that flows beneath this place," Hyam replied. "A strong one."

"The Mistress was right to save you, even if it meant revealing our hand." Bayard rose to his feet. "She tells me you are putting together a battle plan."

Hyam jerked back in his seat. "I didn't—"

"You thought you could hide away the purpose behind four

days of magic?" Bayard smiled. "My grandfather named her Mistress when she was still in her twenties. The old mage who taught her said she was the strongest wizard he had ever known. You would do well to trust her."

"I do, sire. It's just . . . I only have fragments of an idea."

"Bring them with you tomorrow. We gather at noon for a council of war." The Lord of Oberon started to turn away, then remained standing where he was, staring down at Joelle. "You are the emissary's sword bearer?"

"I am, my lord."

"Are the rumors true? You carry a Milantian blade?"

"I do."

"You will show me? No, not here. I will not have such an implement revealed in this hour of ease." To Hyam's surprise, the earl pointed to the ceiling far overhead. "Cast your eye to the right of the high point, midway to the banner with the golden lion. Tell me what you see."

It took Hyam a moment before he realized, "A beam of light courses from his sword?"

Bayard let his arm drop to his side. "There is no record of such, save this one painting. But as a child learning the lessons of long-ago battle, I wondered why the crimson mages were always depicted with an orb in one hand and a sword in the other. Why would the most powerful wizards need a sword? The only answer that has ever satisfied me is there in that painting." The earl studied the hilt rising by Joelle's left shoulder. "Guard your weapon well. And keep it hidden from our enemy's gaze."

44

Hyam had no interest in sharing his splinters of an idea with a group of seasoned generals. He was not ready, nor did he see any benefit, not unless he could determine a few things in advance. So he sent word to the earl, who arrived in the wizard's chamber at dawn. He was accompanied by the biggest man Hyam had ever seen, a red-bearded giant named Fuca. The warrior wore a checked cloak that was gathered at his left shoulder by a battle crest and bound to his waist by a gilded belt holding a battle-ax. Fuca's wrists were encircled by armored braces from which extended snakelike scars. More scars rose from his cloak and disappeared into his hairline. He eyed Hyam with a gaze of crystal-blue death.

Bayard found a soldier's humor in the unease of Hyam and Trace and Joelle. "Fuca was chosen as leader of the badland clans. He did this by wreaking havoc on everyone who stood between him and the title. He used to wear finger bones woven

314

into his hair. I begged him to take them out, as most of them formerly belonged to the clans he now leads."

Fuca revealed a voice of soft thunder. "I feel naked without them."

"I trust Fuca with my life and my fiefdom's future," Bayard said. "Now tell me why we are here."

"I need something for my idea to work," Hyam said. "Something that I don't want revealed to your war council."

"I suppose I should be ever so grateful for your trust," Bayard said wryly.

"His idea is a good one," Mistress Edlyn said. "And his reasons for secrecy are sound."

"Very well. I am ready."

"You brought the map I requested?" Hyam asked.

In reply, the earl unfurled a chart of sewn parchment, big as sailcloth. It completely covered the central stone table. The map showed Falmouth in considerable detail down at the base. The badlands rose in a sweep of valleys and ridges. Most of the vales bore names and townships and coats of arms. Many of the seals were crossed out. Hyam did not need to ask the meaning of the expunged crests.

"This does not include the findings of our last sorties." Bayard stabbed three more valleys. "These clans have been wiped from the earth."

"A few of my people made it through to Falmouth," Fuca rumbled.

"Not many," Bayard countered. "Not enough."

Hyam knew the earl's city had become a haven for the surviving clansmen, and Bayard was using these warriors to strengthen his force. Joelle and Trace had described houses crammed to overflowing and lanes so packed it was hard to make way. Hyam had not seen them. The Mistress Edlyn had ordered him not to leave the castle. They had to assume the city held spies and possibly assassins as well.

Bayard's sorties into the badlands never confronted the enemy, nor did he try. Instead, he sought to keep the roads open and the haven available to all who came. The crimson one's attacks had resulted in a broad ring of destruction with Emporis at its heart. Valleys in every direction had their clans expunged.

"How close does the forest come to Emporis?" Hyam asked.

"Forest?" Both the earl and the clan leader frowned at the query. "What importance do woodlands hold?"

"You describe the badlands as arid and holding poor soil," Hyam said, avoiding the need to answer directly. "I am asking if forests approach the caravan city."

Fuca scowled in concentration. "Scrub pines, aye, they grow along the south ridge here. But you won't find cover for a surprise attack."

"The city rests on a fortified hill," Bayard agreed.

"Plus it is said that before every attack, the crimson one sweeps the land, searching and scouring the hearts of my clansmen with terror."

Hyam insisted, "How close do these pines come to the city's southern gates?"

The two soldiers exchanged looks, clearly worried over placing their trust in one so inexperienced in the ways of war. "A thousand paces. Less. But—"

"Wait, please, and you will understand." He turned to Edlyn. "All right. Let's give this a try."

"Step away from the table, everyone," the Mistress said.

"Do you understand what he is going on about?" Bayard demanded.

"Not entirely, sire. And neither do you. Now stand well back."

Hyam closed his eyes. The orbs—his and the hidden globe of Falmouth—had been set upon a shelf carved from the rock wall and covered with a velvet cloth. He heard Trace and Joelle and Edlyn step over so that they could rest their hands upon the orbs. He heard Edlyn call to her mages in the adjoining room, commanding them to begin their own work. Hyam did not seek to join them, however. He wanted to remain detached. His focus moved through his own orb and aimed downward. Farther and farther he extended his reach, flowing out and along the river of fire.

Hyam rushed with the tide, moving so fast he could not tell how long he was there or how far he went. Only that his course mirrored the map. Finally he announced, "I am there."

"He is where?" Bayard asked peevishly.

"Emporis. Hush, now. We must concentrate. Trace, Joelle?"

"We are ready, Mistress."

"Hyam, do you sense the foe?"

"I can't . . . Yes, there is an orb. But he is not . . . I think he is sleeping. Or disconnected in some other way."

Edlyn sighed with genuine relief. "It is as we have found in our own searches. The crimson one seems to rest at every dawn."

Hyam could feel his heart beating. He felt his feet standing in Elven boots upon ancient flagstones. He felt his hands leaning upon the map stretched across the central table, which was little more than a giant slab of black rock supported by two other slabs. He could hear Bayard muttering to Fuca, who growled an impatient reply. He sensed Joelle and Trace joined to one orb, standing guard over Falmouth Port. Edlyn and her mages were connected through the other, all of them reaching out, following his senses, hovering at the Emporis outskirts. He knew all this, but from a vast distance. For his entire being was swamped with one sensation above all else.

"There is a juncture of rivers beneath the city," Hyam declared.

"What is he going on about?" Bayard demanded.

The Mistress of the hidden orb showed a rare impatience. "You will hush and you will be still. You are witnessing a feat that has not been seen in a thousand years. You are watching a man do what was considered the dominion of the ancients. Now if you must breathe, do so in total silence!"

In the shocked stillness that followed, Edlyn asked, "How many rivers join there, Hyam?"

"Four."

"Can you follow them?"

"I think . . . Yes."

"Do you want me to map them?"

He hesitated, then said, "No, you need to stay on guard."

"Can you remember them all?"

"I don't need to," he realized. And with a slender finger of his attention, he began to trace the lines on the map. Corresponding to the rivers he followed far underground.

The clansman saw the lines appear on the map and muttered, "What manner of sorcery is this?"

Edlyn hissed for silence. But their chatter did not stop, nor did it matter. Hyam found the murmuring to be of no consequence. He raced down one line of power after another, charting their course as he did so.

Then it happened.

The alarm was unmistakable. The rage slammed into his distant awareness, a wash that threatened to strip him from his body. "The enemy has discovered me!"

Even before the words were fully formed, the attack began. A wave of crimson-flecked fury assaulted the castle. The rocks upon which Falmouth stood groaned and shook. The chamber vibrated from the echo of an inhuman roar.

Edlyn shrieked, *"Strike!"*

She and her mages sent wave after wave of force directed at the gates of Emporis. North and south portals were struck simultaneously. Trace began shouting words at Joelle that Hyam did not need to hear, joining their strength into a unified barrier intended to keep the crimson mage at bay. The two diversions worked, for their foe's attention was drawn away from Hyam's quest.

Mistress Edlyn called, "It is time, Hyam!"

"One moment." His own work was not done. His quest was not complete. He needed—

"He is after me!" Joelle's cry was wrenching.

"Hyam, retreat!"

"I'm not—"

Trace showed panic for the very first time. "Now, lad. *Now!*"

He flew back, the distance covered in a single long intake of breath. "I'm back."

The stone chamber shuddered and vibrated. Lines of heated ferocity stabbed the perimeter. Lightning blasted overhead. The rocks of Falmouth groaned in distress.

Then nothing.

"Bayard, sire, go check for damages and comfort your citizens," Edlyn said shakily.

"What just happened?" the earl asked weakly.

"In time, sire. In time. Go. Your people need you."

The two warriors departed, chastened and dazed. Edlyn asked the others, "Everyone is safe?"

When they confirmed, she left the room, only to return and announce, "No injuries among my wizards, save for a few shaken egos."

Hyam stepped to the map, where he was joined by the other three. The chart was now laced with orange lines that formed a diamond pattern across the entire expanse.

But there was no triumph to the achievement. For the lone location where the four broad rivers joined together lay directly beneath their enemy's lair.

The next best alternative within reach was three rivers. Two of which were less than half the width of those flowing beneath Emporis. This juncture lay beneath the ridge holding the pines.

"We do not know if he can tap into that power," Trace said, leaning in beside him.

"If he did, why would he need to sap the life force of vanquished armies?" Edlyn agreed, squinting worriedly at the chart.

Hyam stretched his exhausted frame. "You are willing to risk the battle's outcome on such a chance as that?"

Trace tugged on his beard. "What alternative do we have?"

None was probably the only answer. Hyam started for the door.

"Where are you off to, lad?"

"Rest first," he replied. "Then food."

"The earl will want your report," Edlyn said.

"Soon," he said. "First there is one more task we need to do."

45

Hyam rested for an hour, long enough to regain both strength and clarity. But the sense of vulnerability that always resulted from his mage-work remained, and Trace noticed. They met in the palace's vast kitchen, where a cook fed them fresh-baked bread and platters of cheese and fruit.

Trace observed him with a fretful eye. "You are wounded."

"I am fine."

"You are not fine. You're drawn as thin as parchment by your forays." He turned to where Edlyn sipped tea from a heavy ceramic mug. "Hyam uses no known spells."

"How could he do otherwise," Edlyn replied, "since no one has attempted what he has just achieved."

"He uses no known spells," Trace repeated. "You must know the risk this carries."

"We have no choice," Hyam replied.

Still Trace persisted, "Spells are built with two aims in

mind. First, they harness the orb's force and channel it in a particular direction. Second, they protect the mage from being overwhelmed by this very same power."

"It's not the orb that has power," Hyam replied, "but the earth."

"This power," Trace stubbornly continued, "has the potential of frying the mage from the inside out. I have seen this happen. Once. I never—"

"Stop," Joelle said. "Just stop."

Hyam pushed his plate aside. He had any number of responses. How there were no useful spells because the Long Hall mages kept themselves locked away from the world's needs. How his every deed represented a move into uncharted territory. But he could see how distressed Joelle was, so he simply replied, "So far, the only risk I've run is wearing myself out."

"Which for all we know is the first warning sign—"

"Trace. Enough." This time it was Edlyn who spoke.

"But—"

"Your affection for the young man is touching. But it blinds you to the simple fact that we have no choice. Now hush. You are upsetting Joelle, and your words change nothing."

Hyam found an odd comfort in the tension that enveloped the others. They spoke as they did because they cared for him. He was part of a group who held power, and yet did so with the compassionate ease of those who were not defined by it. If anything, they treated it as a source of responsibility. A reason to reach beyond themselves and care for others.

"I fear I may be Milantian," he confessed. "At least partly."

His words drew them all around. Hyam related the conversation with the Mistress of the Three Valleys Long Hall, his ability with the Milantian tongue, and how not even the Ashanta Seer could determine his heritage.

To his surprise, none seemed particularly disturbed by his admission. Edlyn was the first to speak. "It would explain much."

"Such as how his abilities do not fit any known type of mage," Trace agreed.

"You're forgetting that Milantians have been under a death decree for ten centuries," Hyam pointed out.

"I forget nothing," Edlyn replied.

"They are safe from no one," Hyam went on. "They are the scattered people. If any survive at all."

"You're as bad as the old man," Edlyn scoffed. "The pair of you, fretting over what you can't control."

"As if we didn't have enough to worry about," Joelle agreed.

"The lad has a point. No mage or scholar can speak more than a few words," Trace insisted. "I spoke with the Three Valleys Mistress about this very point. Her Long Hall possessed a library full of Milantian scrolls, all of which Hyam gobbled up in a single winter. No one could find any record of a child gifted in the forbidden tongue. So they hid you the only way possible."

"By forbidding me to speak it again," Hyam recalled. "And forcing me to learn Elven."

"None of this changes a thing," Edlyn said.

"I want to know who I am," Hyam insisted.

"Of course you do. And I want roses to bloom in midwinter." Edlyn smiled at him. "My dear, you have the right to define yourself and your destiny. You have gifts, you have talents, and you have this day to hone both. If you succeed, you just might aid us in saving the realm. In such times as this, who could ask for more?"

They left the castle keep at the strike of noon. The war council was delayed at Hyam's request. The earl and the clan leader accompanied him, as did Trace and Joelle and Edlyn and Adler and Meda and twenty men-at-arms and half a dozen wizards. Hyam had not insisted upon their coming. Any venture beyond the castle keep carried grave risks. The crimson rider knew where they were, and he knew what they intended. But this final task had to be done. Hyam had to do it. He thought it would be good for the others to accompany him, but it was a hunch, and he loathed the idea of risking other people's lives on a guess. So he had confessed his uncertainty and made his request. And they had come.

They took the main road through the village that had grown beyond the city walls. Merchants who had once led caravans clustered here, building corrals for their animals and hiring displaced clansmen to guard the wares piled under canvas tarps. The animals were unlike any Hyam had ever seen, placid desert beasts who watched their passage with limpid gazes. Clans that had spent generations in blood feuds now formed makeshift communities that extended over what formerly had been pastures. Inns built around a trio of hot springs sprouted new wings of tents and thatch. As they passed, many of the commoners knelt in the muck. Soldiers saluted with raised spears. A trio of crossbowmen demanded to know when they were going to take down the crimson monster. Bayard responded to one and all by raising a mailed fist. Fuca gave no sign he saw or heard anything.

The forest had been cut back by the newcomers' growing need for shelter and firewood. They passed through a broad swath of stumps before Hyam signaled for them to halt. "We go on by foot. Just the eight of us."

"Sire," the chief man-at-arms protested.

"Do as he says," Bayard commanded. "Hyam, how long will we be?"

"I have no idea. Only that we must hurry."

"Wait for us," Bayard ordered, and slipped from his horse.

Mistress Edlyn ordered her senior wizard, "Spread out. Bind to the orb. Stay alert."

The mage disliked his orders as much as the sergeant. "And you, Mistress?"

"We are counting on you to keep us safe."

They entered the forest. Ten paces, twenty. Bayard moved up alongside Hyam. "Will you not tell us now why we are here?"

"Soon."

"Why not now?"

"Because you will not believe me."

Fuca snorted, but softly, for he remained bemused by the morning's events. "This forest is tame. We would not even find game this close to the city."

Hyam turned to where Adler and Meda checked their perimeter. "Anything?"

"We are alone, sire."

He asked Joelle, "Is Bryna with us?"

"As you requested, she has come."

Bayard demanded, "Who?"

"All right. Stand back." Hyam stepped forward alone. Facing into just another thicket. He lifted the chain from around his neck, took hold of the crystal whistle, fitted it to his lips, and blew.

There was no sound. No motion. Not even a breath of wind.

Hyam blew a second time. A third.

Then a green warrior stepped from the thicket and said, "Once is enough, Emissary. And it was expected that you would come alone."

They walked the long lane of interlinked trees in awed silence. Six Elven archers walked before them, six behind. Hyam thought his company took the news rather well, that a race thought dead and buried for ten centuries still thrived.

King Darwain and his elders awaited them in front of the great stone watchers. The massive gates leading to the Elven realm were shut and guarded by a company of archers and another of men-at-arms.

Darwain greeted them in the human tongue, which until that moment Hyam did not even know he spoke. "Our safety depends upon secrets we have guarded for a thousand years."

Hyam bowed his apology and said, "The crimson rider prepares for an assault upon the realm."

The elders trembled like saplings attacked by a sudden wind. Darwain replied, "I understand your concerns. But my reservations still stand."

"I have a plan," Hyam said. "But it will only work if we unite."

The Elven king started to protest once more, but his queen said, "Hear what he has to say, my husband."

He nodded slowly. "Speak, then."

"This is Darwain, King of the Elves. Your Majesty, may I introduce Bayard, Earl of Falmouth."

"Your exploits are known to us." Darwain lifted a gloved and bejeweled hand. "I salute the leader of the Oberons and the realm's rightful king."

Bayard was so stunned he probably did not realize he wept. "You speak words I never thought I would hear, Your Majesty."

"May they soon be uttered by the entire realm. Who are your companions?"

"Fuca is leader of the badland clans and one of the fiercest fighters I have ever known." When the battle-hardened chief seemed too dumbstruck to respond, Bayard went on, "Mistress Edlyn is keeper of the hidden orb of Falmouth, and in her own sweet way she matches Fuca for ferocity."

"Shame on you, my lord," she said, then curtseyed deep. "My childhood dreams have been fulfilled this hour, Highness."

"We have long suspected the orb's presence, and until this day would have counted it as a crime against our future." The king glanced at his queen, who nodded gravely. "Now I suppose we must take whatever strength we can, wherever it might be found."

Hyam took that as the best sign he could have hoped for.

"Majesty, may I introduce my companions and the leaders of my own small force, Adler and Meda."

"I thought these false rulers had refused the right of women to bear arms."

Both soldiers dropped to one knee, and Meda said, "They have, Majesty. It is a mystery we have yet to understand."

"The reason is simple enough." It was the queen who responded. "Women fighters are more sensitive to both observing and using magic. The crimson one seeks to cripple the humans before the battle is waged."

"Master Trace is former leader of the Havering Long Hall," Hyam said. "And the Lady Joelle is my trusted companion and link to the Ashanta." He took a long breath, then added, "Majesty, they are with us now."

"What? Here?"

"In the person of one unseen companion, my oldest friend among the Ashanta. Bryna is her name."

"She wishes to address you, Majesty," Joelle said solemnly.

The king pondered the earth at his feet for a time. Then, "The Ashanta may speak."

"Bryna asks if she might be joined by the leader of all Ashanta."

When the king did not reply, his queen said for him, "Permission granted."

There was a quiet rustling of many leaves, and one of the Elves' elders declared, "Highness, more than one has come."

"Majesties, in return for your granting them the boon of entry, they wish to reveal a secret of their own," Joelle said.

A rushing wind shifted the neighboring branches and swept

lower, and lower still. And yet it touched none of them. Finally the leaves to Hyam's right rose in a tight whirlwind. They turned russet, then golden, then blazed in a light as fierce as the wind.

There at the whirlwind's center knelt a score of Ashanta, all wearing the white robes of leadership. They placed both hands upon the lane before them and planted their foreheads in the dirt.

Their voice was a rush of breezes that touched no face nor teased any hair. And yet the sound was clear as the sunlight that surrounded them. "We offer the apology that comes a thousand years too late."

The silence held so long Hyam realized he would either be forced to draw breath or faint. The leader of the Elves also seemed to have difficulty forcing his chest to work once more. He waved at the gates behind him. Instantly his troops stepped aside and the gates opened.

"You are all welcome to enter the Hidden Kingdom," Darwain said.

"I am grateful for your offer, Highness," Hyam said. "But we do not have the time."

The king turned back. "You refuse a royal invitation?"

"Just postpone our acceptance, with your permission," Hyam replied. "The crimson one is hunting us. For a moment only, we may have left him both uncertain and wary. I want to take advantage of this indecision. For this, we need your help."

The king looked genuinely pained. "We are the last of our kind. We are the one surviving remnant of our proud race. Our numbers are too few to risk upon some vague hope."

"Darwain," the queen protested.

"No. On this I will not be swayed. I am sorry, Hyam, but unless the crimson mage assaults our veiled realm, I must refuse—"

"I do not seek your army."

The king hesitated. "Well then, what is it you want?"

As Hyam described his objective, all he could hear were the gaps in his plans. The potential risk for failure. And the very real prospect of not coming out alive.

But even before he was done, the king had turned to his queen and the cluster of elders. All of whom nodded.

Darwain said, "This we can do."

"How much time do you need to prepare?"

"None. Time holds little sway in our realm."

Hyam felt a wash of relief, partly from feeling this crucial element fall into place. But mostly because this ruler of a defeated people found value in his plan. "The Mistress Edlyn and her mages tell us that the crimson mage rests with each dawn. I suggest we attack at tomorrow's daybreak."

"We will be ready," Darwain assured him.

But as he turned away, Joelle said, "Wait. I have a request of my own." She stepped forward, took Hyam's hand, and said, "It's time."

"Joelle, there is much that needs doing and little time—"

"I heard what you did not say. We all did. The risks are great. We may not . . ." She stopped, swallowed, and said to the Elven king, "I ask that you join us as husband and wife."

46

"Nervous, lad?" Adler was grinning.

Hyam had difficulty managing a swallow, much less a single word. So he made do with a nod.

"The man comes looking for war, and what happens but he's blindsided by his own allies!" All the officer's fears over finding himself at the fringes of a forbidden land were gone, replaced now by a vast good humor. "It's war you want and it's war you're going to get!"

Meda snorted. "And here I was wondering how such a charming oaf as yourself managed to stay single."

"Talk about battle strategy—your lass has the makings of a fine general!" Adler laughed out loud. "Hard to say no in the company of all these fine folks!"

"I didn't want to say no," Hyam managed.

"That's the spirit." Adler clapped him on the back. "When there's no other alternative, a warrior commits!"

"Enough," Meda snapped. "We're not gathered around some battle fire."

"Meda is right, you know," Trace agreed. "We stand upon hallowed earth, in a moment that will be remembered by song and myth."

Adler went quiet, but his grin remained firmly planted in place. "Who will stand for you, lad?"

"Master Trace?" Hyam asked.

"I would be honored, my liege," the mage solemnly replied.

The Elven queen approached, followed by four smiling elders, who held cloaks and wreaths of woven forest blossoms. "It is our tradition to mark the joining of lives with robes and crowns fashioned from that which we hold most dear." The woodland garments were fitted in place, and then the queen herself led them forward.

A man whose heritage was hidden from all walked alongside a woman whose heritage had left her excluded from the one people who could fill the gaping wound at the center of her being. Their way was lined by elders of a people who had spent a thousand years shunning all outsiders. Alongside them stood the leader of clans defeated by the crimson foe. They walked toward three leaders who smiled at their approach. The leader of the Ashanta stood to the left of the Elven king, ruler of the people they had allowed to be crushed. To Darwain's right stood Bayard, a man denied his rightful throne by the foe who waited just beyond the Elven veil.

They halted before the leaders beneath a canopy of

cathedral green. Watched by a thousand members of a green race who were no more.

Darwain, King of the Elves, said, "We are gathered here this momentous day to join Hyam and Joelle in the union of man and wife."

47

Their wedding feast was delivered by an unseen servant who left the tray outside their cellar door. The next time the outside world encroached upon their joy was when Meda rapped on the door and announced, "Sire, the hour has arrived."

"We come." Hyam stood with arms outstretched and watched as Joelle laced up the front of his emissary garb. "You have practice at dressing men?"

"You know I don't."

"You do this so well."

She merely looked at him with those grey-violet eyes, and he knew she had set all jests aside. "I want you to hear me. I want you to agree. Without argument."

He detested how the night's sweet joy was vanquished. Though he knew it was necessary, still he hated the moment's arrival. "I am listening."

"I want to come with you."

He started to protest, to object, to deny. But she stilled him with a hand planted upon the crest sewn into the purple leather that covered his chest. "We do not know what you will face. Only that our success depends upon your making this happen."

"Joelle—"

"Who can say what difference it may make, having another's strength to draw on?" She lifted her hand and sealed his words unspoken by placing a finger to his lips. "I know what you are thinking. You will enter and you will do this thing. And you will not survive."

He stood defeated by the depths of her gaze. Unable to break free of her soft touch.

"You are probably right. Why do you think I made the request there in the Elven glade? Because it might have been our only chance. But you will not do this alone. You will not leave me alone. Do you hear me, Hyam? You will not." She replaced her finger with her lips, kissed him softly, and said, "The others await us."

But when they emerged from the chamber, they found only Trace waiting for them. He carried himself with a Master's stern air. "I wish I could forbid what you plan on doing."

"The others are waiting for us."

"My warnings still stand. You can't expect to practice this sort of magery without—"

"There is no other way."

"Then let us postpone the attack."

"You know that's not possible."

Trace tugged angrily on his robes, as though the cloth itself was a foe. "Take the orb, then."

"Another impossibility." Hyam started down the hallway. "What if we defeat the crimson one today?"

"What if we don't?" Trace stepped in front of him once more. "Lad, you are inviting disaster."

Hyam felt as though he had never truly seen Trace before that moment. Not the powerful mage and former Long Hall Master. The man. His face was seamed by years of cares and responsibilities. But not the hour nor his age nor even fresh woes could dampen the light in his clear blue eyes.

Hyam rested a hand on the mage's arm. "I could not wish for a better friend. Now come. The time for argument is ended. The battle awaits."

The gathered force filled the vast plaza that fronted the city's main gates. Hyam had no idea how many they were. More people and more blades and more fierce expressions than he had ever before seen. He spied one of Gimmit's sons, then the others, standing head and shoulders above most of the gathered throng. Hyam resisted the urge to tell them to go back to the sea, where they were safe, where they belonged. Who was he to refuse anyone the right to fight, if that was what they wished? He hoped he had not caused a division between the diminutive sailor and his sons. Then he watched Gault lift the stubby captain onto a ledge by the side wall.

Hyam stood upon the crowded parapet, joined by Trace and Meda and Adler and Joelle and Mistress Edlyn and Bayard and the clan leader. Dama stood on Joelle's other side. The clan leader shouted out words in some badlands tongue, and portions of the throng roared their response. The Earl of Falmouth, heir of the Oberons, spoke then, and Hyam tried hard to listen. But his mind was as scattered as a leaf in a fitful wind. Directly below him gathered the grey-robed mages who had no rightful place in the realm. Some carried staffs, a few held knives. They and Trace and Joelle and Mistress Edlyn and Hyam were the only people in the plaza who did not wear mail and armor. But they all shared the same grim expression as the battle-hardened warriors. Hyam searched one face after another and found great comfort in their resolve. And great fear. So much depended upon him having gotten this right.

Hyam realized the parapet had gone silent, and all the people were watching him. He faltered, his fear a wash that stole away his voice. Then Joelle took hold of his hand, and he realized for the very first moment that he needed her. In this moment and in the battle to come.

Hyam knew what he wanted to say. How he had entered into this conflict alone and afraid. How he had found friends and strength and a purpose. How he hoped all this was enough to ensure them a great victory. How he was still afraid, but he carried their strength with him. And their friendship. And the love of a very good woman.

But Hyam was not made for speeches, nor had he ever addressed such a crowd, all watching and waiting. So he merely lifted the hand not holding Joelle's and cried, "To fight! To win!"

When the cheer died, Bayard called to the gatehouse, "Lower the portal."

In the sudden silence, the crowd waited as the drawbridge creaked down. The only other sounds were the sputtering torches and the huffing of horses. Then far in the distance, a bird of prey gave its piercing cry. Instantly Hyam touched the globe suspended from the satchel over his left shoulder and went out, searching, searching.

When he opened his eyes, everyone on the parapet save Mistress Edlyn was watching him. "Nothing."

"It appears that our foe is resting this dawn," Mistress Edlyn confirmed.

"Then there is not a moment to lose." Bayard lifted his voice. "You know your orders. Our destination is the point where the forest comes closest to the main road. Enter the glade and you will be welcomed by allies. Remember that. The people who await you there are our friends."

Bayard clattered down the stone stairs, followed by the mages and officers. He halted beneath the city's main entryway, checked to his left and right, then focused upon the silent road that vanished into the last hour of dark.

"*Run!*"

48

They ran on foot. The warriors who normally fought from horseback complained at the order. Bayard had not even tried to explain why the horses could not come. But the Elves had warned them that animals shied away from entering the hidden lane. Bayard and Fuca had decided not to tell the warriors they would traverse a mystical path put in place by green mages.

Hyam ran with Dama at his side, uncertain what would happen when he arrived at the thicket but knowing he could not order the dog to wait behind. Dama loped and panted and kept pace with him and Joelle. Hyam did not want to let go of Joelle's hand, for in it he found the slightest hint of the love that had filled his night. "You were right."

She ran easily, though her breathing came hard and fast. "What?"

"To want to come with me. I need—"

"Wait, Hyam. Wait." She tugged on his hand and pulled him to one side of the tide.

On Dama's other side, Trace ran with sprightly grace. The old mage veered over with the dog and asked, "Is something wrong?"

"No," Joelle replied, and waved away anything else the mage might have said. She faced Hyam. "Now speak."

"I wanted to protect you. But this isn't about protection. It's about getting it right."

"You need me."

"Yes, Joelle. I do. Now and every day."

Behind him thundered a steady stream of men and women and blades and huffing breath. But for him there was only the smiling face of a woman dressed in tailored grey with violet trim, the forbidden crest upon her jacket. The dawn light painted her smile with a rosy hue.

"Thank you, Hyam. Now kiss me and let us go and do this thing."

"And win."

"Yes, Hyam. Win and come home."

"I don't understand what any of this is about!" Trace complained. "Does this mean you will heed my warnings?"

"You know I can't, and won't."

"Then let's be off, for the entire world awaits!"

But as they started to rejoin the throng, an idea struck with such force that Hyam shouted, "Wait!"

When the two drew back in beside him, he explained in a rush what he had in mind. Joelle nodded slowly. "I will do this."

Now Hyam was the one to smile. Not that she would try, but succeed. "I know you will."

Trace gave his vilest cackle yet. "This has the hint of battle brilliance."

Hyam found great relief in the mage's approval. "And now we must fly!"

They joined at the back of the rush just in time to see the forward troops falter slightly, then follow their leaders straight into what appeared to be an impenetrable thicket. But the warriors kept moving, and they arrived at the forest's edge and continued forward. Straight into a lane marked by trees whose limbs formed a sheltering canopy high overhead.

At the lane's entrance stood two men in green, their spears planted in the earth, their gazes searching the far horizon. Beyond them rose the vague shape of the ancient Ashanta Seer. The pearl luminescence that surrounded her did nothing to improve either her looks or her disposition.

"You're late!"

Hyam stopped because the dog refused to go farther. "Any sign of our foe?"

"Not yet, but if you were to move any slower, he might still find you." She waved a querulous hand. "Get inside so we can close this portal!"

Hyam dropped to his knees and gripped Dama's pelt. "Guard our way home."

The dog whuffed softly and licked his face. Hyam rose to his feet and stepped through the portal.

"Finally," the Seer huffed.

"Seal the way," one of the Elves commanded.

They were committed.

They assembled in an expanse as vast as Falmouth's main plaza, roofed and sided by green. Bayard and Fuca stood upon a broad ledge fashioned from living roots. Bayard offered his hand, and the Elven king climbed up to stand beside them. The crowd trembled slightly, like a secret wind rushed through and rustled the forest of spears.

Bayard lifted his voice and said, "You see what has been kept concealed for a thousand years. This is what we did not explain, because words would have failed to describe. But listen carefully! What lies beyond that portal, we do not know. So we give you two alternatives. First, if an army of human warriors dares to come against us, we will fight them."

The clan leader lifted his sword, which most soldiers could not have wielded with two hands, much less held aloft one-armed as he did. "You heard the emissary," he bellowed. "We will fight and we will win!"

When the answering roar subsided, Bayard repeated, "Listen carefully! If the foes who rise against us are not human, we will not fight! We will retreat, and survive to fight another day. It is vital that you obey this command!"

Bayard gestured to the clan leader, who loudly agreed, "The clans' valleys are empty now because they fought forces beyond the reach of human arm and sword. If the ghouls rise from the earth, you will retreat! And you will live!"

A voice yelled back, "What victory is there in such a retreat?"

"Aye!" another shouted. "Why did we come this far just to run away?"

"I will answer that." Master Trace started through the crowd.

"Make way for the mage," Bayard called.

Trace was joined by Mistress Edlyn, and the two wizards were helped onto the massive platform. Trace opened the sack he had taken from Hyam's shoulder. "There are powers arrayed against us, as you have heard." He lifted out the glowing violet orb. "I and the Mistress of the hidden orb and her mages will enter into battle against them."

Mistress Edlyn opened her own sack of grey burlap and held aloft the Falmouth globe. Its brilliant silver-white light joined with the violet illumination. The combined radiance was painful to see. It poured through the green sanctuary, revealing every face, every leaf. The gathered leaders of the Ashanta stood on a second ledge at the atrium's other side, etched in a brilliant luminescence all their own.

Edlyn's voice carried a crystal clarity. "Behold the orb that has remained hidden for a thousand years. Our power has been kept alive for just such a moment as this. We stand with you. We will not fail."

Trace pointed across the gathering and continued, "And there stands a company of Ashanta, a folk who in ten centuries have never left their communities. Do you see them, my friends? Do you understand what this means? We are today assembled as we have not been for a thousand years."

As the light faded, the Elven king motioned to his attendants. Two staffs were handed forward. The king planted first one and then the other into the roots upon which they stood. "Your orb, Master Trace."

The globe glowed in his hand with a special hint of springtime mint. Darwain held it a moment, his face bathed in the remarkable blending of green and violet, then set it atop the staff, which grew tendrils up and around the orb, gripping it firmly. "My lady?"

"This is the first time in a thousand years that hands other than ours have held this orb," Mistress Edlyn said.

"I am honored," Darwain said, planting her orb atop the second staff.

Hyam watched the living staff grip the violet orb, seeing his mother's final tapestry come alive before his very eyes. Only there was a difference here. He did not carry the staff into battle. In fact, his plan required that he not touch the orb at all. Hyam felt the first stab of bone-deep terror, for his plan was feeble in the face of their enemy's coming wrath, and there was a very real chance he had gotten it all wrong.

But it was too late to change things, for Darwain gave the staffs holding the orbs back to Trace and Edlyn and said, "So the globes were carried into the last battle against the Milantian foes. Now you are ready for war." Then he turned to the Elven mages and cried, "Release the portal!"

49

The trees parted, the portal opened. Beyond the veil of green lay a harsh yellow light. The change was as shocking as the sudden blast of heat. The army had been warned, and still it faltered.

"Remember your orders," Bayard called, leading from the front. "Stay together. Attack on my command, or retreat if you are called to do so. Victory is ours. Onward!"

Hyam clambered onto the vacated ledge so as to watch their progress and observe the enemy's lair. They were separated from Emporis by a narrow valley that was empty of all save heat and rock and yellow dust. A fitful wind drifted back through the massive portal, carrying with it the scent of creosote and desert pine. The army moved swiftly into position on the bare rock terrace beyond the arid glade. Trace led half the mages to one side of the gathered force, Mistress Edlyn moved opposite him. On a rise behind her clustered the

Ashanta. At the center of the warriors, equidistant between the wizards, stood Bayard and his force.

There was no reason for subterfuge now, no need for further stealth. They were after havoc and alarm. They wanted the enemy taken aback.

Which was why Bayard shouted with all his might, *"Unfurl the banners!"*

A hundred tribal clans lifted standards of valleys that had been reduced to ash and cinder and bones. They were joined by standards of houses once bound by oath and blood to Bayard's forebears. And there at its center, largest of all, rose the forbidden seal of the Oberon kings.

"Sound the trumpets!"

The silence was shattered by the rising clarion. Hyam shivered from its impact. To his ears, the trumpets resonated with an impossible combination of silver and crystal and raw courage.

The enemy saw them. His rage was a hot breath that defied even the sun. Hyam reached for the orb he no longer held and hoped he had done the right thing.

Bayard called, "Advance!"

As he and his force marched into the valley, a swirling mist of rage and death rose from the city's highest tower. It swirled in a delicate tendril that grew and spun and reached out. One strand, then another. Aiming across the valley like flaming meteors.

Mistress Edlyn's voice carried an impossible strength for one so ancient. "Wizards! Attack!"

The mages clutched with magic hands at the two orbs,

sending out lances of violet and silver-white light, spearing the incoming flames and reducing them to faint whispers of dark against the desert sky. More lights launched from Edlyn's bevy, blasts of power that shot across the valley and struck the portals of Emporis with such might the ground beneath the army trembled. Again. A third time. On the fourth, the portico gave a great heaving groan and toppled to the earth.

A rush of shouting warriors spilled through the demolished city gates. Their swords and armor glinted in the ruthless desert light. Bayard glanced back at Edlyn, who shouted, "They are human! They live!"

"Then they are ours!" Bayard lifted his sword. "Attack!"

Edlyn and her mages went back to assaulting the citadel. "Trace! The tower!" the Mistress cried.

While ever more tendrils of flame rose from Emporis, Trace wove strands of his own, spinning them together into a light-lance that carried a searing force, growing and weaving like a master working a loom.

"Trace!"

The lance ripped the air as it shot across the vale. The sound was that of a giant's blade cutting a slice from the world.

At the last minute, the flaming tendrils retreated. They gathered into a massive shield held by a giant's hand. A crimson beast rose above the highest tower of Emporis, forming a monster larger than the city below. The red tendrils were shot with fire and lightning, a crimson beast that deflected the light-lance with one sweep of his giant red orb.

In the valley below, the two armies collided in a rush of steel and cries and fury.

An Elf stepped to the center of the massive portal. She was garbed in mail as pale as moonlight. In her hand she held a green staff, upon which was planted an orb that shone with a fierce green light.

Darwain had slipped up alongside Hyam. "We will keep the portal open as long as possible. As long as the remaining orbs can guarantee my kingdom's safety."

Hyam turned to the Elven king and said, "It's time."

50

The Elven queen requested the honor of leading Hyam and Joelle to their destination. When the king looked ready to object, she said, "You should remain on command at the crucial juncture, sire."

"Return as swiftly as you are able," he said, dismissing her. She bowed and waved them along.

The lane they traversed was narrow by comparison, a high-ceilinged path that descended slightly and then ran smooth and long and true. At its end waited a score of Elven archers who knelt in greeting to their queen.

"They did not volunteer for this duty, they begged," she said.

Hyam bowed to them and wished he was gifted at fine speech, for these warriors deserved more than a simple thanks. There before them rose another cloaked portal, far smaller than the one overlooking the valley. Hyam had no idea what he would find on the other side, even if his destination was where he intended. Abruptly he was caught by the recollection of his first dream of power, when tongues of fire rose from the earth and lashed at him. He shuddered and did his best to push the memories away. The prospect of not surviving the coming attack changed nothing. He had no choice but to try.

The senior archer brought him back to the present by demanding, "How is it you speak our tongue?"

"It was beaten into me. I resisted because I knew it was all wasted effort. Since everyone knows the Elves no longer walk the earth."

The archer did not quite smile. "It is good to know we are led by one who can admit when he is wrong."

"More often than I am right," Hyam said. "More often than I would like."

"I will guard the portal," the queen said. "Though I do not hold the orb, I am able to call upon—"

She was silenced by an unearthly shriek. It rose both through the portal that opened ahead of them and from down the lane behind. The wail rose and was joined by a chorus of inhuman voices.

"What is that?" the Elven archer hissed.

"The rise of the ghouls," Hyam said. "My worst fears have been justified."

"Let us hope they will still obey the Ashanta countermand," the queen said.

Hyam glanced at Joelle, wishing for the impossible, that she would have remained somewhere safe. For even in this moment of gut-churning panic, he knew that unless they were successful, safety was nothing but a momentary myth. "Ready?"

Her gaze held the strength to steady him. "I love you, Hyam."

The queen swept one hand up, drawing away the green curtain. "The hopes of all our races go with you."

As soon as they stepped through the portal, all their senses were assaulted by the battle. Directly overhead swarmed a ferocious pall of misery and ire. Two legs the size of cities rose to support a giant of fire and red smoke.

Lances of brilliant light stabbed the giant, the city, the tower. The air shrieked from the strain and the impact. Searing forces released pungent clouds of sulfuric fumes. All around him, unseen folks screamed and wailed. The ground shook and groaned. Somewhere close, a fire raged.

The Elven king had said that any grove would suffice to anchor their portal. But the larger the coppice, the stronger their bond. And the largest they had located inside Emporis was precisely where Hyam had hoped. He stood at the back of the royal gardens, staring directly into the peaked oak door set into the castle's main keep. The tower from which the smoke and fire rose was directly to his right.

"Spread out," Hyam told the archers. "Guard our way back."

As they moved into position, Hyam said to Joelle, "I will try to lead you."

"I am ready."

It was a grave risk, for she had not managed to connect to the force before, only the orb. And he had never tried to forge such a bond without the orb within reach.

He had also never stood atop the juncture of four great rivers.

He did not search for the orb. He feared such an extension would alert the crimson mage. Everything that happened beyond the city's walls was a diversion designed to grant Hyam this tiny moment in which he had to plunge, hunt, fly down deep into the earth.

Without the orb.

Hyam thought back to the moment he had stood in the field, and the energy that had surged up through his legs, filling him with the power to turn a spade into a wand. He clenched his mind and eyes and body, and hunted.

Instantly he felt it. Only there were not four rivers. There were five. The four currents joined, and from them rose a fount that fed directly into the crimson mage's orb.

Hyam was not even aware he had crouched or that he gripped the earth. All he knew was the energy surged up, forming a sixth flow, coursing into him as well.

Beside him Joelle sang, "I feel it!"

But Hyam could no longer respond. The power gripped him with such ferocity he knew he was being consumed. Just as Trace had warned. Without the orb to serve as a conduit, he was filled with more energy than his human form could contain.

The pain was an animal that consumed him from within. At the same time, his awareness blazed in all directions. Hyam glimpsed with utter clarity how the crimson wizard used his force to deafen the ghouls to the Ashanta's unified commands. And how the Ashanta themselves were shielding the human forces led by Bayard from the ghouls. But the Ashanta's power was waning from the fierce otherworldly onslaught.

Hyam knew he had to act. The crimson one was winning. In an instant it would be too late, and all the forces arrayed against him destroyed.

But he could not move. The light blinded him from within, chained him in place, and melted the flesh from his bones.

From some great distance he heard Joelle scream his name. Her hand reached through the searing force and seized his shoulder. Joelle cried in a voice Hyam had never heard before. Or perhaps she made no sound at all, for his senses were melting from the power that poured through him. Then she unsheathed the Milantian blade and aimed it upward. Diverting the flow of power, draining some of the force away from Hyam. And toward the crimson mage upon the tower ramparts.

It was the one line of assault the mage had not prepared for. The one direction from which he had no line of defense.

Joelle shrieked a battle cry that echoed along the blade, a shimmering force that shone so bright it seared Hyam's closed eyes. He felt the wizard on the citadel falter in utter astonishment and almost be defeated as a result. But not quite, for at the very last moment he withdrew from his assault across the valley, utilizing all his force to forge a magical shield. Joelle's blast of energy was deflected upward, becoming a beacon lost to the desert sky.

Hyam's clarity returned with this draining of some of the power. He enveloped the Elves with his mage-force and cried, "Shoot your bows!"

Instantly the Elves obeyed. Hyam fashioned an arrow of his own from the force that almost overwhelmed him. He was literally burning up from within. Releasing the arrow was a relief, for it granted him an avenue to discharge part of the force. The arrow became a stream of fire that flowed from the bow to the wizard.

The crimson mage gestured with his orb-topped staff, deflecting their missiles as well.

The Elves fired as fast as they could pluck an arrow from their quivers and draw and loose. And each one flew with the power that streamed through Hyam, consuming him in the process.

The crimson mage reached up, and lightning gathered upon his orb. Around him rose a ghoulish cloud of dead warriors, screaming their war cry as they followed the lightning flash straight down, aiming for them.

Joelle did battle with a spear that reached to the heavens, but the mage was besting them all. Hyam extended his arm and allowed the force of four rivers to pour through him. He knew he was burning up. He knew he could not survive much longer. And he knew as well that the crimson mage's orb was holding fast.

The answer came to Hyam with a tragic finality. He knew there was no time to think, for the power would soon consume him utterly.

Hyam reached out with his other hand, crossing the valley

in a single instant beyond time, and plucked the violet orb from Trace's grasp. The old mage cried in forlorn protest. But Hyam was already gone. Streaking back across the vale.

From his position at the tower's base, he kept up a steady rushing torrent of power. Together he and Joelle blinded the crimson mage to the oncoming assault. Until it was too late.

The crimson foe sensed Hyam's new attack at the last possible moment. He had time to shriek his rage and woe. He lifted his own orb. Just as Hyam knew he would.

The two orbs came together in a blast that flattened the tower. The explosion flung them to the earth. Stones melted to crimson lava and rained down around them.

Hyam did not so much release the current as admit his final defeat. He gave in to the blackness and knew no more.

51

The first words Hyam heard were, "No, no, no, lass! *Weave* the spell. Like fabric rising from the loom of your fingers."

"Which is exactly what I was doing."

"You weren't. You were kneading the power like you were making a loaf of bread."

"You weren't even watching."

"What a mess you're making."

"Mistress Edlyn says my work is beautiful."

"The poor lady's mind is finally going. What a pity."

"You're the one who can't see what's happening on the other side of the bed. Peevish and blind."

"I most certainly am not either."

"Peevish, peevish, peevish."

"Be silent, you scamp. Now observe. You *release* the energy. Push it *away* from your fingers. See how it weaves?"

"Ooooh, that's lovely."

"There, you see? I am *not* peevish."

"Let me try again."

"First you must apologize. It isn't fitting for a student to address the master as you did."

"It is if the master is a fussbudget. All right. Here I go."

"Now that is *much* better. Excellent! In another fifty years or so, you might make a half-decent mage. If someone with more patience than I can somehow teach you proper respect."

Hyam drifted away then, carried by the comforting sound of friends. He settled back into the embrace of whatever potion and spell they used to hold him. But not before he caught the faint whisper of loss. Something was gone, leaving behind a sorrow so intense it sliced at his final waking breath.

The next time he rose up, the Mistress of Falmouth said, "He is with us."

"I don't detect any change," Trace said.

Hyam found it easier to speak while keeping his eyes shut, as though he had the energy to speak or see, but not both. He licked dry lips and croaked, "You didn't notice the last time either."

He felt soft hands touch his shoulder, his neck, his cheek, and Joelle whispered into his ear, "My darling, how are you?"

Hyam found it impossible to respond, because the answer was, he was already retreating.

The next time he returned, he was carried aloft by the knowledge that the orb was gone. The thought resonated through his mind, pushing away the lingering tendrils of sleep. The globe was shattered and the point of power lost. But this was not the true problem. Hyam recalled the surge of force rising through him and knew something had been burned away. He felt it like an absent limb. He knew with utter certainty that he would spend the rest of his life reminding himself he had done the right thing, that his sacrifice had been the only route to victory. That his loss was a small price to pay.

He opened his eyes to find Trace there beside him. The room swam gradually into focus. He was back in a windowless chamber, as bleak as the cell he had known as a child. The only difference was the magical illumination that glowed in the side alcove, filling the room with a comforting warmth. That and the smiling mage who lifted his head and helped him drink.

Hyam lifted his right arm, the one that throbbed the worse, and saw it was bandaged from shoulder to hand.

"Edlyn is confident she will save all your fingers," Trace said.

He sighed his satisfaction and managed, "Joelle?"

"She sleeps. She scarcely leaves your side. Either the Mistress or I must command her to eat and rest."

"The crimson one?"

"Destroyed," Trace replied with deep satisfaction. "He and his vile citadel. Flung to the four corners of his once-proud city. His passing was so violent it shook the rocks upon which Falmouth stands."

Hyam licked his lips, then asked the question, not because he hoped but rather because he had to put his hope to rest. "The orb?"

"The orb." Trace sighed with shared pain. "The orb is

no more. Not yours, not his. Both shattered into fragments small as colored dust."

Hyam knew the mage would wait as long as was required, but no amount of time would ease what he had to say. "I've lost it. The magic. It's gone."

"You're healing from a grievous trial, lad. Give yourself—"

"I drew the power of four rivers up through me. Without the orb as a conduit. Just like you warned me. It burned away my ability to do magic. I felt it happen." He took a ragged breath. "I feel it now."

The mage placed a hand upon Hyam's arm. "A word of counsel, lad. The people of Falmouth need you to be happy."

"Happy."

"The foe is defeated. But many are struggling with severe losses of their own. Their hero cannot be seen to wallow in his loss. It would rob them of hope."

"I am no one's hero."

Trace merely looked at him.

"And what of my loss?"

"For the moment, it must remain our secret. Ours and Mistress Edlyn's."

Despite his hollow ache, he could see the truth to Trace's words. "What will I do?"

Trace removed his hand and leaned back, satisfied that the message had been delivered. "I don't know, lad. I truly don't. Yours is a quandary no mage has faced in a thousand years."

The old mage's honesty was enough for Hyam to ease back into slumber. It felt like he was gone just an instant, but when he opened his eyes, Joelle was there to greet him with a kiss and the words, "You're back."

The banquet in his honor was held that night. Hyam was carried in on a padded throne. The massive high-backed chair was covered with layers of furs. Joelle walked alongside him, dressed in a pale gown, and over this a long silver mantle embroidered with emeralds. She had shown it to Hyam as they had settled him into the throne, saying it was a wedding gift from the hidden kingdom. Hyam wore a robe of softest silk so as not to rub the still-healing scars. The back of his throne held a staff, upon which was draped the remnants of his emissary outfit, the leather charred and stained, one arm burned away entirely.

Hyam was first carried to the castle forecourt, where all those gathered in the main keep could see him, know he was indeed alive, and roar their greeting. Then it was back into the hall with its great fires and shouted acclaim and speeches and minstrels and the clamor of hundreds. Hyam dozed through most of it and ate nothing.

When the banquet finally ended, they carried him back and eased him into bed. Joelle embraced him, and held him with those grey and violet eyes, and said with utter conviction, "You will heal, my lord."

"Don't call me that."

"My lord," she said again. "I take this as my duty. To help you become whole."

And for that night, her confidence and her love were enough to settle his heart and soothe him into a sleep beyond loss, beyond wounds, beyond dreams.

52

They built for Hyam and Joelle a house in the border region between Falmouth city and the forest. Joelle went out daily to survey the progress. She shared with him the news that their home was being surrounded by a meadow of wildflowers, and this by trees that grew impossibly fast. All of Falmouth spoke of Hyam's glade, and how it was planted by a folk no one ever saw.

They settled Hyam back into the fur-draped throne and made a procession of carrying him home. They were led by Bayard, Earl of Falmouth. To either side of Hyam and Joelle strode two heralds. One carried the forbidden seal of House Oberon. The other bore a new purple standard, sewn with the Ashanta emblem. Behind them walked all the mages of Falmouth. The street resonated with a song drawn from a different era, written to celebrate a victory a thousand years ago. Kept alive in a city whose very existence had been erased from the realm's records. By a folk considered outcast. Of no account or value to anyone. The conquerors of the crimson foe.

The home itself was very fine, with great beams of varnished elm and strong walls and windows open to the sun and the summer winds. The city's mages sang a benediction and everyone cheered, and all the people called Hyam friend.

Hyam grew in strength and took to walking beyond the stone boundary wall, along the path to the forest. He often stood there with Joelle on one side and Dama on the other, clasping the crystal pipe. But he always turned around without lifting it to his lips.

When the season changed and the leaves fell and rattled about his garden, they came to him. Trace held the gate open for Mistress Edlyn, who seemed to totter a bit as she walked down their front path. They embraced Joelle in turn, accepted her offer of tea, and settled down to either side of Hyam's padded chair. They spoke of harvests and news of the clansmen who had sworn fealty to Bayard as their rightful liege. They spoke of peace and the rebuilding of Emporis, now the northernmost city of Bayard's domain, and the wealth of arriving caravans.

Finally Edlyn set aside her cup and said, "Gimmit has returned from Sutton and Port Royal."

"When?"

"Yesterday."

"He has a new ship," Trace said. "And he has laid the keel for a second, to be skippered by his eldest boy. Gimmit said it was either give the lad his own command or toss him overboard in a heavy sea."

Edlyn went on, "He brought word of yet another unseen foe."

Hyam glanced at Joelle, who until now had done her utmost to keep the outside world at bay. But she only returned his gaze, saying all that was required with silence.

"Cast back your mind to the citadel in Havering," Trace said.

"I'd rather not."

"And I would not ask, except that it is suddenly quite important." The old mage sounded almost cheerful. "The sheriff's son told you that someone was coming from the capital."

"To question me," Hyam recalled.

"Someone powerful enough to order an earl to keep you untouched until they arrived."

"So?"

"Think, lad. The crimson mage was in Emporis. Five hundred leagues from the capital."

"Which means there was another," Joelle said.

"Perhaps," Edlyn countered. "Perhaps merely a spokesperson."

Hyam tried to resist the urge, but his curiosity won out. "What did Gimmit say?"

"Rumors of the dark force still swirl about the palace. King Ravi has not been seen since the day Emporis fell."

"It proves nothing," Hyam said.

"True. But the risk is there."

"What do you want from me?" Hyam lifted the hand now scarred and only partially functioning. "I have lost my power."

"There is no sign of its return?" Edlyn asked.

"It was burned out of me. It is gone."

"The orb is known to hold a healing force," Trace said.

"We tried that while I was still in the castle cellar," Hyam reminded him. "Four times. It did nothing save cause me pain."

"But your wisdom remains, lad. And that is what we most need."

"Join us in the castle keep," Edlyn said. "Help us prepare. In case the rumors are true."

But though they argued and pressed and pleaded, Hyam would not agree. They finally left when he grew too exhausted to listen further.

But as they departed, Hyam asked Trace, "Did you ever know of a wizard named Yagel?"

"Of course!" The old mage smiled delightedly. "Yagel was to be Master of Havering Long Hall, but he never returned from his year among the common folk. We knew him by a different name, of course. Yagel was how he was known before. He was my closest friend among the acolytes—oh my, how long ago was that! I suppose he gave up his Long Hall name when he chose to remain in the outer world. But it could only be the same man as my old friend. Not fat but wide as a beer barrel? I became Master in his stead. There are many a day when I am certain the elders made a terrible choice."

"He fell in love . . ." Something checked him, as though the secret was not his to share.

"I'm glad for him, and for your telling me he's both alive and happy."

"He saved my life."

Trace walked back over and settled a hand upon his shoulder. "For that I am gladdest of all."

53

He expected Gimmit to arrive the next dawn, but it was another five days before the captain appeared. He brought with him a motley crew consisting of three sons, Gault, Adler, and Meda. It was the most people Hyam had seen at one time since the procession, and he disliked how the air felt pressed from the room. Dama must have picked up on his unease, for the dog growled at their entry, the first sound she had made in days.

Gimmit was the only one not concerned. He pointed at Adler and told the dog, "Bite that one if you're hungry. I wouldn't make a decent mouthful."

Hyam knew they had come to discuss the rumors, but he did not give them a chance. Twice they started to speak about the realm beyond the black cliffs, and twice he steered back to safer topics.

But as they accepted defeat and made their farewells, Gimmit was the last to rise. He stopped near the doorway and looked back at Hyam in his high-backed chair. "There will come a day when I grow too old and too feeble to captain my ship. I still manage well enough now, but I can feel the winter's bite, and I know the day's not far off. My boy has built a second cabin where I'll be welcome to sail away my dotage. Which is most likely daft in many people's eyes, and if my dear wife were still here, I'd probably feel different. But she's been gone for years now, and I never did give a tinker's toss for what other people thought."

Gimmit stumped back across the plank flooring to glower at Hyam from close range. "But here's what I do know." He poked Hyam with a stubby finger. "The tide shifts and flows no matter what I say or how much I moan. The only choice I have is how I decide to meet the day."

He nodded once, twice, then turned and started for the door. Then, from the front walk, he bellowed, "Now lift your idle bones out of that chair and get to work!"

The next morning Hyam ventured into the village market, enduring the boisterous welcomes, insisting upon paying for what he selected. The day after, he asked for Matu to be brought up from the palace stables, and his horse arrived with a beautiful mare following behind. The dappled grey was a gift from the earl and had a snow-white mane and a pleasing disposition. He and Joelle took to riding out in the mornings, down to the market and around the sea-draped headlands that rose to join the city walls. Joelle always wore the uniform fashioned for her from Meda's castoffs, with the Milantian sword rising behind her left shoulder. Hyam resisted the urge to tell her to change and leave the sword at home. One glance at the woman's stern expression was enough to know such demands would go unheeded.

Afternoons Hyam rode out with Dama for company, tracing his way along the forest, down to where the meadows met the river and from there out to where the black rock rose like the remnants of some prehistoric growth. There he would sit and watch the sea for hours. Sometimes he felt a glimmer of hope return, as though he could just glimpse a future beyond his loss, a purpose beyond magic.

Then, on the eleventh afternoon, he returned home to find Bryna with his wife.

The friend from his childhood was not there in person, of course. But she was present just the same, and from the way the two women stood in silent communication, Hyam had the distinct impression that her visit was neither singular nor even rare.

He had no idea how he perceived the Ashanta's presence at all. Or what it might signify.

Joelle noticed him standing in the doorway and exclaimed, "You're back!"

He covered his confusion by easing himself down into the high-backed chair. "I am."

"You're hungry and you're tired."

He saw how Bryna watched this exchange, the calm Ashanta mask not quite hiding . . . what? And how did he notice this? Certainly there was nothing about her translucent form to suggest a sense of envy. And yet there was a genuine flavor to Bryna's observation, one of lingering regret over everything she would never know. And with a soft intake of breath, Hyam realized this was part of the Sentry's role. They forfeited the right to wed or love another and gave themselves totally to extending their senses, first out beyond the boundary stones, then as Seers beyond all human boundaries entirely.

Hyam found himself seeing as Bryna might. Joelle bustled about the kitchen, bringing him a brew made from forest herbs. And in that instant he realized they were gifts from Elves who came when he was not home, left in silent homage, a connection forged in their quiet and secret manner. He saw the love in Joelle's eyes and the strain that he had willfully remained blind to. How she had worries and woes of her own, but ones she kept carefully hidden away, so that all she showed him was what he needed most. Love. Support. Healing strength.

"Thank you," he whispered.

Something in the simple words caused her to look up in surprise. And she smiled, and with that smile he saw the great good fortune he had been granted through marriage to this woman. A lady who gifted him with what neither of them thought would ever be theirs to claim. A haven. A home.

"Bryna came to visit," Joelle said.

"Did she?"

"She brought news, but that can wait." Joelle returned to the kitchen, exchanging a smile with the woman she assumed only she could see. "She sends you best wishes from all the Assembly."

"Thank you," he said again, knowing the words were inadequate, but he would do better. In time.

Bryna turned to leave. Hyam sensed a silent communication pass between the two women, one confirmed by how Joelle paused in her preparation of their evening meal to reach out. It was the casual gesture of an old friend, one returned by a woman whose race knew no word for farewell.

And in that moment, Hyam knew both of them needed to hear his words. "I think tomorrow we should go meet with Edlyn."

Joelle's arm dropped, and she turned to him. Her face revealed a deep and visceral longing. Or perhaps it had always been there, and he was only now willing to see. "I can come as well?"

"I would not go without you," he replied. "You need to resume your training."

"You don't mind? I feared, well, it might make you sad."

The hollow ache did not return, for it had never left. He only noticed it more clearly. Even so, "Trace will be happy to pester you again."

She smiled so fiercely her eyes glazed a bit, carried by a yearning she had done her best to deny. "I won't sleep a wink."

Bryna was watching him. She turned to Joelle for a moment, and his wife said, "The Ashanta wish to recognize you at an Assembly."

He had not actually heard the exchange, but there was a subtle resonance, as though he was learning the undertones of a silent tongue. "I think that is an excellent idea, if I can manage."

"If you are unable to travel, they will join you here as they did by the Elven gates. And Hyam—"

"The Elves want me to visit their hidden realm."

She laughed, a melody carried on new aspirations. "How did you know?"

"I didn't, my love."

Bryna turned away once more. As the Ashanta started to leave, she lifted her hand. It could not have been in farewell, for the concept was not known to her. Rather, it was in salutation and acknowledgment. And not to Joelle. To him.

Coming
Spring 2016

Book 2 in the

LEGENDS OF THE REALM
series

1

almouth Port was gripped by an early winter storm. The guards huddled by the iron fire-barrels, though the flames did little good, even down in the sheltered palace forecourt. Upon the battlements, the cold bit like nature's acid. The narrow stone passage that rimmed the city wall was treacherous with fresh ice. The soldiers on duty endured the long hours and searched silent roads. The main street leading from Falmouth's gate to the northern highway was empty, for the wind seemed determined to drive the sleet straight through anyone who dared leave their safe havens. The seasoned troops did a slow circuit of the battlement, then slipped inside the tower room for a bit of warmth and brew heated on the central fire. Which meant only one soldier noticed the solitary man that hour before dawn. At least, when the night was over and the soldier was forced to endure the earl's harsh questions, he was fairly certain the lone traveler had been a man.

The traveler stopped alongside the outermost inn and blacksmith stables. His back was to the distant vales and the lonely route leading to Emporis, the city at the edge of the known world. He stood motionless, as though the night was not struck by the fiercest storm any could recall that early in the winter season. His cloak shivered and rippled, but otherwise the tempest did not touch him. He seemed to study the gates and towers intensely, though the lone soldier could not be certain, for the traveler's face remained hidden beneath a cowl.

The soldier's unease mounted and twice he called for his mates, but the wind clawed the words away. The guard was young and courageous and known for his artistry with blade and bow. But the longer he stood there, the more his belly was gnawed by something he could not name. He gripped his sword's pommel and forced himself not to flee.

Finally the cloaked figure broke off his inspection and turned down a side lane. The soldier felt his chest unlock. He watched the empty road for a time, until his best mate clapped him on the shoulder and told him to go warm himself by the fire. But the young soldier knew he was obliged to take a dreaded move.

Gingerly he descended the icy stairs and pounded upon the door at the tower's base. "Officer of the watch!" Though he shouted, the wind snatched the words away. He could hear nothing, so he pushed open the door and entered the tower's lower chamber. "Begging your pardon, my lady."

Captain Meda had been knighted by the earl following the Battle of Emporis. She had a well-earned reputation as a fierce brawler with a fiery temper. She sprawled on the cot, her weapons heaped upon the watch-table. All but the long knife in her hand. "What is it?"

"Thought I saw something, ma'am."

"Either you saw or you didn't. That's your duty. Not to think. Try again."

"A lone stranger. He stood at the point where the Emporis road meets the smithy's stables. Watched us for a good long time."

Meda swung her feet to the floor. "Is he there now?"

"No, my lady. He turned away." He fidgeted, fearing a good old lashing for what sounded feeble now, here in the warmth and safety of the officer's ready room.

But Meda seemed to find nothing wrong in his report. "No one else noticed?"

"I was the lone guard by the west tower. The gate is sealed, and the storm . . ." He shrugged. "Perhaps it was nothing, Captain."

"Your name. Corporal Alembord, is it not? Recently arrived from . . ."

"Havering. Yes, ma'am. With the last ship."

"Just in time for winter." She offered a tight smile, meant to reassure. "Now tell me why you felt this deserved my attention."

"Something about the man made me clench up tight as a fist. And . . ."

"Go on, Corporal. Speak your mind."

"The cloak he wore wasn't touched by the wind. He stood facing straight into the storm, but the cowl that covered his head—" Alembord halted as the captain leapt from the bed. The snarl on her face caused him to take an involuntary step backward, ramming into the door.

"What was the cloak's color?"

"Couldn't say, Captain. Not in this storm. The torches lining the road were all doused. All I could see was his silhouette."

She reached for the scabbard and belted it to her waist. "Where did he go?"

"Down the side lane." This time, when the snarl reappeared, he knew he was right to have come. "Toward the emissary's home."

"Twenty men, Corporal. Armed and in the forecourt. Three minutes." She flung open the door. "Who is the wizard on duty?"

"Wizard? Ma'am, we're ordered to have nothing to do with that lot down in the palace cellars—"

His words were cut off by a blast that dwarfed the storm and shook the palace. Alembord and the captain were both flung onto the flagstones.

Meda scrambled to her feet and leapt through the door. "Alarm! Sound the alarm!"

Alembord forced his limbs to obey his addled brain. He struggled into the palace forecourt and used his sword's pommel to pound the brass gong. Another blast ripped the darkness, illuminating the troops who scrambled and slithered across the icy stones. Alembord managed to hold to his feet, though he quailed at the sight of sleet turned to flying rubies by the illumination. He rang the alarm and wondered at the sight of lightning that seemed red as the dawn he feared would never come.

The road leading to the forest was empty, which was hardly a surprise, for it meandered past frozen corrals and empty stables and unoccupied hovels. When the crimson mage of Emporis had been defeated a year and a half earlier, the wild border clans had returned to their valley fiefdoms, but only after swearing fealty to Bayard, Earl of Oberon and Lord of Falmouth Port. Some claimed Bayard was also the rightful king of all the realm. But they did so softly, even here in the heart of Oberon's land, for throughout the rest of the human realm, such words carried a death sentence.

The traveler stopped a second time where the emissary's grove met the lane. This would hardly be cause for notice, were it not for the hour and the storm. All the city's dwellers paused here from time to time. Many made it a destination when courting or simply filling an idle hour. Legends were recounted here, about green-skinned people that emerged from the forest and secretly planted the trees. About battles that ravaged the land with forces not seen for over a thousand years. About the man who dwelled in the unseen house within the supernatural glade. None denied the fact that magic had been applied, even though the obscure sciences were officially forbidden throughout the realm. But here, in this place, the power of enchantment rose in silent defiance to all such human laws.

Between the emissary's grove and the western forest stretched a vast expanse of stumps and knee-high new growth.

Over the previous decade, the woodland had been cut back three hundred paces by the refugees. Clansmen who had managed to escape the crimson rider's wrath had cut the forest to make corral fences and crude huts. The emissary's grove had been planted just seventeen months earlier, the same season when the badland refugees returned to their vales and sought to rebuild their lives. Yet the glade that began where the traveler stood was already tall as the city gates, with trunks thick as a warrior's girth. Some who stopped here claimed they could actually hear the trees grow. On this night, however, the only sounds were the shrieking wind, a distant shutter pounding against an empty window, and ice cracking on tree limbs as they danced.

A narrow lane of white stones weaved through the emissary's grove. The stones were another marvel, as none had ever seen the like before. Some claimed they were a gift from the Ashanta, a telepathic race few had ever seen. The Ashanta were said to fashion their fabled cities from these very same stones, which led to much conjecture over what it meant, being laid as a path through a glade all knew to be enchanted. The softly glowing lane curved twice as it passed through the trees, so that the emissary's home and its surrounding gardens remained unseen.

The stranger stood there for a time, long enough for anyone else to freeze solid. Yet he seemed as untouched by the tempest as the emissary's glade. The tall trees blocking the stranger from the home moved less than the traveler's cloak. Were it possible, it might have seemed that the trees watched him intently. Waiting to see what he might do next.

The traveler started forward.

Instantly the trees bowed inward, lacing their branches together.

The traveler backed away. The trees now blocked the lane within a shield of bare winter limbs, woven tight as a wicker wall.

The traveler snarled a curse and opened his cloak. Attached to his belt in the same manner that another might carry a sword was a wand carved with a multitude of symbols and topped by a glass orb the size of a thumbnail.

The wizard raised the wand above his head, aimed the tiny orb at the glade, and droned a few words, enough to light the orb and the woven limbs with a crimson fire.

The branches trembled as the force sought to wrench them apart. But the trees revealed their own power as they resisted the command and the blast and the shaking of the earth. Instead, when the tremors and the fierce red lightning ended, the remaining trees drew together more tightly still.

The wizard roared a spell with such fury his words emerged in a writhing spew of fire. The verbal onslaught joined with the orb, which burned now with a blinding ruby light. Such power could not be contained, and crackled and hissed through the air before blasting into the grove. The earth shook more violently still with the second spell's power.

The first line of trees was demolished. The sleet was tainted by the bitter taste of magical ash. Not even the stumps remained. The nearest empty hovels were also flattened by the backlash.

But beyond this new wasteland rose more trees, and beyond

them more still. Thirty paces deep the grove stretched, every tree now a living guardian. Intent upon sacrificing life for duty.

Again the wizard raged his volcanic spell. Again the lightning blasted. Another line of trees was reduced to flames that hissed and vanished.

The wizard started to unleash another detonation. Then he realized that the glade was now on the move.

Trees to his left and right ripped their roots free of the frozen earth. They moved with the sullen grace of ancients. The earth shivered from the impact of their gnarled limbs striking the frozen ground. They encircled the spot where the traveler stood, closing off his escape.

Then they started in. Now they were the ones on attack.

The wizard lifted his wand high over his head. He shouted words not heard in a thousand years. The tempest plucked at him, stripping the cloak from his body, and then the flesh from his bones.

The wizard and his wand were reduced to crimson flecks. The sentinel trees swatted at the swirling mist, but they might as well have sought to halt the sleet.

In an instant the wizard was gone.

The sentinel trees remained as they were for a time. But when shouts arose from where the forest lane joined the highway, they clumped and they marched and they rejoined the glade.

When the first grey glimmer of daylight forced its way through the tempest, the human soldiers and palace courtiers who gathered by the emissary's white-stone lane could find no sign of anything amiss. Even the ash was gone.

2

Two days later, there was nothing to show for the ferocities that had struck at Falmouth's boundary save the demolished huts, and that damage could have been done by the storm. Hyam and his wife walked beneath a benevolent sky. The light was still strengthening, and the morning was already springtime warm. The trees dripped a noisy pattern as the couple left the glade and turned toward the port.

As they arrived at the main route leading to the city gates, they joined an impatient throng. Farmers and merchants alike jostled and cried and shoved, as was always the case on market days. Joelle greeted the woman who supplied them with farm-fresh cheese as she and her daughters shooed a flock of squawking geese. The prime spots around the city's main squares would be taken within the hour.

Ahead of them, the city rose like the onyx crown of some forbidden warrior race. Falmouth was fashioned from the black rocks upon which it stood. Where some might find the unbroken dark stone forbidding, Hyam thought it held a timeless grace. Beyond the outer walls stretched the narrow lanes that were home to some fifty thousand souls. At the city's heart stood the inner keep, rimmed by broad plazas and fountains, where stood the homes of courtiers and the richest merchants. Beyond that was the ancient second wall, high and so narrow at its crest that guards had to sidle past one another. Since the battle vanquishing the crimson mage of Emporis, the guards remained on constant vigilance.

The palace itself sprouted eleven towers. Since the Battle of Emporis, they were crowned by the banners of those first badland clans who had come to the aid of the Oberons. All of these clan names were officially banned by the king who now possessed the throne in Port Royal. But what the king felt about the earl's defiance no one knew, for the ruler had not been seen since the crimson foe's defeat. Today the standards hung limp and easy in the windless dawn, as though promising a calm to all who dared call Falmouth home.

The palace's central structure was domed, the only such edifice Hyam had ever known. Beneath the dome resided the banquet hall, whose ceilings bore paintings over a thousand years old. The pictures remained vivid because the city's mages kept them so. They recalled dark times and heroic deeds and the joining of races so that the realm might survive to fight another day.

Hyam's wife saluted the guards on duty by the moat bridge. Joelle was not one of them, but she trained with sword and knife as often as her magical duties permitted. She liked the company of soldiers, particularly the women who had flocked to the earl's banner. The king in Port Royal had forbidden all female soldiers from serving within the realm's borders. The Earl of Oberon openly defied this ban, sending word throughout the kingdom that all troops who sought to serve beneath the ancient banners were welcome, men and women alike. Joelle was happiest on the days she could slip away from the stone-lined caverns where the magicians practiced their arts, and join the earl's company in the brash and noisy training ground. They knew her abilities and her role in the Battle of Emporis. They made her welcome. This brought her untold joy. Before her arrival in Falmouth, Joelle had never belonged anywhere.

Captain Meda lolled by the outer moat, a position she had maintained for most of her duty hours since the assault on the glade. Her shield and battle sword leaned against the bridge support. Few women felt comfortable wielding a full-sized blade. But Meda was as seasoned as she was tough, one of the first officers hired by Hyam and a veteran of many battles. She studied the passing crowds with a gaze seamed by years of sun and harsh climes and greeted the couple with, "Where is Dama?"

"Guarding the house," Hyam said.

"You should let her accompany you," Meda said, her eyes never still. "I've never known a better beast for sniffing out danger."

Hyam indicated a trio of lowing calves being forced through the gates. "A wolfhound has no place in Falmouth on market days."

Meda asked, "Any sign of your attacker's return?"

"None." Hyam did not say what he thought, which was, his first alert of the assault had been Meda pounding on their front door.

Joelle replied, "The Elves confirmed there was an attack."

Hyam stared at his wife. "When was this?"

"At dusk yesterday, late in the night, and again before today's dawn. They said some of their sentinel trees had been lost."

"Why am I only hearing about this now?"

"How often have you avoided any mention I make of the Elves or their requests for us to join them? They have waited seventeen months, and still you will not agree to a feast day. I am as tired of making excuses for why you will not meet them as they are of asking."

Meda demanded, "What did the forest folk do this time?"

"Three times they sang to the trees that bordered the lane. They searched the ground for sign." Joelle touched the sword's hilt rising above her right shoulder. "They urged me to carry the Milantian blade."

"I should be told of such events," Hyam groused.

Joelle rolled her eyes, and Meda asked her, "Will I see you on the training grounds today?"

"If Master Trace gives me time to breathe." She tugged on Hyam's hand. "I'm already late."

They did not speak again until they arrived at the inner keep's main portal. Hyam knew Joelle was readying herself for an argument, so he merely asked, "Tonight at dusk?"

"I may be late, and you may not walk back alone."

"We've been through this already."

"But you did not agree." When he tried to turn away, she called, "Hyam!"

"Yes. All right. I'll wait for you."

"And you must let me tell the Elves you will come."

"Soon."

"Today!"

He hugged her, their love a flame that sustained him. Then he turned and walked away. When she called after him, he sketched a wave and kept going. He had no secrets from Joelle. But there was nothing to be gained from explaining again why he avoided the Elves. To be feted by the forest folk meant Hyam would drown in sorrow and remorse yet again. The hours would be made endless by how everyone else sang and danced and celebrated. Hyam suspected the Elves knew this, and honored him by not either pressing or taking offense.

Hyam could not claim the Battle of Emporis had cost him everything. Not when he shared a fine home with the loveliest woman he had ever known. Not when he lived surrounded by friends and was saluted by every warrior in the earl's fief. But some nights he was engulfed by pain so bitter and intense he half wished he had never known magic at all.

The battle had seared away his arcane talents and shattered his orb of power. The losses left him bereft in a manner that none could see and only a handful even comprehend. He lived half a life and struggled daily to convince himself that he could still know joy. Even if his wounds left him crippled.

Hyam rounded the stanchion that anchored the high palace wall and exchanged salutes with a city patrol. To the citizens of Falmouth, he was the reason they lived and walked in safety. He was the victor of Emporis. He now served as adviser to the earl, though he seldom attended the council meetings and never spoke when he did. He was the subject of minstrel tunes, his triumph carried in secret songs that were played throughout the realm. Hyam never discussed how much he yearned for what he had lost, how much he ached. But Joelle knew he seldom slept well. She sensed his yearning for powers and days he would never know again. And she thanked him in her own silent way for how he struggled to look beyond his loss and be happy with all that was still his to claim.

It came to Hyam like a scent carried on a war-torn wind. But there was not the hint of a breeze within the city walls. Nor did he actually smell anything. But he knew it nonetheless, the electric potency of a spell not yet cast, the latent power he had last known when handling an orb the size of an infant's skull. But the crystal globe had been smashed in Emporis, when it struck the enemy's own orb and obliterated the citadel. Hyam had never thought he would taste that sweet pulsing thrill again. He had held the Falmouth orb and been worked over by healing mages countless times. All to no avail. He had almost forgotten how tantalizing the flavor really was.

He ran, stalking the scent like a ravenous wolf.

The crowds thinned as he rounded the keep's eastern side. The squares were smaller here, but also more elegant. Scattered about these neighborhoods were parks ringed with fruit trees and spacious manors. To his astonishment, the magical lure drew him to the house where he had been working for over a year.

Fronting a tree-lined park was a square house, smaller than some, with the Oberon crest adorning the front portal. Despite the dark stone façade and the sense that this home was as old as the city itself, the place held a warmth and peace that had always appealed to Hyam. Even now, when his belly quivered with a hunger he feared would never again be his to claim.

Hyam pushed through the front portal and shouted, "Timmins!"

The maid bustled in from the kitchen, wiping her hands upon a flour-spackled apron. "They're all in the rear yard, your lordship. Every one of them dropped tools and quill the instant the colonel arrived."

Hyam raced down the flagstone hall, past the four grand chambers that served duty as chart room, record room, and two libraries. Normally a city's keeper of records would hardly occupy such a villa. But Falmouth's chief scribe was also the earl's older cousin. The two had been friends since childhood. Bayard, Earl of Oberon, was a fighter and keen strategist who treated history as a road map to his next victory. Timmins was a scholar by choice and temperament.

Hyam slammed through the rear portal to find the scribe and three offspring and six apprentices clustered about a dusty wagon, joined by Timmins's thickset wife and a dozen grinning soldiers.

The scribe cried, "There you are at last. I've searched everywhere!"

"You haven't done anything of the sort," his daughter Shona chided. "Good morning, Hyam. How is Joelle?"

"Fine, she's fine." He nodded a greeting to Colonel Adler, once the officer in charge of Hyam's band and recently appointed head of the earl's castle guard. But Hyam's attention remained fixed upon the wagon. He pushed his way through the crowd and leaned over the wagon's side.

"A veritable treasure trove!" Timmins tended to speak excitedly over anything to do with the written word. "The legends have come alive before our very eyes!"

The soldiers were mud-spattered and road-weary. They held mugs of cider and munched happily on bread and cheese, enjoying the scribe's antics. Timmins was a favorite of most who called the palace home.

Adler said to Hyam, "Meda tells me you slept straight through an attack."

"Of course he did!" Timmins bent down to lift a grandson clamoring at his feet. "That's all the man does! Most mornings Hyam walks into the scriptorium and asks for a quilt and pillow!"

"You talk utter rubbish," his daughter said. "Hyam works harder than all of your apprentices together."

"Well, that's hardly saying a thing, is it." Timmins peered myopically at Hyam. "How could you possibly have slept through a blast that woke the entire city?"

Hyam paid him no mind. Timmins was as outrageous as he was poetic and rewarded his friends with fierce affection. The youth of Falmouth vied for apprenticeships, even when they spent their first two years out beyond the city walls, turning the skins of butchered animals into the softest vellum. For even these youngest were taught morning and night, and Timmins was counted among the city's finest teachers. He instructed in history and law and proper writing and brought in mathematicians and builders and others for the subjects where he had no ability. He called everyone dunderheads, including the earl. He was never satisfied, no matter how great the effort. He was happiest when peering over a lost scroll and or a book abandoned for centuries. He made the past come alive and put flesh to the long-dead bones of myths and legends. The wizard Trace counted him the wisest of men. He had friends everywhere.

Hyam had no idea what he expected to find in the wagon bed. All he could say for certain was the source of power lay there before him. The dusty tarp was thrown back to reveal several dozen scrolls scattered amid clay shards. Four intact clay vessels were propped on blankets and lashed to the wagon's sides. The vessels would have stood taller than Hyam if held upright. But such a position would have been impossible, for their bases were curved and pointed like crude clay spears.

"These dunderheads actually broke one of the precious amphorae," Timmins groused. "Didn't you know you carried the wealth of centuries?"

"The pot was already broken," Adler replied. "And they're nothing but a bunch of scrolls so old their script has vanished with the years."

Hyam reached for the nearest scroll and instantly felt the power course through him. He shivered with palpable delight.

"Never mind that lot," Timmins cried, and pointed at the top of the nearside vessel. "Observe the crest on this amphora! The past is come to life!"

But Hyam would not draw his eyes away. The scroll was so ancient the act of unrolling caused tiny flecks to fall off like dry scales. Even so, the unfurled document stole away his breath. His fingers trembled so badly he feared he would rip the vellum further. So he propped himself on the wheel spoke, leaned over the side, and settled the scroll on the wagon bed. Gingerly he unfurled it one handbreadth at a time.

Adler set down his mug and leaned over to study the nearest clay vessel. Shona stepped over to stand alongside him. She was sixteen, the youngest of Timmins's brood, and a beauty. The scribe doted on her, though he complained to all within reach that she remained the one scroll he could never read. Her three older brothers were all married with children of their own. If Shona had any interest in men or matrimony, she hid it well.

A crest was stamped in gold leaf upon the vessel's rim, and then repeated twice in the clay itself. Adler read, "Property of the merchant of Alyss."

"Not *Alice*, you dunderhead. This is no maiden's diary, no matter how fair she might once have been. Ah-*liss*. The most famous of cities."

"Never heard of it." Adler traced a hand about the sloping base. "Why is this jug shaped so oddly?"

Shona replied, "Amphorae were shaped to fit snug along a ship's curved hull. Imagine hundreds of these clumped together like eggs in a crate of their own making. They were used to carry the most valuable of liquids, finest wines and rare oils and refined fragrances."

One of the apprentices asked, "So where is this Alyss, anyway?"

"You really are the worst dunderhead who has ever tried to eat me out of house and home," Timmins replied. "Come over here so I can thunk your thick skull."

Shona was blessed with her father's questing mind and her uncle's fair looks. She also held Hyam in something akin to awe. "Alyss was the largest trading city of the lost realm."

Adler said, "You are speaking of the empires destroyed by the Milantian invasion?"

"The very same. Alyss was a city of unimaginable wealth. Poems describe how many of the palaces were roofed in pure gold."

Adler said, "So these scrolls . . ."

Timmins finished, "Are over a thousand years old!"

Shona traced one finger along the nearest amphora's wax stopper. "The question is, why would they use amphorae to store scrolls? Even the most valuable were transported in chests."

"Perhaps some of the scrolls in the vessels that remain intact and sealed will be legible." Timmins almost danced in place. "Would that not be a wonder to carry us through the winter!"

Hyam reluctantly broke away from his study. "You can't read this?"

That turned them all around. Timmins demanded, "Read what?"

Gingerly he lifted the vellum. "It's clear enough to me."

Timmins and his daughter crowded in to either side. Shona asked, "You see text? Truly?"

"And designs." Hyam resumed his inspection of the ancient vellum. "Do they not seem to move before your eyes?"

Timmins leaned over until his nose almost touched the scroll. "I see nothing save blank vellum." He slipped back to earth and exchanged a long look with his daughter. For once, the scribe was both somber and still.

Shona said doubtfully, "Perhaps it is the sun's angle. Move aside, Hyam." She slipped into his place, squinted, declared, "Still nothing."

Hyam touched one of the scroll's designs. The image was traced by the same fire that accelerated his heart rate. "Truly, none of you can see what's written here?"

"I have no idea what you're talking about," Shona replied.

Timmins said softly, "Tell us what you see."

"The script is Milantian," Hyam replied. "It appears to be a teaching scroll."

"For what discipline?"

Hyam looked from one perplexed face to the next. "War."

Thomas Locke is a pseudonym for Davis Bunn, an award-winning novelist whose work has been published in twenty languages. Critical acclaim for his novels includes four Christy Awards for excellence in fiction. Davis divides his time between Oxford and Florida and holds a lifelong passion for speculative stories. Learn more about the author and his books at www.tlocke.com.

EXPLORE THE
WORLD OF

THOMAS
LOCKE

Subscribe to the Blog

Find Previews of
Upcoming Releases

And More

tlocke.com

Get to know Joelle and follow her story
in this ebook exclusive . . .

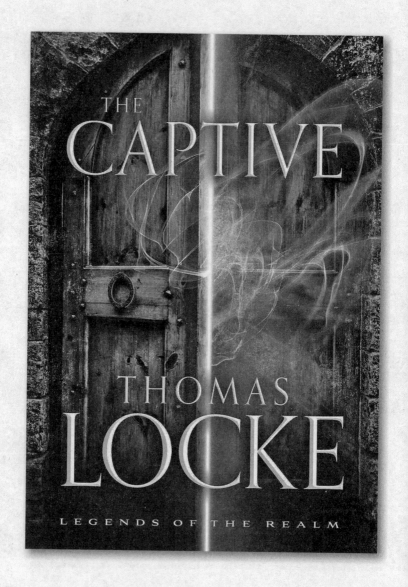

COMING SOON

FROM

THOMAS
LOCKE

TRIAL RUN

Book 1 in the Fault Lines Series

"An explosive read."

"A thrilling ride . . . groundbreaking fiction."

"A gripping and intense experience."

Scientists, corporations, and the government
are chasing a dangerous and mind-bending technology,
and perception and reality become entangled.
But one warning remains clear:
what you don't know can kill you.

4-16

Be the First to Hear about Other New Books from REVELL!

Sign up for announcements about new and upcoming titles at

RevellBooks.com/SignUp

Don't miss out on our great reads!

Revell

a division of Baker Publishing Group

www.RevellBooks.com